A Book Of

OPERATING SYSTEMS

Semester IV : Paper - I

For Third Year B.Sc. Computer Science
As Per Revised Syllabus
Effective from June 2015

Ms. Manisha Bharambe
M.Sc. (Computer Science), M.Phil. (IT)
Associate Professor
Department of Computer Science,
MES Abasaheb Garware College,
PUNE - 4

Mrs. Veena Gandhi
M.C.S., M.Phil. (Computer Science), UGC-NET
Lecturer in Computer Science Department,
Abeda Inamdar Senior College,
PUNE - 1

NIRALI PRAKASHAN
ADVANCEMENT OF KNOWLEDGE

N0895

OPERATING SYSTEMS

ISBN 978-93-5164-910-6

Second Edition : January 2017

© : Authors

Published By : Polyplate

NIRALI PRAKASHAN

Abhyudaya Pragati, 1312, Shivaji Nagar

Off J.M. Road, PUNE – 411005

Tel - (020) 25512336/37/39, Fax - (020) 25511379

Email : niralipune@pragationline.com

➤ DISTRIBUTION CENTRES

PUNE

Nirali Prakashan : 119, Budhwar Peth, Jogeshwari Mandir Lane, Pune 411002, Maharashtra
Tel : (020) 2445 2044, 66022708, Fax : (020) 2445 1538
Email : bookorder@pragationline.com, niralilocal@pragationline.com

Nirali Prakashan : S. No. 28/27, Dhyari, Near Pari Company, Pune 411041
Tel : (020) 24690204 Fax : (020) 24690316
Email : dhyari@pragationline.com, bookorder@pragationline.com

MUMBAI

Nirali Prakashan : 385, S.V.P. Road, Rasdhara Co-op. Hsg. Society Ltd.,
Girgaum, Mumbai 400004, Maharashtra
Tel : (022) 2385 6339 / 2386 9976, Fax : (022) 2386 9976
Email : niralimumbai@pragationline.com

➤ DISTRIBUTION BRANCHES

JALGAON

Nirali Prakashan : 34, V. V. Golani Market, Navi Peth, Jalgaon 425001,
Maharashtra, Tel : (0257) 222 0395, Mob : 94234 91860

KOLHAPUR

Nirali Prakashan : New Mahadvar Road, Kedar Plaza, 1st Floor Opp. IDBI Bank
Kolhapur 416 012, Maharashtra. Mob : 9850046155

NAGPUR

Pratibha Book Distributors : Above Maratha Mandir, Shop No. 3, First Floor,
Rani Jhanshi Square, Sitabuldi, Nagpur 440012, Maharashtra
Tel : (0712) 254 7129

DELHI

Nirali Prakashan : 4593/21, Basement, Aggarwal Lane 15, Ansari Road, Daryaganj
Near Times of India Building, New Delhi 110002 Mob : 08505972553

BENGALURU

Pragati Book House : House No. 1, Sanjeevappa Lane, Avenue Road Cross,
Opp. Rice Church, Bengaluru – 560002.
Tel : (080) 64513344, 64513355,Mob : 9880582331, 9845021552
Email:bharatsavla@yahoo.com

CHENNAI

Pragati Books : 9/1, Montieth Road, Behind Taas Mahal, Egmore,
Chennai 600008 Tamil Nadu, Tel : (044) 6518 3535,
Mob : 94440 01782 / 98450 21552 / 98805 82331,
Email : bharatsavla@yahoo.com

niralipune@pragationline.com | www.pragationline.com

Also find us on ⓕ www.facebook.com/niralibooks

Preface ...

We take an opportunity to present this book entitled as **"Operating Systems"** to the students of T.Y.B.Sc. Computer Science as per the revised syllabus, June 2015.

The book covers theory of Introduction to Operating Systems, Process Management, Multithreaded Programming, Process Synchronization, Process Scheduling, Deadlocks, Memory Management and File System.

A special word of thanks to Shri. Dineshbhai Furia, Mr. Jignesh Furia for showing full faith in us to write this book. We also thank to Mr. Amar Salunkhe, Mr. Akbar Shaikh, Ms Chaitali Takle of M/s Nirali Prakashan for their excellent co-operation.

Although every care has been taken to check mistakes and misprints, any errors, omission and suggestions from teachers and students for the improvement of this text shall be most welcome.

Our efforts shall be more than rewarded if this book proves beneficial to the students.

Authors

Syllabus ...

7. Memory Management [11]

7.1 Background – Basic hardware, Address binding, Logical versus physical address space, Dynamic loading, Dynamic linking and shared libraries

7.2 Swapping

7.3 Contiguous Memory Allocation – Memory mapping and protection, Memory allocation, Fragmentation

7.4 Paging – Basic Method, Hardware support, Protection, Shared Pages

7.5 Segmentation – Basic concept, Hardware

7.6 Virtual Memory Management – Background, Demand paging, Performance of demand paging, Page replacement – FIFO, OPT, LRU, Second chance page replacement

8. File System [7]

8.1 File concept

8.2 Access Methods – Sequential, Direct, Other access methods

8.3 Directory and Disk Structure – Storage structure, Directory overview, Single level directory, Two level directory, Tree structure directory, Acyclic graph directory, General graph directory

8.4 Allocation Methods – Contiguous allocation, Linked allocation, Indexed allocation

8.5 Free Space Management – Bit vector, Linked list, Grouping, Counting, Space maps

Contents ...

Introduction

Contents ...

Objectives...

- To Understand the Various Ways of Structuring an Operating System
- To Learn the Concept of Virtual Machine
- To Study How Operating Systems are Booted?

1.1 | INTRODUCTION

- In first semester, we have already learned the concept of operating system. An operating system acts as an interface between the user of a computer and the computer hardware.
- The purpose of an operating system is to provide an environment in which a user can execute programs in a convenient and efficient manner.
- The operating system provides certain services to programs and to the users of those programs in order to make their tasks easier.
- In this chapter, we will learn how operating system structure is evolved from simple structure to virtual machines.

1.2 | OPERATING SYSTEM STRUCTURE

- As an operating system is large and complex, it is divided in sub-components. Each of these components should have a well-described portion of the system, with carefully defined inputs, outputs, and function.

- In this section, we will discuss how these components are interconnected and structured into a kernel.

1.2.1 Simple Structure

- Simple structure of operating system has not well-defined structure.

- MS-DOS is an example of simple structure operating system as shown in Fig. 1.1.

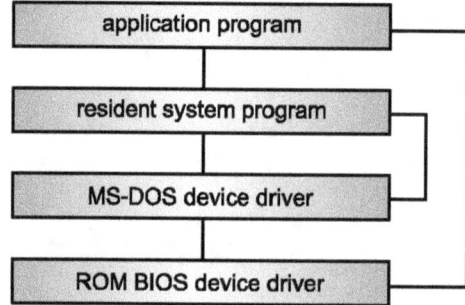

Fig. 1.1: MS-DOS layer structure

- It was written to provide the most functionality in the least space, so it was not carefully divided into modules.

- Although it has some structure, interfaces and levels of functionality are not well separated.

- The application programs communicate directly with disk drives to perform I/O operations.

- MS-DOS which uses Intel 8088, not having dual mode and no hardware protection. The base hardware is accessible.

- The original UNIX operating system also has simple structure like MS-DOS. The UNIX OS consists of two separable parts:

  1. Systems programs, and

  2. The kernel.

- Kernel consists of everything below the system-call interface and above the physical hardware.

- It provides the file system, CPU scheduling, memory management, and other operating-system functions; a large number of functions for one level.

- Fig. 1.2 shows original UNIX system.

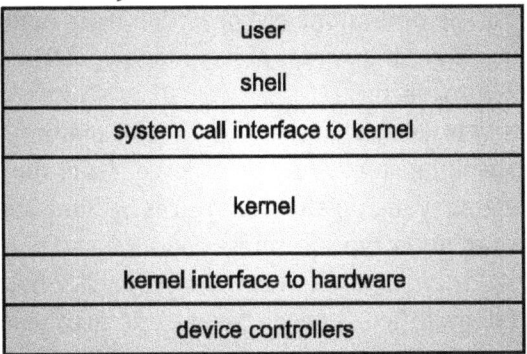

Fig. 1.2: UNIX system structure

1.2.2 Layered Approach

- The operating system is divided into a number of layers or levels, each built on top of lower layers.
- The bottom layer (layer 0), is the hardware; the top layer (layer N) is the user interface.
- With modularity, layers are selected such that each uses functions and services of only lower-level layers.
- **Example:** A layered design was first used in the THE (Technische Hogeschool Eindhoven) operating system designed by a team led by Edsger W. Dijkstra.
- Fig. 1.3 shows layered approach of an operating system.

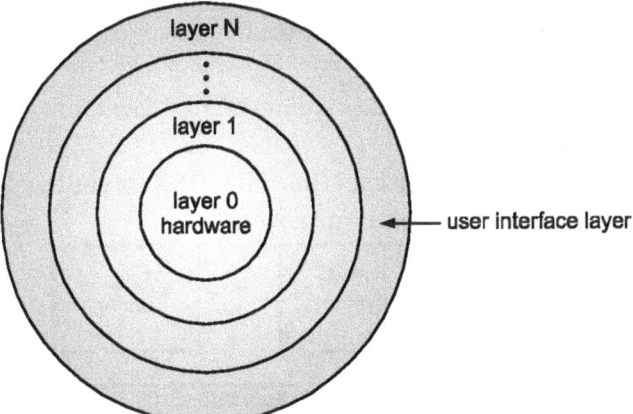

Fig. 1.3: Layered approach of O.S.

Advantages of Layered Approach:

1. Simplicity in design and implementation.

2. Debugging is easy. Debugging is done from Layer 0 to Layer n. Once the first layer debugging is done, then second layer is debugged and so on. When the error is found, the error is only of that layer, because bottom layers are already debugged.

3. Each layer hides the existence of data structures, operations and hardware from higher-level layers. The operations are provided from higher-level layers to lower-level layers. So each layer is abstract object made up of data and operations.

Disadvantages of Layered Approach:

1. A layer can use only lower-level layers, so careful planning is necessary. Example, device driver for backing store must be at lower level than memory management routine because memory management requires backing store.

2. Efficiency is less than other type. Suppose a system call occurs at layer 3 which has passed to layer 2, then layer 1 and finally to hardware. At each layer, the parameters may be modified, so each layer adds overhead to the system call and system calls take longer time than non-layer operating system.

1.2.3 Microkernels

- As UNIX expanded, the kernel becomes large and it is difficult to manage. The microkernel approach is used by operating system. In the mid-1980s, researchers at Carnegie Mellon University developed an operating system called Mach that modularized the kernel using the microkernel approach.

- It structures the operating system by moving all non-essential components from the kernel and implementing them as system and user-level programs into user space.

- So small core OS is running at kernel level and OS Services built from many independent user-level processes.

- Main function of microkernels is to provide communication facility between the client program and various services running in user mode, communication is achieved by message passing

- It provides minimal process and memory management, in addition to a communication facility.

- **Examples:** Tru64 UNIX, Mac OS X kernel (Darwin), QNX (real-time operating system).

- Fig. 1.4 shows architecture of a typical microkernel.

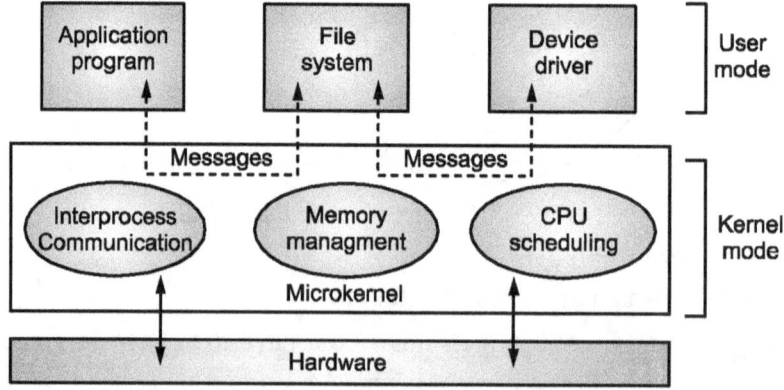

Fig. 1.4: Architecture of a typical microkernel

Advantages:

1. To provide communication facility between the client program and various services running in user mode through message passing.
2. Extending of operating system is easier, since all new services are added to user space and kernel modification is not required.
3. It is portable due to small size of kernel, it is easy to port operating system from one hardware to other.
4. More secure and reliable.

Disadvantages:

1. Performance of microkernels suffer due to increased system function overhead.
2. Performance overhead of user space to kernel space communication.

1.2.4 Modules   (Oct. 16)

- Most modern operating systems involve loadable kernel modules.
- The idea behind this is to provide core services to the kernel while other services are implemented dynamically, as the kernel is running.
- Linking services dynamically is preferable to adding new features directly to the kernel.
- Features of Loadable kernel modules are:
  1. It uses object-oriented approach.
  2. Each core component is separate.
  3. Each component talks to the others over known interfaces.
  4. Each component is loadable as needed within the kernel.
  5. Overall, similar to layers but more flexible.
- **Example:** Solaris, Linux, Mac OS X, Apple Mac OS X uses hybrid structure. Linux also uses loadable kernel modules, primarily for supporting device drivers and file systems.
- The Solaris operating system structure is shown in Fig. 1.5.

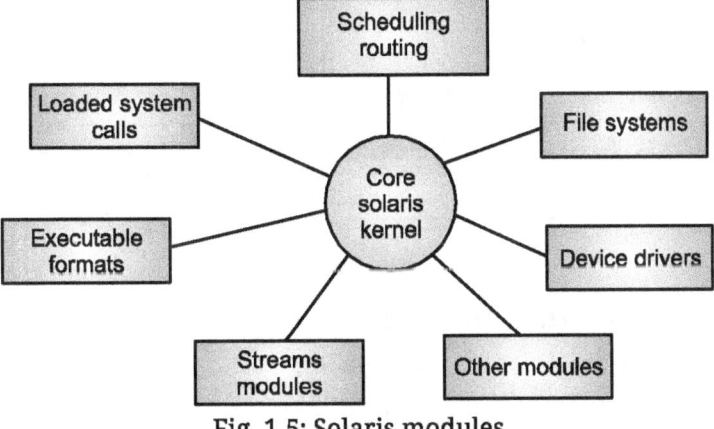

Fig. 1.5: Solaris modules

1.3 | VIRTUAL MACHINES

1.3.1 Introduction

- The original meaning of virtual machine is the creation of a number of different identical execution environments on a single computer, each of which exactly emulates the host computer. This provides each user with the illusion of having an entire computer, but one that is their "private" machine, isolated from other users, all on a single physical machine.

- A virtual machine takes the layered approach to its logical conclusion. It treats hardware and the operating system kernel as though they were all hardware.

- A virtual machine provides an interface identical to the underlying bare hardware.

- The operating system creates the illusion of multiple processes, each executing on its own processor with its own (virtual) memory.

- The resources of the physical computer are shared to create the virtual machines.

For example:

- CPU scheduling can create the appearance that users have their own processor.

- Spooling and a file system can provide virtual card readers and virtual line printers.

- A normal user time- sharing terminal serves as the virtual machine operator's console.

- Fig. 1.6 shows the virtual machine model.

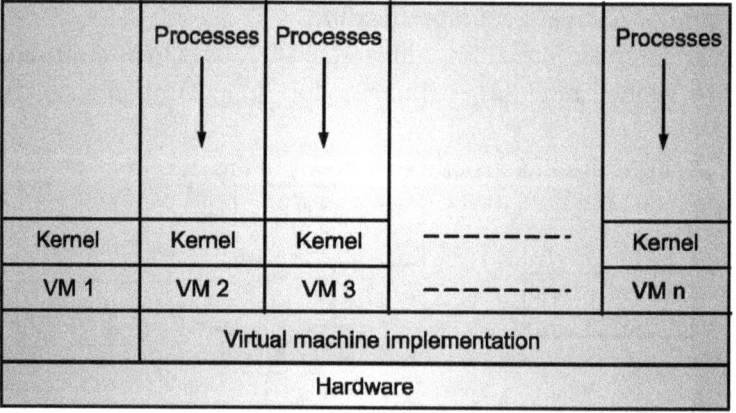

Fig. 1.6: Virtual machine

- **Example: JVM (Java Virtual Machine):** The JVM is a specification for an abstract computer. The JVM consists of a class loader, a class verifier, and a Java interpreter that executes the architecture-neutral bytecodes.

- Fig. 1.7 shows JVM.

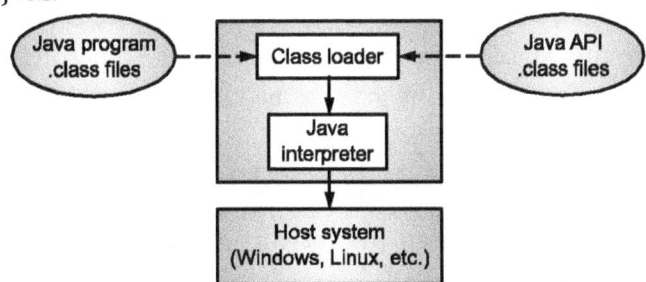

Fig. 1.7: Java Virtual Machine

1.3.2 Benefits   (April 16)

- Benefits of virtual machines are listed below:
    1. **Protection:** Virtual machine provides protection to system resources and a robust level of security. Also each virtual machine is isolated from other virtual machines.
    2. **Easy development**: System development is done on the virtual machine, instead of on a physical machine and so does not disrupt normal system operation.
    3. **Sharing hardware**: multiple execution environments (different operating systems) can share the same hardware.
    4. **Easy communication**: Virtual machine can share the information through virtual communication network. Direct sharing of resources is not required.
    5. **Consolidation:** It involves taking two or more separate systems and running them in virtual machines on one system.
    6. **Portability:** "Open Virtual Machine Format", standard format of virtual machines, allows a VM to run within many different virtual machine (host) platforms.
    7. **Usefulness:** It is useful for developing and testing. It is perfect vehicle for operating-systems research, development, and teaching.

1.3.3 Disadvantages

- Disadvantages of virtual machines are listed below:
    1. The virtual machine concept is difficult to implement due to the effort required to provide an exact duplicate to the underlying machine.
    2. Timing can be an issue – slower than real machine.
    3. Hardware support is needed.
    4. Multiple VMs running on a single physical machine can deliver unstable performance.

1.4 SYSTEM BOOT   (April 16, Oct. 16)

- Operating system must be made available to hardware so hardware can start it. The procedure of starting a computer by loading the kernel is known as system booting.

- The program called bootstrap program or bootstrap loader is used to locate the kernel and loads it into main memory and starts execution.

- When computer turn on or reset, the instruction register is loaded with memory location where, bootstrap program is present. The program is in read only form and stored in ROM.

  o Bootstrap program is used to determine the state of the machine.

  o Bootstrap program is used to initialize the all aspects of the systems, from CPU registers to device controllers.

  o Since, bootstrap is stored in ROM, the changing of bootstrap code requires changing the ROM (Read Only Memory) hardware chips. Therefore, EPROM (Erasable Programmable Read-Only-Memory) is used, but it is expensive. All forms of ROM are called firmware.

  o The large operating system like Mac OS X, Windows, UNIX, the bootstrap loader is stored in firmware and operating system is on disk.

  o The bootstrap has a bit of code that reads a single block from disk into memory and executes code from that block called boot block. The program stored in boot block is used to load the entire operating system into memory.

  o Grub is an example of open-source bootstrap program on LINUX system.

SUMMARY

- ➤ A system as large and complex as a modern operating system must be designed carefully.

- ➤ Simple structure of operating system has not well-defined structure. MS-DOS, UNIX is an examples of simple structure operating system.

- ➤ In layered approach, the operating system is divided into a number of layers (levels), each built on top of lower layers. With modularity, layers are selected such that each uses functions and services of only lower-level layers. A layered design was first used in the THE (Technische Hogeschool Eindhoven) operating system designed by a team led by Edsger W. Dijkstra.

➢ Microkernels approach structures the operating system by moving all non-essential components from the kernel and implementing them as system and user-level programs into user space. Example, Tru64 UNIX, Mac OS X kernel (Darwin), QNX (real-time operating system).

➢ Modular approach involves loadable kernel modules. The idea behind this is to provide core services to the kernel while other services are implemented dynamically, as the kernel is running. Example: Solaris, Linux, Mac OS X.

➢ A virtual machine takes the layered approach to its logical conclusion. It treats hardware and the operating system kernel as though they were all hardware. The operating system creates the illusion of multiple processes, each executing on its own processor with its own (virtual) memory. The resources of the physical computer are shared to create the virtual machines.

➢ The procedure of starting a computer by loading the kernel is known as system booting. The program called bootstrap program or bootstrap loader is used to locate the kernel and loads it into main memory and starts execution

PRACTICE QUESTIONS

1. Explain the layered structure of operating system.
2. State the advantages and disadvantages of layered operating system.
3. Compare layered operating system with microkernels operating system.
4. Write a note on microkernels.
5. State the advantages of microkernels.
6. State two examples of microkernels.
7. State two examples of modules.
8. Write any two features of modules.
9. Write benefits of virtual machine.
10. Write a note on virtual machine.
11. What is system boot? How it is implemented?
12. What is bootstrap loader? What is function of bootstrap loader?
13. What is the purpose of command interpreter and why it is separated from the kernel?
14. What is the main advantage for an operating system designer of using virtual machine architecture?
15. In what ways the modular kernel approach similar to the layered approach and in what ways they differ.

16.   What is the main function of microkernels?

Ans.   Refer to Section 1.2.3.

17.   What is a virtual machine? Give two examples of virtual machine. List any three benefits of virtual machine.

Ans.   Refer to Section 1.3.

18.   List two benefits of Virtual Machine.

Ans.   Refer to Section 1.3.2.

■■■

Process Management

Contents ...

Objectives...

- To Understand Concept of Process and Process Model
- To Learn Process Control Block (PCB)
- To Study Importance of Process Scheduling and Different Types of Schedulers
- To Learn various Operation on Processes
- To Understand Methods of Interprocess Communication

2.1   INTRODUCTION

- A process is a smallest unit of work that is scheduled by operating system.
- A process needs resources, such as CPU time, memory, files and I/O devices, to accomplish its task. These resources are allocated either when the program is created, or when it is executing.

- Operating system enable processes to share and exchange information protect the resources of each process from other processes and enable synchronization among processes.

- To meet these requirements, process management is required which is integral part of an operating system.

- In this chapter, we will discuss about process concept, process model, process scheduling and inter process communication etc.

2.2 | PROCESS CONCEPT

- A process is a program in execution. It is an instance of an application execution.

- A process is also referred as job of batch system or task of time-sharing system. The process contains text section, data section, heap and stack.

- A single program may create two processes; they are nevertheless considered two separate execution sequences.

- For instance, several users may be running different copies of the mail program, or the same user may invoke many copies of the editor program. Each of these is a separate process, and, although the text sections are equivalent, the data sections vary.

- The "ps" command on Unix will list processes on UNIX systems as shown in Fig. 2.1.

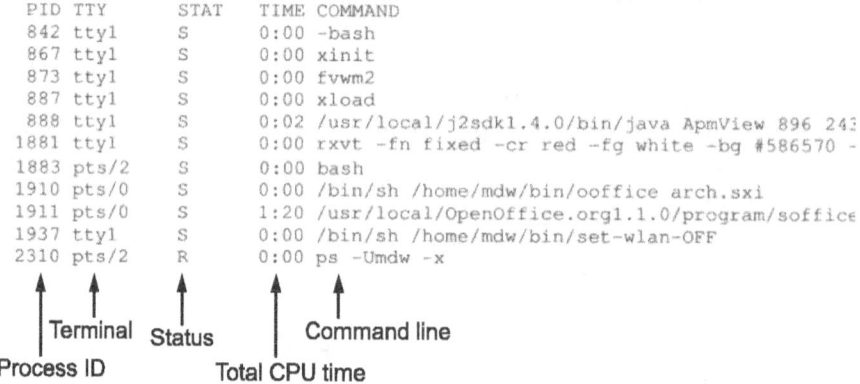

```
PID TTY      STAT    TIME COMMAND
842 tty1      S      0:00 -bash
867 tty1      S      0:00 xinit
873 tty1      S      0:00 fvwm2
887 tty1      S      0:00 xload
888 tty1      S      0:02 /usr/local/j2sdk1.4.0/bin/java ApmView 896 243
1881 tty1     S      0:00 rxvt -fn fixed -cr red -fg white -bg #586570 -
1883 pts/2    S      0:00 bash
1910 pts/0    S      0:00 /bin/sh /home/mdw/bin/ooffice arch.sxi
1911 pts/0    S      1:20 /usr/local/OpenOffice.org1.1.0/program/soffice
1937 tty1     S      0:00 /bin/sh /home/mdw/bin/set-wlan-OFF
2310 pts/2    R      0:00 ps -Umdw -x
```

Terminal Status   Command line

Process ID   Total CPU time

Fig. 2.1: Process on Unix operating system

Difference between Program and Process:

Sr. No.	Program	Process
1.	Program is set of instructions to be executed by processor.	Process is a program in execution.
2.	Program is a passive entity such as the contents of a file stored on disk.	Process is an active entity with a program counter specifying the next instruction to execute.

contd. ...

3.	Program is static entity as it made up of program statements.	Process is dynamic entity.
4.	Program occupy fixed place in storage or main memory.	Process changes its state during execution.

2.2.1 Process

- We known that, a process is program in execution.
- A process is defined as "an entity which represents the basic unit of work to be implemented in the system".
- The Fig. 2.2 shows the structure of a process. The process includes:
  1. Text section.
  2. Stack: Contains temporary data.
  3. Data section: It contains global variables.
  4. A heap: It is a memory dynamically allocated during runtime.
- It also includes the current activity, as represented by the value of the program counter and the contents of the processor's registers.
- When a program executable file is loaded into a memory, a program becomes a process.
- The process contains program counter which specify the next instruction to be executed.
- If N users are running n copies of the one program, then each of these is a separate process.
- If one user invokes many copies of one program, then also each of these is a separate process. In such situations, the text sections of process are same, but stack, heap and data section varies.

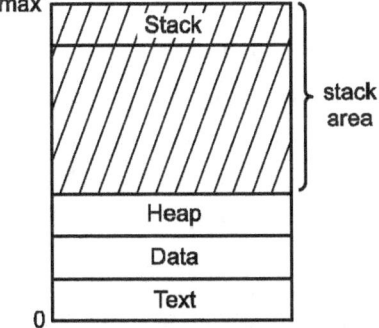

Fig. 2.2: Structure of a process

2.2.2 Process States

- As a process executes, it changes state. The process state reflects the current status of the process:
    1. **New (Dormant):** The programs not yet submitted to the operating system are dormant. The process is being created and not tracked by the operating system.
    2. **Ready:** The process is ready after creation. The process is waiting to be assigned to a processor (CPU) is called ready state.
    3. **Active:** The running process executes the sequence of machine instructions. (Instructions are being executed).
    4. **Waiting:** Waiting for an input/output to complete.
    5. **Halted:** Halted may be because it is complete or because of error.
- Fig. 2.3 shows various process state.

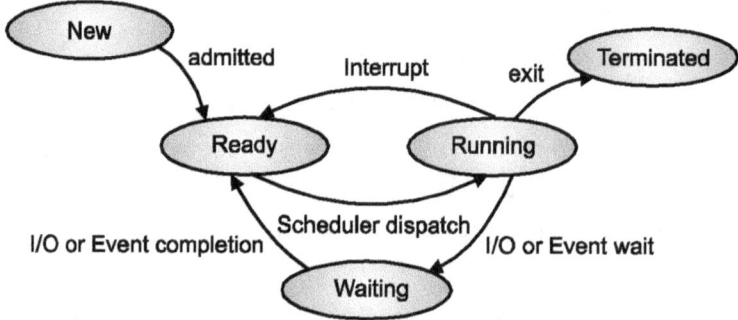

Fig. 2.3: Process state diagram

- When the process is selected by the scheduler, it is loaded into memory means the process is in new state or admitted.
- After the process is admitted or in new state, it is in ready state and the process control block is created by scheduler. The process is waiting for CPU.
- When the process is allocated to the CPU and executed, then it is in running state.
- During the execution of process, if process requires some input output operations then it is in wait state if I/O device is not available for the operation.
- After completion of I/O operation, the process is again in steady state, waiting for the CPU.
- During execution if interrupt occurs then process change running to ready state.
- After completion of execution the process is in terminated or halted state.

2.2.3 Process Control Block (PCB)   (April 16)

- In order to execute instruction operating system has to create processes. For creating process, operating system maintains a process table.

- Process table contains an array of structures, with one entry per process. There is a separate process control block (PCB) for each process.
- Information in a PCB is updated during the transition of process states. It is created when a user creates a process and it is terminated or halted from the system when the process is killed.
- Fig. 2.4 shows a Process Control Block (PCB) or Task Control Block (TCB).

Pointer	Process current state
Process ID (number)	
Process priority	
Registers	
Program counter	
I/O ststus information	
Accounting information	
Memory limits	
Other information	

Fig. 2.4: Process Control Block (PCB)

- Information stored in a PCB includes some or all of the following:
  1. **Pointer:** This is pointer to PCB of next process in the ready queue.
  2. **Process state:** Current state of the process. It may be new, ready, running, waiting or halted. As the process changes its state, this parameter of PCB also changes.
  3. **Process ID:** This is a number allocated by the operating system to the process on creation.
  4. **Process priority:** Sometimes, it is required to complete the process immediately (high priority) than lower priority processes. This priority is set by system manager.
  5. **Register:** Number of CPU registers depends upon the architecture of the computer. There are general purpose registers, accumulators, condition code registers, etc.
     These all are saved in case an interrupt is occurred, to preserve the status. So that the process can continue, with wherever it had left.
  6. **Program counter:** This is the address of next instruction to be executed.
  7. **I/O status information:** The information includes I/O requests, I/O device allocated to the process, a list of open files and information about outstanding requests.
  8. **Accounting information:** This stores number of resource used, time limit, amount of real and CPU time used, process or job number, etc.
  9. **Memory limits:** Information about page table, bound registers or base register.
  10. **Other information:** Current directory, address of different scheduling queues, etc.

- As there is any change that affects any of the information related to a process, those changes are immediately reflected in the respective PCB. A PCB is always stored in the monitor memory.
- Fig. 2.5 shows relationship between the different pieces of data that constitute a process.

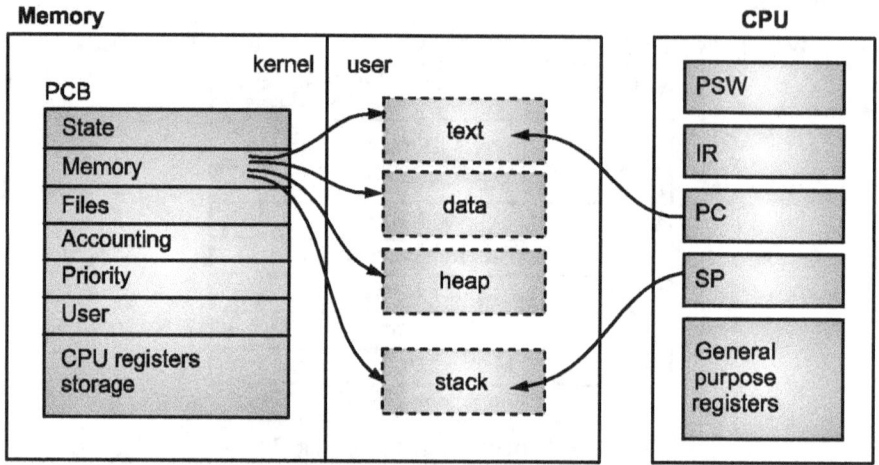

Fig. 2.5: Relationship between the different pieces of data of process

2.3 | PROCESS SCHEDULING

- The objective of multiprogramming is to keep to CPU busy for maximum time and achieve maximum CPU utilization.

- In uniprocessor system, only one process is there and any time it may get the attention of the CPU. But in multiprogramming as only one process may get attention of the CPU at a time, other processes have to wait. So the process scheduling is necessary and it is done by operating system. The method of selecting a process to be allocated to CPU is called Process Scheduling.

2.3.1 Scheduling Queue

- In multiprogramming, several processes are there in ready or waiting state. These processes form a queue. The various queues maintained by operating system are: Job Queue, Ready Queue, and Device Queue.
  1. **Job queue**: As the process enter the system, it is put into a job queue. This queue consists of all processes in the system.
  2. **Ready queue**: The processes that are residing in main memory and are ready and waiting to execute are kept on a list called the ready queue. This queue is generally stored as a linked list. A ready-queue header contains pointers to the first and final PCBs in the list. Each PCB includes a pointer field that points to the next PCB in the ready queue in Fig. 2.6 (a).

3. **Device queue:** A process may have an input/output request, and the device requested may be busy. In such case, the input/output request in maintained is the device queue. It contains all those processes that are waiting for a particular I/O device. Each device has its own device queue. In case of dedicated devices, the device queue will never have more process in it. In case of sharable devices, several processes may be in the ready queue.

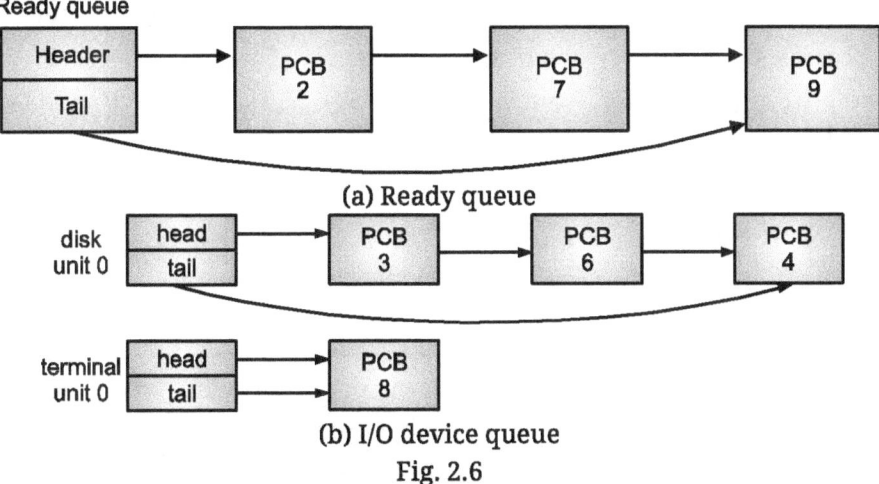

(a) Ready queue

(b) I/O device queue

Fig. 2.6

•   CPU scheduling is represented by a queuing diagram as shown in Fig. 2.7. In Fig. 2.7, queues are represented as rectangles and resources are represented as circles. Directed arrows represent the flow of the processes in the system.

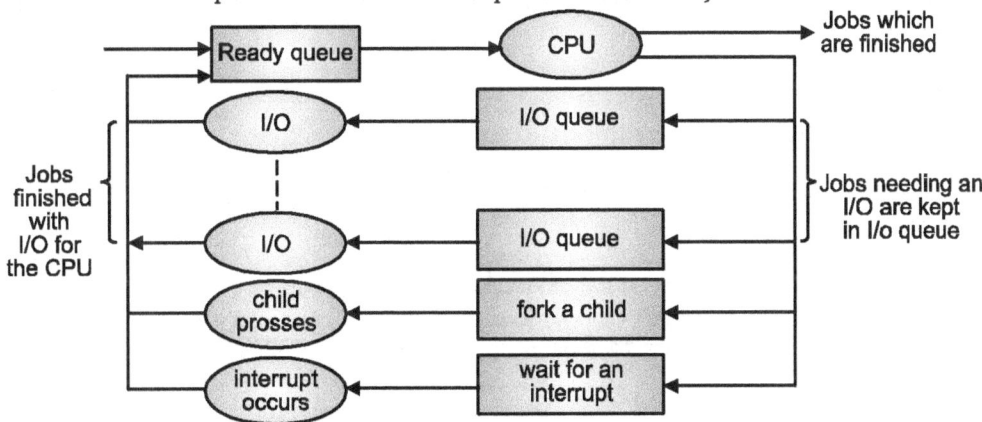

Fig. 2.7: Process scheduling queues

•   A process that enters the system, it is placed in ready queue. It waits there for the CPU. When the process is executing on the CPU, many events occurs like:

1. The process have I/O request, and then it placed in I/O queue.

2. The process can create a new sub process and wait for finish that process.

3. If the interrupt occur, then the process is put back in the ready queue.

4. After the CPU is utilized by the process, it may finish its execution and leave the system at which time it is removed from all queues and has its PCB and resources deallocated.

- The process scheduling must perform the following functions:

1. It keeps track of the process states (either running, ready or waiting) of all the processes. This is done by the traffic controller.

2. It selects process from ready queue for execution. This task is done by the scheduler.

3. It allocates the CPU to process.

4. When running process requires, any I/O resources or an interrupt occurs or it exceeds its time quantum then processor releases the process.

2.3.2 Types of Schedulers   (April 13)

- When a process is created, it moves from one scheduling queue to other. The operating system must select processes from these queues in some way. The job of the appropriate scheduler is to select the process for execution.

- Schedulers are special system softwares which handles process scheduling in various ways.

- Scheduler's main task is to select the jobs to be submitted into the system and to decide which process to run.

- There are three different types of scheduler as shown in Fig. 2.8 namely long-term scheduler, medium-term scheduler and short-term scheduler.

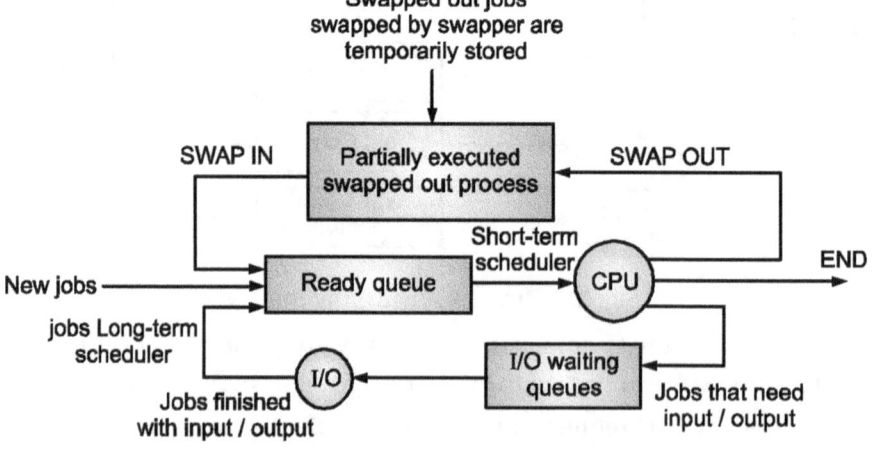

Fig. 2.8: Types of Schedulers

1. **Long-term Scheduler (Job Scheduler):**

- The long-term scheduler selects the job or process to be executed from job pool on a secondary storage device and loads them into memory for execution. The long-term scheduler executes less frequently.

- The long-term scheduler is invoked when the process leaves the system. Because of the longer duration between executions, the long-term scheduler can afford to take more time to decide which process should be selected for execution.

- It also provides a good process mix of I/O bound and CPU bound processes to the short-term scheduler. The I/O bound process means the process requires more I/O than CPU and CPU bound process means the process require more CPU than I/O.

- If all processes are CPU bound, the I/O waiting queue will almost be empty, and if the all processes are I/O bound, then ready queue will almost be empty, and the short-term scheduler will have little to do. Hence, the system with the best performance will have a combination of CPU bound and I/O bound processes.

- The above tasks are summarized as follows:

  o The long-term scheduler communicates directly with the job pool.

  o It selects number of jobs from the pool and loads them in the memory for execution.

  o Long-term scheduler controls degree of multiprogramming. (Degree of multiprogramming is number of programs that can reside in the memory of the computer at a time).

  o It needs to be invoked only when a job leaves the system. Therefore, it is invoked less frequently as compared to short term scheduler.

  o It has the responsibility of selecting proper mix of input/output bound and CPU bound jobs, so that CPU utilization is good.

2. **Short-term Scheduler (CPU Scheduler):**

- Short-term scheduler selects a job from ready queue and submits it to CPU.

- As the short-term scheduler selects only one job at a time, it is invoked very frequently.

- In case of input/output bound jobs as the ready queue is almost empty, short-term scheduler has very less work to do.

- The systems like time sharing do not have long-term scheduler. The jobs are placed directly in the ready queue for the short-term scheduler. But such some systems have an additional type of scheduler called as medium-term scheduler.

3. **Medium-term Scheduler:**   (Oct. 16)

- Following are the situations in which medium-term scheduler is required:

  o Sometimes, it is required to remove some number of jobs from memory temporarily and reduce degree of multiprogramming.

  (Degree of multiprogramming may have to be changed to have a proper job mix of input/output bound and CPU bound jobs to increase CPU utilization).

  o Sometimes, while executing the program, it is found that, memory requirements of the program are changed. Therefore, the job is to be removed from the memory temporarily. Later, the process can be reintroduced into memory, and its execution can be continued where it left off.

- Swapping is term associated with the medium-term scheduler by which processes are temporarily removed and then brought back to the ready queue.

- The dispatcher is the actual component that gives control of the CPU to the process selected by short-term scheduler.

Comparison between Schedulers:

Sr. No.	Long Term Scheduler	Short Term Scheduler	Medium Term Scheduler
1.	It is a job scheduler.	It is a CPU scheduler.	It is a process swapping scheduler.
2.	It controls the degree of multiprogramming.	It provides lesser control over degree of multiprogramming.	It reduces the degree of multiprogramming.
3.	It is almost absent or minimal in time sharing system.	It is also minimal in time sharing system.	It is a part of Time sharing systems.
4.	Speed is lesser than short term scheduler.	Speed is fastest among other two.	Speed is in between both short and long term scheduler.
5.	It selects processes from pool and loads them into memory for execution.	It selects those processes which are ready to execute.	It can re-introduce the process into memory and execution can be continued.

2.3.3 Context Switch

- Switching the CPU from one process to another process requires saving the state of old process and loading the saved state of new process. This task is known as Context Switch.

- Context of a process represented in the PCB. The context of the interrupted old process must require saving the state.

When Context Switch Occurs?

- Whenever, an interrupt arrives, the CPU must do a state-save of the currently running process, and then switch into kernel mode to handle the interrupt, and then do a state-restore of the interrupted process.

- Similarly, a context switch occurs when the time slice for one process has expired and a new process is to be loaded from the ready queue. This will be instigated by a timer interrupt, which will then cause the current process's state to be saved and the new process's state to be restored.

- Saving and restoring states involves saving and restoring all of the registers and program counter(s), as well as the process control blocks described above.

- Context-switch time is overhead; the system does no useful work while switching.

- Context switch times vary from machine to machine, depending on the memory speed, number of CPU registers, and the existence of special instructions. It highly depends on the hardware support. It ranges from 1 to 1000 microseconds:

- Some CPU provides multiple sets of registers (e.g. sun UltraSPARC). A context switch simply involves changing the pointer to the current register set. If active processes are more than register sets, the system resorts to copying register data to and from memory.

- Fig. 2.9 shows the concept of context switch.

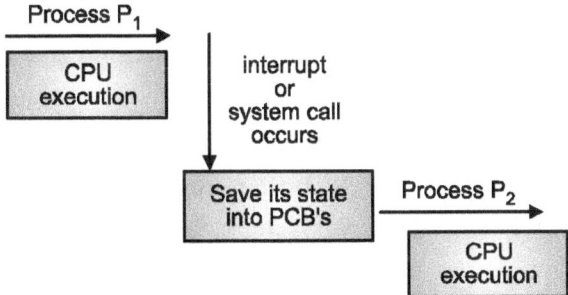

Fig. 2.9: Concept of context swtich

- When process P_1 is executing and system call from operating system occurs (e.g. I/O request) then status of process P_1 is saved into different registers and process is send to fulfill the outstanding request.

- At that time, operating system process P_2 for execution. When process P_2 requires I/O then again operating system switches to P_1 from where it was left off. This switching time from one process to other is called **context switch.**

2.4 │ OPERATIONS ON PROCESSES   (April 13)

- In the system, the processes are created and deleted dynamically. There are two operations provided by operating system on processes:
  1. Process creation, and
  2. Process termination.

2.4.1 Process Creation

- When the process is executes, it may create several new processes, via. a create process system call. The creating process is called a parent process and the new process is called child process.
- If there are many processes created then they all are children processes of parent process. The child process is turn can create further child processes.
- It is a tree structure as shown in Fig. 2.10.

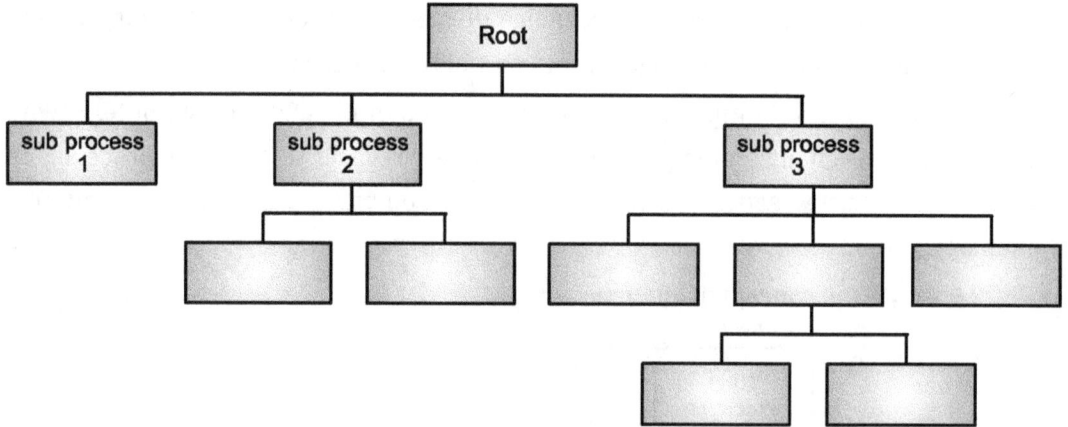

Fig. 2.10: A tree of processes

- Each process is given an integer identifier, termed its process identifier, or PID. The parent PID (PPID) is also stored for each process.
- On typical UNIX systems the process scheduler is termed sched, and is given PID 0. The first thing it does at system startup time is to launch init, which gives that process PID 1. Init then launches all system daemons and user logins, and becomes the ultimate parent of all other processes.
- On UNIX, the command,

```
$> ps - el
```

will list complete information for all processes currently active in the system.
- When a process creates a sub process, the sub process obtains the resources from its parent or from the operating system directly.

- There are two options for the parent process after creating the child:

  1. Wait for the child process to terminate before proceeding. The parent makes a wait( ) system call, for either a specific child or for any child, which causes the parent process to block until the wait( ) returns. UNIX shells normally wait for their children to complete before issuing a new prompt.

  2. Run concurrently with the child, continuing to process without waiting. This is the operation seen when a UNIX shell runs a process as a background task. It is also possible for the parent to run for a while, and then wait for the child later, which might occur in a sort of a parallel processing operation

- Two possibilities for the address space of the child relative to the parent:

  1. The child may be an exact duplicate of the parent, sharing the same program and data segments in memory. Each will have their own PCB, including program counter, registers, and PID. This is the behavior of the fork system call in UNIX.

  2. The child process may have a new program loaded into its address space, with all new code and data segments. This is the behavior of the spawn system calls in Windows. UNIX systems implement this as a second step, using the exec system call.

Example:

- The UNIX operating system follows a certain procedure to achieve above implementations as shown in Fig. 2.11.

- In UNIX, each process has a unique integer number called process identifier or process-id. A child is created by the FORK system call. The FORK operation is used to split a sequence of instructions into two concurrently executable instruction sequences. The parent process can be easily communicated with new process because the new process consists of a copy of the address space of the original process. From the instruction after the FORK call, the parent and child processes continue execution.

- When the child process is created, the return code of the FORK call is zero and when the child is returned to the parent, the return code is non-zero. FORK usually returns the identification of the child to the parent process and the parent can use that identifier to identify the child. The relation between processes created by FORK is executed from a single segment of code and child usually initially obtains a copy of the variables of its parent.

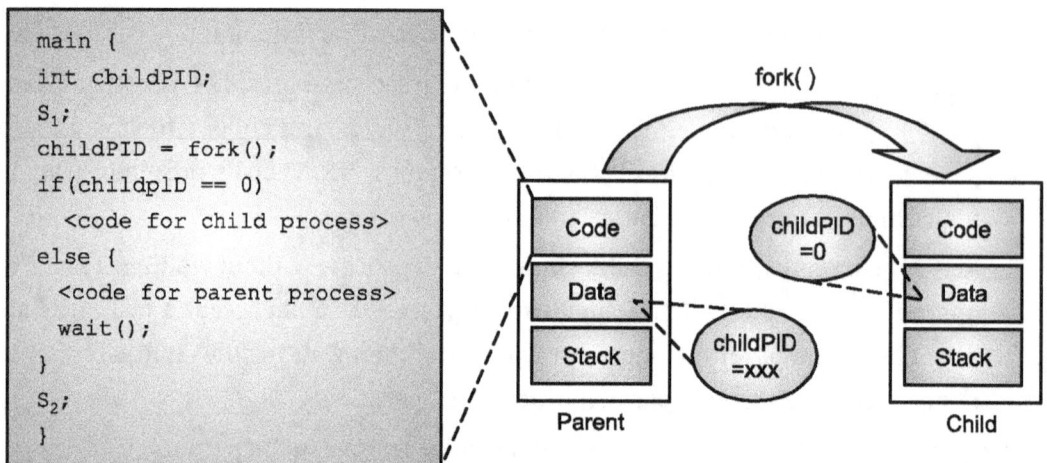

Fig. 2.11: Fork() system call

- The EXECLP system call is used after a FORK call by one of the two processes to replace the processes memory space with a new program. This call loads a binary file into memory and starts its execution. So two processes can be easily communicates with each other.
- Fig. 2.12 below shows the fork and exec process on a UNIX system

```
#include<sys/types.h>
#include<stdio.h>
#include<unistd.h>
int main()
{
pidt pid;
/* fork a child process */
pid = fork();
if (pid < 0){ /* error occurred */
fprintf(stderr, "Fork Failed");
return 1;
}
else if (pid == 0){ /* child process */
execlp("/bin/wc","wc",NULL);
}
else{ /* parent process */
/* parent will wait for the child to complete */
wait(NULL);
printf("Child Complete");
}
return 0;
}
```

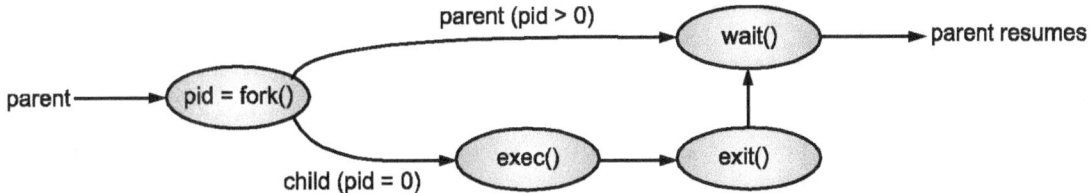

Fig. 2.12: Creating a separate process using the UNIX fork()system call.

2.4.2 Process Termination

- After execution ends, the process is terminated. The operating system terminates the process using EXIT system call typically returning int.
- This int is passed along to the parent if it is doing a wait( ), and is typically zero on successful completion and some non-zero code in the event of problems.

```
child code:
int exitCode;
exit( exitCode ); //return exitCode; has the same effect when executed from
                main( )
parent code:
        pid_t pid;
        int status
        pid = wait( &status );    // pid indicates which child exited.
```

- When the process is terminated, all the resources such as memory, I/O files are deallocated or free by the operating system. The process termination status and execution times are returned to the parent if the parent is waiting for the child to terminate, or eventually returned to init if the process becomes an orphan. Processes which are trying to terminate but which cannot because their parent is not waiting for them are termed zombies. These are eventually inherited by init as orphans and killed off. Modern UNIX shells do not produce as many orphans and zombies as older systems used to.
- Another system call is ABORT. Usually, this call can be invoked by only the parent of the process that is to be terminated.
- There are many reasons for terminating the execution of child process by parent such as:
  1. The child has crossed the limit of usage of the resources it has been allocated.
  2. The child process no longer required.
  3. In response to a KILL command or other unhandled process interrupt.
  4. If the parent-terminates, then operating system does not allows a child to continue execution.
- A process terminates normally or abnormally when a process is terminates, then all its children must be terminated. This is called cascading termination.

2.5 | INTERPROCESS COMMUNICATION

- The concurrent executing processes are two types:

    1. **Independent processes:** They cannot affect or be affected by other executing processes.

    2. **Cooperating processes:** They can affect or be affected by other executing processes in the system. Co-operating processes can share the data with other processes. Co-operating processes requires Interprocess Communication (IPC) mechanisms.

- The co-operation between the processes is required because of the following reasons:

    1. **Information sharing:** The same information (e.g. a shared file) can be shared by many processes.

    2. **Computation speedup:** In multiprocessing system, the same task is divided into number of substasks and subtasks runs parallel to speed up the execution.

    3. **Modularity:** To construct a system in modular way, the system functions are divided into separate processes or threads and these processes wants to communicate with each other.

    4. **Convenience:** If user wants to do parallel task (e.g. editing, printing) at same time.

- Co-operating processes require some type of inter-process communication, which is most commonly one of two types:

    1. Shared memory, and

    2. Message passing.

- In **shared memory model**, memory is shared by cooperating processes. Shared Memory is faster once it is set up, because no system calls are required and access occurs at normal memory speeds. However it is more complicated to set up, and doesn't work as well across multiple computers. Shared memory is generally preferable when large amounts of information must be shared quickly on the same computer. Example—POSIX system.

- In **message passing model**, cooperating process are communicating by means of message exchange Message Passing requires system calls for every message transfer, and is therefore slower, but it is simpler to set up and works well across multiple computers. Message passing is generally preferable when the amount and/or frequency of data transfers is small, or when multiple computers are involved.

- Fig. 2.13 shows the communication models. Example – Mach system.

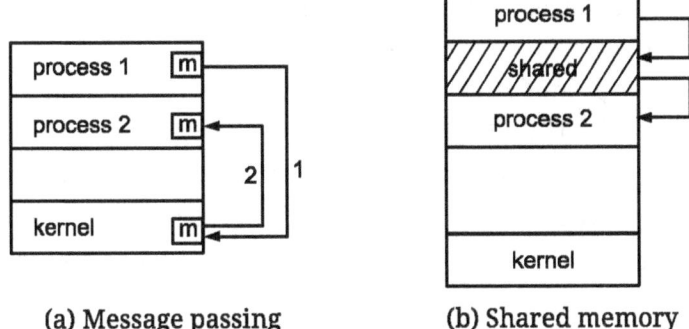

      (a) Message passing   (b) Shared memory

Fig. 2.13: Interprocess communication

2.5.1 Shared Memory Systems

- In this, the communicating processes must establish a region of shared memory. The region is established by the process that is creating the shared memory region in its address space.

- The processes that want to communicate using shared memory region must attach to their address space.

- The processes can exchange the information by reading and writing data in the shared area.

- Let us consider producer – consumer problem which arises in interprocess communication.

Producer – Consumer Problem:

- A process is a program in execution. It is an active entity. A sequential process may be in one of the following four states.

    Running   :   Instructions are being executed.

    Blocked   :   Process waiting for some event to occur.

    Ready   :   Process is waiting to be assigned to a processor.

    Deadlocked   :   Process is waiting for some event that will never occur.

- There are two categories of the processes which are commonly found in an operating system a producer process and a consumer process.

- For example, a print program produces characters that are consumed by printer driver. A compiler may produce assembly code, which is consumed by an assembler. The assembler in turn, may produce object modules, which are consumed by the loader.

- To allow producer and consumer to run concurrently, we must provide a pool of buffers that will be filled by producer and emptied by consumer. Producer can produce in one buffer and consumer can consume from other buffer.
- The unbound-buffer producers/consumers problem places no limit on the number of buffers. (This is practically difficult to achieve).
- The bounded-buffer problem assume that there are some fixed n number of buffers.
- Two pointers in and out are used. They are initialized to zero.
- Producer will first check if buffer is not full, then it will produce an item, add it and increment the in pointer.
- Consumer will check if pool is empty. Condition is (in = out).

The producer code will be,

```
repeat

    produce an item in next-item

    while in + 1 mod n = out do skip;

    (because buffer is full).

        buffer [in] = next_ item

    in:=  in + 1   mod n

    until false.
```

The consumer code will be,

```
repeat

        while in = out do skip;

        next _ item _ consume:= buffer [out]

        out:= out + 1 mod n;

    consume the item in next _item _ consume

until false ;
```

- (Recall this solution is nothing but a circular queue of size n; in and out are rear and front respectively, producer and consumer are same as add-queue ( ) and del-queue ( )).
- If producer and consumer want to share some common data, then care must be taken so that simultaneous access to same data does not lead to wrong execution or computation.
- For example, if counter is a common integer one process may add value to it and the other process which is interested in previous value of count will get this new updated value.

2.5.2 Message Passing Systems

- Message passing mechanism is used for communication of processes without sharing the same address space.

- Message passing provides two operations:

  1. send, and

  2. receive.

- Messages can be either fixed size or variable size. If the message is fixed size, then system implementation is straight forward.

- If the message is variable size, then system level implementation is complex.

- To communicate processes, the communication link must exist between processes. Following are several methods to implement a link logically.

  o   Direct or indirect communication,

  o   Synchronous or asynchronous communication, and

  o   Automatic or explicit buffering.

1. **Direct Communication:**

- The process that wants to communicate must explicitly name the sender or recipient.

- The send() and receive() primitives are as follows:

  o   send (P1, message) → send a message to process P1.

  o   receive (P2, message) → receive a message from process P2.

- This is symmetric scheme. Properties of a communication link in symmetric scheme:

  (i)   Automatically establish between every pair of processes.

  (ii) Associated with exactly two processes.

  (iii) Only one link between two processes.

- Properties of a communication link in asymmetric scheme:

  (i)   receive (id, message) → receive message from any process.

2. **Indirect Communication:**

- In this, the messages are sent to and receive from mailboxes or ports. Multiple processes can share the same mailbox or boxes. Only one process can read any given message in a mailbox.

- Initially the process that creates the mailbox is the owner, and is the only one allowed to read mail in the mailbox, although this privilege may be transferred.

- The OS must provide system calls to create and delete mailboxes, and to send and receive messages to/from mailboxes. Each mailbox has unique identifier.

- The send and receive primitives are as follows:
  (i)   send (A, message) → send a message to mailbox A.
  (ii) receive (A, message) → receive a message from mailbox A.
- **A Communication Link:**
  o   Established between a pair of processes only if both processes have a shared mailbox.
  o   A link can be associated with more than two processes.
  o   Each pair of processes can have number of links.

3. **Synchronization:**

- Different combination of send() and receive() are possible. The message passing is either blocking (synchronous) or non-blocking (asynchronous).
  (i) Blocking send: The sending process is blocked until the message is received by receiving process or by the mailbox.
  (ii) Non-blocking send: The sending process send a message and operation resumes.
  (iii) Blocking receive: The receiver block until message is available.
  (iv) Non-blocking receive: The receiver block can receive message.

4. **Buffering:**

- The messages are stored in a queue. These queues can be implemented for following capacity configurations:
  (i) Zero capacity: This is blocking send stage. The queue has a maximum length of zero.
  (ii) Bounded capacity: The queue has finite length and the maximum no. of messages is stored in a queue equal to length of queue. Sender can continue execution without waiting, if queue is not full. If queue is full, sender must block till queue will have sufficient space.
  (iii) Unbounded capacity: The queue length is infinite. The sender never blocks and any no. of messages can receive and send.

SUMMARY

➤ A process is a program in execution. It is an instance of an application execution.
➤ Program and Process are different. Program is set of instructions to be executed by processor. Program is a passive entity such as the contents of a file stored on disk whereas process is an active entity with a program counter specifying the next instruction to execute.
➤ The process contains text section, data section, heap and stack.

➤ As a process executes, it changes state. The process state reflects the current status of the process. The process can be any one of states like New (Dormant), Ready, Active, Waiting and Halted.

➤ For creating process, operating system maintains a process table. Process table contains an array of structures, with one entry per process. So there is a separate process control block (PCB) for each process. Information in a PCB is updated during the transition of process states. PCB includes Pointer, Process state, Process ID, Process priority, Register, Program counter, I/O status information, Accounting information and Memory limits.

➤ The method of selecting a process to be allocated to CPU is called Process Scheduling.

➤ In multiprogramming, several processes are there in ready or waiting state. These processes form a queue. The various queues maintained by operating system are: Job Queue, Ready queue and Device Queue.

➤ When a process is created, it moves from one scheduling queue to other. The job of the appropriate scheduler is to select the process for execution. There are three different types of scheduler long-term scheduler, medium-term scheduler and short-term scheduler.

➤ The long-term scheduler selects the job or process to be executed from job pool on a secondary storage device and loads them into memory for execution. The long-term scheduler executes less frequently. It controls degree of multi-programming.

➤ Short-term scheduler selects a job from ready queue and submits it to CPU. As the short-term scheduler selects only one job at a time, it is invoked very frequently.

➤ Swapping is term associated with the medium-term scheduler by which processes are temporarily removed and then brought back to the ready queue.

➤ Switching the CPU from one process to another process requires saving the state of old process and loading the saved state of new process. This task is known as Context Switch.

➤ There are two operations provided by operating system on processes: Process creation and Process termination.

➤ When a process creates a sub process, the sub process obtains the resources from its parent or from the operating system directly.

➤ In UNIX, each process has a unique integer number called process identifier or process-id. A child is created by the FORK system call. The FORK operation is used to split a sequence of instructions into two concurrently executable instruction sequences. The parent process can be easily communicated with new process because the new process consists of a copy of the address space of the original process.

➤ After execution ends, the process is terminated. The operating system terminates the process using EXIT system call typically returning int.

➢ The concurrent executing processes are two types i.e., Independent processes, Cooperating processes.

➢ Independent processes cannot affect or be affected by other executing processes.

➢ Cooperating processes can affect or be affected by other executing processes in the system.

➢ Co-operating processes can share the data with other processes. Cooperating processes require some type of inter-process communication, which is most commonly one of two types: Shared memory and Message passing.

➢ In shared memory model, memory is shared by cooperating processes. Shared Memory is faster once it is set up, because no system calls are required and access occurs at normal memory speeds.. Shared memory is generally preferable when large amounts of information must be shared quickly on the same computer. Example, POSIX system.

➢ In message passing model, cooperating process are communicating by means of message exchange Message Passing requires system calls for every message transfer. Message passing is generally preferable when the amount and/or frequency of data transfers is small, or when multiple computers are involved. Example – Mach system.

PRACTICE QUESTIONS

1. Define:
   (i) Cascading termination
   (ii) FORK system call
   (iii) Device queue
   (iv) Ready queue
   (v) Context switch

2. Write the functions of:
   (i) Long-term scheduler
   (ii) Short-term scheduler
   (iii) Short-term scheduler

3. Explain the structure and importance of Process Control Block (PCB).

4. What is a scheduler? What are the different types of schedulers? Describe each in brief.

5. Describe the difference between the short-term, medium-term and long-term scheduling. Indicate clearly their position in the process state diagram. When does the operating system call each of them?

6. What is a process? State and explain in brief different types of process states.

7. Write a note on message passing.

8. Define terms:
    (i)   Bounded capacity
    (ii) Zero capacity
    (iii) Co-operating processes
    (iv) Independent processes

9. State two types of processes used for interprocess communication.

10. Why co-operation between the processes is required?

11. Compare message passing and shared memory.

12. State two models used in interprocess communication.

13. Write a note on interprocesses communication models.

14. Explain the properties of communication link in direct and indirect communication.

15. State two primitives used for message passing.

16. **Multiple Choice Questions**:
    (i)   A child is created by _____ system call.
          (a) fork   (b) create   (c) exit   (d) execlp
    (ii) _____ scheduler loads the job from secondary storage to memory.
          (a) short-term   (b) long-term   (c) medium-term   (d) all.
    (iii) The list in which jobs are waiting for CPU is called _____
          (a) scheduler   (b) CPU   (c) PCB   (d) dispatcher.
    Ans.: (i) a   (ii) b   (iii) c.

17. **State True or False:**
    (i)   A process is a program in execution.
    (ii) Short-term scheduler loads the process from secondary storage to memory.
    (iii) The time is required for CPU to switch from one process to other.
    (iv) The process is allocated to the CPU is called running state of the process.
    Ans.: (i) True (ii) False (iii) True (iv) True.

18. What is process? List the different types of process states.

Ans. Refer to Sections 2.2 and 2.2.2.

19. What is scheduler? Explain medium-term scheduler in detail.

Ans. Refer to Section 2.3.2.

20. What do you mean by context switch?

Ans. Refer to Section 2.3.3.

21.  ```
     p = fork ( );
     printf ("Hi");
     ```
     This program segment prints Hi two times on screen. Justify.

Ans. True. fork () will create one child process. It creates a new copy of the running program and both continue running the same instructions, which is to print "hi" two times.

22. Explain PCB with proper diagram.

Ans. Refer to Section 2.2.3.

23. Give the diagrammatic representation for - Swapping of two processes using a disk as a backing store.

Ans. Refer to Section 2.3.2.

24. Which are different events in which process switches from running state to waiting state?

Ans. Refer to Section 2.2.2.

25. What is co-operating process? Explain in brief two fundamental models of interprocess communication.

Ans. Refer to Section 2.5

26. State the role of medium-term process scheduler.

Ans. Refer to Section 2.3.2 (Point 3).

27. "Any executable file on a disk is called as a process" True/False – Justify)

Ans. False. When executable file has been run by CPU, then it becomes a process.

28. Define short term scheduler with queuing diagram.

Ans. Refer to Section 2.3.2 (Point 2).

29. What are the two common models of interprocess communication?

Ans. Refer to Section 2.5.

30. What will happen if all processes are I/O bound in system?

Ans. Refer to Section 2.3.2.

UNIVERSITY QUESTIONS AND ANSWERS

1. Which scheduler controls the degree of multiprogramming? How?

    (April 2013) (1 M)

Ans. Refer to Section 2.3.2.

2. Write a primary function of Medium term scheduler. **(April 2015) (1 M)**

Ans. Refer to Section 2.3.2 (Point 3).

■■■
     ```

Multithreaded Programming

Contents ...

Objectives...

- To Understand the Benefits of Multithreaded Programming
- To Learn the Concept of Multi-core Programming
- To Study different Multithreaded Models

3.1 | INTRODUCTION

- Concurrency can be implemented by structuring an application as a set of concurrent processes. However, use of traditional processes in this manner is considerable overheads due to process management and scheduling functions.
- A traditional process has one thread of execution. The operating system keeps track of the memory map, saved registers, and stack pointer in the process control block and the operating system's scheduler is responsible for making sure that the process gets to run every once in a while. Threads are a low cost alternative to processes for certain kinds of concurrent applications.
- Using Threads, the overhead of context-switching is also reduced.
- Threads provide a way to improve application performance through parallelism. In this chapter, we will discuss the concept of threads and threaded models.

3.2 | OVERVIEW

- A thread is a flow of execution through the process code, with its own program counter, system registers and stack.
- A thread is also called as light weight process.
- It is also defined as a "unit of concurrency within a process and had access to the entire code and data parts of the process". Thus, thread of the same process can share their code and data with one another.
- A thread is used to utilize CPU more effectively.
- A process may be multithreaded, where the same program contains multiple concurrent threads of execution. If the processes are multithreaded, it can perform more than one task at a time.
- The items that the operating system must store that are unique to each thread are:
  1. Thread ID,
  2. Saved registers, stack pointer, instruction pointer,
  3. Stack (local variables, temporary variables, return addresses),
  4. Signal mask, and
  5. Priority (Scheduling information).

Difference between Process and Thread:

Sr. No.	Process	Thread
1.	Process is heavy weight or resource intensive.	Thread is light weight taking lesser resources than a process.
2.	Process switching needs interaction with operating system.	Thread switching does not need to interact with operating system.
3.	In multiple processing environments each process executes the same code but has its own memory and file resources.	All threads can share same set of open files, child processes.
4.	If one process is blocked then no other process can execute until the first process is unblocked	While one thread is blocked and waiting, second thread in the same task can run.
5.	Multiple processes without using threads use more resources.	Multiple threaded processes use fewer resources.
6.	In multiple processes each process operates independently of the others.	One thread can read, write or change another thread's data.

- The Fig. 3.1 shows the single threaded and multithreaded processes.

code	data	stack
files		registers

Thread

(a) Single-threaded process

code	data	files
stack	stack	stack
registers	registers	registers

Thread

(b) Multithreaded process

Fig. 3.1: Single threaded and multithreaded processes

- Operating system supports multiple threads of execution within a single process. Most operating system kernels are multithreaded. Example, **Solaris** operating system is a multithreaded; it creates a set of thread for interrupt handling. **Linux** uses set of thread for managing the amount of free memory. WINDOWS XP, Mac OS X are support multithreaded models. In many situations, multithreaded is preferable than single threaded (DOS is single threaded).

Example:

- Consider web server. The web-server has to process request from many clients. Clients can request for the web pages or images or audio-video clips etc. If server run as a single process (threaded) then for each client request, it has to create a separate process to service that request. It is time consuming. Therefore, multithreaded processes are used by server.

- For each client request, server is creating new thread rather than creating process. The multithreaded processes are also used by remote procedure call server.

- When server receives a message from client, the remote server services the message using separate thread.

- The Fig. 3.2 shows the multithreaded server architecture.

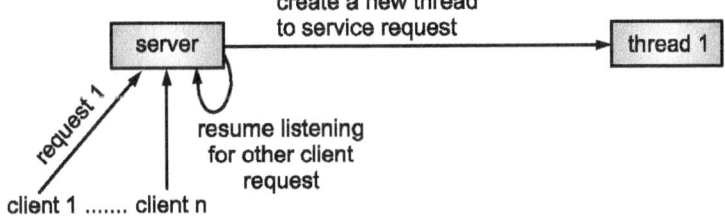

Fig. 3.2: Multithreaded servlet architecture

- When client 1 request for a service, server creates a new thread to service that request and then resume listening for other client request.

- The operating system also treats threads exactly like processes except for one difference – it does not save and restore the execution environment while switching between threads.

- Uses of Threads in a Single-User Multiprocessing System:

  1. Foreground to background work,

  2. Asynchronous processing,

  3. Speed of execution, and

  4. Modular program structure.

3.2.1 Benefits of Multithreaded Programming   (April 2016, Oct. 16)

- Various benefits of multithreaded programming are listed below:

  1. **Responsiveness:** Thread management is performed through a thread library. This library provides function to create and terminate threads, to synchronize their activities and to permit them to make request to the operating system. So multithreading is an interactive application, allow user interaction in one thread while some other operation is performing with another thread. The program is continued to run even if part of it is blocked.

  2. **Resource sharing:** Threads share the memory and the resources of the process to which they belong. Less address space is required.

  3. **Economy:** Threads does not save and restore the execution environment, so context switch time is less. Separate processes are not need to create for each request.

  4. **Scalability:** In multiprocessor systems, threads are running in parallel on different processes, so multithreading is beneficial.

3.2.2 Multicore Programming

- In a single core system, one processor runs multiple threads. The threads are executed in interleaved manner, because processor can run only on thread at a time.

- In a multicore system, more than one processors are in the system. The threads are executed in parallel manner. Each processor can run one thread at a time.

- Example, if system has 3 processors, then 3 threads are executed at the same time.

- The Fig. 3.3 shows the single-core and multicore systems. In single-core, concurrent execution occurs and in multicore, parallel execution occurs.

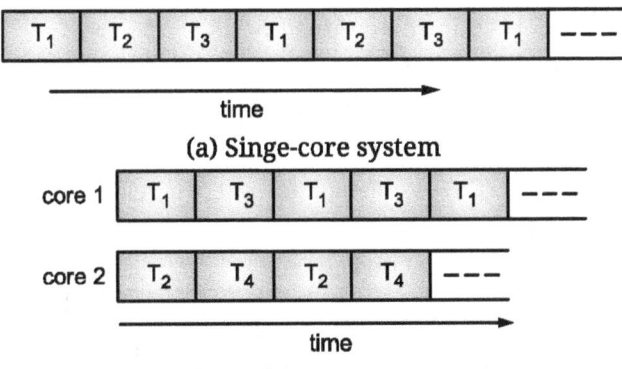

(a) Singe-core system

(b) Multi-core system

Fig. 3.3: Thread execution

- For parallel execution of threads, the designer of operating system must write proper scheduling algorithm.
- There are five challenging areas which have to be considered by application programmer while designing a new program for multicore systems. They are as follows:

   1. **Dividing activities:** While dividing the program into separate tasks, the programmer examines the features of applications and find how the tasks are divided.

   2. **Data splitting:** Data is also divided into separate task and run on the separate core.

   3. **Balance:** The programmer must ensure that the task can perform equal work of equal value. The tasks should be balance on multiple cores to run.

   4. **Data dependency:** The task dependency is examined by programmer and the dependent task may be run on the same core and properly synchronized.

   5. **Testing and debugging:** Testing and debugging of multi-threaded application is more difficult than single threaded application. The programmer must take care, when the program is running on multicore system.

3.3 | MULTITHREADING MODELS   (April 13)

- The threads are implemented using two approaches:
   1. Kernel level threads, and
   2. User level threads.

1. Kernel Level Threads:

- In this case, thread management done by the Kernel. There is no thread management code in the application area.
- Kernel threads are supported directly by the operating system.
- The Kernel maintains context information for the process as a whole and for individuals' threads within the process.

- Scheduling by the Kernel is done on a thread basis.
- The Kernel performs thread creation, scheduling and management in Kernel space.
- Kernel thread is created using create-thread call. The kernel creates a new thread and assigns it an id. The call returns with the id of the thread.
- A Thread Control Block (TCB) is needed for each thread and scheduler use thread control block for scheduling.
- The Fig. 3.4 shows the kernel level threads.

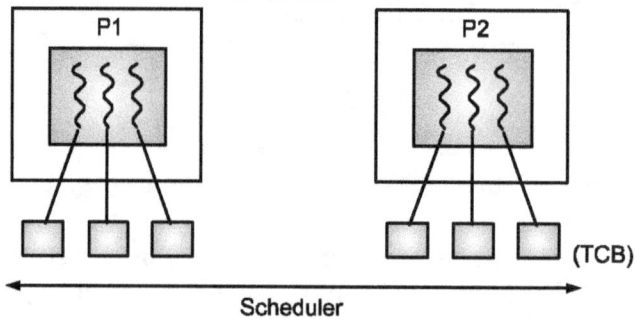

Fig. 3.4: Kernel level

- For Example, Windows XP, Solaris, Linux, Mac OS X.

Advantages:

(i)   Kernel can simultaneously schedule multiple threads from the same process on multiple processes.

(ii) If one thread in a process is blocked, the Kernel can schedule another thread of the same process.

(iii) Kernel routines themselves can multithreaded.

Disadvantages:

(i)   Kernel threads are generally slower to create and manage than the user threads.

(ii) Transfer of control from one thread to another within same process requires a mode switch to the Kernel.

2. **User Level Threads:**

- In this case, application manages thread management. Kernel is not aware of the existence of threads.
- The thread library contains code for creating and destroying threads, for passing message and data between threads, for scheduling thread execution and for saving and restoring thread contexts.
- The application begins with a single thread and begins running in that thread.
- A process does not create a thread using a **create thread** call.
- The process manages its own threads. The **id** of the user-level thread is not known to the kernel.

- Thread management is performed through a thread library and no burden on application of programmer.
- User threads are supported above the kernel and are managed without kernel support.
- The Fig. 3.5 shows the user level threads.

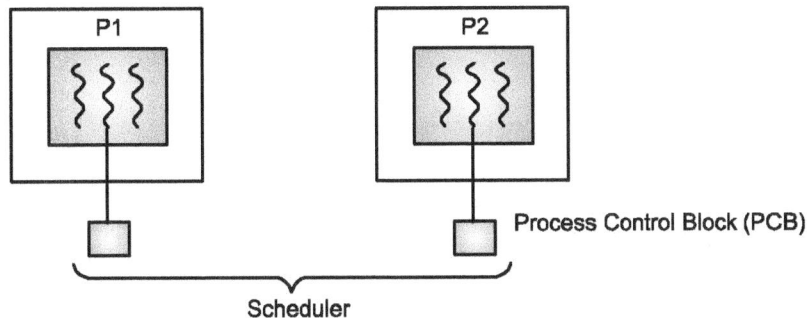

Fig. 3.5: User level threads

Advantages:

(i) Thread switching does not require Kernel mode privileges.

(ii) User level thread can run on any operating system.

(iii) Scheduling can be application specific in the user level thread.

(iv) User level threads are fast to create and manage.

Disadvantages:

(i) In a typical operating system, most system calls are blocking. If a thread were to block in a system call, it would block the process containing the thread. In effect, all threads of the process would get blocked.

(ii) Multithreaded application cannot take advantage of multiprocessing.

Difference between User Level Thread and Kernel Level Thread: (April 13)

Sr. No.	User level threads	Kernel level threads
1.	User level threads are faster to create and manage.	Kernel level threads are slower to create and Manage.
2.	Implementation is by a thread library at the user level.	Operating system supports creation of Kernel threads.
3.	User level thread is generic and can run on any operating system.	Kernel level thread is specific to the operating System.
4.	Multi-threaded application cannot take advantage of multiprocessing.	Kernel routines themselves can be Multithreaded.

- There are three common ways to establish the relationship between user thread and kernel thread i.e., Many-to-one, One-to-one and Many-to-many.

3.3.1 Many-to-One Model

- In this model, many user level threads multiplexes to the Kernel thread of smaller or equal numbers i.e., many-to-one model maps many user-level threads to one kernel-level thread.

- The number of Kernel threads may be specific to either a particular application or a particular machine.

- Example, Green threads for Solaris.

- Fig. 3.6 shows many-to-one model concept.

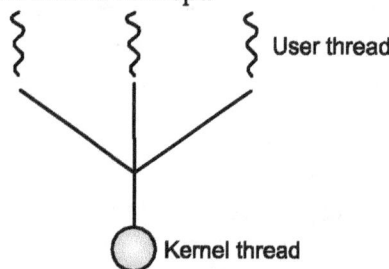

Fig. 3.6: Many-to-one model

Advantages:

1. Thread management is done by thread library in user space.

2. It is efficient because thread management is done by thread library.

Disadvantages:

1. The disadvantage is entire process will block if a thread makes blocking system call.

2. Multiple threads are not able to run in parallel since only one thread can be accessed by kernel at a time.

3.3.2 One-to-One Model   (April 15)

- There is one to one relationship of user level thread to the kernel level thread i.e. Each user threads maps to a kernel thread.

- The Fig. 3.7 shows one-to-one model.

- Example, LINUX, OS/2, Windows NT and windows 2000 use one to one relationship model.

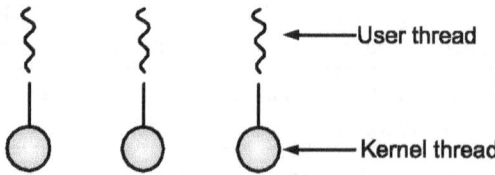

Fig. 3.7: One-to-One Model

Advantages:

1. This model provides more concurrency than the many to one model.

2. When one thread makes a blocking call, the entire process will not block and concurrent execution of thread is possible.

3. It support multiple thread to execute in parallel on microprocessors.

Disadvantages:

1. The disadvantage is, for each user thread, the kernel thread is required.

2. Creating a kernel thread is overhead and performance of application degrades.

3.3.3 Many-to-Many Model   (April 15, 16)

*   In this model, many user level threads multiplexes to the Kernel thread of smaller or equal numbers.

*   The number of Kernel threads may be specific to either a particular application or a particular machine.

*   Example, IRIX, HP-VX and Tru 64 UNIX.

*   The Fig. 3.8 shows many-to-many model which maps many user held threads to a smaller or equal number of kernel threads.

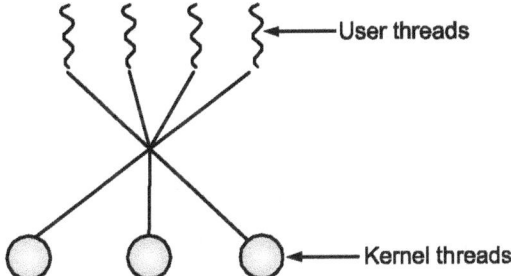

Fig. 3.8: Many-to-many model

Advantages:

1. Developers can create any number of threads and corresponding kernel threads can run in parallel on a multiprocessor.

2. Process will not block, since a thread performs a blocking system call, the kernel can schedule another thread for execution.

3. For large number of threads, many-to-many model is efficient than one-to-one.

4. For greater concurrency, this model is efficient than many-to-one.

5. The variation of this model is sometimes called two-level model.

Disadvantages:

1. Multiple threads of kernel are an overhead for OS.

2. Low performance.

SUMMARY

➤ A thread is a flow of execution through the process code, with its own program counter, system registers and stack.

➤ A thread is also called as light weight process. It is used to utilize CPU more effectively.

➤ It act as a unit of concurrency within a process and had access to the entire code and data parts of the process. Thus thread of the same process can share their code and data with one another.

➤ A process may be multithreaded, where the same program contains multiple concurrent threads of execution. If the processes are multithreaded, it can perform more than one task at a time.

➤ Operating system supports multiple threads of execution within a single process. That operating system kernel is multithreaded.

➤ In a single core system, one processor runs multiple threads. The threads are executed in interleaved manner, because processor can run only on thread at a time.

➤ In a multicore system, more than one processors are in the system. The threads are executed in parallel manner. Each processor can run one thread at a time.

➤ The threads are implemented using two approaches: Kernel level threads and User level threads.

➤ In kernel level threads, thread management done by the Kernel. There is no thread management code in the application area. Kernel threads are supported directly by the operating system.

➤ In user level threads, application manages thread management. Kernel is not aware of the existence of threads. The thread library contains code for creating and destroying threads, for passing message and data between threads, for scheduling thread execution and for saving and restoring thread contexts.

➤ There are three common ways to establish the relationship between user thread and kernel thread: Many-to-one, One-to-one and Many-to-many

➤ Many-to-one model maps many user-level threads to one kernel-level thread.

➤ In one-to-one model, there is one to one relationship of user level thread to the kernel level thread.

➤ In many-to-many model, many user level threads multiplexes to the Kernel thread of smaller or equal numbers.

PRACTICE QUESTIONS

1. Compare user-level and kernel level threads.
2. Explain many-to-one model of multithreading.
3. State any two example of one-to-one model.

4. Can a multithreaded solution using multiple user-level threads achieve better performance on a multiprocessor system than on a single-processor system? Explain.

5. What resources are used when a thread is created?

6. Under what circumferences user-level and kernel-level threads type better than the other.

7. In many-to-many model, no. of user-level threads are greater than kernel levels threads-state true or false.

8. Which are the challenging areas faced by application programmer while designing multicore system program.

9. Explain the benefits of multithreaded programming or what the advantages of multithreaded programming are.

10. What do you mean by multicore programming.

11. Differentiate single core and multicore system.

12. Define Thread.

13. Differentiate between single threaded process and multithreaded process.

14. Explain multithreaded server architecture with an example.

15. **Multiple choice questions:**

    (i) Which of the following components of a program state are shared across threads in multithreaded process ? _____

         (a) Register values   (b) Heap memory

         (c) Global variable   (d) Stack

    (ii) Which of the following operating system not uses the kernel level thread _____

         (a) WindowsXP   (b) MS-DOS

         (c) Linux   (d) Solaris

    (iii) Which of the following is not used many-to-many model of multithreading.

         (a) IRIX   (b) HP-VX

         (c) Tru64UNIX   (d) Green threads for solaris

    Ans.: (i) a and d, (ii) b, (iii) d.

16. What is difference between process based model and thread based model?

Ans. Refer to Section 3.2.

17. What are the benefits of multithreading programming? Explain any one of Multithreading models.

Ans. Refer to Section 3.2.1.

18. Explain the following multithreading models.

    (a) One-to-one model

    (b) Many-to-many model.

Ans. Refer to Sections 3.3.2 and 3.3.3.

19. Multi-threaded programs are good candidate for a deadlock. Justify.

Ans. True. Multithreaded programs are good candidates for deadlock because multiple threads can compete for shared resources.

20. List two benefits of multithreaded programming.

Ans. Refer to Section 3.2.

21. State two benefits of multi-threading.

Ans. Refer to Section 3.2.

22. Explain Many-to-Many multithreading model.

Ans. Refer to Section 3.3.3.

UNIVERSITY QUESTIONS AND ANSWERS

  1.   Define term kernel-thread and user-thread.   **(April 2013) (1M)**

Ans.   Refer to Section 3.3.

  2.   Explain any two types of Multithreading.   **(April 2015) (5M)**

Ans.   Refer to Sections 3.3.2 and 3.3.3.

■■■

Process Scheduling

Contents ...

Objectives...

- To Understand Concept of CPU scheduling, i.e. the Basis for Multiprogramming Operating Systems
- To Learn Evaluation Criteria for Selecting a CPU-Scheduling Algorithm for a Particular System
- To Study various CPU Scheduling Algorithms like FCFS, SJF, RR, etc.
- To Know How to Schedule Threads?

4.1 INTRODUCTION

- The assignment of physical processors to processes allows processors to accomplish work.
- In multi-programming environment, many processes are in memory.
- The problem of determining when processors should be assigned and to which processes is called processor scheduling or CPU scheduling.
- When more than one process is run able, the operating system must decide which one first.
- The part of the operating system concerned with this decision is called the scheduler, and algorithm it uses is called the scheduling algorithm.
- Scheduling is a important function of operating system.
- The process scheduling is the activity of the process manager that handles the removal of the running process from the CPU and the selection of another process on the basis of a particular strategy.
- In this chapter, we discuss about CPU scheduling and scheduling algorithms.

4.2 BASIC SCHEDULING CONCEPTS

- In batch operating system, the batch of jobs is submitted to system sequentially.
- The CPU executes each job sequentially. The other job or process has to wait until the CPU is free and can be rescheduled.
- In multiprogramming system, many programs are present in memory.
- The CPU executes one program at a time. If that program requires I/O then operating system switches the CPU to another.
- At that time switching time is requires to switch among the processes.
- The other process has to wait; the operating system takes the CPU away from that process. This cycle is continued.
- In this manner processes are executed concurrently. Here, CPU is primary resource used and its scheduling is very important.
- The main objectives of scheduling are:
  1. Enforcement of fairness in allocating resources to processes.
  2. Enforcement of priorities to processes.
  3. Make best use of available system resources.
  4. Give preference to processes holding key resources.
  5. Give preference to processes exhibiting good behavior.
  6. Degrade gracefully under heavy loads.

4.2.1 CPU and I/O Burst Cycle   (April 16)

- The success of CPU scheduling depends on the following observed property of processes: the process execution is cycle of CPU execution and I/O wait.

- Processes alternate back and forth between these two states as shown in Fig. 4.1.

- When the process is allocated to CPU after selecting from ready queue; it starts with CPU burst. (i.e. time for process is allocated to CPU).

- The CPU burst is followed by I/O burst when process required I/O.

- Again CPU burst (when I/O is finished), then I/O burst and so on.

- The last CPU burst will end with a system request to terminate execution.

- The duration of CPU burst vary from process to process or computer to computer.

- If the program is I/O bound, then it has short CPU burst, when the program or process is CPU bound then it has very short I/O burst.

- This distribution is important in selecting appropriate CPU scheduling algorithms discussed in further section.

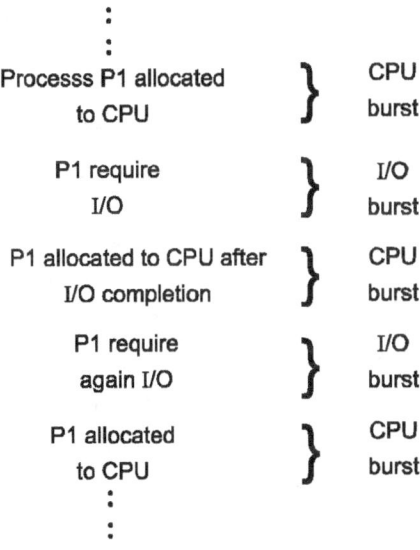

Fig. 4.1: CPU and I/O burst

4.2.2 CPU Scheduler

- CPU scheduler or short-term scheduler selects the process from ready queue allocates to CPU for execution.

- This selection of process is not in FIFO order but it depends on CPU scheduling algorithms.

4.2.3 Pre-emptive and Non-preemptive Scheduling   (Oct. 16)

- The scheduling schemes are of two types:
    1. Pre-emptive scheduling, and
    2. Non-preemptive scheduling.
- When a CPU allocates a process and releases the process after completion or the process switches from running state to waiting state (request for I/O) then it is non-preemptive scheduling scheme.
- When a process switches from running state to the ready state (e.g. when interrupt occurs) or switches from waiting to ready; then it is pre-emptive scheduling scheme. The pre-emptive means the process is pre-empted or interrupted.

Disadvantages of Pre-emptive Scheduling:

1. The scheduling cost is increases.
2. When two processors are sharing same data. One process is updating the data and at that time the pre-emption occurs then it will affect on the other process which is reading same data.
3. Pre-emption also has an affect on the design of the operating system kernel i.e. the important kernel data may be changed.

- **Example:** Windows 95 and subsequent versions of windows used preemptive scheduling. Non-preemptive scheduling (cooperative scheduling) is used only on certain hardware platforms because it does not required special hardware like timer.

4.2.4 Dispatcher   (April 13, 15, 16, Oct. 16)

- Dispatcher is a component which involves in the CPU scheduling.
- The dispatcher is the module that actually gives control of the CPU to the process selected by the short-term scheduler.
- The following are functions performed by dispatcher:
    1. Loading the register of the process.
    2. Switching operating system to the user mode.
    3. Restart the program by jumping to the proper location in the user program.
- The dispatcher needs to be as fast as possible, as it is run on every context switch.
- The time taken by dispatcher to stop one process and start another process to run is called dispatch latency time.   (April 13, Oct. 13)

4.3 | SCHEDULING CRITERIA   (April 13, 16)

- Scheduling algorithm is one which selects some job from ready queue based on some criteria and submits it to the CPU.

- There are many different CPU, Scheduling algorithms are available and different CPU scheduling algorithms have different properties and may favour one class of processes over another.

- To choose a particular algorithm for a particular situation, we must consider the properties of the various algorithms. For comparing CPU - scheduling algorithms many criteria have been suggested.

- The characteristics used for comparison can make a substantial difference in the determination of the best algorithm.

- The scheduling criteria are listed below:

   1. **CPU utilization:** It gives the information about how much time the CPU is busy. CPU time is the most expensive resource of computer system. So keep the CPU and other resources as busy as possible. This utilization may range from 0% to 100%. Less the time CPU is idle, more is its utilization.

   2. **Throughput:** It is amount of work done or number of jobs done in a unit of time or number of processes completes their execution per unit time. If throughput is more, then the algorithm is better.

   3. **Turnaround time:** For a process, the important criterion is how long it takes to execute that process. Turnaround time is the interval from the time of submission to the time of completion. i.e. The amount of time to execute a particular process from its entry time. Smaller the turnaround time better is the algorithm. It is sum of job service time and waiting time.   **(April 16)**

   4. **Waiting time:** Waiting time is the amount of time a job or process is waiting in the ready queue. More the waiting time, more is the turnaround time. A good system/algorithm should have the aim to have a small waiting time.

   5. **Response time:** Response time is the time interval from submission of the job, to time when the first response was produced. This response is not the complete output. By the time first response is produced, computer may start computing next result. This major criterion is used because sometimes turnaround time is delayed because of slow output device and algorithm is not judged properly. To guarantee that all users get good service, we may want to minimize the maximum response time.

- In order to maximize CPU utilization and throughput, to minimize turnaround time, waiting time and response time, we need to optimize the average measure using scheduling algorithms.

4.4 | SCHEDULING ALGORITHMS   (April 13)

- The different scheduling algorithms are:
  1. FCFS (First Come First Serve).
  2. SJF (Shortest Job First).
     - Pre-emptive, and
     - Non-pre-emptive.
  3. Priority scheduling
  4. RR (Round Robin) scheduling
  5. Multi-level queues scheduling
  6. Multi-level feedback queues scheduling.
- To find out performance of the scheduling algorithms, we can use Gantt charts.
- Gantt chart is nothing but a chart use to describe a schedule. It will represent the sequence in which the jobs will be scheduled by the CPU.

4.4.1 FCFS (First Come First Serve) Scheduling

- The simplest among all is the FCFS scheduling algorithm.
- The process that requests the CPU first, is allocated CPU first. Jobs are processed in the order of their arrival in the ready queue.
- It can be implemented with FIFO (First In First Out) queue.
- The FCFS scheduling algorithm is non-pre-emptive. Once the CPU has been allocated to a process, that process keeps the CPU until it wants to release the CPU, either by terminating or by requesting I/O.
- In time-sharing system it is not useful because process will hold the CPU until it finishes or changes a state to wait state.
- Performance of FCFS is often very poor because a process with a long CPU burst will hold up other processes. Moreover, it can affect overall throughput since I/O on processes in the waiting state may complete; while the CPU bound process is still running.
- Average waiting time for FCFS algorithm is not minimal, and it also varies substantially if the process CPU burst time vary greatly.

Example:

Jobs	Burst Time	Arrival Time
1	2	1
2	3	0
3	4	2

- Above given is the CPU burst time and arrival time of each job present in the ready queue.
- To calculate turnaround time and wait time, we will first draw the Gantt chart.

J 2	J 1	J 3
0 3	5	9

Jobs	Turnaround time	Wait time
1	(5 – 1) = 4	3 – 1 = 2
2	(3 – 0) = 3	0 – 0 = 0
3	(9 – 2) = 7	5 – 2 = 3
	14	5

Average turnaround = $\frac{14}{3}$ = 4.66.

Average wait time = $\frac{5}{3}$ = 1.66.

- Note that turnaround time is the difference between time of completion of a job and its arrival time.
- Wait time is time for which job was waiting in the ready queue i.e. difference of starting time of job and its arrival time.
- If arrival time is not given in the same example then arrival of each job is assumed to be zero.

Gantt chart would be:

J 1	J 2	J 3
0 2	5	9

Jobs	Turnaround Time	Wait Time
1	(2 – 0) = 2	(0 – 0) = 0
2	(5 – 0) = 5	(2 – 0) = 2
3	(9 – 0) = 9	(5 – 0) = 5
	16	7

Average turnaround = $\frac{16}{3}$ = 5.33.

Average wait time = $\frac{7}{3}$ = 2.33.

4.4.2 SJF (Shortest Job First) Scheduling

- Jobs or processes are processed in the ascending order of their CPU burst times.
- Every time the job with smallest CPU burst-time is selected from the ready queue.
- If the two processes having same CPU burst then they will be scheduled according to FCFS algorithm

- Performance of this algorithm is very good in comparison to FCFS.
- The SJF scheduling algorithm is probably optimal; it gives minimal average waiting time for a given set of processes. By moving short process before a long one, the waiting time of short process decreases. Consequently average waiting time reduces.

Drawbacks:

1. As it is optimal algorithm it cannot be implemented in short-term CPU scheduling.
2. This algorithm expects jobs to be submitted with their burst time. Many times it is practically not possible that, one will predict the correct burst time of a job.
3. Aging is another problem where big jobs are waiting for long-time in the CPU.

- SJF can be evaluated in two different manners.
   1. **Non-pre-emptive SJF:** In this method if CPU is executing one job, it is not stopped in between before completion.
   2. **Pre-emptive SJF:** In this method while CPU is executing a job, if a new job arrives with smaller burst time, then the current job is pre-empted (sent back to ready queue) and the new job is executed. It is also called Shortest Remaining Time First (SRTF).

Example:

Jobs	Burst Time	Arrival Time
1	4	0
2	1	1
3	2	2
4	1	3

1. **Non-pre-emptive SJF:**

- At ø time unit only one job (J1) is in the ready queue. So we must start with J1.
- J2 and J4 has same burst times, therefore by applying FCFS we will consider J2 before J4.
- As it is non-pre-emptive, J1 will not be pre-empted before completion.

Gantt chart would be:

J 1	J 2	J 4	J 3

0   4   5   6   8

Jobs	Turnaround Time	Wait Time
1	(4 − 0) = 4	(0 − 0) = 0
2	(5 − 1) = 4	(4 − 1) = 3
3	(8 − 2) = 6	(6 − 2) = 4
4	(6 − 3) = 3	(5 − 3) = 2
	17	9

Average turnaround time = $\dfrac{17}{4}$ = 4.25.

Average wait time = $\dfrac{9}{4}$ = 2.25.

2. Pre-emptive SJF:

- At zero time units there is only one job in the ready queue. Therefore we must start with J1.
- At one time unit a new job J2 arrives with smaller burst time therefore J1 will be pre-empted and J2 will complete its execution.
- At two time units J3 arrives and CPU starts executing it. J3 has a burst time of two units.
- After one unit of it is over (i.e. at 3 time units) J4 arrives with 1 as burst time.
- Now if we compare balance burst time of J3 (i.e. 2 – 1) and burst time of J4 (i.e. 1) both is exactly same.
- Applying FCFS, J3 will continue. At the end J4 will be executed and then balance of J1.
- Gantt chart would be:

Brought back for balance execution

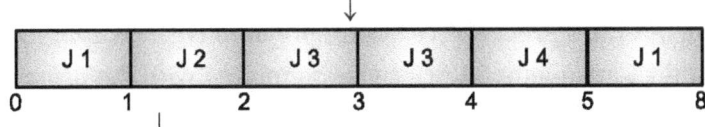

Pre-empted

Jobs	Turnaround Time	Wait Time
1	(8 – 0) = 8	(0 – 0) + (5 – 1) = 4
2	(2 – 1) = 1	(1 – 1) = 0
3	(4 – 2) = 2	(2 – 2) = 0
4	(5 – 3) = 2	(4 – 3) = 1
	13	5

Average turnaround time = $\dfrac{13}{4}$ = 3.25.

Average wait time = $\dfrac{5}{4}$ = 1.25.

Little explanation about Wait Time and Turnaround Time:

- In the above mentioned example J1 started its execution at zero time units but as it was pre-empted, it's execution was over at 8 time units. Therefore, turnaround time for J1 is 8 – 0 = 8.
- J1 is arrived at zero time units and immediately started executing. Therefore, wait time for J1 is (0 – 0) = 0.
- But when J1 was pre-empted, it was again waiting in the ready queue for CPU. This time (5 – 1) if added to previous wait time.

    ∴   Total wait time of J1 = (0 – 0) + (5 – 1) = 4.

4.4.3 Priority Scheduling

- Along with arrival time and the burst time, sometimes some more information is submitted along with jobs i.e. the priority of the job.
- While processing, the jobs are scheduled in the descending order of their priorities i.e. first the highest priority job is considered and at the end the lowest priority job is considered.
- Equal priority processes are scheduled with FCFS algorithm.
- SJF algorithm is a special case of Priority scheduling algorithm where priority is the predicted next CPU burst time.
- Priorities are roughly categorized into internal and external priorities.
- Internal priorities are based on burst time, memory requirements, number of open files etc. measurable quantities.
- External priorities are human created e.g. seniority, influence of any person, etc. In our syllabus only internal priorities are considered.
- The priority scheduling can be either pre-emptive or non-pre-emptive.
- When process enters into the ready queue, its priority is compared with the priority of the current running process.
- In a pre-emptive priority scheduling algorithm, at any time, the CPU is allocated one process and if the priority of the newly arrived process is higher than the priority of the currently running process, the process which was allocated is interrupted and return to the queue. The higher priority job is started for execution.
- A non-preemptive priority - scheduling algorithm will simply put the new process at the head of the ready queue.
- A problem with priority scheduling algorithm is indefinite blocking or starvation. Here, the low priority process may be indefinitely locked out by the higher priority processes. In general, completion of a process within finite time of its creation cannot be guaranteed with this scheduling policy.
- A solution to the problem of starvation of low priority processes is aging.   (Oct. 16)
- Aging is process in which the priority of each process is gradually increased after the process spends a certain amount of time in the system. Even a process with an initial priority 0, get the higher priority in the system and it would be executed.
- Example:

Jobs	Burst Time	Priority
1	4	4
2	6	1 (Highest)
3	2	3
4	3	5 (Lowest)

Note: • If there are more than one jobs with same priority apply FCFS.

• If along with priorities highest and lowest is not specified, please do not forget to make your own assumption and specify it before you solve the problem.

Gantt chart for the above example would be:

Arrival of all jobs assumed to be zero.

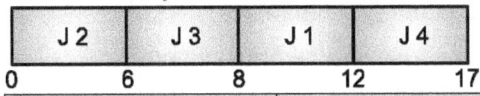

Jobs	Turnaround Time	Wait Time
1	(12 – 0) = 12	(8 – 0) = 8
2	(6 – 0) = 6	(0 – 0) = 0
3	(8 – 0) = 8	(6 – 0) = 6
4	(17 – 0) = 17	(12 – 0) = 12
	43	26

Average turnaround time = $\dfrac{43}{4}$ = 10.75.

Average wait time = $\dfrac{26}{4}$ = 6.5.

4.4.4 Round Robin (RR) Scheduling   (April 15)

• Mostly, this scheduling algorithm is used for time-sharing system.

• The process time is divided into time slice or time quantum.

• The process from ready queue is selected in FCFS order.

• Each one allocates its time slice.

• If the process is not finished within time slice then again it is placed at the end of the ready queue.

• When the other processes are waiting in ready queue, the allocated process is not take more than one time slice.

• The RR scheduler picks the first process from the ready queue, sets a timer to interrupt after one time quantum and dispatches the process.

• In this a fixed time slot is given to each process. After this time slot is over CPU is given to the next process, this takes place in the circular manner.

• Round robin scheduling is a preemptive version of first-come, first-served scheduling.

• Processes are dispatched in a first-in-first-out sequence but each process is allowed to run for only a limited amount of time.

- Most important thing for this algorithm is proper selection of time quantum. If time quantum is too small, then most of the time is wasted in context switching (time required switching from one job to other, this includes time to preserve the status of current job and give new job to CPU). If time quantum is too big, then processing is almost FCFS.

- Proper selection of time quantum gives equal priority to all jobs.

- At the end of each time quantum context switch is required to save old process status in registers and load new one. So the time quantum should be large with respect to the context switch time. If time quantum is less, then context switch time is more.

- Turn-around time is also depends on the time quantum. It can be improved if most jobs finish their next CPU burst in a single time quantum. For example, given three jobs of 10 time slice each and a quantum of 1 time unit, the average turnaround time = 29. If the time quantum is 10, then the average turn-around time drops to 20. If context switch is added in, then for smaller time quantum we get more turnaround time.

Example:

Jobs	CPU burst time
1	3
2	4
3	5

Time quantum = 2

If time quantum is not given, you are allowed to assume some value and specify your assumption.

Gantt chart would be,

Arrival time of all jobs is considered to be 0 (zero).

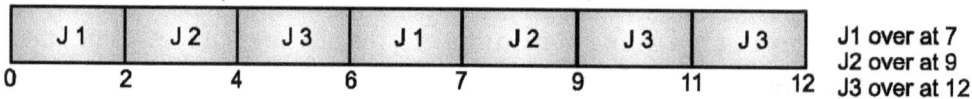

| J1 | J2 | J3 | J1 | J2 | J3 | J3 | J1 over at 7 |
|----|----|----|----|----|----|----| J2 over at 9 |

0   2   4   6   7   9   11   12   J3 over at 12

Jobes	Turnaround Time
J1	(7 – 0) = 7
J2	(9 – 0) = 9
J3	(12 – 0) = 12
	= 28

Jobes	Wait time
J1	$(0 – 0) + (6 - 2) = \quad 4$
J2	$(2 – 0) + (7 – 4) = \quad 5$
J3	$\underline{(4 – 0) + (9 – 6) = \quad 7}$
	$= \quad 16$

$\therefore \qquad$ Average turnaround time $\ = \dfrac{28}{3} = 9.33.$

$\qquad\qquad$ Average wait time $\ = \dfrac{16}{3} = 5.33.$

- While proceeding to next job, current job is brought back to the ready queue. All this time when job is in ready queue is added to the wait time of the job.

- If arrival time is given, user must take care of not entering a job into the Gantt chart before it arrives e.g. if arrival time of job Ji is 4 time units, then Ji should not be there onto the Gantt chart for 0 to 4 time units.

# 4.4.5 Multi-Level Queue (MLQ) Scheduling				(April 13)

- In this kind of algorithm:

  o All jobs are divided into different categories viz. system jobs, interactive, batched (non-interactive), editing, etc.

  o Ready queue is partitioned into number of sections, one for each of the category present.

  o Each such queue may have separate/different scheduling algorithm.

  o Each queue has jobs with some common property.

  o Priorities are specified for the queue.

  o One by one all queues are processed in descending order of priority.

  o Jobs assigned to a queue remain permanently in the same queue. They are not allowed to move from one queue to other.

  o Until and unless all jobs from high priority queue are not over, scheduling for low priority does not start.

  o Sometime a fixed time slot is given to each job.

  o While scheduling a particular job, if any high priority job entered the queue, then current job is pre-empted. Therefore, this scheduling is also called as fixed priority pre-emptive scheduling.

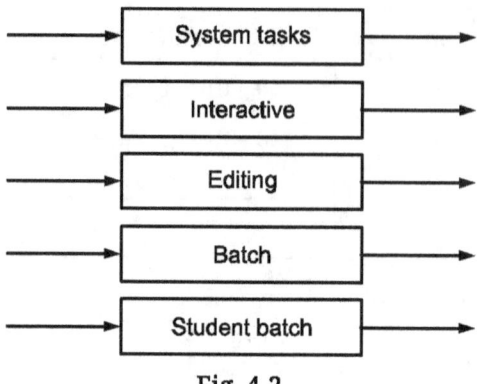

Fig. 4.2

4.4.6 Multilevel Feedback Queue Scheduling

- Multi-level feedback queue scheduling is an enhancement of MLQ.

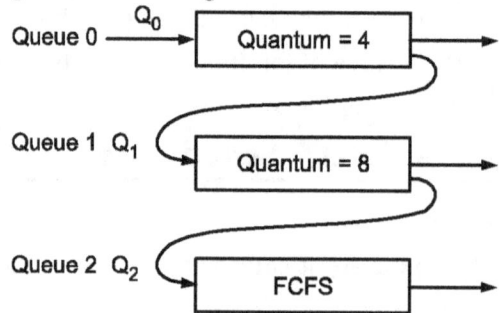

Fig. 4.3: Multilevel feedback queue

- In this scheme, processes can move between different queues.
- The various processes are separated in different queues on the basis of their CPU burst times.
- The top priority queue is given smallest CPU time quantum.
- If the quantum expires before the process terminates, it is then placed at the back of the next lower queue.
- Again, if it does not complete, it is put to the last priority queue. The processes in this queue run on FCFS scheduling.
- If a process uses too much CPU times, it will be moved to a lower priority queue. This leaves I/O bound and interactive processes in the higher priority queues.
- If a process waits for long time in a lower priority queue, then it is moved to a higher priority queue. This form of aging prevents starvation.
- As shown in Fig. 4.3, different queues are maintained with different fixed time slots.
- All jobs are first placed into first queue (queue = 0).

- Each job in Q_0 will be given a time slot of say 4 time units. If a job could not finish within this slot, it will be moved to the tail of next queue i.e. queue 1.
- After all jobs from queue are processed and queue 0 is empty, processing for queue 1 will start.
- All jobs from queue 1 are processed from its head to tail. They all are again given a fixed time slot of say 8 units each.
- Jobs not been able to complete in this slot are shifted to tail of queue 2. Queue 2 is processed on FCFS basis, after queue 1 is empty.
- In short, the highest priority is given to the jobs with smallest CPU burst time. Jobs with very big CPU burst time always sink to the last queue, queue 2 in this example. In queue 2 they will be processed on FCFS basis for the balance of their burst time.
- This is also a pre-emptive algorithm e.g. while processing job from queue 1, if a job arrives in queue 0 , job in queue 0 will pre-empt job in queue 1.

Parameters:
- The below are the parameters for a multilevel feedback queue scheduler:
    - The number of queues.
    - The scheduling algorithm for each queue.
    - The method used to determine when to upgrade a process to a higher-priority queue.
    - The method used to determine when to demote a process to a lower priority queue.
    - The method used to determine which queue a process will enter when that process needs service.

4.5 | THREAD SCHEDULING

- The scheduling of user-level threads and scheduling of kernel-level threads are different.
- For many-to-many and many-to-one model, the thread library schedules user-level threads. This scheme is called Process-Contention Scope (PCS).
- The threads are scheduled onto available Light Weight Process (LWP).
- In kernel-level model, the kernel-thread is scheduled by operating system to decide which kernel thread to schedule onto a CPU; the kernel uses System-Contention Scope (SCS).
- One-to-one model uses only SCS.
- PCS uses preemptive priority algorithm for scheduling a thread.
- The higher priority thread will select first. PCS also preempt the thread, when currently running thread has low priority than one of the thread.
- Some thread libraries may allow the programmer to change the priority of threads.

4.5.1 pthread Scheduling

- pthread allows either PCS or SCS scheduling during thread creation.
- The contention scope values of pthread are:
    - ♦ PTHREAD_SCOPE_PROCESS (in PCS scheduling)
    - ♦ PTHREAD_SCOPE_SYSTEM (in SCS scheduling)
- In PCS, the system implements many-to-many model and PTHREAD_SCOPE_PROCESS schedules the user-level threads onto available LWPs.
- In SCS, the system implements one-to-one model and PTHREAD_SCOPE_SYSTEM scheduling will create and bind an LWP for each user-level thread and maps to one-to-one policy.
- Pthread uses two functions for setting and getting the contention scope policy.
    1. pthread_attr_setscope (pthread_attr_t * attr, int scope)
        - 1st argument is the pointer to the attribute set for the thread.
        - 2nd argument is to set the scope either PTHREAD_SCOPE_PROCESS or PTHREAD_SCOPE SYSTEM.
    2. pthread_attr_getscope (pthread_attr_t * attr, int * scope)
        - 1st argument is same.
        - 2nd argument contains a pointer to the value which is already set by 1st function.
        - Example: Linux and MacOSX systems allows only PTHREAD_SCOPE_SYSTEM contention value.

UNIVERSITY SOLVED PROBLEMS

Problem 1: Consider the following set of processes that arrive in the ready queue at the same time.

Processes	CPU Time
P1	8
P2	2
P3	1
P4	10
P5	3

Find out turnaround time and wait time for each of the process using FCFS (First Come First Served), SJF (Shortest Job First) and Round Robin (Quantum = 1).

Solution: Arrival time of all jobs assumed to be 0 **FCFS**.

Gantt Chart:

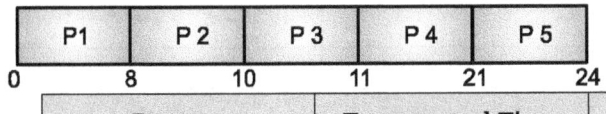

Process	Turnaround Time	Wait Time
P1	$(8 - 0) = 8$	$(0 - 0) = 0$
P2	$(10 - 0) = 10$	$(8 - 0) = 8$
P3	$(11 - 0) = 11$	$(10 - 0) = 10$
P4	$(21 - 0) = 21$	$(11 - 0) = 11$
P5	$(24 - 0) = 24$	$(21 - 0) = 21$

SJF: Pre-emptive or not pre-emptive is not specified. Therefore assumed to be non-pre-emptive.

Gantt chart:

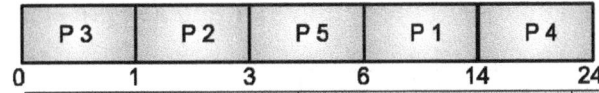

Processes	Turnaround Time	Wait Time
P1	$(14 - 0) = 14$	$(6 - 0) = 6$
P2	$(3 - 0) = 3$	$(1 - 0) = 1$
P3	$(1 - 0) = 1$	$(0 - 0) = 0$
P4	$(24 - 0) = 24$	$(14 - 0) = 14$
P5	$(6 - 0) = 6$	$(3 - 0) = 3$

Round Robin with quantum 1.

Gantt Chart:

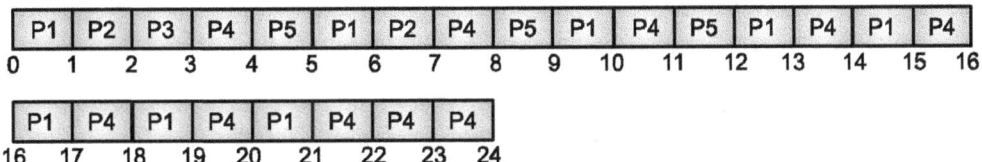

Processes	Turnaround Time
P1	$(21 - 0) = 21$
P2	$(7 - 0) = 7$
P3	$(3 - 0) = 3$
P4	$(24 - 0) = 24$
P5	$(12 - 0) = 12$

Processes	Wait Time
P1	(0 – 0) + (5 – 1) + (9 – 6) + (12 – 10) + (14 – 13) + (16 – 15) + (18 – 17) + (20 – 19) = 13
P2	(1 – 0) + (6 – 2) = 5
P3	(2 – 0) = 2
P4	(3 – 0) + (7 – 4) + (10 – 8) + (13 – 11) + (15 – 14) + (17 – 16) + (19 – 18) + (21 – 20) = 14
P5	(4 – 0) + (8 – 5) + (11 – 9) = 9

Problem 2: Consider snapshot of the system: (April 08)

Job	Arrival time	Burst time
1	0	8
2	1	4
3	2	9
4	3	5

Compute average turn around time using pre-emptive SJF and non-pre-emptive SJF.

Solution: Pre-emptive SJF.

Job 1	Job 2	Job 4	Job 1	Job 3

0   1   5   10   17   26

Average turnaround time:

Job	Completion time - Arrival time
1	(17 – 0) = 17
2	(5 – 1) = 4
3	(26 – 2) = 24
4	(10 – 3) = 7

$$\text{Average turn around time} = \frac{17 + 4 + 24 + 7}{4}$$

$$= \frac{52}{4} = 13$$

Non-pre-emptive SJF:

Job 1	Job 2	Job 4	Job 1

0   8   12   17   26

$$\text{Average turn around time} = \frac{(8 – 0) + (12 – 1) + (17 – 2) + (26 – 3)}{4}$$

$$= \frac{8 + 11 + 15 + 23}{4}$$

$$= \frac{57}{4}$$

$$= 14.25$$

Problem 3: The following series of processes with the given estimated run times arrive in the ready queue in the order shown. For the FCFS and SJF scheduling policies, calculate the waiting time and wait time/run time ratio of each process. Comment on the results.

Job	Estimated runtime
1	10
2	50
3	2
4	100
5	5

Solution:

(i) **FCFS:** If the jobs arrive shortly one after the other in the order job1, job2, job3, job4, job5 the result shown in the following Gantt chart:

Job 1	Job 2	Job 3	Job 4	Job 5

0   10   60   62   162   167

The waiting time is 0 time units for Job1, 10 time units for Job2, 60 time units for Job3, 62 time units for Job4, and 162 time units for Job5.

Thus, the wait time/runtime ratio for job1 = 0,

The wait time/runtime ratio for Job2 = $\frac{10}{50}$ = 0.2,

The wait time/runtime ratio for Job3 = $\frac{60}{2}$ = 30,

The wait time/runtime ratio for Job4 = $\frac{62}{100}$ = 0.62,

The wait time/runtime ratio for Job5 = $\frac{162}{5}$ = 32.4

(ii) **SJF:** The result of the above example, using SJF scheduling is shown in the following Gantt chart:

Job 3	Job 5	Job 1	Job 2	Job 4

0   2   7   17   67   167

The waiting time is 7 for Job1, 17 time unit for Job2, 0 time unit for Job3, 67 time unit for Job4, and 2 time unit for Job 5.

Thus, wait time/runtime ratio,

for   Job1   = $\frac{7}{10}$ = 0.7

for   Job2   = $\frac{17}{50}$ = 0.34

for   Job3   = $\frac{0}{2}$ = 0

for   Job4 $= \dfrac{67}{100} = 0.67$

for   Job5 $= \dfrac{2}{5} = 0.4$

From the above result, it is found that, SJF is a optional scheduling algorithm in terms of minimizing the average waiting time of a given work load.

Problem 4: Five jobs arrive at time 0, in the order given.

Jobs	Burst Time
1	10
2	29
3	3
4	7
5	12

Considering FCFS, SJF and RR (quantum = 10) scheduling algorithms for this set of jobs, which algorithms would give the minimum average waiting time ?

Solution:

(a) For FCFS, we would execute the jobs as:

1	2	3	4	5

0   10   39   42   49   61

Jobs	Waiting time
1	0
2	10
3	39
4	42
5	49
	140

The average waiting time is then,

$$\dfrac{140}{5} = 28$$

(b) For SJF (non-pre-emptive) we execute the jobs as:

3	4	1	5	2

0   3   10   20   32   61

Jobs	Waiting time
1	10
2	32
3	0
4	3
5	20
	65

The average waiting time is,

$$\frac{65}{5} = 13$$

(c) With RR (quantum = 10), we start job 2, but pre-empt it after 10 time units, putting it in the back of the queue.

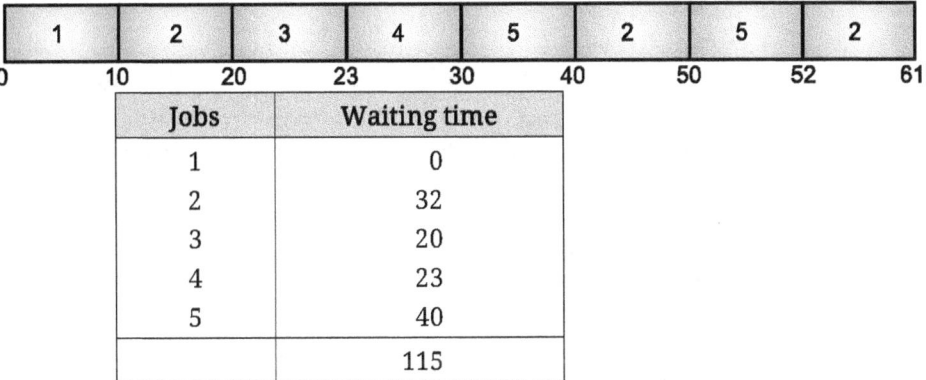

Jobs	Waiting time
1	0
2	32
3	20
4	23
5	40
	115

The average waiting time $= \dfrac{115}{5} = 23$

Problem 5: Consider the following snapshot.

Process	Burst time	Arrival time
P1	5	1
P2	3	0
P3	2	2
P4	4	3
P5	2	13

Compute average turnaround time and average waiting time with RR algorithm with time slice = 2.

Solution: Gantt chart:

P 2	P 1	P 3	P 4	P 2	P 1	P 4	P 5	P 1
0 2	4	6	8	9	11	13	15	16

$$\text{Average turn around time} = \frac{(16 - 1) + (9 - 0) + (6 - 2) + (13 - 3) + (15 - 13)}{5}$$

$$= \frac{15 + 9 + 4 + 10 + 2}{5} = \frac{40}{5} = 8$$

$$\text{Average waiting time} = \frac{(15 - 4 - 1) + (8 - 2 - 0) + (4 - 2) + (11 - 2 - 3) + (13 - 13)}{5}$$

$$= \frac{10 + 6 + 2 + 6 + 0}{5}$$

$$= \frac{24}{5} = 4.8$$

Problem 6: Consider the following set of processes with CPU burst time given in milliseconds.

Process	Burst time	Arrival time	Priority
P1	8	0	4
P2	6	1	6
P3	7	3	3
P4	9	3	1 (highest)

Illustrate the evaluation of these process using non-preemptive SJF and priority preemptive CPU scheduling algorithm. Also calculate average waiting time.   **(5 M)**

Solution: 1. Non-preemptive SJF:

Gantt Chart:

P 1	P 2	P 3	P 4

0   8   14   21   30

$$\text{Average turn around time} = \frac{(8-0)+(14-1)+(21-3)+(30-3)}{4}$$

$$= \frac{8+13+18+27}{4}$$

$$= \frac{66}{4} = 16.5$$

$$\text{Average waiting time} = \frac{(0-0)+(8-1)+(14-3)+(21-3)}{4}$$

$$= \frac{0+7+11+18}{4} = \frac{36}{4} = 9$$

2. Priority preemptive algorithm:

Gantt chart:

P 1	P 4	P 3	P 1	P 2

0   3   12   19   24   30

$$\text{Average turn around time} = \frac{(24-0)+(30-1)+(19-3)+(12-3)}{4}$$

$$= \frac{24+29+16+9}{4}$$

$$= \frac{78}{4} = 19.5$$

$$\text{Average waiting time} = \frac{(19-3-0)+(24-1)+(12-3)+(3-3)}{4}$$

$$= \frac{16+23+9+0}{4}$$

$$= \frac{48}{4}$$

$$= 12$$

Problem 7: Consider the following set of process with CPU burst time given in milliseconds.

Process	Burst time	Arrival time
P1	5	1
P2	3	0
P3	2	2
P4	4	3
P5	8	2

Illustrate the execution of these process using FCFS and preemptive SJF. Calculate average turn around time and average waiting time.   (5 M)

Solution: 1. FCFS:

P 2	P 1	P 3	P 5	P 4

0   3   8   10   18   22

$$\text{Average turn around time} = \frac{(8-1)+(3-0)+(10-2)+(22+3)+(18-2)}{5}$$

$$= \frac{7+3+8+19+16}{5}$$

$$= \frac{53}{5} = 10.6$$

$$\text{Average waiting time} = \frac{(3-1)+(0-0)+(8-2)+(18-3)+(10-2)}{5}$$

$$= \frac{2+0+6+15+8}{5}$$

$$= \frac{31}{5} = 6.2$$

2. Preemptive SJF:

Gantt chart:

P 2	P 3	P 4	P 1	P 5

0   3   5   9   14   22

$$\text{Average turn around time} = \frac{(14-1)+(3-0)+(5-2)+(9-3)+(22-2)}{5}$$

$$= \frac{45}{5} = 9$$

$$\text{Average waiting time} = \frac{(9-1)+(0-0)+(3-2)+(5-3)+(14-2)}{5}$$

$$= \frac{23}{5} = 4.6$$

Problem 8: Consider the following set of process with CPU burst time given in milliseconds.

Process	Burst time	Arrival time
P1	1	5
P2	0	7
P3	3	3
P4	2	10

Illustrate the execution of these process using RR (with time quantum = 3 ms) and shortest remaining time first. Calculate average turn around time and average waiting time.

Solution: 1. RR CPU Scheduling:

Gantt chart:

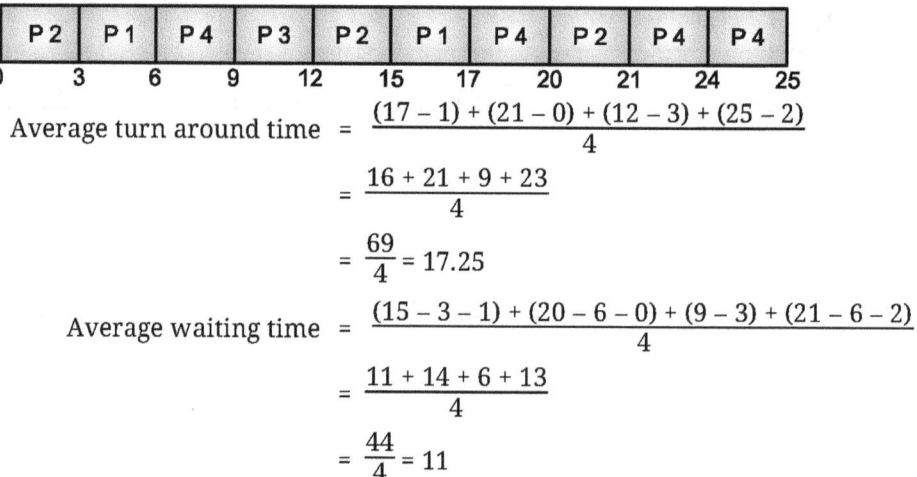

$$\text{Average turn around time} = \frac{(17-1)+(21-0)+(12-3)+(25-2)}{4}$$

$$= \frac{16+21+9+23}{4}$$

$$= \frac{69}{4} = 17.25$$

$$\text{Average waiting time} = \frac{(15-3-1)+(20-6-0)+(9-3)+(21-6-2)}{4}$$

$$= \frac{11+14+6+13}{4}$$

$$= \frac{44}{4} = 11$$

2. **SJF or SRTF: (Preemptive)**

Gantt chart: Preemptive SJF is also called shortest remaining time first.

P 2	P 1	P 3	P 2	P 4
0	1	6	9	15	25

$$\text{Average turn around time} = \frac{(6-1)+(15-0)+(9-3)+(25-2)}{4}$$

$$= \frac{5+15+6+23}{4} = \frac{49}{4} = 12.25$$

$$\text{Average waiting time} = \frac{(1-1)+(9-1-0)+(6-3)+(15-2)}{4}$$

$$= \frac{0+8+3+13}{4}$$

$$= \frac{24}{4} = 6$$

Problem 9: Consider the following set of process with CPU burst time given in milliseconds.

Process	Burst time	Arrival time	Priority
P1	2	0	3
P2	3	1	1
P3	4	2	4 (Highest)
P4	3	3	2

Illustrate the execution of these process using non-preemptive SJF and non-preemptive priority. Calculate average turn around time and average waiting time.

Solution: 1. Non-preemptive SJF:

Gantt Chart:

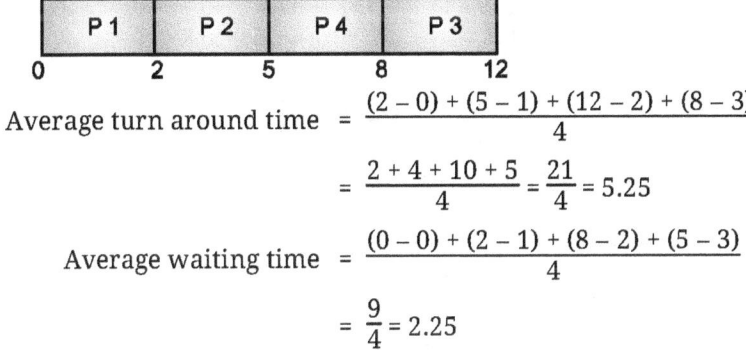

$$\text{Average turn around time} = \frac{(2-0)+(5-1)+(12-2)+(8-3)}{4}$$

$$= \frac{2+4+10+5}{4} = \frac{21}{4} = 5.25$$

$$\text{Average waiting time} = \frac{(0-0)+(2-1)+(8-2)+(5-3)}{4}$$

$$= \frac{9}{4} = 2.25$$

2. Non-preemptive priority:

Gantt chart:

$$\text{Average turn around time} = \frac{(2-0)+(12-1)+(6-2)+(9-3)}{4}$$

$$= \frac{2+11+4+6}{4} = \frac{23}{4} = 5.75$$

$$\text{Average waiting time} = \frac{(0-0)+(9-1)+(2-2)+(6-3)}{4}$$

$$= \frac{8+0+3}{4}$$

$$= \frac{11}{4}$$

$$= 2.75$$

Problem 10: Consider the following set of process with CPU burst time given in milliseconds.

Process	Burst time	Arrival time
J1	1	5
J2	0	7
J3	3	3
J4	2	10

Compute average time around time using RR (time quantum = 2) and shortest remaining time first. **(Oct. 16) (5 M)**

Solution: 1. RR:

Gantt chart:

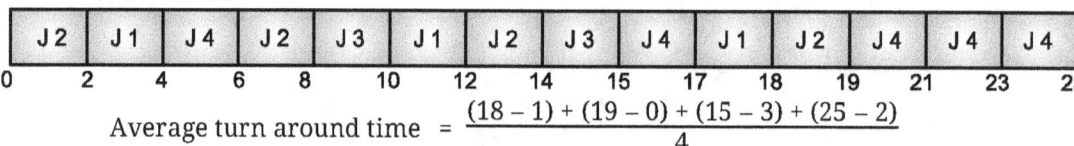

$$\text{Average turn around time } = \frac{(18-1)+(19-0)+(15-3)+(25-2)}{4}$$

$$= \frac{17+19+12+23}{4} = \frac{71}{4} = 17.75$$

2. Shortest remaining time first:

Gantt chart:

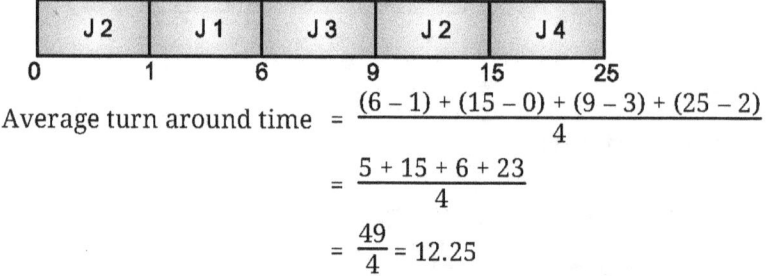

$$\text{Average turn around time } = \frac{(6-1)+(15-0)+(9-3)+(25-2)}{4}$$

$$= \frac{5+15+6+23}{4}$$

$$= \frac{49}{4} = 12.25$$

Problem 11: Consider the following snapshot of a system:

Process	CPU Burst time	Arrival time
P1	5	3
P2	2	0
P3	2	4
P4	3	5

Draw the Gantt chart and find average waiting time for the following scheduling algorithms:

(i)   Preemptive SJF.

(ii) Round Robin (time quantum = 2). **(5 M)**

Solution:

(i) **Preemptive SJF:** Gantt chart

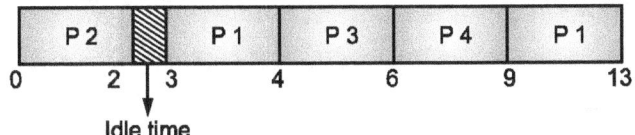

Waiting time:

Process	Waiting time	
P1	$(3 - 3) + (9 - 4)$	= 5 +
P2	$(0 - 0)$	= 0 +
P3	$(4 - 4)$	= 0 +
P4	$(6 - 5)$	= 1
Total waiting time		= 6
Average waiting time	= 6/4	= 1.5

(ii) **RR (Time quantum = 2):** Gantt chart

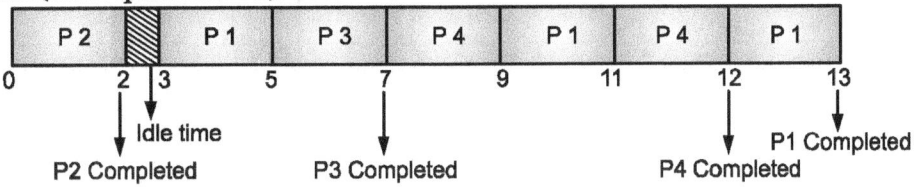

Waiting time:

Process	Waiting time	
P1	$(3 - 3) + (9 - 5) + (12 - 11)$ =	5 +
P2	$(0 - 0)$	= 0 +
P3	$(5 - 4)$	= 1 +
P4	$(7 - 5) + (11 - 9)$	= 4
Total waiting time	= 10	
Average waiting time	= 10/14 = 2.5	

Problem 12: Consider the following snapshot of a system:

Process	Burst time	Arrival time
P_1	5	1
P_2	3	0
P_3	2	2
P_4	4	3
P_5	2	13

Compute the average turn around time and average waiting time using:

(i) SJF (Non-preemptive).

(ii) Round Robin (Time Quantum = 2).   **(5 M)**

Solution:

(i) SJF (Non-preemptive):

P 2	P 3	P 4	P 1	P 5

0   3   5   9   14   16

$$\text{Turn around time} = (14 - 3) + (3 - 0) + (5 - 2) + (9 - 3) + (15 - 13)$$

$$\text{Avg. TT} = \frac{(11) + (3) + (3) + (6) + (3)}{5} = \frac{26}{5} = 5.2$$

$$\text{Waiting time} = \frac{(9 - 1) + (0 - 0) + (3 - 2) + (5 - 3) + (14 - 13)}{5}$$

$$= \frac{8 + 1 + 2 + 1}{5}$$

$$\text{Avg. waiting time} = 2.4$$

(ii) Round Robin (Time quantum = 2):

P 2	P 1	P 3	P 4	P 2	P 1	P 4	P 5	P 1

0   2   4   6   8   9   11   13   15   16

P3 Completed   P2 Completed   P4 Completed   P1 Completed

P5 Completed

$$\text{Average Turn around TT} = \frac{(16 - 1) + (9 - 0) + (6 - 2) + (13 - 3) + (15 - 13)}{5}$$

$$= \frac{15 + 9 + 4 + 10 + 2}{5}$$

$$\text{Average TT} = 8$$

$$\text{Average Waiting Time} = \frac{[(15 - 11) + (9 - 4) + (2 - 1)] + [(8 - 2) + 0]}{5} \\ + [4 - 2] + [(11 - 6) + (6 - 3) + [13 - 13]$$

$$\text{Average Waiting Time} = \frac{10 + 6 + 2 + 8 + 0}{5} = 5.2$$

Problem 13: Consider the following set of processes, with the length of CPU burst time and arrival time in milliseconds.

Process	Burst time	Arrival time
P_1	5	1.5
P_2	1	0
P_3	2	2
P_4	4	3

Illustrate the execution of these processes using pre-emptive SJF CPU scheduling algorithm. Calculate average waiting time and average turn around time. Give the contents of Gantt chart.   (5 M)

Solution: Preemptive SJF:

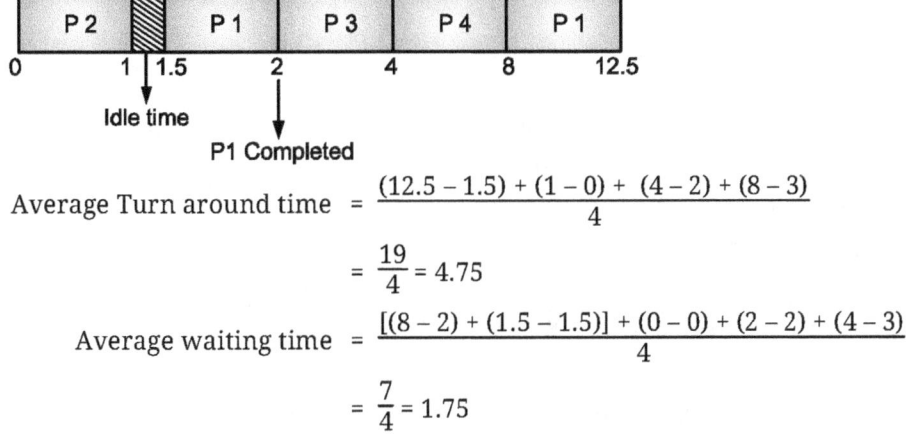

$$\text{Average Turn around time} = \frac{(12.5 - 1.5) + (1 - 0) + (4 - 2) + (8 - 3)}{4}$$

$$= \frac{19}{4} = 4.75$$

$$\text{Average waiting time} = \frac{[(8 - 2) + (1.5 - 1.5)] + (0 - 0) + (2 - 2) + (4 - 3)}{4}$$

$$= \frac{7}{4} = 1.75$$

Problem 14: Consider the following set of processes, with the length of CPU burst time and arrival time in milliseconds.

Process	Burst time	Arrival time	Priority
P1	4	0	3
P2	3	2	1 (lowest)
P3	7	1	4 (highest)
P4	15	3	2

Illustrate the execution of these processes using pre-emptive priority algorithm. Draw Gantt chart and calculate average turn around time and waiting time.   (5 M)

Solution: Preemptive priority algorithm:

P 1	P 3	P 1	P 4	P 2
0   1   8   11   26   29

P1 Completed

$$\text{Average Turnaround time} = \frac{(11 - 0) + (29 - 2) + (8 - 1) + (26 - 3)}{4}$$

$$= \frac{68}{4} = 17$$

$$\text{Average waiting time} = \frac{[(8 - 1) + (0 - 0)] + (26 - 0) + (1 - 1) + (11 - 3)}{4}$$

$$= \frac{41}{4} = 10.25$$

Problem 15: Consider the following set of processes, with the length of CPU burst time and arrival time in milliseconds.

Process	Burst time	Arrival time
P1	4	2
P2	6	0
P3	2	1

Illustrate the execution of these processes using Round Robin (RR) CPU scheduling algorithm (quantum = 3 milliseconds). Calculate average waiting time and average turn around time. Give the contents of gantt chart. **(5 M)**

Solution: Round Robin Algorithm:

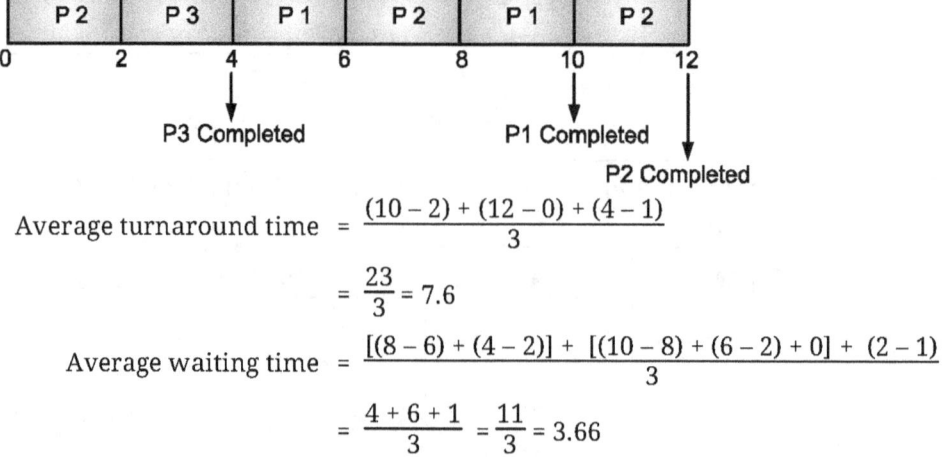

$$\text{Average turnaround time} = \frac{(10-2)+(12-0)+(4-1)}{3}$$

$$= \frac{23}{3} = 7.6$$

$$\text{Average waiting time} = \frac{[(8-6)+(4-2)]+[(10-8)+(6-2)+0]+(2-1)}{3}$$

$$= \frac{4+6+1}{3} = \frac{11}{3} = 3.66$$

Problem 16: Consider the following snapshot of the system.

Process	Burst time	Priority	Arrival time
P1	10	3	0
P2	5	0 (high)	4
P3	2	1	3
P4	16	2	5
P5	8	4 (low)	2

Schedule the above set of processes according to:

(i)   Non-preemptive priority scheduling algorithm.

(ii) Preemptive priority scheduling algorithm.

Draw proper Gantt chart and find average turnaround time and waiting time.

(April 13) (5 M)

Solution: (i) Non-preemptive priority:

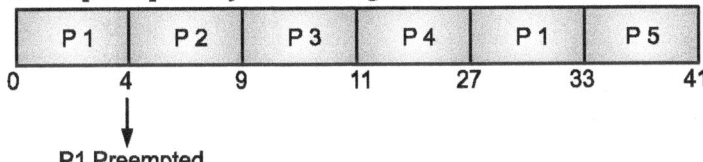

| P 1 | P 2 | P 3 | P 4 | P 5 |

0   10   15   17   33   41

$$\text{Average Turn around time} = \frac{(10-0)+(15-4)+(17-3)+(33-5)+(41-2)}{5}$$

$$= \frac{102}{5} = 20.4$$

$$\text{Average waiting time} = \frac{[(0-0)]+(10-4)+(15-3)+(17-4)+(33-2)}{5}$$

$$= \frac{62}{5} = 12.4$$

(ii) **Preemptive priority scheduling:**

| P 1 | P 2 | P 3 | P 4 | P 1 | P 5 |

0   4   9   11   27   33   41

↓

P1 Preempted

$$\text{Average turnaround time} = \frac{(33-0)+(9-4)+(11-3)+(27-5)+(41-2)}{5}$$

$$= \frac{107}{5} = 21.4$$

$$\text{Average waiting time} = \frac{[(27-4)+(0-0)+(4-4)+(9-3)+(11-5)+(33-2)]}{5}$$

$$= \frac{66}{5} = 13.2$$

Problem 17: Consider the following set of processes with the length of CPU burst time and arrival time in milliseconds:

Process	Burst time	Arrival time	Priority
P_1	5	1	1 (h)
P_2	6	0	2
P_3	2	1	1
P_4	4	0	3 (*l*)

Illustrate the execution of these processes using pre-emptive priority and FCFS scheduling algorithm.

Calculate waiting time and turnaround time for each process and calculate average waiting time and average turnaround time.

Give the contents of Gantt chart.   (April 15) (5 M)

Solution:

(i) Pre-emptive priority algorithm:

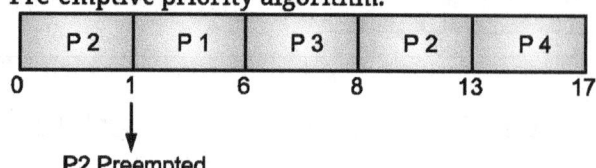

P2 Preempted

$$\text{Average turnaround time} = \frac{(6-1)+(13-0)+(8-1)+(17-0)}{4}$$

$$= \frac{42}{4} = 10.5$$

$$\text{Average waiting time} = \frac{(1-1)+[(8-1)+0]+(6-1)+(13-0)}{4}$$

$$= \frac{25}{4} = \frac{25}{4} = 6.25$$

(ii) FCFS algorithm:

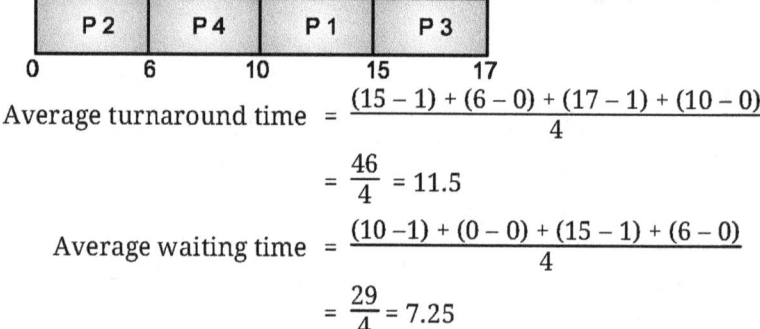

$$\text{Average turnaround time} = \frac{(15-1)+(6-0)+(17-1)+(10-0)}{4}$$

$$= \frac{46}{4} = 11.5$$

$$\text{Average waiting time} = \frac{(10-1)+(0-0)+(15-1)+(6-0)}{4}$$

$$= \frac{29}{4} = 7.25$$

SUMMARY

➢ In multi-programming environment, many processes are in memory. The problem of determining when processors should be assigned and to which processes is called processor scheduling or CPU scheduling.

➢ The success of CPU scheduling depends on the following observed property of processes: The process execution is cycle of CPU execution and I/O wait. Processes alternate back and forth between these two states.

➢ CPU scheduler or short-term scheduler selects the process from ready queue allocates to CPU for execution.

➢ The scheduling schemes are of two types: Pre-emptive scheduling and Non-preemptive scheduling.

➢ When a CPU allocates a process and releases the process after completion or the process switches from running state to waiting state (request for I/O) then it is non-preemptive scheduling scheme.

➤ When a process switches from running state to the ready state (e.g. when interrupt occurs) or switches from waiting to ready; then it is pre-emptive scheduling scheme. The pre-emptive means the process is pre-empted or interrupted.

➤ The dispatcher is the module that actually gives control of the CPU to the process selected by the short-term scheduler.

➤ The time taken by dispatcher to stop one process and start another process to run is called dispatch latency time.

➤ Scheduling algorithm is one which selects some job from ready queue based on some criteria and submits it to the CPU.

➤ Scheduling criteria are CPU Utilization, Throughput, Turnaround time, waiting time and Response time.

➤ In order to maximize CPU utilization and throughput, to minimize turnaround time, waiting time and response time, we need to optimize the average measure using scheduling algorithms.

➤ The different scheduling algorithms are: FCFS (first come first served), SJF (shortest job first), Priority, RR (Round Robin),Multi-level queues and Multi-level feedback queues.

➤ In FCFS scheduling, the process that requests the CPU first, is allocated the CPU first. Thus, the name First-Come-First-Served. The implementation of FCFS is easily managed with a FIFO queue. FCFS scheduling algorithm is non-preemptive.

➤ In SJF, the process with the least estimated execution time is selected from the ready queue for execution. It associates with each process, the length of its next CPU burst. SJF algorithm can be preemptive or non-preemptive.

➤ In priority scheduling, a priority is associated with all processes.▯ Processes are executed in sequence according to their priority. CPU is allocated to the process with highest priority. Priority scheduling can be preemptive or non-preemptive.

➤ In Round Robin scheduling, processes are dispatched in FIFO but are given a small amount of CPU time known as Time Quantum or Time Slice. If a process does not complete before its time slice expires, the CPU is preempted and is given to the next process in the ready queue. Round Robin scheduling is always preemptive as no process is allocated the CPU for more than given time quantum.

➤ Multi-Level Queue scheduling classifies the processes according to their types. Multi-Level Feedback Queue scheduling is an enhancement of MLQ. In this scheme, processes can move between different queues. The various processes are separated in different queues on the basis of their CPU burst times.

➤ The process scheduler schedules only the kernel threads.

➤ User threads are mapped to kernel threads by the thread library - The OS (and in particular the scheduler) is unaware of them.

PRACTICE QUESTIONS

1. Explain functioning of multilevel queues.
2. Consider the following snapshot of a system.

Jobs	Arrival Time	CPU Burst Time
1	0	7
2	1	2
3	2	5
4	3	4

Compute turn around time using RR with quantum 3 and SJF (non-pre-emptive).

3. Consider following snapshot of the system.

Jobs	Arrival Time	CPU Burst Time
1	0.0	8
3	0.5	5
3	1.0	2

Compute average turn around time and average wait time using (1) FCFS, (2) SJF (pre-emptive).

4. Comment on the principle disadvantages of each of these scheduling methods: FCFS, SJF, RR.

5. What advantage is there in having different time quantum sizes on different levels of a multilevel queuing system ?

6. Assume that the following jobs are to be executed with one processor.

Job	Burst time	Priority	Arrival time
1	5	2	0
2	2	4 (lowest)	3
3	1	3	3
4	3	1 (highest)	4

Give the turn around time for each job using

(i)   Pre-emptive shortest job first algorithm.

(ii) Non-pre-emptive priority algorithm.

7. Assume that you have the following jobs to be executed with one processor.

Job	Arrival Time	Burst Time
1	0	12
2	2	3
3	5	8
4	5	5
5	7	6

Calculate the average turnaround fine and total wait time using pre-emptive SJF scheduling algorithm.

8. Consider following snapshot of a system:

Job	Arrival time	CPU Burst time
J_1	1	5
J_2	0	7
J_3	3	3
J_4	2	10

Compute average turn around time using round robin with time slot = 2 and shortest remaining time first algorithm.

(**Ans.** with RR A.T.A.T. = 18.75

with SRTN A.T.A.T. = 12.25)

9. Consider the following set of processes, with the length of the CPU-burst time given in milliseconds:

Process	Burst Time	Priority
P_1	10	3
P_2	1	1
P_3	2	3
P_4	1	4
P_5	5	2

The processes are assumed to have arrived in the order P_1, P_2, P_3, P_4, P_5 all at time 0.

(a) Draw four Gantt charts illustrating the execution of these processes using FCFS, SJF, a non-pre-emptive (a smaller priority number implies a higher priority), and RR (quantum = 1) scheduling.

(b) What is the turnaround time of each process for each of the scheduling algorithms in part a?

    (c)   What is the waiting time of each process for each of the scheduling algorithms in part a?

    (d)   Which of the schedules in part a results in the minimal average waiting time (over all processes).

10. Define the difference between pre-emptive and non-pre-emptive scheduling. State why strict non-pre-emptive scheduling is unlikely to be used in a computer centre.

11. Explain the concept of a priority used in scheduling. Why is priority working usually chosen for real time processes?

12. Define process contention scope.

13. Write a note on Thread Scheduling.

14. State two contention scope values used by pthread.

15. State two functions for setting and getting the contention scope value in pthread.

16. Give examples of operating system with user pthreads.

17. Multiple Choice Questions:

    (i)   The time required to submit the process to CPU and finish it, is called _____

       (a) turn around time   (b) waiting time

       (b) throughput   (d) response time

    (ii) _____ algorithm is non-pre-emptive only.

       (a) SJF   (b) priority

       (c) RR   (d) FCFS

    (iii) _____ gives control of the CPU to the process selected by the short-term scheduler.

       (a) scheduler   (b) dispatcher

       (c) context switch   (d) linux

    Ans.: (i) a, (ii) d, (iii) b.

18. State true or false:

    (i)   Round-Robin algorithm is appropriate for time-sharing system.

    (ii) RR algorithm is non-pre-emptive.

    (iii) SJF is pre-emptive or non-pre-emptive.

    (iv) In Window 2000, operating system using pre-emptive, priority based scheduling algorithm.

    (v) Priority scheduling suffers from starvation.

    (vi) FCFS is optimize algorithm.

    (vii) One-to-one model uses only SCS.

    Ans.: (i) True, (ii) False, (iii) True, (iv) True, (v) True, (vi) False, (vii) True.

19. Consider the following set of process with CPU burst time given in milliseconds.

Process	Burst time	Arrival time
P1	1	5
P2	0	7
P3	3	3
P4	2	10

Illustrate average time around time using

(i) RR (time quantum = 3)

(ii) Shortest remaining time first.

Calculate Average Time Around Time.

Ans. Refer to Solved Problems Answer of Problem 10.

20. What is Aging?

Ans. Refer to Section 4.4.3.

21. Give any four criteria for computing various scheduling algorithms.

Ans. Refer to Section 4.3.

22. Explain in detail multilevel queues and multilevel feedback queues.

Ans. Refer to Sections 4.4.5 and 4.4.6.

23. Define: Turnaround time.

Ans. Refer to Section 4.3.

24. Performance of Round Robin (RR) scheduling algorithm depends on the size of time quantum. Justify.

Ans. Refer to Section 4.4.4.

25. Define dispatch latency time. Explain the function of dispatcher in brief.

Ans. Refer to Section 4.2.4.

26. Why SJF algorithm cannot be implemented at the level of short-term CPU scheduling?

Ans. Refer to Section 4.4.2.

27. Explain multilevel queue scheduling with diagram.

Ans. Refer to Section 4.4.5.

UNIVERSITY QUESTIONS AND ANSWERS

1. What is dispatch latency?   (April 2013, Oct. 2013) (1 M)

Ans. Refer to Section 4.2.4.

2. Explain in brief multi-level queue scheduling.   **(April 2013) (2 M)**

Ans. Refer to Section 4.4.5.

3. RR is non-preemptive. True/False? Justify.   **(April 2015) (1 M)**

Ans. Refer to Section 4.4.4.

4. What is the role of dispatcher?   **(April 2015) (1 M)**

Ans. Refer to Section 4.2.4.

■■■

Process Synchronization

Contents ...

Objectives...

- To Understand Problems in Execution of Cooperating Processes that Shares a Logical Address Space
- To Introduce the Critical-Section Problem, Whose Solutions can be Used to Ensure the Consistency of Shared Data
- To Explore Several Tools like Semaphore to Solve Process Synchronization Problems
- To Study Several Classical Process - Synchronization Problems

5.1 | BACKGROUND

- Concurrent execution of the statements means simultaneous or parallel execution of more than statements.

- Concurrent access often need access to shared data and shared resources.

- If there is no controlled access to shared data, it may result in data inconsistency.

- Maintaining data consistency requires mechanism to ensure the orderly execution of co-operating processes.

- A cooperating process is one that can affect or be affected by other processes in the system. Cooperating processes can either directly share a logical address space or be allowed to share data through files or messages.

- In this chapter, we would discuss various mechanisms for execution of cooperating processes that share a logical address space.

- In this chapter, we would discuss the general issue of concurrency both within a single process and concurrency across processes.

- Process syncrhonisation means sharing system resources by processes in a such a way that, concurrent access to shared data is handled thereby minimizing the chance of inconsistent data.

5.1.1 Interprocess Communication   (April 13, Oct. 16)

- As processes frequently need to communicate with other processes therefore, there is a need for a well-structured communication, without using interrupts among processes.

- Consider producer - consumer problem in which two processes share a fixed-size buffer.

- One process produces information and puts it in the buffer, while the other process consumes information from the buffer.

- These processes do not take turns accessing the buffer, they both work concurrently. Herein lays the problem.

- What happens if the producer tries to put an item into a full buffer? What happens if the consumer tries to take an item from an empty buffer? In order to synchronize these processes, we will block the producer when the buffer is full, and we will block the consumer when the buffer is empty.

```
process producer

{


while (true) {

while (count == BUFFER_SIZE);

++count;

buffer[in] = item;

in = (in + 1) % BUFFER_SIZE;

}

}

process consumer

{

while (true)

    {

while (count == 0);

--count;

item = buffer[out];

out = (out - 1) % BUFFER_SIZE;

    }

}
```

- Assume count = 5 and both producer and consumer execute the statements ++count and --count.
- What will be Result? count could be set to 4, 5, or 6 (but only 5 is correct).
- Although both Producer and Consumer routines are correct separately, they may not function correctly when executed concurrently.
- We would arrive at this inconsistent state because we allowed both processes to manipulate the variable counter concurrently.

5.1.2 Race Condition   (April 16)

- Consider a simple example as shown in Fig. 5.1.
- Assume that two processes are being run, each process occasionally requests that line be printed on the single printer.
- Depending on scheduling of process P1 or P2, all the printout of process P1 may precede or follow the printout of process P2.
- But most likely the printout of each will be interspersed on the printer paper if they are interleaved.

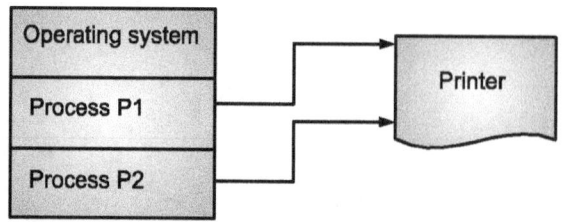

Fig. 5.1: Race condition

- **Definition:** "A situation where multiple processes access and manipulate the same data concurrently and the outcome of the execution depends on the order in which the instructions execute".

- To guard against the race condition, we need to ensure that only one process at a time can be manipulating the common resource.

- To obtain this, we need some form of process synchronization.

- The process which completes its task should release the resource and the process which requires the resources and resources are not available (currently in use) would automatically switch to wait state.

5.2 | CRITICAL SECTION PROBLEM   (April 13, 16)

- The key to preventing trouble involved in shared storage is find some way to prohibit more than one process from reading and writing the shared data simultaneously. That part of the program where the shared memory is accessed is called the Critical Section.

- To avoid race conditions and flawed results, one must identify codes in Critical Sections in each thread.

- **Definition Critical Section:** Consider a system consisting of n co- operating processes {P1....,Pn}. Each process has a segment of code, called a critical section, in which the process may be changing common variable, updating a table, writing a file, and so on.

- **Definition Critical Section Problem:** The critical-section problem is to design a protocol that the processes can use to cooperate. Each process must request permission to enter its critical section.

- The execution of the critical section must be mutually exclusive; while one process is in its critical section, other process should not be allowed to enter its own critical section.

- Every process should take permission of operating system to enter its own critical section.

- There should be an exit point to the critical section.

- The balance code after the critical section is called as remainder section.

- The solution to critical section problem must satisfy following requirements:

  1. **Mutual exclusion:** When one process is in its critical section, other process should not be allowed to enter its critical section.

  2. **Progress:** If no process is in critical section and, there are some processes requesting to enter their critical sections, then all requesting processes except the one which are in its remainder section can participate in the selection decision. (The processes which are in their remainder section, have recently finished with their critical section. So the processes again should not be immediately given the chance to enter their critical section.)

  3. **Bounded waiting:** A bound must exist on the number of times that other processes are allowed to enter their critical sections after a process has made a request to enter its critical section and before that request is granted.

- Assume that each process executes at a nonzero speed.

- No assumption concerning relative speed of the n processes.

- There are number of software and hardware solutions to solve critical section problem.

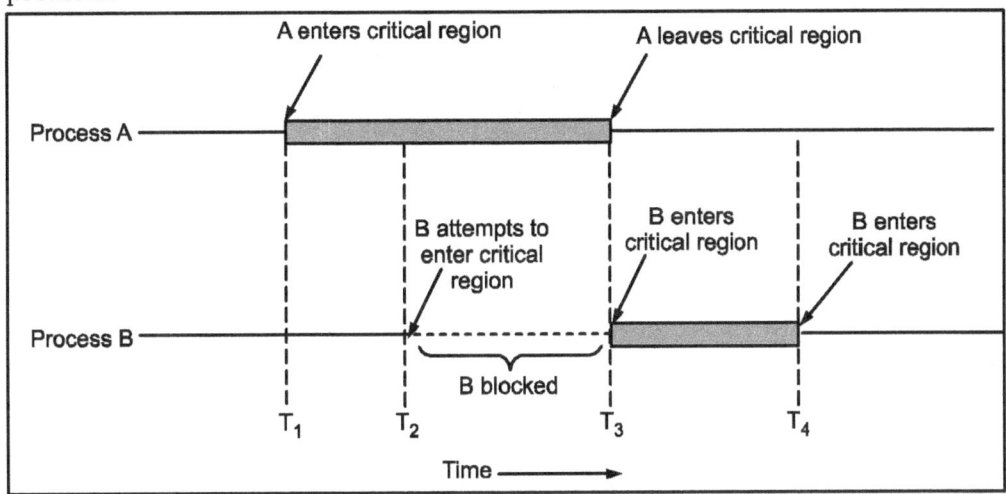

Fig. 5.2: Mutual exclusion by using critical section

The general structure of Process Pi is as follows:

```
do
{
    Entry section
        Critical section
    Exit section
remainder section
} while (TRUE);
```

- Two general approaches are used to handle critical sections in operating system:
  1. Preemptive kernels, and
  2. Non-preemptive kernels.
- A preemptive kernel allows a process to be preempted while it is running in the kernel mode.
- A non-preemptive kernel does not allow a process running process running in kernel mode ,to be preempted a kernel mode process will run until it exits kernel mode ,blocks or voluntarily yields control of the CPU.
- Obviously, a non-preemptive kernel is essentially free from race conditions on kernel data structures, as only one process is active in the kernel at a time.
- We cannot say the same about preemptive kernels, so they must be carefully designed to ensure that shared kernel data are free from race conditions.
- Preemptive kernels are especially difficult to design for SMP architectures, since in these environments it is possible for two kernel mode processes to run simultaneously on different processors.
- Preemptive kernel is preferred over a non-preemptive one.
- A preemptive kernel is more suitable for real-time programming, as it will allow real-time process to preempt a process currently running in the kernel. Furthermore, a preemptive kernel may be more responsive, since there is less risk that a kernel-mode process will run for an arbitrarily long period before relinquishing the processor to waiting processes.
- But, this effect can be minimized by designing kernel code that does not behave in this way.
- Windows XP and Windows 2000 are non-preemptive kernels and the traditional UNIX kernel. Linux 2.6 onwards changed to preemptive kernel.

5.2.1 Peterson's Solution (For Two Processes)

- It is restricted to two processes that alternate execution between their critical and remainder section.
- Assumption that the LOAD and STORE instructions are atomic; that is, cannot be interrupted.
- The two processes *Pi* an *Pj* share two variables:
  o   `int turn;`
  o   `Boolean flag[2]`
- The variable turn indicates whose turn it is to enter the critical section.

- The flag array is used to indicate if a process is ready to enter the critical section. flag[i] = true implies that process Pi is ready.

```
while (true)

    {

        flag[i] = TRUE;

        turn = j;

        while ( flag[j] && turn == j);

        critical section

        flag[i] = FALSE;

        remainder section

    }
```

- **Explanation:** Turn is a common integer initialized to one or zero. (it can take values 0 or1 only). This solution is for two processes Pi and Pj .Process Pi can enter its critical section if turn = i. Process Pj can enter its critical section if turn is =j.

- To enter the critical section, process *Pi* first sets flag[i] to true and then sets turn to value j so that *Pj* can enter the critical section. If both processes try to enter at same time, turn will be set to both i and j at same time. Only one of these assignments will last; the other will occur but will be overwritten immediately. The eventual value of turn decides which of the two processes are allowed to enter its critical section first. This solution satisfies three requirements of critical section problem.

- **Mutual Exclusion:**
  o Each Pi enters its critical region only if either flag[j]==false or turn==i.
  o Each Pi enters its critical region with flag[i]==true.
  o Both Pi and Pj cannot enter their critical region at the same time.

- **Progress:**
  o Pi can be stuck only if either flag[j]==true and turn==j

- **Bounded Waiting:**
  o Pi will enter the critical region after at most one entry by Pj.
  o A process will not wait longer than one turn for entrance to the critical section. After giving priority to the other process, this process will run to completion and set its flag to false, thereby allowing the other process to enter critical section.

5.2.2 Bakery Algorithm

- This uses the concept which is used in bakeries to serve customers. When a customer enters in a bakery, he is given a token in ascending order of number.

- While providing the service, the customer with smallest token number is served first.
  1. It is generalization for n processes.
  2. Each process has an id. Process ids are ordered.
  3. Before entering its critical section, a process receives a number. The holder of the smallest number enters its critical section.
- The common data structures are:

```
Var choosing: array [0..n-1] of Boolean;
number: [0..n-1] of integer.
The structure for process Pi is as follows:

Repeat
choosing[i] = true
 number[i] = max (number [0],..., number [n-1]) +1;
 choosing [i] =false;

for j:= 0 to n-1 do
begin
 while choosing[j] do skip;
 while ((number[j]≠0) && (number[ j ] , j < (number[i], i) ))
 do skip;
end;
Critical section
number[i] =0
 remainder section;
Until false;
```

Explanation:

- Processes can enter into their critical section on FCFS (First Come First Serve) basis.
- The number of value of the process willing to enter is set to max of all plus 1.
- While one process is in critical section, other is not allowed to enter.
- After critical section of a process is over, its number value is set to zero.
- This algorithm does not ensure, if two processes are given same number or not. They will also be treated on FCFS basis.

5.3 | SEMAPHORE   (April 13, 16, Oct. 16)

- Semaphore is introduced by Dijkstra in 1965.
- The various hardware-based solutions to the critical region problem are complicated for application programmers to use.

- It can be solved using synchronization tool, called a semaphore that does not require busy waiting.
- It restricts the sequence or order of execution of the statements.
- **Definition:** A semaphore is a protected variable, apart from initialization whose value can be accessed and altered only by the two atomic operations Wait() (i.e. P) and Signal() (or V).
- The signal() & wait() operations are as follows:

```
wait(S)
    {
        while (S <= 0) ;
        // no-operation
        S--;
    }
signal(S)
    {
        S++;
    }
```

- **Wait (S):** It decrements the value of semaphore variable S. As soon as it becomes negative, wait operation completes. It must be executed indivisibly.
- **Signal (S):** It increments the value of semaphore variable S, as an indivisible operation.
- When one process modifies the semaphore value, no other process can simultaneously modify that same semaphore value. It is less complicated to use.

5.3.1 Usage

- Semaphore can be of two type's binary semaphore and counting semaphore.
1. **Binary Semaphore:**
- Binary semaphore can range only between 0 and 1. Binary semaphore is also known as mutex lock that provides mutual exclusion.
- We can use binary semaphores to deal with critical section problem for multiple processes.
- The n processes share a semaphore mutex initialized to 1. Each process Pi is organized as shown below:

```
do
{
Wait (mutex)
//Critical section
Signal (mutex)
//remainder section
}
while(TRUE);
```

2. Counting Semaphore:

- The value of counting semaphore can range over an unrestricted domain.
- It can be used to control access to a given resource consisting of finite number of instances.
- The semaphore is initialized to number of resources available.
- Each process that wishes to use resource performs wait () operation. When process releases resource, it performs a signal ().
- Counting Semaphore S can be implemented in terms of binary semaphore.
- Data Structures used:

  var   S1: binary-semaphore;

           S2: binary-semaphore;

           S3: binary-semaphore;

           C: integer;

- Initialization:

      S1 = S3 =1;

      S2 = 0;

      C = initial value of semaphore S;

- **Wait Operation can be Defined as follows:**

```
wait(S3);
wait(S1);
C:= C-1;
if (C < 0)
{
    signal (S1);
    wait(S2);
}
    else signal (S1);
    signal (S3);
```

- **Signal Operation can be Defined as follows:**

```
wait(S1);
C = C + 1;
if (C <= 0)
    signal (S2);
    signal (S1);
```

- Semaphore is also used to solve many synchronization problems.
- For example, consider process P1 and P2 are concurrently running and share a common semaphore synch initialized to zero.
- Consider statements of P1 and P2.

Process P1	Process P2
S1;	wait (synch);
signal (synch);	S2;

- The process P2 will execute S2 only after the P1 executes S1 and signal (synch).

Explanation:

- Synch is initialized to zero.
- Synch=0
- If S1 is executed first then signal (synch) operation will take place.
- By signal () operation synch = 1
- Before S2 is executed wait (synch) operation will take place.
- This operation check value of synch <= 0.
- But as synch =1
- Next statement synch: = synch-1 will be executed
- So S2 can be executed after S1 is executed.

Now consider the reverse situation:

- Let start with synch =0
- If S2 is to be executed, then wait (synch) will be executed.
- Now as synch is 0, while synch<=0 condition is true and do skip will allow to continue.
- Therefore S2 cannot be started. S2 will have to wait till synch is>0 and that will be made only after S1 completes its execution.
- P2 cannot be started before P1 completed its execution. Actually processes which are made to wait, by operation wait must start after operation signal is executed.

5.3.2 Implementation

- The critical aspect of semaphore is that they be executed automatically. We must guarantee that no two processes can execute wait () and signal () operations on the semaphore at the same time. This is critical section problem.
- While one process is in its critical section, another process that tries to enter its critical section must loop continuously in the entry code. This continuous looping is problem in multiprogramming environment.

- In multi- programming environment, only one CPU is shared among processes. A process which is waiting utilizes the CPU only to execute wait loop which is nothing but wastage of CPU cycles. This is called as problem of busy waiting.
- To overcome need of busy waiting; wait() and signal() operations are modified. With each semaphore, there is an associated waiting queue.
- Each entry in a waiting queue has two data items: value (of type integer) and pointer to next record in the list
- C structure of semaphore is as follows:

```
typedef struct
{
    int value;
    struct process *list;
}semaphore;
```

- Two operations:
  1. **block:** Place the process invoking the operation on the appropriate waiting queue.
  2. **wakeup:** Remove one of processes in the waiting queue and place it in the ready queue.
- A process which is waiting is blocked and added to list of blocked processes.
- The process which is blocked by operation wait(), will be restarted by wakeup operation which is included in signal() operation.

Implementation of Wait:

```
wait (semaphore *s)
{
    s → value--;
    if (s → value < 0)
    {
        add this process to waiting queue
        block();
    }
}
```

Implementation of Signal:

```
Signal (semaphore *s)
{
    s→value++;
    if (s → value < = 0)
    {
        remove a process P from the waiting queue
        wakeup(P);
    }
}
```

- In a uniprocessor environment (only one CPU), critical section problem can be solved by inhibiting interrupts during execution of wait() and signal() (P or V) operation. So only currently running process executes until interrupts are re-enabled.

- In a multiprocessor environment, inhibiting interrupts will not work. Commands from different processes may be interleaved in some arbitrary way. If the hardware does not support any special instructions, we can provide any of the correct software solution for the critical –section problem.

5.3.3 Deadlocks and Starvation   (April 16)

- If the semaphore is implemented with waiting queue, then two or more processes waiting longer time for the event that can be caused only by one of the waiting processes. Here, that event is signal () operation. The situation is called deadlock.

- Consider a example, if there are two processes P1 and P2, each accessing two semaphores S1 and S2 which are initialized to 1.

Process P1	Process P2
wait(S1)	wait (S2)
wait(S2)	wait (S1)

- Let process P1 executes wait(S1) and then process P2 executes wait(S2). When P1 executes wait (S2), it must wait until P2 executes signal (S2). Similarly, when P2 executes wait (S1), it must wait until P1 executes signal (S1). So P1 and P2 are deadlocked.

- The processes which are waiting indefinitely within the semaphore is called starvation.

- This can be handled by allocating the resources and releasing the resources.

- The resource acquisition and the releasing the resource by operating system at proper time or the operating system associate the priority to each process.

5.4   CLASSIC PROBLEMS OF SYNCHRONIZATION

- In this section, number of synchronization problems can be solved by using semaphores.

5.4.1 Bounded-Buffer Problem
(Producer and Consumer Problem)   (Oct. 16)

Producer:
- Creates item and adds to the buffer.
- Do not want to overflow the buffer.

Consumer:
- Removes items from buffer (consumes it).
- Do not want to get ahead of producer.

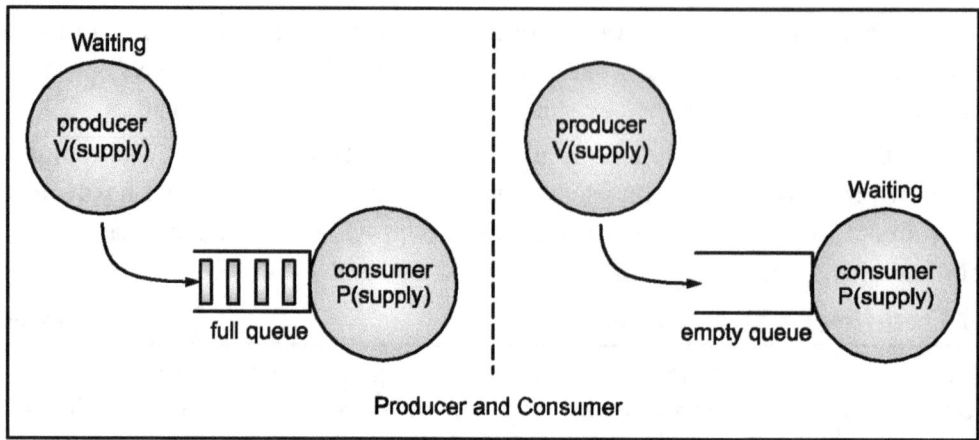

Fig. 5.3: Producer and Consumer problem

- Bounded-buffer assumes that there is a fixed buffer size.
- Consumer waits for new item, producer waits if buffer is full.
- Producers and consumers are much like Unix pipes.
- The bounded buffer problem can be handled using semaphores, mutex semaphore provide mutual exclusion. empty and full semaphores count number of empty and full buffers respectively.

Initialize Semaphore Full: = 0,

Semaphore empty: =n

Semaphore mutex: = 1

Producer	Consumer
while(true)	while(true)
{	{
...	wait (full);
produce an item in nextp	wait (mutex);
...	...
wait (empty);	remove an item from buffer to nextc
wait (mutex);	...
...	signal (mutex);
add nextp to buffer	signal (empty);
...	...
signal (mutex);	consume the next item in nextc
signal (full);	...
}	}

Explanation:
1. While one process is producing or consuming, mutex value is made 0 and after producing and consuming is over; it is set back to 1. Therefore, mutual exclusion is preserved.
2. For producer, if empty=0, then process cannot continue. It is made to wait and after producing is over; full is incremented.
3. For consumer, exactly reverse is the case. If full =0; then process cannot continue. At the end, empty is incremented.

5.4.2 The Reader/Writer Problem

- A data set is shared among a number of concurrent processes.
- Some processes may want to read the data, whereas others may want to write the data.
- These two types of processes are referred as:
  1. **Readers** only read the data set; they do not perform any updates
  2. **Writers** can both read and write.
- The reader/writer problem is to allow multiple readers to read at the same time; but only one single writer can exclusively access the shared data at the same time. Such control can be achieved using semaphores.

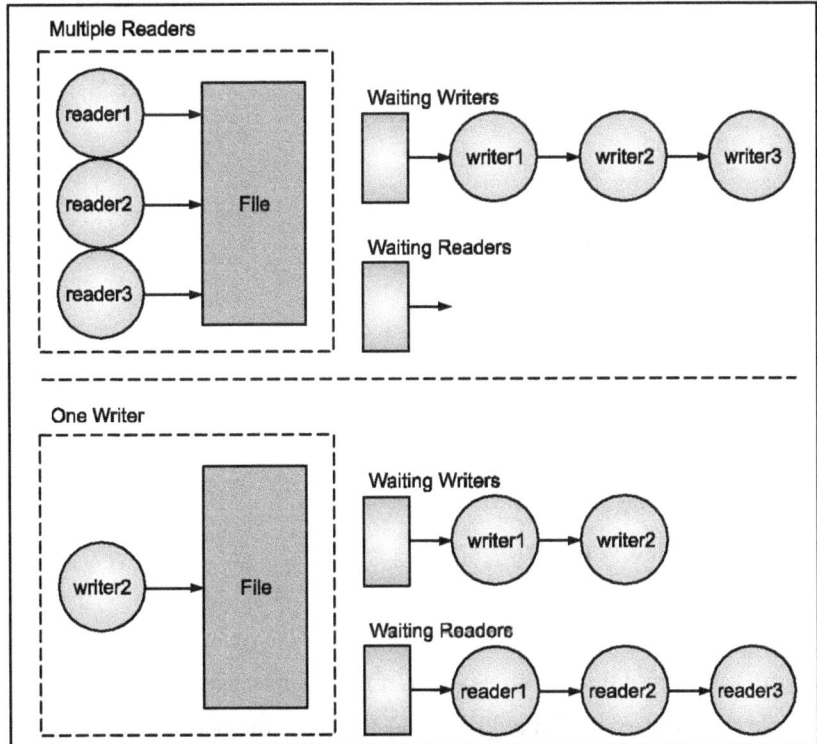

Fig. 5.4: Reader –Writer problem

- mutex and wrt are common semaphores shared by all processes. readcount is a common integer which keeps count of concurrent reader processes.

Semaphore mutex=1.	
Semaphore wrt=1.	
integer readcount =0	

Reader	Writer
| ```
while(true)
{
    wait (mutex)
    readcount ++;
    if (readcount == 1)
    wait (wrt);
    signal (mutex)
    // reading is performed
    wait (mutex);
    readcount - -;
    if (readcount == 0)
    signal (wrt);
    signal (mutex);
}
``` | ```
while(true)
{
    wait (wrt);
    // writing is performed
    signal (wrt);
}
``` |

Explanation:

Case 1: More than one process is reading:

We start with mutex =1and wrt = 1 and readcount = 0.

Suppose A is a process that wants to read. Process will execute following steps:

1. wait (mutex) → mutex=0.
2. readcount: = readcount +1 => readcount=1
   One process is reading
3. If readcount =1 then wait(wrt)
4. signal (mutex) => mutex=1
5. Reading of process A will begin

- Now some other process B want to read then it will also execute same set of steps:
  1. wait(mutex)=> mutex=0(Since Process A has set mutex to 1)
  2. readcount = readcount +1 => readcount=2

3. If readcount = 1 then wait(wrt)this condition does not hold.

4. signal(mutex) => mutex=1

5. Reading of Process B start .

Such any number of processes can read simultaneously.

Case 2: Process A is reading and Process B is trying to write:

- Process A will execute reader structure by which

- mutex=0 , wrt=0 and readcount=1 and process A will start reading.

- Now while process A is reading, if process B is trying to write, B will execute following steps:

      wait(wrt)

- Process can not proceed because wrt is made 0 by Process A, therefore Process B is blocked.

Case 3: Process A is writing and Process B is trying to write:

- We start with wrt =1

- Process A will execute following steps:

    1. wait(wrt) =>wrt=0

    2. Writing started.

- Now suppose Process B also wants to write, it will execute following steps:

    1. wait(wrt)

    2. Process B is blocked because wrt value is made 0 by process A.

Case 4: Process A is writing and Process B is trying to read:

- We start with wrt =1, mutex=1 and readcount =0

- If process A is writing:

    1. wait(wrt) => wrt=0

    2. Writing started

- Now process B will execute following steps to start reading:

    1. wait(mutex) =>mutex =0.

    2. readcount=readcount+1 => readcount=1

    3. If readcount =1then wait(wrt)

- Process B is blocked because wrt value made 0 by process A.

- After reading or writing of process is over, mutex and wrt values are again set to proper values.

5.4.3 Dining Philosopher Problem   (April 15, 16)

- It is popular and classic synchronization problem of concurrency control. The problem can be stated as follows:
  - Consider five philosophers spend their lives alternating between thinking and eating.
  - They are seated around a circular table. In the centre of table is a bowl of rice, and table is laid with five single chopsticks.
  - Each philosopher has access to the chopsticks at her left and right. In order to eat, a philosopher must be in possession of both chopsticks.
  - A philosopher may only pick up one chopstick at a time. Each philosopher attempts to pick up the left chopstick and then the right chopstick.
  - When done eating, a philosopher puts both chopsticks back down on the table and begins thinking.
  - Since the philosophers are sharing chopsticks, it is not possible for all of them to be eating at the same time.
  - Now consider each philosopher as process and chopsticks are as resources. It is a simple presentation of the need to allocate several resources among several processes in a deadlock-free and starvation-free manner.

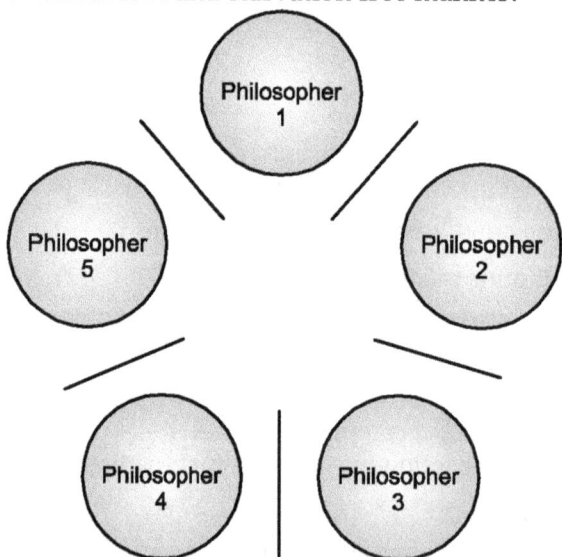

Fig. 5.5: Dining Philosopher Problem

- This problem can be solved as follows:

Shared Data:

- Bowl of rice (data set).
- Semaphore chopstick [5] initialized to 1.

The Structure of Philosopher is:

```
while (true)
{
    wait ( chopstick[i] );
    wait ( chopStick[ (i + 1) % 5] );
        // eat
    signal ( chopstick[i] );
    signal (chopstick[ (i + 1) % 5] );
        // think

}
```

- Although this solution guarantees that no two neighbours are eating simultaneously i.e. mutual exclusion, but it is not deadlock free. The deadlock can be handled by following solutions:

  1. Allow most four philosophers to be sitting simultaneously at the table.
  2. Allow a philosopher to pick up her chopsticks only if both chopsticks are available.
  3. Odd philosopher picks up first her left chopsticks and then her right chopstick, whereas an even philosopher picks up her right chopstick and then her left chopstick.

5.4.4 Problems with Semaphore

- Although semaphores provide a convenient and effective mechanism for process synchronization, using them incorrectly can result in timing errors that are difficult to detect, since these errors happen only if some particular execution sequence takes place and these sequences do not always occur.
- Consider the semaphore solution to the critical section problem. All processes share a semaphore variable mutex which is initialized to 1.Each process must execute wait(mutex) before entering critical section and signal(mutex) afterward.
- Suppose that a process interchanges the order in which the wait() and signal() operations on semaphore mutex are executed, resulting following operations:

```
signal (mutex)
    ............
critical section
    ............
wait (mutex)
```

In this situation, several processes may be executing in their critical section simultaneously, violating the mutual-exclusion requirement.

- Suppose that a process replaces signal(mutex) with wait(mutex) resulting following operations:

```
wait (mutex)
    ............
critical section
    ............
wait (mutex)
```

In this case, a deadlock will occur.

- Suppose that a process omits the wait() or signal(mutex) or both then mutual exclusion is violated and deadlock will occur.

SUMMARY

➢ A cooperating process is one that can affect or be affected by other processes in the system.

➢ Cooperating processes can either directly share a logical address space or be allowed to share data through files or messages.

➢ Race conditions occurs in a situation where multiple processes access and manipulate the same data concurrently and the outcome of the execution depends on the order in which the instructions execute.

➢ To guard against the race condition, we need to ensure that only one process at a time can be manipulating the common resource. To obtain this, we need some form of process synchronization.

➢ To avoid race conditions and flawed results, one must identify codes in Critical Sections in each thread.

➢ Consider a system consisting of n co- operating processes {P1....,Pn}. Each process has a segment of code, called a critical section, in which the process may be changing common variable, updating a table, writing a file, and so on.

➢ The solution to critical section problem must satisfy following requirements: i.e., mutual exclusion, progress and bounded wait.

➢ Two general approaches are used to handle critical sections in operating system: Preemptive kernels and Non-preemptive kernels

➢ Preemptive kernel is preferred over a non-preemptive one.

➢ Semaphore is introduced by Dijkstra in 1965. The various hardware-based solutions to the critical region problem are complicated for application programmers to use. It can be solved using synchronization tool, called a semaphore that does not require busy waiting.

➢ A semaphore is a protected variable, apart from initialization whose value can be accessed and altered only by the two atomic operations Wait() (i.e. P) and Signal() (or V).

➤ Semaphore can be of two type's binary semaphore and counting semaphore.

➤ Binary Semaphore: Binary semaphore can range only between 0 and 1. Binary semaphore is also known as mutex lock that provides mutual exclusion.

➤ Counting Semaphore: The value of counting semaphore can range over an unrestricted domain.

➤ Number of synchronization problems like bounded buffer problem, the reader writer problem, the dining philosopher problem etc can be solved by using semaphores.

PRACTICE QUESTIONS

1. What is critical section problem?
2. Write note on race condition.
3. What are drawbacks of solution of critical section problem?
4. Write note on semaphore.
5. What are different types of semaphore? Explain its usage and implementation.
6. Discuss the following problems in concurrent programming and explain the use of semaphore in these problems:
   (i) The producer-consumer problem
   (ii) The reader-writer problem
   (iii) Dining Philosopher problem
7. What is problem with semaphores?
8. Define the terms:
   (i) Race condition.
   (ii) Bounded wait.
   (iii) Critical section.
   (iv) Deadlock.
   (v) Binary semaphore.
   (vi) Counting Semaphore.
   (vii) Deadlock.
   (viii) Co-operating process.
9. State True or False:
   (i) Semaphore is powerful interprocess synchronization tool
   (ii) The execution of critical section must be sharable.
   (iii) A race condition exists when processes are running simultaneously.
   (iv) Semaphore can be accessed by atomic operation block() and sleep().
   (v) Counting semaphore can be implemented by using binary semaphore.
   Ans.: (i) True (ii) False (iii) True (iv) False (v) True

10. Explain Bounded buffer problem? Give structure of producer and consumer.
Ans. Refer to Section 5.4.1.

11. What is critical section of process?
Ans. Refer to Section 5.2.

12. Which two standard atomic operations can access semaphore value?
Ans. Refer to Section 5.3.

13. What is critical section of problem? Give Peterson's solution to solve critical section problem.
Ans. Refer to Section 5.2.

14. What is semaphore?
Ans. Refer to Section 5.3.

15. What is critical section problem? Explain the following term in the context of it (i) mutual exclusion (ii) progress (iii) bounded wait.
Ans. Refer to Section 5.2.

16. Explain the role of wait ( ) and signal ( ) operations used in semaphores.
Ans. Refer to Section 5.3.

17. Which three requirements must be satisfied while designing a solution to the critical section problem? Explain each in detail.
Ans. Refer to Section 5.2.

18. What is race condition?
Ans. Refer to Section 5.1.2.

19. What is a semaphore? How semaphore can be used to solve the Dining Philosopher problem of concurrency control?
Ans. Refer to Sections 5.3 and 5.4.3.

20. What is critical section of a process?
Ans. Refer to Section 5.2.

UNIVERSITY QUESTIONS AND ANSWERS

1. What is semaphore and what is purpose of it?   (April 2013) (1M)
Ans. Refer to Section 5.3.

2. What is critical section problem? What are the conditions that must be satisfied while designing solution to critical section problem? List various ways to handle it.   (April 2013) (5 M)
Ans. Refer to Section 5.2.

3. Write a short note on Dinning Philosophers problem.   (April 2015) (5 M)
Ans. Refer to Section 5.4.3.

■■■

Deadlocks

Contents ...

Objectives...

- To Understand Concept of Deadlock and Conditions for Deadlock to Occur
- To Learn Methods for Handling Deadlocks like Deadlock Prevention, Deadlock Avoidance and Deadlock Detection
- To Know How to Recover from Deadlock

6.1 | INTRODUCTION   (April 15)

- In multiprogramming environment, Process A needs the resource which is held by other Process B. On the other hand, the other Process B also needs the resource held by the Process A. If both processes are waiting for each other to release the resource, then the situation is called a deadlock as shown in Fig. 6.1.

- None of the processes can run, none of them can release any resources, and none of them can be awakened. It is important to note that the number of processes, kind of resources possessed and requested are unimportant.

- The resources may be either physical or logical. Examples of physical resources are Printers, Tape Drivers, Memory Space, and CPU Cycles. Examples of logical resources are Files, Semaphores and Monitors.

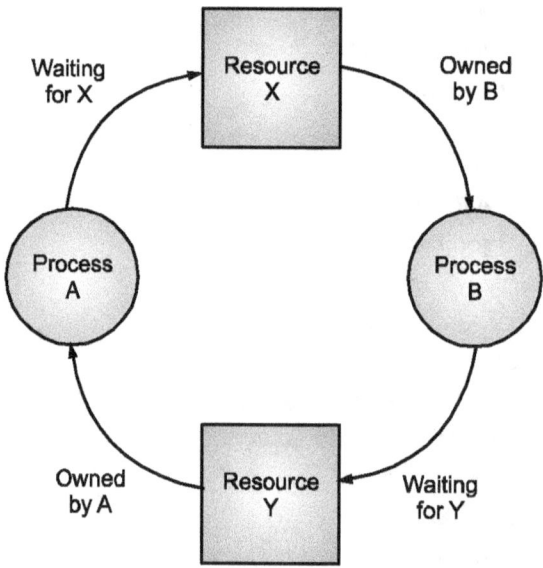

Fig. 6.1: Situation of Deadlock

- In this chapter, we would discuss the technique for dealing with deadlocks. These techniques are deadlock prevention, deadlock avoidance and deadlock detection and recovery.

6.2 | SYSTEM MODEL

- Any system consists of finite number of resources which are distributed among the processes. For example, if a system have 5 printers, then the resource is printer and it has 5 instances.

- If a Process P require an instance of a resource type printer, then it is allocated to Process P (if free) to satisfy the request.

- If the instances of printer are not free; means all the printers are allocated to other processes, then Process P has to wait until any other process release it. So a process must request a resource before using it, and must always release the resource after using it.

- A process may request any number of resources to carry out its task.

- A process cannot request the number of resources greater than the number of resources present in the system. For example, if the system having 3 printer and the process request 4 printers, then request is not granted.

- Under the normal mode of operation, any resource is utilized by a process in following manner:

  o **Request:** A process request for a resource. If it is available, it is immediately granted; otherwise the process must wait for it.

  o **Use:** After a request is granted, process uses the resource.

  o **Release:** The Process releases the resource after it is used.

- The following Fig. 6.2 shows the above sequence.

---

1. Process P1 is requesting resource R1

2. If Resource R1 is free, then request made by P1 is granted. Process P1 use resource R1.

3. Process P1 releases resource R1 and may be used by P2.

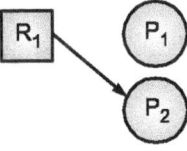

Fig. 6.2: System Model

Definition of Deadlock: (April 15, Oct. 16)

- A set of processes is in a deadlock state when every process in the set is waiting for an event that can only be caused by another process in the set.

- For example, there are two tape drives, in some system. There are two processes, each holding one more tape. Now each of the process needs one more tape drive. Now both the processes are waiting for each other to release a tape drive. This is a deadlock situation.

6.3 | DEADLOCK CHARACTERIZATION

6.3.1 Necessary Conditions

- Coffman (1971) identified **four conditions** that must hold simultaneously for there to be a deadlock.

    1. **Mutual Exclusion Condition**: The resources involved are non-shareable. Only one process at a time can use a resource.

        Explanation: At least one resource (thread) must be held in a non-shareable mode, that is, only one process at a time claims exclusive control of the resource. If another process requests that resource, the requesting process must be delayed until the resource has been released.

    2. **Hold and Wait Condition**: a process holding at least one resource is waiting to acquire additional resources held by other processes.

        Explanation: There must be a process that is holding a resource already allocated to it; while waiting for additional resource that are currently being held by other processes.

    3. **No-Preemptive Condition**: Resources already allocated to a process cannot be preempted.

        Explanation: Resources cannot be removed from the processes until its completion or released voluntarily by the process holding it.

    4. **Circular Wait Condition**: The processes in the system form a circular list or chain; where each process in the list is waiting for a resource held by the next process in the list.

        Explanation: A set $\{P_0, P_1, ..., P_n\}$ of waiting processes must exist such that P_0 is waiting for resource held by P_1, P_1 is waiting for a resource held by P_2,......P_{n-1} is waiting for a resource held by P_n and P_n is waiting for a resource held by P_0.

- It is necessary to understand that all four conditions must be satisfied simultaneously for a deadlock to occur. If any one of them does not occur, a deadlock can be avoided.

- Consider an example of the traffic on road as shown in Fig. 6.3.

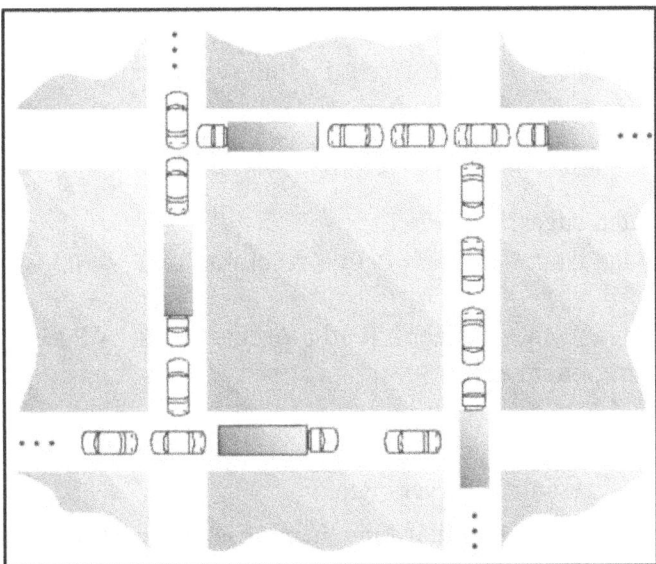

Fig. 6.3: Traffic deadlock

- Consider each section of the street as a resource.

    1. **Mutual exclusion** condition applies, since only one vehicle can be on a section of the street at a time.

    2. **Hold-and-wait** condition applies, since each vehicle is occupying a section of the street, and waiting to move on to the next section of the street.

    3. **No-preemptive** condition applies, since a section of the street that is occupied by a vehicle cannot be taken away from it.

    4. **Circular wait** condition applies, since each vehicle is waiting on the next vehicle to move. That is, each vehicle in the traffic is waiting for a section of street held by the next vehicle in the traffic.

- The simple rule to avoid traffic deadlock is that a vehicle should only enter an intersection if it is assured that it will not have to stop inside the intersection.

- It is not possible to have a deadlock involving only one single process. The deadlock involves a circular "hold-and-wait" condition between two or more processes, so "one" process cannot hold a resource, yet be waiting for another resource that it is holding.

- In addition, deadlock is not possible between two threads in a process, because it is the process that holds resources, not the thread that is, each thread has access to the resources held by the process.

6.3.2 Resource-Allocation Graph   (April 15)

- It is nothing but directed graph, which is used to describe resources allocated to a particular process in a system.

- The graph is made up of:
  - A set of processes P = {P$_1$, P$_2$, ..., P$_n$}. This set contains all the processes in the system.
  - A set of resources R = {R$_1$, R$_2$, ..., R$_n$}. This contains all the resources present in the system.
  - A set of directed edges.
  - A directed edge from a process P$_i$ to a resource R$_j$. (P$_i$ → R$_j$) is called as a request edge.
  - A directed edge from a resource R$_j$ to a process P$_i$ (R$_j$ → P$_i$) is called as allocation edge or an assignment edge.

Conventions:
1. Process is represented by circle.
2. Resource is represented by rectangle.
3. Number of resources of similar type (instances) is represented by dots.
4. Process may be holding a resource or may be requesting for a resource.
5. When process P$_i$ requests an instance of resource type R$_j$, a request edge is inserted in the resource-allocation graph.
6. When this request can be fulfilled, the request edge is instantly transformed to an assignment edge.
7. When the process no longer needs access to the resource, it releases the resource; as result, assignment edge is removed.
8. If the graph contains no cycle, then no process in the system is deadlocked.
9. If graph contains cycle, then deadlock may exist.

- The resource allocation graph as shown in Fig. 6.4 depicts the following situation:

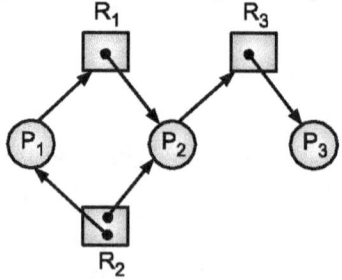

Fig. 6.4: Resource Allocation Graph

  - P = (P$_1$, P$_2$, P$_3$)
  - R = (R$_1$, R$_2$, R$_3$)
  - E = Request Edge = {P$_1$ → R$_1$, P$_2$ → R$_3$}

    Assignment Edge = {R$_1$ → P$_2$, R$_3$ → P$_3$, R$_2$ → P$_1$, R$_2$ → P$_2$}

Process States:

1. Process P_1 is holding an instance of resource type R_2 and is waiting for an instance of resource type R_1.

2. Process P_2 is holding an instance of resource type R_1 and is waiting for an instance of resource type R_3.

3. Process P_3 is holding an instance of resource type R_3.

- As graph contains no cycle, system is deadlock free.

- Consider Fig. 6.5 in which Process P_3 requests an instance of resource type R2. At this point, two minimal cycles exist in the system:

  $P_1 \rightarrow R_1 \rightarrow P_2 \rightarrow R_3 \rightarrow P_3 \rightarrow R_2 \rightarrow P_1$

  $P_2 \rightarrow R_3 \rightarrow P_3 \rightarrow R_2 \rightarrow P_2$

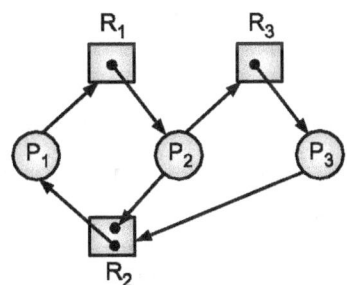

Fig. 6.5: Resource allocation graph with deadlock

- Processes P_1, P_2 and P_3 are deadlocked. Process P_2 is waiting for the resource R_3, which is held by process P_3. Process P_3 is waiting for either process P_1 or P_2 to release resource R_2. Also process P_1 is waiting for process P_2 to release resource R_1. So system is in deadlock.

- Consider resource allocation graph shown in Fig. 6.6 which contains cycle, $P_1 \rightarrow R_1 \rightarrow P_2 \rightarrow R_2 \rightarrow P_1$. However there is no deadlock. Process P_3 may release the resource R_2. Then that resource R_2 can allocated to P_2, breaking the cycle.

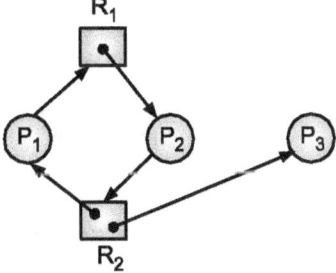

Fig. 6.6: Resource allocation graph with cycle but no deadlock

- If graph contains cycle, then check the following:
  - If there is one instance per resource type, then there is a deadlock.
  - If resource type has multiple instances, then there may or may not be deadlock.

6.4 | METHODS FOR HANDLING DEADLOCK   (Oct. 16)

- There are two common methods for dealing with the deadlock situation.
  1. Don't allow the system to enter a deadlock state.
  2. Allow the system to enter a deadlock state and recover.
- The deadlock handling techniques are deadlock prevention, deadlock avoidance, and deadlock detection and recovery.
- Deadlock prevention algorithm disallows one of four necessary conditions for deadlock.
- Deadlock avoidance algorithm do not grant resource request if resource-allocation have potential have lead to deadlock.
- Deadlock Detection and Recovery algorithm always grants resource request when possible. It periodically checks for a deadlock. If deadlock exists, recover from it.
- We would discuss these techniques in the following sections.

6.4.1 Deadlock Prevention

- We have already discussed in Section 6.2 each of four necessary conditions hold, for occurrence of deadlock.
- A deadlock can be prevented if either of four conditions is prevented from taking place.
- By ensuring that at least one of these conditions cannot hold, we can prevent the occurrence of a deadlock.
- Let us consider each of them separately.
  1. **Mutual exclusion:** The mutual exclusion condition must hold for non-sharable resources. That is, several processes cannot simultaneously share a single resource. This condition is difficult to eliminate because some resources, such as the tape drive and printer, are inherently non-shareable. Note that shareable resources like read-only-file do not require mutually exclusive access and thus cannot be involved in deadlock. Processes never need to wait for a sharable resource. So try to use maximum resources in sharable mode.
  2. **Hold and wait:** In order to prevent this condition to hold, we must guarantee that, a process holding some resource does not request for more resources. This can be achieved by either of holding following protocols:

(i)   The first protocol is that a process request be granted all of the resources it needs at once, prior to execution. This strategy requires that all of the resources a process will need must be requested at once. The system must grant resources on "all or none" basis. If the complete set of resources needed by a process is not currently available, then the process must wait until the complete set is available. While the process waits, however, it may not hold any resources. Thus the "wait for" condition is denied and deadlocks simply cannot occur.

Drawbacks:

(a)   This strategy can lead to serious waste of resources. For example, a program requiring ten tape drives must request and receive all ten drives before it begins executing. If the program needs only one tape drive to begin execution and then does not need the remaining tape drives for several hours. Then substantial computer resources (9 tape drives) will sit idle for several hours.

(b)   It can cause indefinite postponement (starvation). Since not all the required resources may become available at once.

(c)   As well as process must be able to specify all the future requirements of the resources. This may not be possible.

(ii) Second protocol is to disallow a process from requesting resources whenever it has previously allocated resources. A process will first request the source it requires, use it and release it. Then the process will request for second source it need, use it then release it and so on. By this solution also hold and wait conditions does not take place. But drawback of this method is a process may have to wait for a long time, in case of popular resource. A process may suffer starvation.

3. **No preemption:** This condition can also be avoided by either of two solutions:

(i)   In the first solution, if process P_1 is holding some resource and waiting for few more resources. If the resources for which P_1 is waiting are currently not available, then P_1 release all its resources. All released resources are added to request list of process P_1. Now P_1 will restart only when it will get all the resource from it's request list (i.e. previously allocated and new resources together). Thus no pre-emption is avoided when P_1 is pre-empted.

(ii) In the second solution, if a process P, holding some resources and waiting for some additional resources. If they are available then given to process P. If they are held by other process, that is waiting for few more resources. Then this other process will be pre-empted and the resources will be given to Process P. In simple words, in first solution, Process P itself forcefully pre-empted and in second solution, it forces other process to pre-empt.

In both ways, the forceful preemption of process may lead to an inconsistent state of system. When a process release resources, the process may lose all its work to that point. One serious consequence of both strategies is the possibility of indefinite postponement (starvation). A process might be held off indefinitely as it repeatedly requests and releases the same resources.

4. **Circular wait**: the circular wait can be denied by imposing a total ordering on all of the resource types than forcing. This strategy impose that each process requests resources in a numerical order (increasing or decreasing) of enumeration. If several instances of same resource type are needed, a single request for all of them is issued. With this rule, the resource allocation graph can never have a cycle. For example, provide a global numbering of all the resources, as shown below:

1	≡	Card reader
2	≡	Printer
3	≡	Plotter
4	≡	Tape drive
5	≡	Card punch

(i)   Now the rule is this: processes can request resources whenever they want to, but all requests must be made in numerical order.

(ii) A process may request first printer and then a tape drive (order: 2, 4), but it may not request first a plotter and then a printer (order: 3, 2). The problem with this strategy is that it may be impossible to find an ordering that satisfies everyone.

6.5 | DEADLOCK AVOIDANCE

- If detail information about the processes and resources is available, then it is possible to avoid deadlock. For example, which process will require which resources, possibly in what sequence etc. This information may help to decide the sequence in which the processes can be executed to avoid deadlock.

- Each request can be analyzed on the basis of number of resources currently available, currently allocated and future request which may come from other process. From this information, system can decide whether or not a process should wait.

- The deadlock avoidance algorithm dynamically examines the resource- allocation state from the available information to ensure that there is no circular wait. The resource-allocation state is defined by the number of available and allocated resources and the maximum demands of the processes.

6.5.1 Safe State   (April 13)

- A state is safe if the system can allocate resources to each process in some order and still avoid a deadlock.

- A system is in a safe state; if there exists a safe sequence.

- **Definition:** Safe Sequence: A sequence of processes $<P_1, P_2, ..., P_n>$ is a safe sequence for current allocation state if, for each process Pi, the resource requests that P_i can still make can be satisfied by the currently available resources plus the resources held by all P_j have finished with $j < i$.

- If resources that P_i needs are not available, then P_i can wait until all P_j have finished.

- When P_j terminates, P_i will obtain its resources and completes the task.

- When P_i terminates, P_{i+1} obtain its resources and so on.

- If no such sequence exists, then system is in unsafe state.

- A system without safe sequence is unsafe.

- A safe state is not deadlocked state. Conversely deadlocked state is unsafe state. Thus unsafe system may lead to deadlock as shown in Fig. 6.7.

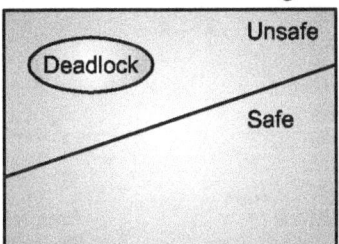

Fig. 6.7: Safe, unsafe and deadlock state spaces.

6.5.2 Resource-Allocation Graph Algorithm

- This algorithm uses a variant of resource allocation graph for single instance of resource type.

- In this algorithm, apart from all set and edges from resource allocation graph, one more edge is used. This edge is called as a claim edge. A claim edge (P_1, R_j) indicates that process P_i may request resource R_j, sometime in future.

- A claim edge is represented by a dashed line. All the claim edges must appear in graph before P_i starts execution.

- When process Pi requests for a resource R_j, then the claim edge $<P_i, R_j>$ is converted to request edge $<P_i, R_j>$ (dashed line converted to regular line).

- A resource is granted only when, conversion of request edge $<P_i, R_j>$ to assignment edge $<R_j, P_i>$ does not form any cycle in the graph.

- If graph contains cycle, then system is in unsafe state.
- Consider the following example, in Fig. 6.8, Processes P_1 and P_2 claim for resources before execution.
  - In Fig. 6.8 (a), Process P_1 requests Resource R_A. So claim edge $<P_1, R_A>$ is converted into request edge $<P_1, R_A>$.
  - In Fig. 6.8 (b), request made by Process P_1 for Resource R_A is granted. So request edge $<P_1, R_A>$ is converted into assignment edge $<R_A, P_1>$.
  - In Fig. 6.8 (c), Process P_2 requests Resource R_B. So claim edge $<P_2, R_B>$ is converted into request edge $<P_2, R_B>$.
  - In Fig. 6.8 (d), if request made by Process P_2 for Resource R_B is granted, it forms cycle in the graph. So allocation is denied, even if R_B is available.

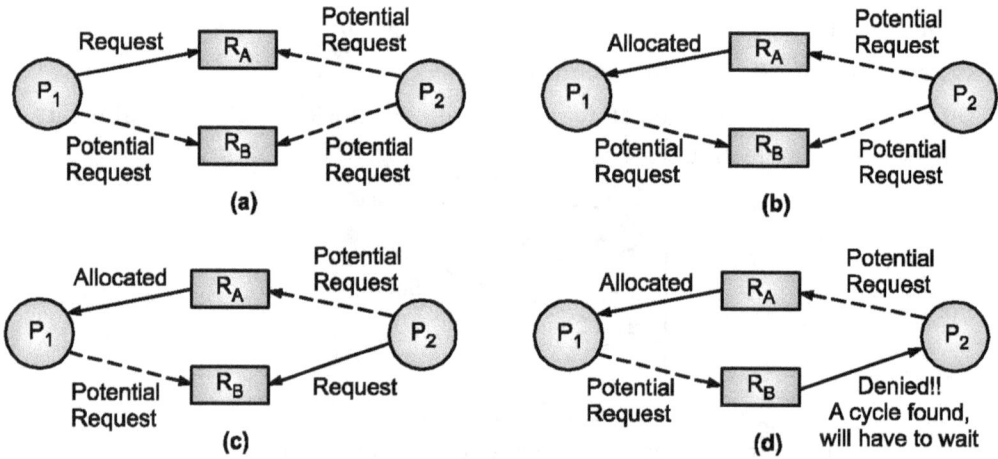

Fig. 6.8: Resource allocation graph for deadlock avoidance

6.5.3 Banker's Algorithm   (April 13)

- The avoidance algorithm used for several instances of the resources is called as Banker's algorithm developed by Dijkstra [1965].
- It has been named as Banker's algorithm, because this algorithm could be used in a banking system to ensure that the bank never allocates its available cash in such way that it can no longer satisfy the requirement of all customers (means available cash is always > customer requirement).
- Each process must a priori claim for maximum use. When a process requests a resource, it may have to wait.

- When a process gets all its resources it must return them in a finite amount of time.
- Several data structures are used to implement Banker's algorithm. Let n be number of processes and m be number of resource types.

  1. **Available:** A vector of length m indicating the number of available resources of each type. If Available [j] = k means there are k instances of resource type R_j available.

  2. **Max:** A n × m matrix defining the maximum demand of each process. If Max [i, j] = k, then process P_i may request at most k instances of resource type R_j.

  3. **Allocation:** A n × m matrix defining number of resources of each type currently allocated to each process. If Allocation [i, j] = k then process P_i is currently allocated k instances of resource type R_j.

  4. **Need:** A n × m matrix indicating the remaining resource need of each process. if Need [i, j] = k, then process P_i may need k more instances resource type R_j, in order to complete its task.

6.5.3.1 Safety Algorithm

- Let **Work** and **Finish** be vectors of length m and n, respectively.

  1. Initialize Work = Available

     Finish [i] = false for i = 0, 1, ..., n – 1.

  2. Find i such that both:

     (a) Finish [i] = = false

     (b) $Need_i \leq Work$

     If no such i exists, go to step 4.

  3. Work = Work + Allocation$_i$, Finish[i] = true, go to step 2.

  4. If Finish [i] == true for all i, then the system is in a safe state.

- This algorithm requires order of m × n^2 operation to check whether system is in safe state.

6.5.3.2 Resource – Request Algorithm

- This algorithm determines if requests can be safely granted.
- Let Request$_i$ be request vector for process P_i. If Request$_i$ [j] = k then process P_i wants k instances of resource type Rj.

1. If $Request_i \leq Need_i$ go to step 2. Otherwise, raise error condition, since Process has exceeded its maximum claim.

2. If $Request_i \leq Available$, go to step 3. Otherwise P_i must wait, since resources are not available.

3. Pretend to allocate requested resources to P_i by modifying the state as follows:

    Available = Available – $Request_i$;

    $Allocation_i$ = $Allocation_i$ + $Request_i$;

    $Need_i$ = $Need_i$ – $Request_i$

    If safe state $\Rightarrow$ the resources are allocated to P_i.

    If unsafe state $\Rightarrow$ P_i must wait, and the old resource-allocation state is restored.

-   **Example:** Consider the following snapshot of system, A, B, C and D are the resource type.

	Allocation			
	A	B	C	D
P_0	0	0	1	2
P_1	1	0	0	0
P_2	1	3	5	4
P_3	0	6	3	2
P_4	0	0	1	4

	MAX			
	A	B	C	D
P_0	0	0	1	2
P_1	1	7	5	0
P_2	2	3	5	6
P_3	0	6	5	2
P_4	0	6	5	6

Available			
A	B	C	D
1	5	2	0

-   Answer the following questions using Banker's Algorithm:

    1. What is the contents of Need array?

    2. Is the system in safe state? If yes give the safe sequence.

    3. If a request from process P1 arrives for (0, 4, 2, 0) can it be granted immediately?

    Solution:

    The content of need array is as follows:

    Need[i][j] = Max[i][j] – Allocation[i][j]

	Max			
	A	**B**	**C**	**D**
P_0	0	0	1	2
P_1	1	7	5	0
P_2	2	3	5	6
P_3	0	6	5	2
P_4	0	6	5	6

	Allocation			
	A	**B**	**C**	**D**
P_0	0	0	1	2
P_1	1	0	0	0
P_2	1	3	5	4
P_3	0	6	3	2
P_4	0	0	1	4

	Need			
	A	**B**	**C**	**D**
P_0	0	0	0	0
P_1	0	7	5	0
P_2	1	0	0	2
P_3	0	0	2	0
P_4	0	6	4	2

2. To check whether system is in safe state, Banker's safety algorithm is used.

Initialize Finish = { False, False, False, False, False,}

Work = Available = {1,5,2,0}

Let i=0

Finish[0] == False

Check Need(P_0) <= Work

{0,0,0,0} <= {1,5,2,0}=>true

Therefore, Process P_0 can be granted required resources.

So Work = Work + Allocation[P_0] (After P_0 finishes its task, it will release resources)

Work = {1,5,2,0} + {0,0,1,2}

= {1,5,3,2}

Finish = { True, False, False, False, False}

Safe Sequence = {P_0}

Let i=1

Finish[1] == False

Check Need(P_1) <= Work

{0,7,5,0} <= {1,5,3,2} =>False

Therefore Process P_1 can not be given resources. P_1 must wait.

Let i=2 Finish[2] == False

Check Need(P_2) <= Work

{1,0,0,2} <= {1,5,3,2} =>true

Therefore, Process P_2 can be granted required resources.

So Work = Work + Allocation[P_2] (After P_2 finishes its task, it will release resources)

Work = {1,5,3,2} + {1,3,5,4}

= {2,8,8,6}

Finish = { True, False, True, False, False}

Safe Sequence ={P_0,P_2}

Let i=3 Finish[3] == False

Check Need(P_3) <= Work

{0,0,2,0} <= {2,8,8,6}=>true

Therefore, Process P_3 can be granted required resources.

So Work = Work + Allocation[P3] (After P_3 finishes its task, it will release resources)

Work = {2,8,8,6} + {0,6,3,2}

= {2,14,11,8}

Finish = { True, False, True, True, False}

Safe Sequence ={P_0,P_2,P_3}

Let i=4, Finish[4] == False

Check Need(P_4) <= Work

{0,6,4,2} <= {2,14,11,8}=>true

Therefore, Process P_4 can be granted required resources.

So Work = Work + Allocation[P_4] (After P_4 finishes its task, it will release resources)

Work = {2,14,11,8} + {0,0,1,4}

= {2,14,12,12}

Finish = { True, False, True, True, True}

Safe Sequence ={P_0,P_2,P_3,P_4}

Again Check Finish[1] == False

Check Need(P_1) <= Work

{0,7,5,0} <= {2,14,12,12}=>true

Therefore, Process P_1 can be granted required resources.

So Work = Work + Allocation[P_1] (After P_1 finishes its task, it will release resources)

Work = {2,14,12,12} + {1,0,0,0}

= {3,14,12,12}

Finish = { True, True, True, True, True}

Safe Sequence = {P_0,P_2,P_3,P_4,P_1}

Yes, system is in safe state.

3. If request from process P_1 arrives for {0,4,2,0) can it granted immediately?

Resource – request algorithm is used to check request can be granted immediately.

1. Request(P_1) < = Need(P_1) => {0,4,2,0} <= {0,7,5,0} => True
2. Request(P_1) < = Available(P_1) => {0,4,2,0} <= {1,5,2,0} => True
3. Then system pretends to have allocated the requested resources to process P_1 by modifying the state as follows:

    Available = Available – Request(P_1);

    Allocation$_i$ = Allocation$_i$ + Request(P_1);

    Need(P_1) = Need(P_1) – Request(P_1)

	Allocation			
	A	B	C	D
P_0	0	0	1	2
P_1	1	4	2	0
P_2	1	3	5	4
P_3	0	6	3	2
P_4	0	0	1	4

	Need			
	A	B	C	D
P_0	0	0	0	0
P_1	0	3	3	0
P_2	1	0	0	2
P_3	0	0	2	0
P_4	0	6	4	2

	Available			
A	B	C	D
1	1	0	0

- Now again check whether system is in safe state, by using Banker's safety algorithm and find safe sequence.

Initialize Finish = { False, False, False, False, False,}

Work = Available = {1,1,0,0}

Let i=0

Finish[0] == False

Check Need(P_0) <= Work

{0,0,0,0} <= {1,1,0,0} =>true

Therefore, Process P_0 can be granted required resources.

So Work = Work + Allocation[P_0] (After P_0 finishes its task, it will release resources)

Work = {1,1,0,0} + {0,0,1,2}

= {1,1,1,2}

Finish = { True, False, False, False, False}

Safe Sequence = {P_0}

Let i=1

Finish[1] == False

Check Need(P_1) <= Work

{0,3,3,0} <= {1,1,1,2} => False

Therefore, Process P_1 can not be given resources. P_1 must wait.

Let i=2 Finish[2] == False

Check Need(P_2) <= Work

{1,0,0,2} <= {1,1,1,2} => true

Therefore, Process P_2 can be granted required resources.

So Work = Work + Allocation[P_2] (After P_2 finishes its task, it will release resources)

Work = {1,1,1,2} + {1,3,5,4}

= {2,4,6,6}

Finish = { True, False, True, False, False}

Safe Sequence = {P_0,P_2}

Let i=3 Finish[3] == False

Check Need(P_3) <= Work

{0,0,2,0} <= {2,4,6,6} =>true

Therefore, Process P_3 can be granted required resources.

So Work = Work + Allocation[P_3] (After P_3 finishes its task, it will release resources)

Work = {2,4,6,6} + {0,6,3,2}

= {2,10,9,8}

Finish = { True, False, True, True, False}

Safe Sequence = {P_0,P_2,P_3}

Let i=4, Finish[4] == False

Check Need(P_4) <= Work

{0,6,4,2} <= {2,10,9,8}=>true

Therefore, Process P_4 can be granted required resources.

So Work = Work + Allocation[P_4] (After P_4 finishes its task, it will release resources)

Work = {2,10,9,8} + {0,0,1,4}

= {2,10,10,12}

Finish = { True, False, True, True, True}

Safe Sequence ={P_0,P_2,P_3,P_4}

Again Check Finish[1] == False

Check Need(P_1) <= Work

{0,3,3,0} <= {2,10,10,12} => true

Therefore, Process P1 can be granted required resources.

So Work = Work + Allocation[P_1] (After P_1 finishes its task, it will release resources)

Work = {2,10,10,12} + {1,4,2,0}

= {3,14,12,12}

Finish = { True, True, True, True, True}

Safe Sequence = {P_0,P_2,P_3,P_4,P_1}

Yes, system is in safe state. So, request of Process P_1 can be granted immediately.

6.6 | DEADLOCK DETECTION

- The systems that do not implement algorithms for deadlock prevention or avoidance must implement an algorithm for deadlock detection and recovery.

- The system must maintain information about:

  1. Process status: resource allocated and requested by a process.

  2. An algorithm to detect the deadlock.

- There are two algorithms i.e. Single instance resource type and Several instances of a resource type.

6.6.1 Single Instance Resource Type

- If all resources have single instance in a system, then deadlock detection algorithm uses variant of resource allocation graph, known as wait-for-graph.

- This graph contains only processes, resources are removed. An edge from process P_i to process P_j exists in wait-for-graph if and only if the corresponding resource allocation graph contains two edges $P_i \rightarrow R_q$ and $R_q \rightarrow P_j$ for some resource type R_q. If wait-for-graph contains cycle, then deadlock exists in system.

- To detect a deadlock, system needs to maintain wait-for-graph and periodically invoke an algorithm that searches for cycle in the graph.

- The algorithm requires an order of n^2 operations where n is number of vertices.

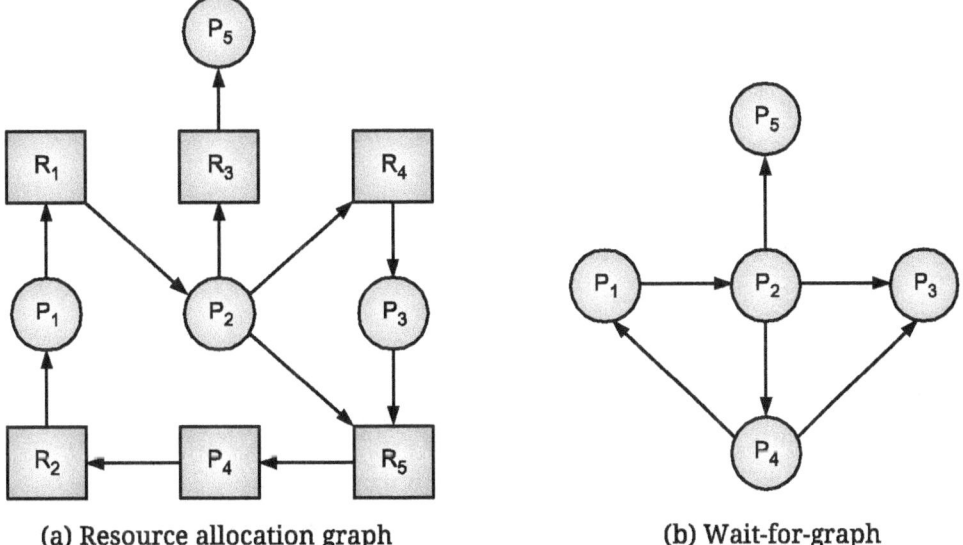

(a) Resource allocation graph   (b) Wait-for-graph

Fig. 6.9

- In the Fig. 6.9, wait-for-graph is shown corresponding to resource allocation graph. In wait-for-graph:

  Edge $P_1 \rightarrow P_2$ exists since there is corresponding edge from $P_1 \rightarrow R_1$ and $R_1 \rightarrow P_2$

  Edge $P_2 \rightarrow P_3$ exists since there is corresponding edge from $P_2 \rightarrow R_4$ and $R_4 \rightarrow P_3$

  Edge $P_3 \rightarrow P_4$ exists since there is corresponding edge from $P_3 \rightarrow R_5$ and $R_5 \rightarrow P_4$

  Edge $P_4 \rightarrow P_1$ exists since there is corresponding edge from $P_4 \rightarrow R_2$ and $R_2 \rightarrow P_1$

  Edge $P_2 \rightarrow P_5$ exists since there is corresponding edge from $P_2 \rightarrow R_3$ and $R_3 \rightarrow P_5$

- As there is cycle $P_1 \rightarrow P_2 \rightarrow P_4 \rightarrow P_1$ in wait-for-graph, Process P_1, P_2 and P_4 are deadlocked.

6.6.2 Several Instances of the Resource Type

- The deadlock detection algorithm uses same data structures as Banker's algorithm:
  - Available = A vector of length m indicating number of available resources of each type.
  - Allocation = An n × m matrix indicating the number of resources of each type currently allocated to each process.
  - Request = A n × m matrix indicating the current request of each process. If Request[i][j] = k then process P_i is requesting k more instances of resource type Rj.

Algorithm:

Step 1: Let Work and Finish be vectors of length m and n, respectively. Initialize Work = Available. For i = 1, 2, ..., n, if Allocation$_i \neq 0$, then Finish[i] = false; otherwise, Finish[i] = true.

Step 2: Find an index i such that both:

(a) Finish[i] == false

(b) Request$_i \leq$ Work

If no such i exists, go to step 4.

Step 3: Work = Work + Allocation$_i$, Finish[i] = true go to step 2.

Step 4: If Finish[i] == false, for some i, $1 \leq i \leq n$, then the system is in deadlock state. Moreover, if Finish[i] == false, then Pi is deadlocked.

- Algorithm requires an order of $O(m \times n^2)$ operations to detect whether the system is in deadlocked state.

Example: Consider the system with 3 resources types A,B, and C with 7, 2, 6 instances respectively. Consider the following snapshot:

	Allocation				Request				Total Resources		
	A	B	C		A	B	C		A	B	C
P_0	0	1	0	P_0	0	0	0		7	2	6
P_1	2	0	0	P_1	2	0	2				
P_2	3	0	3	P_2	0	0	1				
P_3	2	1	1	P_3	1	0	0				
P_4	0	0	2	P_4	0	0	2				

Answer the following questions:

1. What are the contents of Available array?
2. Is there any deadlock?

Solution: The content of Available array is as follows:

Available = Total Resources – Total Allocation

Total Allocation = {7,2,6}

	Allocation		
	A	B	C
P_0	0	1	0
P_1	2	0	0
P_2	3	0	3
P_3	2	1	1
P_4	0	0	2
	7	2	6

Available = {7, 2, 6} – {7, 2, 6}

= {0, 0, 0}

Now execute the deadlock detection algorithm.

Initialize Finish = {False, False, False, False, False}   Work = Available = {0,0,0}
Let i=0   Check Finish[0] == False   Check Request(P_0) <= Work   {0,0,0} <= {0,0,0}=>true   So Work = Work + Allocation[P0]   Work = {0,0,0} + {0,1,0}   = {0,1,0}   Finish = { True, False, False, False, False}

Let i=1

Finish[1] == False

Check Request(P_1) <= Work

{2,0,2} <= {0,1,0} =>False

Finish = { True, False, False, False, False}

Let i=2;

Finish[2] == False

Check Request(P_2) <= Work

{3,0,3} <= {0,1,0} => False

Finish = { True, False, False, False, False}

Let i=3;

Finish[3] == False

Check Request(P_3) <= Work

{2,1,1} <= {0,1,0} =>False

Finish = { True, False, False, False, False}

Let i=4;

Finish[4] == False

Check Request(P_4) <= Work

{0,0,2} <= {0,1,0} =>False

Finish = { True, False, False, False, False}

As Finish[i] == False for process P_1, P_2, P_3 and P_4, system is in deadlock state.

Process P_1, P_2, P_3 and P_4 are deadlocked.

6.6.3 Deadlock Detection Usage Algorithm

- When should we invoke the detection algorithm depends on:
  1. how often is a deadlock likely to occur.
  2. how many processes will be affected by deadlock when it happens.
- If deadlocks occur frequently, then the algorithm should be invoked frequently.
- Deadlocks only occur when some process makes a request which cannot be granted, (if this request completes a chain of waiting processes).
  1. **Extreme:** Invoke the algorithm every time a request is denied
  2. **Alternative:** Invoke the algorithm at less frequent time intervals:
     o Once per hour.
     o Whenever CPU utilization < 40%.
     o Disadvantage: cannot determine exactly which process 'caused' the deadlock.

6.7 | RECOVERY FROM DEADLOCK   (April 15)

- When deadlock detection algorithm detects a deadlock in system, some recovery scheme must be used to recover the system from deadlock.

- The recovery scheme may use either of the following approaches.

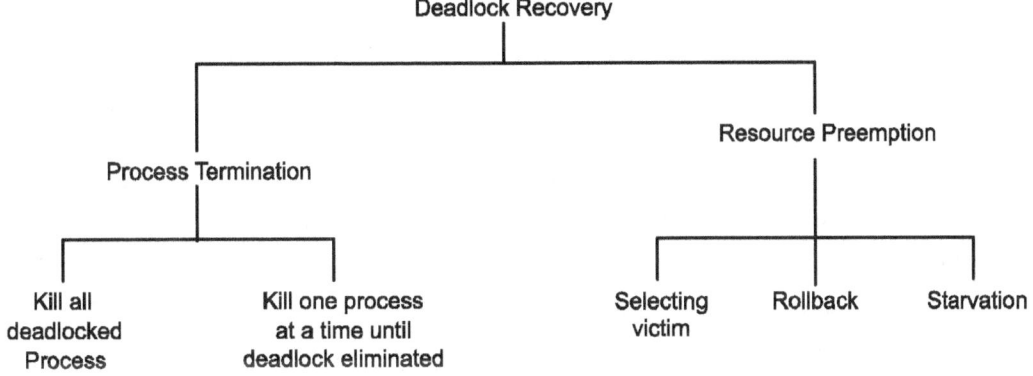

Fig. 6.10: Deadlock Recovery Scheme

- The Fig. 6.10 shows the different ways for breaking a deadlock.

   o The first option in deadlock recovery is to kill one or more processes in order to break the circular wait.

   o The next option is to pre-empt some resources from one or more of the deadlocked processes.

6.7.1 Process Termination

- The process can be terminated by two ways:

   1. **Kill all deadlocked processes:** This scheme is very expensive way of breaking a deadlock

   2. **Kill one process at a time until the deadlock is eliminated:** This scheme involves lot of overhead, since after killing each process; deadlock detection algorithm must be invoked to determine whether any processes are still deadlocked.

- While killing the process one must take care, because partial completion of the process may leave the system in inconsistent state.

- Many factors are involving in taking the decision of the process selection:

   1. Priority of the process.

   2. Cost involved in the killing the process (how much the process has completed and how much time it will need to completion?)

   3. Which resources and what type of resources are held by the process?

   4. How many total processes will be involved in roll back?

6.7.2 Resource Pre-emption

- In this method successively, some resource are pre-empted and given to other processes unless a deadlock is broken.
- This method requires three major decisions to be taken.

    1. **Selecting a victim:** May be selected based on following criteria:

        (i) **Priority:** Resources of low priority processes will be pre-empted.

        (ii) **Own cost:** Process that has completed very less of its execution will pre-empt its resources.

        (iii) **Cost affecting other processes**: How many maximum processes can restart their execution if resources of a particular process P are pre-empted?

    2. **Rollback:** The process, from which resource or resources are pre-empted, will not be able to continue execution, such process is roll backed partially or completely, to some safe state.

    3. **Starvation:** A process may be held for long time waiting for its resources; then process is said to be starved. So care must be taken so that some process is not selected again and again as victim. To achieve this, the cost factor may contain the number of roll backs of the process. This count will also be considered while selecting the victim.

Difference between Deadlock and Starvation:

Sr. No.	Deadlock	Starvation
1.	A set of processes is in a deadlock state when every process in the set is waiting for an event that can only be caused by another process in the set.	A process may be held for long time waiting for its resources.
2.	All four conditions-Mutual Exclusion, Hold and Wait, No Preemption and circular wait, occur simultaneously, and then deadlock occurs.	Due to higher priority of process, lower priority process selected as victim again and again and has to wait for long time. It is also known as indefinite postponement.
3.	It is not possible to have a deadlock involving only one single process.	It is possible to have a starvation involving only one single process.
4.	If a deadlock occurs, system can not progress further since two or more processes may be blocked.	If a starvation occurs, system can progress with other processes.

contd. ...

| 5. | To avoid a deadlock, one of the method can be implemented:
• Deadlock Prevention
• Deadlock Avoidance
• Deadlock detection and recovery | To avoid starvation:
• Priority of process is increased periodically (Aging)
• Count of number of rollback is kept so that same process should not be selected as victim again and again |

- Let us summarize three different techniques for handling a Deadlock:

Factors	Deadlock Prevention	Deadlock Avoidance	Deadlock Detection and Recovery
Method	This method ensures that at least one of four conditions should not be held.	This method does not grant a resource request if it leads to deadlock.	This method allows entering a deadlock but implements algorithm which invoked periodically to detect deadlock and recover from it.
Handling of process's requests	It prevents a deadlock by restraining how requests can be made. These restrains ensure that one of conditions can not occur.	The system requires a prior information regarding overall potential use of each resource for each process. Then system dynamically considers the every request and decides whether it is safe to grant request to a process.	Process's request can be satisfied by: Process preemption or Resource Preemption of other process.
Advantages	• No preemption necessary • Don't require runtime information • Useful for processes that performs single burst of activity	• No preemption necessary • Proper resource utilization • Good system throughput	• Every request of process granted. • Facilitates online handling

contd. ...

| Dis-advantages | • Low Resource utilization
• Starvation
• low system throughput
• Disallow incremental resource requests | • Future resource requirement must be known.
• Some times process's requests are not granted, though resources are available. Since it may lead to a deadlock in future. | • Overhead includes run-time cost of maintaining necessary information
• Execution deadlock detection algorithm periodically incur overhead in computation time.
• Losses inherent in recovery from deadlock. |

UNIVERSITY SOLVED PROBLEMS

Problem 1: Consider a system with 5 processes $\{P_0, P_1, P_2, P_3, P_4\}$ and four resources types $\{A, B, C, D\}$. There are 3 instances of type A, 14 instances of type B, 12 instances of type C and 12 instances of type D. The allocation and maximum demand matrices are as follows:

	Allocation			
	A	**B**	**C**	**D**
P_0	0	6	3	2
P_1	0	0	1	2
P_2	1	0	0	0
P_3	1	3	5	4
P_4	0	0	1	4

	Max			
	A	**B**	**C**	**D**
P_0	0	6	5	2
P_1	0	0	1	2
P_2	0	7	5	0
P_3	2	3	5	6
P_4	0	6	5	6

Answer the following questions having Banker's algorithm.

1. What are the contents of need array?

2. Is a system in a safe state?

3. Is the request from process P_4 arrives for (0, 0, 4, 1) can the request be immediately granted?   **(April 05)**

Solution:

Total Resources	–	Total Allocation	=	Available
A B C D		A B C D	=	A B C D
3 14 12 12	–	2 9 10 12	=	1 5 2 0

1. Need = Max – Allocation

	Need					Max					Allocation			
	A	**B**	**C**	**D**		**A**	**B**	**C**	**D**		**A**	**B**	**C**	**D**
P_0	0	0	2	0		0	6	5	2		0	6	3	2
P_1	0	0	0	0	=	0	0	1	2	–	0	0	1	2
P_2	0	7	5	0		1	7	5	0		1	0	0	0
P_3	1	0	0	2		2	3	5	6		1	3	5	4
P_4	0	6	4	2		0	6	5	6		0	0	1	4

2. Now using Banker's Safety Algorithm.

$$\text{Work} \ = \ \text{Available} = \{1, 5, 2, 0\}$$
$$\text{Finish} \ = \ \{F, F, F, F, F\}$$

(i) Let i = 0, Finish[i] = F,

$$\text{Need } (P_0) < \ = \ \text{Work} \Rightarrow \{0, 0, 2, 0\} < = \{1, 5, 2, 0\}$$
$$\text{So work} \ = \ \text{Work} + \text{Allocation}$$
$$= \ \{1, 5, 2, 0\} + \{0, 6, 3, 2\}$$
$$\text{Work} \ = \ \{1, 11, 5, 2\}$$

(After P_0 finishes, it will release resources)

$$\text{Finish} \ = \ \{T, F, F, F, F\}$$
$$\text{Safe sequence} \ = \ \{P_0\}$$

(ii) Let i = 1, Finish[1] = F

$$\text{Need } (P_1) < \ = \ \text{Work} \Rightarrow \{0, 0, 0, 0\} < = \{1, 11, 5, 2\}$$
$$\text{So work} \ = \ \text{Work} + \text{Allocation}$$
$$= \ \{1, 11, 5, 2\} + \{0, 0, 1, 2\}$$
$$\text{Work} \ = \ \{1, 11, 6, 4\}$$

(After P_1 finishes, it will release resources)

$$\text{Finish} \ = \ \{T, T, F, F, F\}$$
$$\text{Safe sequence} \ = \ \{P_0, P_1\}$$

(iii) Let i = 2, Finish[2] = F

$$\text{Need } (P_2) < \ = \ \text{Work} \Rightarrow \{0, 7, 5, 0\} < = \{1, 11, 6, 4\}$$
$$\text{So work} \ = \ \text{Work} + \text{Allocation}$$
$$= \ \{1, 11, 6, 4\} + \{1, 0, 0, 0\}$$
$$\text{Work} \ = \ \{2, 11, 6, 4\}$$

(After P_2 finishes, it will release resources)

$$\text{Finish} \ = \ \{T, T, T, F, F\}$$
$$\text{Safe sequence} \ = \ \{P_0, P_1, P_2\}$$

(iv) Let i = 3, Finish[3] = F

$$\text{Need } (P_3) < = \text{Work} \Rightarrow \{1, 0, 0, 2\} < = \{2, 11, 6, 4\}$$

$$\text{So work} = \text{Work} + \text{Allocation}$$

$$= \{2, 11, 6, 4\} + \{1, 3, 5, 4\}$$

$$\text{Work} = \{3, 14, 11, 8\}$$

$$\text{Finish} = \{T, T, T, T, F\}$$

$$\text{Safe sequence} = \{P_0, P_1, P_2, P_3\}$$

(v) Let i = 4, Finish[4] = F

$$\text{Need } (P_4) < = \text{Work} \Rightarrow \{0, 6, 4, 2\} < = \{3, 14, 11, 8\}$$

$$\text{So work} = \text{Work} + \text{Allocation}$$

$$\Rightarrow \{3, 14, 11, 8\} + \{0, 0, 1, 4\}$$

$$= \{3, 14, 12, 12\}$$

$$\text{Finish} = \{T, T, T, T, T\}$$

$$\text{Safe sequence} = \{P_0, P_1, P_2, P_3, P_4\}$$

∴ System is in safe state.

3. If request (0, 0, 4, 1) from P_4 arrives. According to Resource Request Algorithm,

(i) $\text{Request } (P_4) = \text{Need } 4 \Rightarrow$

$$\{0, 0, 4, 1\} < = \{0, 0, 6, 4\} \Rightarrow \text{True go to Step 2}$$

(ii)   Check if $\text{Request } (P_4) < = \text{Available}$

$$\{0, 0, 4, 1\} < = \{1, 5, 2, 0\} \Rightarrow \text{No}$$

So P_4 has to wait since resources are not available.

∴   Request cannot be granted immediately.

Problem 2: Consider a system with 7 processes A through G and six types of resources R through W with one resource for each type. Resource ownership is as follows:

A   holds R and wants S

B   holds nothing but wants T

C   holds nothing but wants S

D   holds U and wants S and T

E   holds T and wants V

F   holds W and wants S

G   holds V and wants U

Is the system deadlocked, and if so, which processes are involved?

Solution: Resource – Allocation graph is as follows:

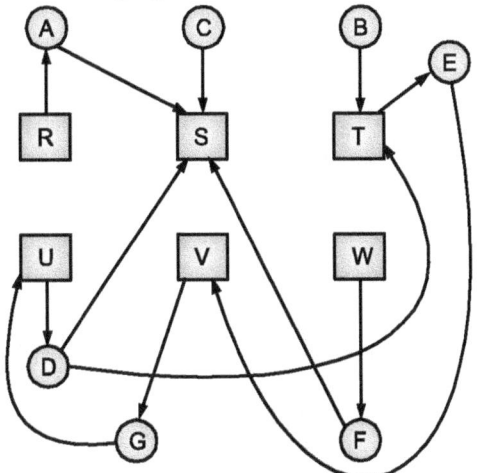

Fig. 6.11 (a): Allocation graph

Wait – for – Graph for above resource allocation graph is:

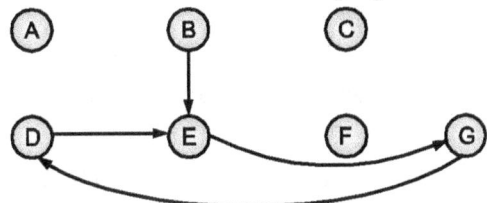

Fig. 6.11 (b): Resource allocation graph

As cycle exists in graph O → E – G – D; processes D, E, G are involved in a deadlock.

Problem 3: Consider given snapshot of system. A system has 5 processes and 3 types of resources A, B, C.

	Allocation				Max				Available		
	A	B	C		A	B	C		A	B	C
P_0	0	1	0		7	5	3		3	3	2
P_1	2	0	0		3	2	2				
P_2	3	0	2		9	0	2				
P_3	2	1	1		2	2	2				
P_4	0	0	2		4	3	3				

Answer the following questions using Banker's Algorithm:

1. What is the contents of matrix need?

2. Is the system in safe state?

3. If request from process P_1 arrives as (1, 0, 2) can the request be granted immediately?

Solution:

1. The contents of Need Matrix,

    Need = Max. – Allocation

	Need		
	A	B	C
P_0	7	4	3
P_1	1	2	2
P_2	6	0	0
P_3	0	1	1
P_4	4	3	1

2. Now using Banker's Safety Algorithm,

$$\text{Work} = \text{Available} = \{3, 3, 2\}$$
$$\text{Finish} = \{F, F, F, F, F\}$$

(i)   Let i = 0,   Finish[0] = F

$$\text{Need } (P_0) < = \text{Work} \Rightarrow \{7, 4, 3\} < = \{3, 3, 2\}$$

No, P_0 cannot be given resources. P_0 has to wait.

(ii)   Let i = 1,   Finish[1] = F

$$\text{Need } (P_1) < = \text{Work} \Rightarrow \{1, 2, 2\} < = \{3, 3, 2\}$$

∴ $$\text{Work} = \text{Work} + \text{Allocation}$$
$$= (3, 3, 2) + (2, 0, 0)$$
$$= (5, 3, 2)$$

[P_1 releases resources after its condition]

$$\text{Finish} = \{F, T, F, F, F\}$$
$$\text{Safe sequence} = \{P_1\}$$

(iii)   Let i = 2,   Finish[2] = F

$$\text{Need } (P_2) < = \text{Work} \Rightarrow \{6, 0, 0\} < = \{5, 3, 2\}$$

No, P_2 has a wait.

(iv)   Let i = 3   Finish[3] = F

$$\text{Need } (P_3) < = \text{Work} \Rightarrow \{0, 1, 1\} < = \{5, 3, 2\}$$

∴ $$\text{Work} = \text{Work} + \text{Allocation}$$
$$= (5, 3, 2) + (2, 1, 1)$$
$$= (7, 4, 3)$$

After P_3 finishes, it releases resources

$$\text{Finish} = \{F, T, F, T, F\}$$
$$\text{Safe sequence} = \{P_1, P_3\}$$

(v)   Let i = 4   Finish[4] = F

Need $(P_4) <$ = Work $\Rightarrow$ {4, 3, 1} < = {7, 4, 3} $\Rightarrow$ Yes

∴   Work = Work + Allocation

= (7, 4, 3) + (0, 0, 2)

= (7, 4, 5)

After P_4 finishes, it releases resources

Finish = {F, T, F, T, T}

Safe sequence = {P_1, P_3, P_4}

(vi)   Let i = 0

Need $(P_0) <$ = Work $\Rightarrow$ {7, 4, 3} < = {7, 4, 5}

∴   Work = Work + Allocation

= (7, 4, 5) + (0, 1, 0)

= (7, 5, 5)

After P_0 finishes, it releases resources

Finish = {T, T, F, T, T}

Safe sequence = {P_1, P_3, P_4, P_0}

(vii) Let i = 2

Need $(P_2) <$ = Work $\Rightarrow$ {6, 0, 0} < = {7, 5, 5}

∴   So work = Work + Allocation

= (7, 5, 5) + (3, 0, 2)

= (10, 5, 7)

Finish = {T, T, T, T, T}

Safe sequence = {P_1, P_3, P_4, P_0, P_2}

∴ Yes, system is in safe state.

3. If request from process P_1 arrives for (1, 0, 2), can it granted immediately?

According to Resource request algorithm:

(i)   Request $(P_1) <$ = Need (P_1)

(1, 0, 2) < = (1, 2, 2)

(ii)   Request $(P_1) <$ = Available

(1, 0, 2) < = (3, 3, 2) which is true.

Then system pretends to fulfill request, then modify resource allocation state as follows:

(a)   Available = Available – Request (P_1)

(b)   Allocation (P_1) = Allocation (P_1) + Request (P_1)

(c)   Need (P_1) = Need (P_1) – Request (P_1)

	Allocation		
	A	B	C
P_0	0	1	0
P_1	3	0	2
P_2	3	0	2
P_3	2	1	1
P_4	0	0	2

	Need		
	A	B	C
	7	4	3
	0	2	0
	6	0	0
	0	1	1
	4	3	1

	Available		
	A	B	C
	2	3	0

Now, check system is in safe state

$$Work = Available = \{2, 3, 0\}$$

$$Finish = \{F, F, F, F, F\}$$

(i) Let i = 0,   Finish[0] = F

$$Need (P_0) < = Work \Rightarrow \{7, 4, 3\} < = \{2, 3, 0\}$$

No, P_0 has to wait for resources.

(ii) Let i = 1,   Finish[1] = F

$$Need (P_1) < = Work \Rightarrow \{0, 2, 0\} < = \{2, 3, 0\}$$

∴ $$Work = Work + Allocation$$

$$= (2, 3, 0) + (3, 0, 2)$$

$$= (5, 3, 2)$$

After P_1 finishes, it releases resources

$$Finish = \{F, T, F, F, F\}$$

$$Safe\ sequence = \{P_1\}$$

(iii) Let i = 2,   Finish[2] = F

$$Need (P_2) < = Work \Rightarrow \{6, 0, 0\} < = \{5, 3, 2\}$$

No, P_2 has to wait for resources.

(iv) Let i = 3,   Finish[3] = F

$$Need (P_3) < = Work \Rightarrow \{0, 1, 1\} < = \{5, 3, 2\}$$

∴ $$Work = Work + Allocation$$

$$= (5, 3, 2) + (2, 1, 1)$$

$$= (7, 4, 3)$$

After P_3 finishes, it releases resources

$$Finish = \{F, T, F, T, F\}$$

$$Safe\ sequence = \{P_1, P_3\}$$

(v) Let i = 4,   Finish[4] = F

Need $(P_4) <$ = Work $\Rightarrow$ {4, 3, 1} < = {7, 4, 3}

∴   Work = Work + Allocation

= (7, 4, 3) + (0, 0, 2)

= (7, 4, 5)

After P_4 finishes, it releases resources

Finish = {F, T, F, T, T}

Safe sequence = {P_1, P_3, P_4}

(vi)   Let i = 0,   Finish[0] = F

Need $(P_0) <$ = Work $\Rightarrow$ {7, 4, 3} < = {7, 4, 5}

∴   Work = Work + Allocation

= (7, 4, 5) + (0, 1, 0)

= (7, 5, 5)

After P_0 finishes, it releases resources

Finish = {T, T, F, T, T}

Safe sequence = {P_1, P_3, P_4, P_0}

(vii)   Let i = 2,   Finish[2] = F

Need $(P_2) <$ = Work $\Rightarrow$ {6, 0, 0} < = {7, 5, 5}

∴   Work = Work + Allocation

= (7, 5, 5) + (3, 0, 2)

= (10, 5, 7)

Safe sequence = {P_1, P_3, P_4, P_0, P_2}

Yes, system is in safe state. So request can be granted immediately.

Problem 4: Consider the following snapshot of a system:

Process	Allocation			Max.			Available		
	A	B	C	A	B	C	A	B	C
P0	2	3	2	9	7	5	3	3	2
P1	4	0	0	5	2	2			
P2	5	0	4	1	1	0 4			
P3	4	3	3	4	4	4			
P4	2	2	4	6	5	5			

Answer the following questions using Banker's algorithm:

(i) What is the content of Need Matrix?

(ii) Is the system in a safe state? If yes, give the safe sequence.   (5 M)

Solution:

1. Need = Max – Allocation

	Need		
	A	B	C
P_0	7	4	3
P_1	1	2	2
P_2	6	0	0
P_3	0	1	1
P_4	4	3	1

	Max		
	A	B	C
	9	7	5
	5	2	2
	11	0	4
	4	4	4
	6	5	5

	Allocation		
	A	B	C
	2	3	2
	4	0	0
	5	0	4
	4	3	3
	2	2	4

2. Now using Banker's Safety Algorithm.

$$\text{Work } = \text{ Available } = \{3, 3, 2\}$$
$$\text{Finish } = \{F, F, F, F, F\}$$

(i)   Let i = 0,   Finish[0] = F

$$\text{Need } (P_0) < = \text{ Work } \Rightarrow \{7, 4, 3\} < = \{3, 3, 2\}$$

No, P_0 cannot be given resources. P_0 has to wait.

(ii)   Let i = 1,   Finish[1] = F

$$\text{Need } (P_1) < = \text{ Work } \Rightarrow \{1, 2, 2\} < = \{3, 3, 2\}$$

∴   Work = Work + Allocation

$$= (3, 3, 2) + (2, 0, 0)$$
$$= (5, 3, 2)$$

[P_1 releases resources after its condition]

$$\text{Finish } = \{F, T, F, F, F\}$$
$$\text{Safe sequence } = \{P_1\}$$

(iii)   Let i = 2,   Finish[2] = F

$$\text{Need } (P_2) < = \text{ Work } \Rightarrow \{6, 0, 0\} < = \{5, 3, 2\}$$

No, P_2 has a wait.

(iv)   Let i = 3   Finish[3] = F

$$\text{Need } (P_3) < = \text{ Work } \Rightarrow \{0, 1, 1\} < = \{5, 3, 2\}$$

∴   Work = Work + Allocation

$$= (5, 3, 2) + (2, 1, 1)$$
$$= (7, 4, 3)$$

After P_3 finishes, it releases resources

$$\text{Finish } = \{F, T, F, T, F\}$$
$$\text{Safe sequence } = \{P_1, P_3\}$$

(v)   Let i = 4   Finish[4] = F

Need (P_4) < = Work $\Rightarrow$ {4, 3, 1} < = {7, 4, 3} $\Rightarrow$ Yes

$\therefore$ Work = Work + Allocation

= (7, 4, 3) + (0, 0, 2)

= (7, 4, 5)

After P_4 finishes, it releases resources

Finish = {F, T, F, T, T}

Safe sequence = {P_1, P_3, P_4}

(vi)   Let i = 0

Need (P_0) < = Work $\Rightarrow$ {7, 4, 3} < = {7, 4, 5}

$\therefore$ Work = Work + Allocation

= (7, 4, 5) + (0, 1, 0)

= (7, 5, 5)

After P_0 finishes, it releases resources

Finish = {T, T, F, T, T}

Safe sequence = {P_1, P_3, P_4, P_0}

(vii) Let i = 2

Need (P_2) < = Work $\Rightarrow$ {6, 0, 0} < = {7, 5, 5}

$\therefore$ So work = Work + Allocation

= (7, 5, 5) + (3, 0, 2)

= (10, 5, 7)

Finish = {T, T, T, T, T}

Safe sequence = {P_1, P_3, P_4, P_0, P_2}

$\therefore$ Yes, system is in safe state.

Problem 5: Consider a system with 5 processes {P_0, P_1, P_2, P_3, P_4} and four resources types {A, B, C, D}. There are 3 instances of type A, 14 instances of type B, 12 instances of type C and 12 instances of type D. The allocation and maximum demand matrices are as follows:

	Allocation					Max			
	A	B	C	D		A	B	C	D
P_0	0	6	3	2	P_0	0	6	5	2
P_1	0	0	1	2	P_1	0	0	1	2
P_2	1	0	0	0	P_2	0	7	5	0
P_3	1	3	5	4	P_3	2	3	5	6
P_4	0	0	1	4	P_4	0	6	5	6

Answer the following questions having Banker's algorithm.

1. What are the contents of need array?

2. Is a system in a safe state?

3. Is the request from process P_4 arrives for (0, 0, 4, 1) can the request be immediately granted?   **(April 15)**

Solution:

Total Resources	–	Total Allocation	=	Available
A B C D		A B C D	=	A B C D
3 14 12 12	–	2 9 10 12	=	1 5 2 0

1. Need = Max – Allocation

	Need			
	A	**B**	**C**	**D**
P_0	0	0	2	0
P_1	0	0	0	0
P_2	0	7	5	0
P_3	1	0	0	2
P_4	0	6	4	2

	Max			
	A	**B**	**C**	**D**
	0	6	5	2
	0	0	1	2
	1	7	5	0
	2	3	5	6
	0	6	5	6

	Allocation			
	A	**B**	**C**	**D**
	0	6	3	2
	0	0	1	2
	1	0	0	0
	1	3	5	4
	0	0	1	4

2. Now using Banker's Safety Algorithm.

$$\text{Work} = \text{Available} = \{1, 5, 2, 0\}$$
$$\text{Finish} = \{F, F, F, F, F\}$$

(i) Let i = 0, Finish[i] = F,

$$\text{Need}(P_0) < = \text{Work} \Rightarrow \{0, 0, 2, 0\} < = \{1, 5, 2, 0\}$$
$$\text{So work} = \text{Work} + \text{Allocation}$$
$$= \{1, 5, 2, 0\} + \{0, 6, 3, 2\}$$
$$\text{Work} = \{1, 11, 5, 2\}$$

(After P_0 finishes, it will release resources)

$$\text{Finish} = \{T, F, F, F, F\}$$
$$\text{Safe sequence} = \{P_0\}$$

(ii) Let i = 1, Finish[1] = F

$$\text{Need}(P_1) < = \text{Work} \Rightarrow \{0, 0, 0, 0\} < = \{1, 11, 5, 2\}$$
$$\text{So work} = \text{Work} + \text{Allocation}$$
$$= \{1, 11, 5, 2\} + \{0, 0, 1, 2\}$$
$$\text{Work} = \{1, 11, 6, 4\}$$

(After P_1 finishes, it will release resources)

$$\text{Finish} = \{T, T, F, F, F\}$$

$$\text{Safe sequence} = \{P_0, P_1\}$$

(iii) Let i = 2, Finish[2] = F

$$\text{Need } (P_2) < = \text{Work} \Rightarrow \{0, 7, 5, 0\} < = \{1, 11, 6, 4\}$$

$$\text{So work} = \text{Work} + \text{Allocation}$$

$$= \{1, 11, 6, 4\} + \{1, 0, 0, 0\}$$

$$\text{Work} = \{2, 11, 6, 4\}$$

(After P_2 finishes, it will release resources)

$$\text{Finish} = \{T, T, T, F, F\}$$

$$\text{Safe sequence} = \{P_0, P_1, P_2\}$$

(iv) Let i = 3, Finish[3] = F

$$\text{Need } (P_3) < = \text{Work} \Rightarrow \{1, 0, 0, 2\} < = \{2, 11, 6, 4\}$$

$$\text{So work} = \text{Work} + \text{Allocation}$$

$$= \{2, 11, 6, 4\} + \{1, 3, 5, 4\}$$

$$\text{Work} = \{3, 14, 11, 8\}$$

$$\text{Finish} = \{T, T, T, T, F\}$$

$$\text{Safe sequence} = \{P_0, P_1, P_2, P_3\}$$

(v) Let i = 4, Finish[4] = F

$$\text{Need } (P_4) < = \text{Work} \Rightarrow \{0, 6, 4, 2\} < = \{3, 14, 11, 8\}$$

$$\text{So work} = \text{Work} + \text{Allocation}$$

$$\Rightarrow \{3, 14, 11, 8\} + \{0, 0, 1, 4\}$$

$$= \{3, 14, 12, 12\}$$

$$\text{Finish} = \{T, T, T, T, T\}$$

$$\text{Safe sequence} = \{P_0, P_1, P_2, P_3, P_4\}$$

∴ System is in safe state.

3. If request (0, 0, 4, 1) from P_4 arrives. According to Resource Request Algorithm,

(i) $\quad$ Request (P_4) = Need 4 $\Rightarrow$

$\quad\quad$ $\{0, 0, 4, 1\} < = \{0, 0, 6, 4\} \Rightarrow$ True go to Step 2

(ii) Check if Request $(P_4) < =$ Available

$\quad\quad$ $\{0, 0, 4, 1\} < = \{1, 5, 2, 0\} \Rightarrow$ No

So P_4 has to wait since resources are not available.

∴ $\quad$ Request cannot be granted immediately.

Problem 6: Consider the following sets P, R and E:

$P = \{P_1, P_2, P_3\}$

$R = \{R_1, R_2, R_3, R_4\}$

$E = \{P_1 \rightarrow R_1, P_2 \rightarrow R_3, R_1 \rightarrow P_2, R_2 \rightarrow P_2, R_2 \rightarrow P_1\}$

Also consider the following number of instances per resource type:

(i) One instance of resource type R_1 and R_3.

(ii) Two instances of resource type R_2.

(iii) Three instances of resource type R_4.

Construct the Resource - allocation graph for the above problem. Check whether the system is in the deadlock.   **(Oct. 16)**

Solution:

$R = \{R_1, R_2, R_3, R_4\}$

$E = \{P_1 \rightarrow R_1, P_2 \rightarrow R_3, R_1 \rightarrow P_2, R_2 \rightarrow P_2, R_2 \rightarrow P_1\}$

Resource instances:

- One instance of resource typeR_1
- Two instances of resource typeR_2
- One instance of resource typeR_3
- Three instances of resource typeR_4

Process States:

- Process$P_1$is holding an instance of resource type R2 and is waiting for an instance of resource type R1.
- Process P2 is holding an instance of R1 and an instance of R2 and is waiting for an instance ofR3.

The resource allocation graph for above instance is as follows:

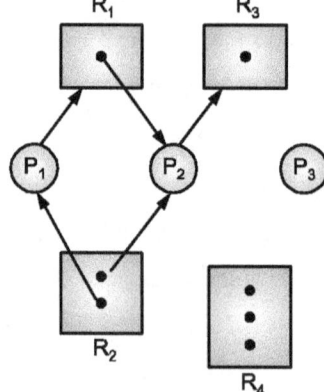

Fig. 6.12

Since, above resource allocation graph does not contain cycle, so no process in system is deadlocked. So there is no deadlock.

Problem 7: Consider given snapshot of system. A system has 5 processes and 3 types of resources A, B, C.

	Allocation				Max				Available		
	A	B	C		A	B	C		A	B	C
P_0	0	1	0		7	5	3		3	3	2
P_1	2	0	0		3	2	2				
P_2	3	0	2		9	0	2				
P_3	2	1	1		2	2	2				
P_4	0	0	2		4	3	3				

Answer the following questions using Banker's Algorithm:

1. What is the contents of matrix need?
2. Is the system in safe state?
3. If request from process P1 arrives as (1, 0, 2) can the request be granted immediately?

Solution:

1. The contents of Need Matrix

   Need = Max. – Allocation

	Need		
	A	B	C
P_0	7	4	3
P_1	1	2	2
P_2	6	0	0
P_3	0	1	1
P_4	4	3	1

2. Now using Banker's Safety Algorithm,

$$\text{Work} = \text{Available} = \{3, 3, 2\}$$

$$\text{Finish} = \{F, F, F, F, F\}$$

(i)   Let i = 0,   Finish[0] = F

            Need (P_0) < = Work $\Rightarrow$ {7, 4, 3} < = {3, 3, 2}

No, P_0 cannot be given resources. P_0 has to wait.

(ii)   Let i = 1,   Finish[1] = F

Need $(P_1) < \ = $ Work $\Rightarrow$ {1, 2, 2} < = {3, 3, 2}

∴   Work = Work + Allocation

= (3, 3, 2) + (2, 0, 0)

= (5, 3, 2)

[P_1 releases resources after its condition]

Finish = {F, T, F, F, F}

Safe sequence = {P_1}

(iii)   Let i = 2,   Finish[2] = F

Need $(P_2) < \ = $ Work $\Rightarrow$ {6, 0, 0} < = {5, 3, 2}

No, P_2 has a wait.

(iv)   Let i = 3   Finish[3] = F

Need $(P_3) < \ = $ Work $\Rightarrow$ {0, 1, 1} < = {5, 3, 2}

∴   Work = Work + Allocation

= (5, 3, 2) + (2, 1, 1)

= (7, 4, 3)

After P_3 finishes, it releases resources

Finish = {F, T, F, T, F}

Safe sequence = {P_1, P_3}

(v)   Let i = 4   Finish[4] = F

Need $(P_4) < \ = $ Work $\Rightarrow$ {4, 3, 1} < = {7, 4, 3} $\Rightarrow$ Yes

∴   Work = Work + Allocation

= (7, 4, 3) + (0, 0, 2)

= (7, 4, 5)

After P_4 finishes, it releases resources

Finish = {F, T, F, T, T}

Safe sequence = {P_1, P_3, P_4}

(vi)   Let i = 0

Need $(P_0) < \ = $ Work $\Rightarrow$ {7, 4, 3} < = {7, 4, 5}

∴   Work = Work + Allocation

= (7, 4, 5) + (0, 1, 0)

= (7, 5, 5)

After P_0 finishes, it releases resources

Finish = {T, T, F, T, T}

Safe sequence = {P_1, P_3, P_4, P_0}

(vii)   Let i = 2

$$\text{Need } (P_2) < \ = \text{Work} \Rightarrow \{6, 0, 0\} < \ = \{7, 5, 5\}$$

$$\therefore \qquad \text{So work} = \text{Work} + \text{Allocation}$$

$$= (7, 5, 5) + (3, 0, 2)$$

$$= (10, 5, 7)$$

$$\text{Finish} = \{T, T, T, T, T\}$$

$$\text{Safe sequence} = \{P_1, P_3, P_4, P_0, P_2\}$$

∴ Yes, system is in safe state.

3. If request from process P_1 arrives for (1, 0, 2), can it granted immediately?

According to Resource request algorithm:

(i) $\text{Request } (P_1) < \ = \text{Need } (P_1)$

$(1, 0, 2) < \ = (1, 2, 2)$

(ii) $\text{Request } (P_1) < \ = \text{Available}$

$(1, 0, 2) < \ = (3, 3, 2)$ which is true.

Then system pretends to fulfill request, then modify resource allocation state as follows:

(a) $\text{Available} = \text{Available} - \text{Request } (P_1)$

(b) $\text{Allocation } (P_1) = \text{Allocation } (P_1) + \text{Request } (P_1)$

(c) $\text{Need } (P_1) = \text{Need } (P_1) - \text{Request } (P_1)$

	Allocation				Need				Available		
	A	B	C		A	B	C		A	B	C
P_0	0	1	0		7	4	3		2	3	0
P_1	3	0	2		0	2	0	–			
P_2	3	0	2		6	0	0				
P_3	2	1	1		0	1	1				
P_4	0	0	2		4	3	1				

Now, check system is in safe state

$$\text{Work} = \text{Available} = \{2, 3, 0\}$$

$$\text{Finish} = \{\Gamma, \Gamma, \Gamma, \Gamma, \Gamma\}$$

(i)   Let i = 0,   Finish[0] = F

$$\text{Need } (P_0) < \ = \text{Work} \Rightarrow \{7, 4, 3\} < \ = \{2, 3, 0\}$$

No, P_0 has to wait for resources.

(ii)   Let $i = 1$,   Finish[1] = F

$$\text{Need } (P_1) < = \text{Work} \Rightarrow \{0, 2, 0\} < = \{2, 3, 0\}$$

$\therefore$ Work = Work + Allocation

$$= (2, 3, 0) + (3, 0, 2)$$

$$= (5, 3, 2)$$

After P_1 finishes, it releases resources

$$\text{Finish} = \{F, T, F, F, F\}$$

$$\text{Safe sequence} = \{P_1\}$$

(iii)   Let $i = 2$,   Finish[2] = F

$$\text{Need } (P_2) < = \text{Work} \Rightarrow \{6, 0, 0\} < = \{5, 3, 2\}$$

No, P_2 has to wait for resources.

(iv)   Let $i = 3$,   Finish[3] = F

$$\text{Need } (P_3) < = \text{Work} \Rightarrow \{0, 1, 1\} < = \{5, 3, 2\}$$

$\therefore$ Work = Work + Allocation

$$= (5, 3, 2) + (2, 1, 1)$$

$$= (7, 4, 3)$$

After P_3 finishes, it releases resources

$$\text{Finish} = \{F, T, F, T, F\}$$

$$\text{Safe sequence} = \{P_1, P_3\}$$

(v)   Let $i = 4$,   Finish[4] = F

$$\text{Need } (P_4) < = \text{Work} \Rightarrow \{4, 3, 1\} < = \{7, 4, 3\}$$

$\therefore$ Work = Work + Allocation

$$= (7, 4, 3) + (0, 0, 2)$$

$$= (7, 4, 5)$$

After P_4 finishes, it releases resources

$$\text{Finish} = \{F, T, F, T, T\}$$

$$\text{Safe sequence} = \{P_1, P_3, P_4\}$$

(vi)   Let $i = 0$,   Finish[0] = F

$$\text{Need } (P_0) < = \text{Work} \Rightarrow \{7, 4, 3\} < = \{7, 4, 5\}$$

$\therefore$ Work = Work + Allocation

$$= (7, 4, 5) + (0, 1, 0)$$

$$= (7, 5, 5)$$

After P_0 finishes, it releases resources

$$\text{Finish} = \{T, T, F, T, T\}$$

$$\text{Safe sequence} = \{P_1, P_3, P_4, P_0\}$$

(vi)   Let i = 2,   Finish[2] = F

Need (P_2) < = Work $\Rightarrow$ {6, 0, 0} < = {7, 5, 5}

∴   Work = Work + Allocation

= (7, 5, 5) + (3, 0, 2) = (10, 5, 7)

Safe sequence = {P_1, P_3, P_4, P_0, P_2}

Yes, system is in safe state. So request can be granted immediately

Problem 8: Consider a system with four processes P1, P2, P3, P4 and four resource types A, B, C, D with one instance of each type. Resource ownership is as follows:

P1 holds A and wants C

P2 holds B

P3 holds D wants B

P4 holds C wants D

Is system deadlocked?

(Draw resource-allocation graph and wait-for graph)   (5 M)

Solution:

R = {A, B, C, D}

E = {P1 →C1, P4 →D, P3 →B, A →P1, C →P4, D →P3, B → P2}

Resource instances:

- One instance of resource type A,B,C,D

Process states:

- Process P1is holding an instance of resource type A and is waiting for an instance of resource type C.
- Process P2 is holding an instance of B.
- Process P3 is holding an instance of resource type D and is waiting for an instance of resource type B
- Process P4 is holding an instance of resource type C and is waiting for an instance of resource type D

The resource allocation graph for above instance is as follows:

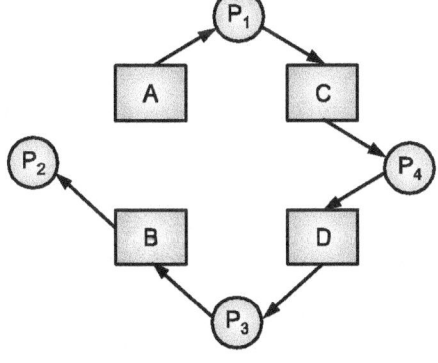

Fig. 6.13

Wait-for-Graph for above instance is as follows:

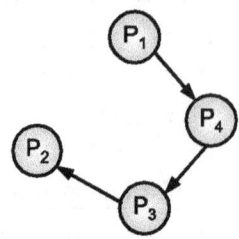

Fig. 6.14

As wait-for-Graph does not contain cycle, System has no deadlock.

Problem 9: Consider the following snapshot of the system:

Process	Allocation				Max			
	A	B	C	D	A	B	C	D
P0	0	3	2	4	6	5	4	4
P1	1	2	0	1	4	4	4	4
P2	0	0	0	0	0	0	1	2
P3	3	3	2	2	3	9	3	4
P4	1	4	3	2	2	5	3	3
P5	2	4	1	4	4	6	3	4

A system has total 10, 20, 13, 15 instances of resource types A, B, C, D respectively.

Answer the following using Banker's algorithm:

(i) What is content of need and available matrix?

(ii) Is the system in safe state>

(iii) If a request from process P1 arrives for (2, 2, 3, 3), can it be granted immediately?

(April 13) (5 M)

Solution:

Total Resources   −   Total Allocation   =   Available

   A   B   C   D   A   B   C   D   =   A B C D

   10 20 12 15   −   7   16 8   13   =   3 4 4 2

1. Need = Max – Allocation

	Need					Max					Allocation			
	A	B	C	D		A	B	C	D		A	B	C	D
P_0	6	2	2	0		6	5	4	4		0	3	2	4
P_1	3	2	4	3	=	4	4	4	4		1	2	0	1
P_2	0	0	1	0		0	0	1	2		0	0	0	0
P_3	0	6	1	2		3	9	3	4		3	3	2	2
P_4	1	1	0	1		2	5	3	3		1	4	3	2
P5	2	2	2	1		4	6	3	5		2	4	1	4

2. Now using Banker's Safety Algorithm.

$$\text{Work} = \text{Available} = \{3, 4, 4, 2\}$$
$$\text{Finish} = \{F, F, F, F, F, F\}$$

(i) Let i = 0, Finish[i] = F,

$$\text{Need } (P_0) < = \text{Work} \Rightarrow \{6, 2, 2, 0\} < = \{3, 4, 4, 2\}$$

No, P_0 has to wait for resources.

(ii) Let i = 1, Finish[1] = F

$$\text{Need } (P_1) < = \text{Work} \Rightarrow \{3, 2, 4, 3\} < = \{3, 4, 4, 2\}$$

No, P1 has to wait for resources.

(iii) Let i = 2, Finish[2] = F

$$\text{Need } (P_2) < = \text{Work} \Rightarrow \{0, 0, 1, 0\} < = \{3, 4, 4, 2\}$$
$$\text{So work} = \text{Work} + \text{Allocation}$$
$$= \{3, 4, 4, 2\} + \{0, 0, 0, 0\}$$
$$\text{Work} = \{3, 4, 4, 2\}$$

(After P_2 finishes, it will release resources)

$$\text{Finish} = \{F, F, T, F, F, F\}$$

Safe sequence = { P_2}

(iv) Let i = 3, Finish[3] = F

$$\text{Need } (P_3) < = \text{Work} \Rightarrow \{0,6,1, 2\} < = \{3, 4, 4, 2\}$$

No, P3 has to wait for resources.

(v) Let i = 4, Finish[4] = F

$$\text{Need } (P_4) < = \text{Work} \Rightarrow \{1, 1, 0, 1\} < = \{3, 4, 4, 2\}$$
$$\text{So work} = \text{Work} + \text{Allocation}$$
$$\Rightarrow \{3, 4, 4, 2\} + \{1, 4, 3, 2\}$$
$$= \{4, 8, 7, 4\}$$

(After P4 finishes, it will release resources)

$$\text{Finish} = \{F, F, T, F, T, F\}$$

Safe sequence $= \{P_2, P_4\}$

(vi) Let i = 5, Finish[5] = F

$$\text{Need (P5)} < = \text{Work} \Rightarrow \{2, 2, 2, 1\} < = \{4, 8, 7, 4\}$$

$$\text{So work} = \text{Work} + \text{Allocation}$$

$$\Rightarrow \{4, 8, 7, 4\} + \{2, 4, 1, 4\}$$

$$= \{6, 12, 8, 8\}$$

(After P5 finishes, it will release resources)

$$\text{Finish} = \{F, F, T, F, T, T\}$$

Safe sequence $= \{P_2, P_4, P5\}$

(vii) Let i = 0, Finish[0] = F

$$\text{Need (P0)} < = \text{Work} \Rightarrow \{6, 2, 2, 0\}\} < = \{6, 12, 8, 8\}$$

$$\text{So work} = \text{Work} + \text{Allocation}$$

$$\Rightarrow \{6, 12, 8, 8\} + \{0, 3, 2, 4\}$$

$$= \{6, 15, 10, 12\}$$

(After P0 finishes, it will release resources)

$$\text{Finish} = \{T, F, T, F, T, T\}$$

Safe sequence $= \{P_2, P_4, P5, P0\}$

(vii) Let i = 1, Finish[1] = F

$$\text{Need (P1)} < = \text{Work} \Rightarrow \{3, 2, 4, 3\} < = \{6, 15, 10, 12\}$$

$$\text{So work} = \text{Work} + \text{Allocation}$$

$$\Rightarrow \{6, 15, 10, 12\} + \{1, 2, 0, 1\}$$

$$= \{7, 17, 10, 13\}$$

(After P1 finishes, it will release resources)

$$\text{Finish} = \{T, T, T, F, T, T\}$$

Safe sequence $= \{P_2, P_4, P5, P0, P1\}$

(viii) Let i = 3, Finish[3] = F

$$\text{Need (P3)} < = \text{Work} \Rightarrow \{0, 6, 1, 2\} < = \{7, 17, 10, 13\}$$

$$\text{So work} = \text{Work} + \text{Allocation}$$

$$\Rightarrow \{7, 17, 10, 13\} + \{3, 3, 2, 2\}$$

$$= \{10, 20, 12, 15\}$$

(After P3 finishes, it will release resources)

$$\text{Finish} = \{T, T, T, T, T, T\}$$

Safe sequence $= \{P_2, P_4, P5, P0, P1, P3\}$

$\therefore$ Yes, system is in safe state.

If request (2, 2, 3, 3) from P1 arrives, then according to Resource Request Algorithm,

(i)   Request (P1) <= Need 4 $\Rightarrow$

               (2, 2, 3, 3) < = {3, 2, 4, 3} $\Rightarrow$ True go to Step 2

(ii)   Check if Request (P1) < = Available

               (2, 2, 3, 3) < = {3, 4, 4, 2} $\Rightarrow$ No

So P1 has to wait since resources are not available.

∴   Request cannot be granted immediately.

SUMMARY

➤ A set of processes is in a deadlock state when every process in the set is waiting for an event that can only be caused by another process in the set.

➤ For example, there are two tape drives, in some system. There are two processes, each holding one more tape. Now each of the process needs one more tape drive. Now both the processes are waiting for each other to release a tape drive. This is a deadlock situation.

➤ Under the normal mode of operation, any resource is utilized by a process in following manner:

1. **Request:** A process request for a resource. If it is available, it is immediately granted; otherwise the process must wait for it.

2. **Use:** After a request is granted, process uses the resource.

3. **Release:** The Process releases the resource after it is used.

➤ Coffman identified four conditions that must hold simultaneously for there to be a deadlock are Mutual Exclusion Condition, Hold and Wait Condition , No-Preemptive Condition and Circular Wait Condition.

➤ Resource allocation graph is directed graph, which is used to describe resources allocated to a particular process in a system. It contains set of processes P, set of resources R = {R_1, R_2, ..., R_n}, request edge and allocation edge or an assignment edge.

➤ If Resource allocation graph contains cycle, then deadlock may exist.

➤ The deadlock handling techniques are deadlock prevention, deadlock avoidance, and deadlock detection and recovery.

➤ Deadlock prevention algorithm disallows one of four necessary conditions for deadlock.

➤ Deadlock avoidance algorithm do not grant resource request if resource-allocation have potential have lead to deadlock.

➤ Deadlock Detection and Recovery algorithm always grants resource request when possible. It periodically checks for a deadlock. If deadlock exists, recover from it.

➤ A state is safe if the system can allocate resources to each process in some order and still avoid a deadlock.

➤ A system is in a safe state; if there exists a safe sequence.

➤ Safe Sequence:A sequence of processes <P_1, P_2, ..., P_n> is a safe sequence for current allocation state if, for each process Pi, the resource requests that P_i can still make can be satisfied by the currently available resources plus the resources held by all P_j have finished with j < i.

➤ A system without safe sequence is unsafe.

➤ A safe state is not deadlocked state. Conversely deadlocked state is unsafe state. Thus unsafe system may lead to deadlock.

➤ The deadlock avoidance algorithm used for several instances of the resources is called as Banker's algorithm developed by Dijkstra.

➤ Deadlock detection algorithm is used to detect the deadlock. There are two algorithms:

➤ Single instance resource type uses wait-for-graph

➤ Several instances of a resource type uses data structure of bankers algorithm.

➤ When deadlock detection algorithm detects a deadlock in system, some recovery scheme must be used to recover the system from deadlock.

➤ The recovery scheme may use either of the following approaches: Process Termination and Resource Preemption.

PRACTICE QUESTIONS

1. What is deadlock? What are different methods to handle a deadlock?
2. Explain necessary conditions for a deadlock to occur.
3. Explain deadlock prevention strategies.
4. Explain deadlock avoidance technique for a single instance of each resource type.
5. What is wait-for-graph? Explain with example.
6. List few schemes for deadlock recovery.
7. Discuss the different data structures used in Bankers algorithm.
8. What is difference between deadlock and starvation?
9. Define the terms:
   - Starvation
   - Request Edge
   - Claim Edge
   - Allocation Edge
   - Rollback
   - Safe Sequence
10. Consider a system consisting of four resources of the same type that are shared by three processes, each of which needs at most two resources. Show that the system is deadlock-free.
11. **Multiple Choice Questions:**
    (i) Which of the following is not necessary condition in deadlock _____.
       (a) Hold and Wait   (b) Circular Wait
       (c) Mutual Exclusion   (d) Safe State

(ii) In resource- allocation graph, if there is edge from process to resource, then it is known as _____.
   (a) claim edge   (b) Request Edge
   (c) Allocation edge   (d) None

(iii) In resource-allocation graph, if there is edge from resource to process, then it is known as _____.
   (a) claim edge   (b) Request Edge
   (c) Allocation edge   (d) None

(iv) Banker's safety Algorithm is used for _____.
   (a) Deadlock detection   (b) Deadlock Prevention
   (c) Deadlock Avoidance   (d) Recovery

(v) Wait-for-graph is used for _____ in the system.
   (a) Deadlock detection   (b) Deadlock Prevention
   (c) Deadlock Avoidance   (d) Recovery

Ans.: (i) (d) (ii) (b) (iii) (c) (iv) (c) (v) (a)

12. **State True or False:**
   (i)   When process request for resource, it is immediately granted.
   (ii) Deadlock occurs in Multiprogramming.
   (iii) A safe state is deadlock state.
   (iv) Rollback is one of the deadlock recovery scheme.
   (v)   If wait-for-graph contains cycle, then there exists a deadlock in the system.
   (vi) Prevention of Hold and Wait causes more resource utilization.
   (vii) Forceful preemption of process causes inconsistent state of system.

   Ans.: (i) False (ii) True (iii) False (iv) True (v) True (vi) False (vii) True

13. What is a wait-for-graph? Draw wait-for-graph for the following:

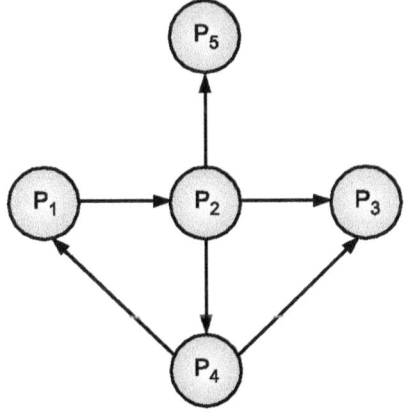

Fig. 6.15

Ans.: Refer to Section 6.6.1.

14. List the sequence of operations in which process can utilize a resource under normal mode of operations.

Ans. Refer to Section 6.2.

15. Write note on recovery from deadlock.

Ans. Refer to Section 6.7.

16. Define request edge and claim edge.

Ans. Refer to Section 6.6.1.

17. Explain the term "Rollback and select a victim" in the context of deadlock recovery.

Ans. Refer to Section 6.7.2.

18. What is the role of Max and Need array used in Banker's Algorithm?

Ans. Refer to Section 6.5.3.

19. Write a short note on deadlock prevention strategies.

Ans. Refer to Section 6.4.1.

20. Explain recovery from a deadlock in brief.

Ans. Refer to Section 6.7.

21. Define safe sequence.

Ans. Refer to Section 6.5.1.

UNIVERSITY QUESTIONS AND ANSWERS

1. Justify: "System must avoid deadlock".   (April 2013) (1 M)

Ans. Refer to Section 6.5.1.

2. Wait for graph is used for deadlock avoidance in the system True/False? Justify.

                                                                        (April 2015) (1 M)

Ans. False. It is used in deadlock detection and to Section 6.6.

3. Define starvation.   (April 2015) (1 M)

Ans. Refer to Section 6.7.2.

4. What is resource allocation graph? Explain in brief.   (April 2015) (2 M)

Ans. Refer to Section 6.3.2.

5. What is deadlock? Explain deadlock recovery in detail.   (April 2015) (5 M)

Ans. Refer to Sections 6.1 and 6.7.

■■■

Memory Management

Contents ...

Objectives...

- To Understand Basic Concept like Physical and Logical Address Space, Basic Method for Memory Utilization like Dynamic Loading and Linking etc.
- To Learn Concept of Swapping
- To Know Different Memory Management Schemes like Contiguous Allocation, Paging and Segmentation etc.
- To Study Virtual Memory Management Technique

7.1 INTRODUCTION

- Main memory is storage area of quickly accessible data which is shared by CPU and I/O devices.
- Main memory is a large array of words or bytes. Each word or byte has its own address. For any program to be executed, it must be in main memory along with data.
- CPU reads instruction from main memory during instruction fetch cycle and performs read and write operation in main memory during data fetch cycle. Thus, it is storage device that CPU is able to address and access directly.
- To improve the utilization of the CPU and the speed of the computer's response to its users, we must keep several processes in memory; i.e. we must share memory. Thus, multi-programming creates need of memory management.
- Operating system is responsible for the following activities in connection with memory management:
  1. To keep track of all memory locations- free or allocated. If allocated, to which process and how much.
  2. Deciding which processes and data to move into and out of memory.
  3. Allocating and de-allocating memory space as needed according to various memory management techniques and algorithms.
- There are various memory management schemes and techniques for managing memory. In selecting memory management scheme, various issues like hardware design, protection, binding of symbolic addresses to physical addresses, distinguishing logical and physical addresses, dynamic loading and linking etc. must be considered.

7.1.1 Basic Hardware

- Main memory and registers are only the storage that CPU can access directly. For any instruction in execution and any data being used by instruction must be in one of these storage devices.

- Registers are accessible generally in one clock of CPU.

- But main memory take more cycles of CPU to complete as CPU has to wait for data which is required for completing.

- To avoid this situation, a fast memory i.e. cache is added between main memory and CPU.

- In addition to speed of accessing memory, we must also ensure correct operation has to protect operating system from user access and user process from one another.

- This protection must be provided by the hardware. Two registers, base and limit register can be used to provide protection as shown in Fig. 7.1.

- The base register holds the starting base address or smallest legal physical memory address and limit register specifies size of the range.

- For example, if base register holds address 300040 and limit register contains range 120900 then process can access legal addresses from 300040 to 420940.

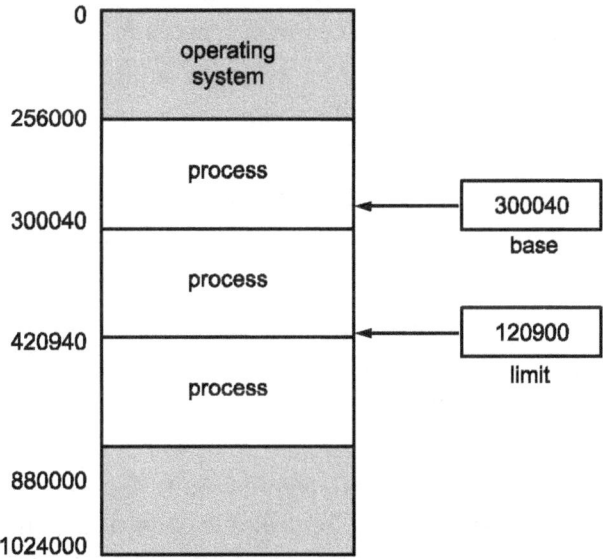

Fig. 7.1: A base and a limit register define a logical address space

- Protection of memory space is accomplished by comparing every address generated by user's program with these registers.

- Any attempt made by user's program to access operating system's memory or other user's memory results in a trap to the operating system as shown in Fig. 7.2.

- Thus, this method prevents a user program from modifying code or data of operating system or other users.
- The base and limit registers can be loaded by operating system using special privileged instruction in kernel mode.

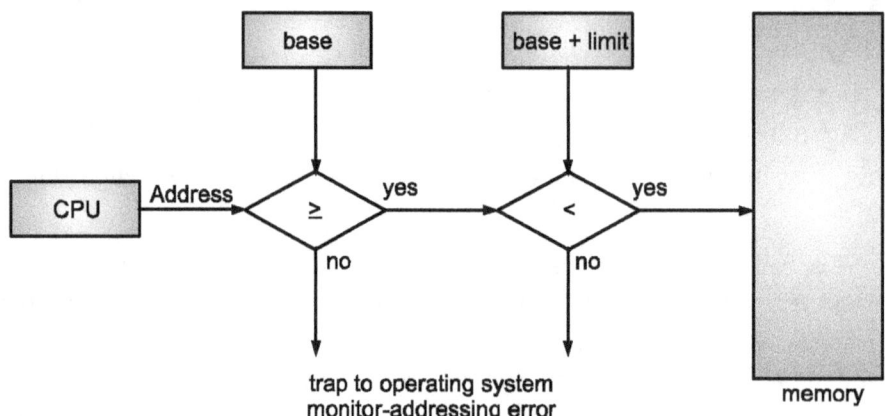

Fig. 7.2: Hardware address protection with base and limit registers

7.1.2 Address Binding

- Generally, programs reside in executable form on the disk. For execution, program must be brought into memory and placed within process.
- So, to create active process in memory, symbolic addresses generated by program must be mapped into the process address space. This mapping is known as address binding.
- As process is executed, it accesses instructions and data from memory.
- Classically binding of instructions and data can be done at any step, (shown in Fig. 7.3) as follows:
  - **Compile Time:** If you know at compile time where the process will reside in memory, then absolute code can be generated. If starting location changes, then it will be necessary to recompile this code. In MS-DOS, .COM files are bound at compile time.
  - **Load Time:** If it is not known at compile time where the process will reside memory, then compiler generates relocatable code. Then binding is delayed until load time. If the starting address is changed, only reload the code to changed address.
  - **Execution Time:** If the process can moved during its execution from one memory segment to another, then binding must be delayed until run time. Special hardware is needed to implement this scheme.

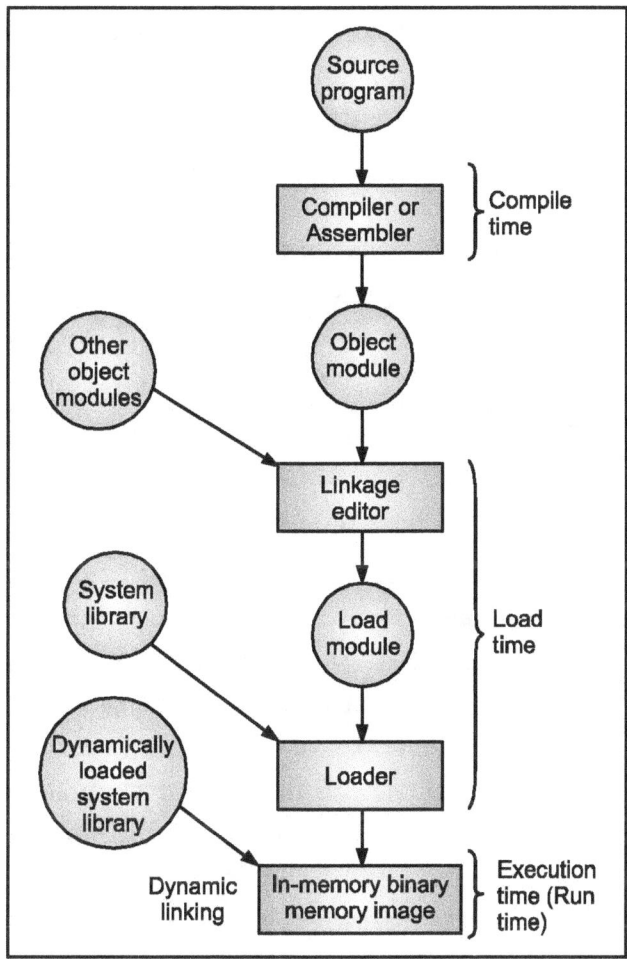

Fig. 7.3: Address binding

7.1.3 Logical Versus Physical Address Space   (April 13, Oct. 16)

- An address generated by the CPU is commonly known as Logical Address or virtual address.

- The address seen by the memory unit that is one loaded into the memory- address-register of the memory is commonly referred as the Physical Address.

- The compile time and load time address binding generates the identical logical and physical addresses.

- However, the execution time address binding scheme generates differing logical and physical addresses as process moves from one memory segment to another.

- The set of all logical addresses generated by a program is known as Logical Address Space.

- The set of all physical addresses corresponding to these logical addresses is Physical Address Space.

- Now, the run time mapping from virtual address to physical address is done by a hardware device known as Memory Management Unit (MMU).

- Different methods like contiguous allocation, paging, segmentation etc. can perform such mapping. The simplest memory mapping scheme is shown in the Fig. 7.4.

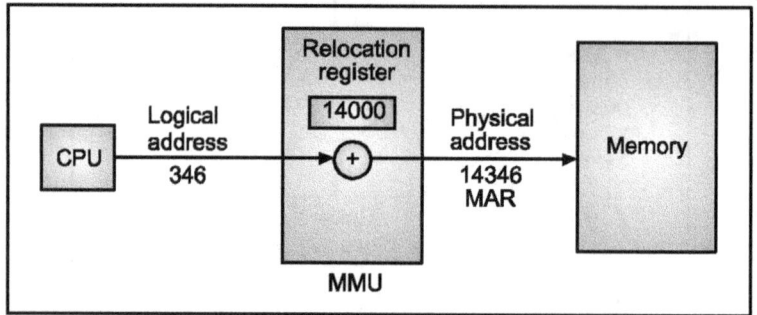

Fig. 7.4: Dynamic relocation using relocation register

- Here, base register is known as relocation register. The value in the relocation register is added to the address generated by a user process at the time it is sent to memory.

- Let's understand this situation with the help of example: If the base register contains the value 14000, then an attempt by the user to address location 346 is mapped to location 14346.

- The user program never sees the real physical address space, it always deals with the Logical address.

- Logical address is in the range (0 to max) and Physical address is in the range(R to R+max) where R is the value of relocation register.

- As it is clear from the above text that user program supplies only logical address, these logical address must be mapped to physical address before they are used.

7.1.4 Dynamic Loading

- For process to execute, the entire program and data must be in physical memory.

- So the size of process is limited to size of physical memory.

- But all routines of program are not required at a time or program may contain some error routines which may be never called.

- To obtain better memory utilization, routines can be loaded in main memory as required. This is known as dynamic loading.

- Thus, in dynamic loading:
  - o A routine is not loaded until it is called.
  - o All routines are kept on disk in relocatable load format.
  - o Only main routine is loaded into memory and is executed.
  - o When routine needs to call another routine, the calling routine checks whether that routine has been loaded. If not, then relocating linking loader is called to load the desired routine and updates program's address table.

Advantages of Dynamic Loading:
1. Unused routine is never loaded.
2. Better memory utilization.
3. Useful when large amount of code is needed to handle infrequently occurring cases.
4. Logical to physical address binding is at runtime.
5. No special support from the operating system is required, can be implemented through program design.

7.1.5 Dynamic Linking and Shared Libraries

- In static linking, system language libraries are treated as like any other object module and are combined by the loader into binary program image.

Dynamic Linking:
- In dynamic linking, linking is postponed until execution time. This feature is usually useful in system libraries such as language subroutine libraries.
- Without this facility, each program on system must include one copy of language library.
- With dynamic linking, a stub is included in the image for each library routine reference.
- The stub is a small piece of code that indicates how to locate the appropriate memory-resident library routine or how to load the library if the routine is not already present.
- When stub is executed, it checks to see whether the needed routine is already in memory. If not, the program loads the routine into memory. Either way, the stub replaces itself with address of the routine and executes the routine.
- Thus, the next time that particular code segment is reached, the library routine is executed directly, incurring no cost for dynamic linking.

Advantages:
1. All processes that use a language library execute only one copy of the library code in memory
2. The above feature can be extended to library updates(such as bugs fixes)

3. A library may be replaced by a new version, and all programs that reference the library will automatically use the new version.

4. Without this support, such programs would need to be re-linked to gain access to the new library.

Shared Libraries:

- More than one version of a library may be loaded into memory, and each program uses its version information to decide which copy of library to use. Major changes increments the version number and minor changes retain the same version number.

- Thus, only programs that are compiled with new library version are affected by the incompatible changes incorporated in it.

- Other programs linked before the new library was installed will continue using the older library. This system is also known as shared libraries.

7.2 | SWAPPING   (Oct. 16)

- The process to be executed must be in main memory.

- A process can be swapped temporarily out of memory to a backing store, and then brought back into memory for continued execution. This process is known as swapping.

- Swapping requires backing store.

- Backing store is fast disk large enough to accommodate copies of all memory images for all users; must provide direct access to these memory images as shown in Fig. 7.5.

- System maintains a ready queue of ready-to-run processes which have memory images on disk.

- When CPU scheduler decides to execute a process, dispatcher checks to see whether next process in the queue is in memory.

- If it is not, the dispatcher swaps out a process currently in memory and swaps in desired process along with context of process.

- If static binding is used, then process that swapped out will be swapped in same memory space it occupied previously.

- In case of dynamic binding, process can be easily moved in different locations.

- Variant part of swapping policy is roll out, roll in used for priority-based scheduling algorithms.

- Lower-priority process is swapped out so higher-priority process can be loaded and executed.

- Context switch time is fairly high in swapping system. For example, we assume that the user process is 10MB, and the standard hard disk with a transfer rate of 40MB per second, actual transfer would to and from memory would take:

  10000kb/40000kb per sec = ¼ second = 250 milliseconds.

- Assume we expect 8 millisecond of delay; each swap will take 258 milliseconds. And we need two swaps (in and out) therefore it takes 516 milliseconds. Thus major part of swap time is transfer time; total transfer time is directly proportional to the amount of memory swapped.

- Swapping is constrained by some factors like never swap a process with pending I/O or execute I/O operations. Because if we swap out a process which is executing or waiting I/O operations and swap in desired process, then I/O operation might attempt to use memory that belongs to desired process.

- Currently, standard swapping is used in few systems. It requires too much swapping and less execution. Modified versions of swapping are found on many systems (i.e., UNIX, Linux, and Windows).

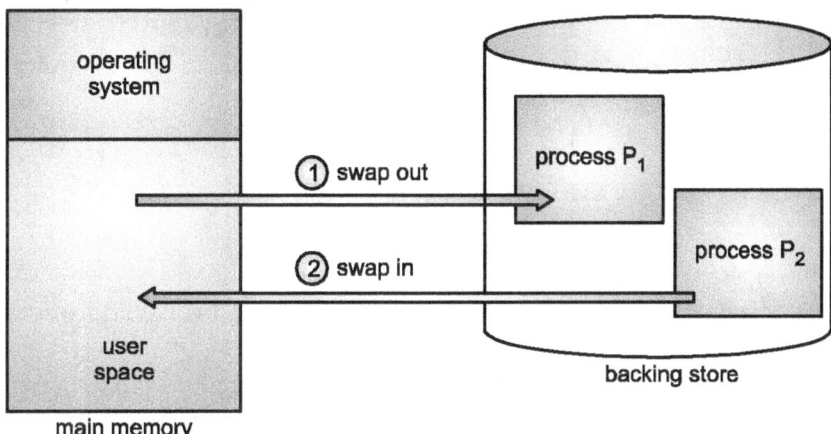

Fig. 7.5: Swapping of two processes using a disk as a backing store

7.3 | CONTIGUOUS MEMORY ALLOCATION

- Operating System allows accommodation of multiple processes in memory.

- Memory needs to be allocated efficiently in order to allow as many processes into memory as possible.

- If not enough processes are in memory, multiprogramming will not be effective and the CPU will be idle most of the time.

- Main memory usually divided into two partitions as shown in Fig. 7.6 i.e.,

  1. Resident operating system, usually held in low memory with interrupt vector.

  2. User processes then held in high memory.

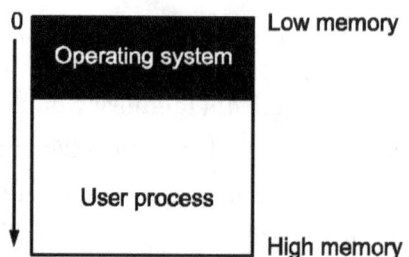

Fig. 7.6: Memory partition

- Therefore, we need to discuss memory mapping and protection, contiguous memory allocation method.

7.3.1 Memory Mapping and Protection

- Relocation registers are used to protect user processes from each other, and from changing operating-system code and data.

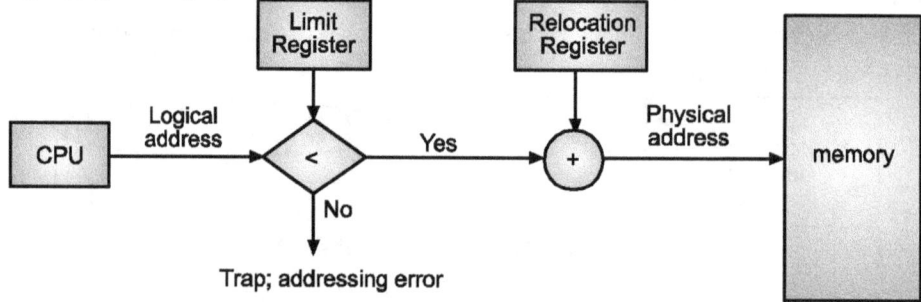

Fig. 7.7: Hardware support for relocation and limit registers

- Relocation register contains value of smallest physical address.
- Limit register contains range of logical addresses – each logical address must be less than the limit register.
- MMU maps the logical address dynamically by adding the value in the relocation register to generate physical address which is sent to memory.
- When the CPU scheduler selects a process for execution, the dispatcher loads the relocation and limit registers with the correct values as part of the context switch.
- The relocation register scheme provides an effective way to allow the operating system size to change dynamically. For example, Transient code such as device drivers are loaded as needed. So it is not kept in memory.
- With help of relocation register, this code can be loaded during program execution. So size of operating system changes dynamically.

7.3.2 Memory Allocation

- Memory can be partitioned by two approaches:
  1. Single partition allocation, and
  2. Multiple partition allocation.

7.3.2.1 Single Partition Allocation

- This is simplest method of memory management. The memory is divided in two sections one section for operating system and second section for user program as shown in Fig. 7.6.

- In order to provide a contiguous area of free storage for user program, operating system is loaded at one end (usually in low or bottom part).

- The relocation registers points to first location in user's partition.

- User's logical address is adjusted by hardware to produce physical address.

- Address binding is delayed until execution time.

- Relocation register value is static during program execution. Hence all of the Operating system must be in memory.

- A new program (user process) is loaded only when operating system passes control to it.

- After receiving control, it starts running until its completion or termination due to I/O or some error.

- When this program is completed or terminated, the operating system may load another program for execution.

- Protection of operating system from user process is achieved through limit register.

- It is set to highest address occupied by operating system code.

- Memory address generated by user process to access certain memory location is compared with limit register.

- If address is more than limit register, then trap will be generated and permission is denied.

Advantages:

1. It is simplest method.

2. Sharing of data and code is very easy.

Disadvantages:

1. It only supports single process environment, for example MS-DOS(i.e. It does not support multiprogramming.

2. Less utilization of CPU. CPU will be sitting idle during I/O operation.

3. Less utilization of memory. Since only one program is residing at a time in memory, it may not occupy whole memory.

7.3.2.2 Multiple Partition Allocation Method   (April 15, Oct. 16)

- In multi-programming environment, several programs reside in main memory at a time.

- To support multiprogramming, main memory is divided into several partitions; each of which is allocated to a single process.

- The number of programs residing in memory will be bound by the number of partitions. Depending upon how and when partitions are created, there may be two types of approaches:

  1. Multiple contiguous fixed (static) partition allocation, and

  2. Multiple contiguous variable (dynamic) partition allocation.

7.3.2.2.1 Multiple Contiguous Fixed (Static) Partition Allocation

- In this method, memory is divided into several partitions of fixed size that size never changes.

- Each partition method holds one process. This method is originally used in the IBM OS/360 operating system. It is also known as multiprogramming with fixed number of tasks (MFT).

- Jobs are assigned to these fixed partitions by either of the following methods:

  1. There will be a separate ready queue for each of regions. A region will be big enough to satisfy memory requirement of all jobs in its own queue. In this scheme, a system will have to pre-pass over the common ready queue, in which all the jobs were initially placed. And then assign each of these jobs to the queue of appropriate region. Each queue is scheduled separately.

     Example: One queue for 2K, one queue for 6K, and a queue for 12K. When a job arrives then it is put on the appropriate queue if there is no memory partition available. If a job of 4K arrives and there is no partition of size 4K then it is put in the queue of larger partition (6K) as shown in following Fig. 7.8.

					Monitor
Q2	------	2K	1K	2K	2K
Q6	------	3K	4K	4K	6K
Q8	------	11K	7K	8K	12K

Fig. 7.8: MFT with separate queues for each partition

2. In the other scheme, all the jobs are placed in only one queue. Whenever a partition is free, job selected by FCFS, round robin, or priority algorithm is assigned to the partition as shown in following Fig. 7.9.

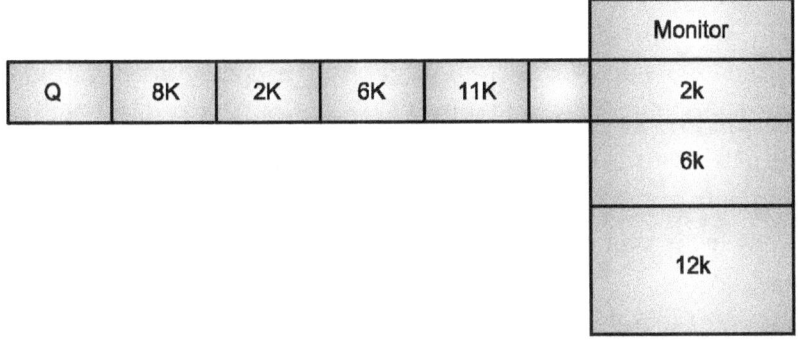

Fig. 7.9: MFT with one queue

- If while one job is executing, and a high priority job from appropriate partition is swapped out \rolled out and high priority job is swapped \rolled in. After this job is over, generally the swapped out job is brought back in the same region.
- This is because; otherwise that job will again have to undergo relocation, and calculation of new address space for it. If after a memory is assigned to a job, the memory requirements of the job increase, then either of following situations takes place.
  - o An error message is given to the user and a job is terminated.
  - o Control returns to the user along with error. And user decides either to modify or exit.
  - o System can:
    1. Swap out the job,
    2. Wait for lager region,
    3. Swap into lager region,
    4. Continue.
  - o Overall performance of MFT depends upon correct selection of region size.
  - o There are two major things to be selected and decided:
    1. How many regions to have?
    2. What will be the size of each region?
  - o The decision regarding the size of the region is generally based on educated guess of the memory requirement of input programs.
  - o For which one may have to study the kind and types of job which will be submitted to the system.

- Generally, the set of region is searched to determine which region is best to allocate. First fit, best fit and worst fit are most common strategies used to select a free region from the set of available regions.

  1. **First-fit:** The first -fit approach allocate the first free partition large enough to accommodate the process. Searching can start either at the beginning of the set of holes or where the previous first fit search ended.

  2. **Best-fit:** The best fit approach allocates the smallest free partition that meets the requirements of the process. Under consideration we must search the entire list, unless the list is kept ordered by size. This strategy produces the smallest leftover partition.

  3. **Worst-fit:** The worst – fit approach allocate the largest free partition. Again, we must search the entire list, unless it is sorted by size .this strategy produced to largest leftover partition, which may be more useful than the smaller than leftover partition from a best – fit approach.

Problems with MFT:

- Process can not demand more memory than allocated partition.
- It does not support for dynamic relocation.
- It dose not support a system having dynamically data structures such as queue, stack and heap etc.
- It suffers from internal fragmentation, (Fragmentation is discussed in next Section 7.3.3).

7.3.2.2.2 Multiple Contiguous Variable (Dynamic) Partition Allocation

- In this scheme, region or partition size is not fixed; it can vary dynamically.
- It creates partition according to requirements of process. It is also known as multiprogramming with variable number of tasks (MVT).
- Operating system maintains a table indicating which parts of the memory are free and which are allocated.
- Whenever a job requests for the memory, the table indicating the current status of the memory is referred.
- If memory is available, then the job is assigned to partition according to job scheduling policy and the table is updated to reflect the new status.
- When the job terminates, it releases the memory occupied by it. Therefore, at any instance of time, the snapshot of memory will show blocks of allocated memory and free holes distributed all over the memory as shown in Fig. 7.10.

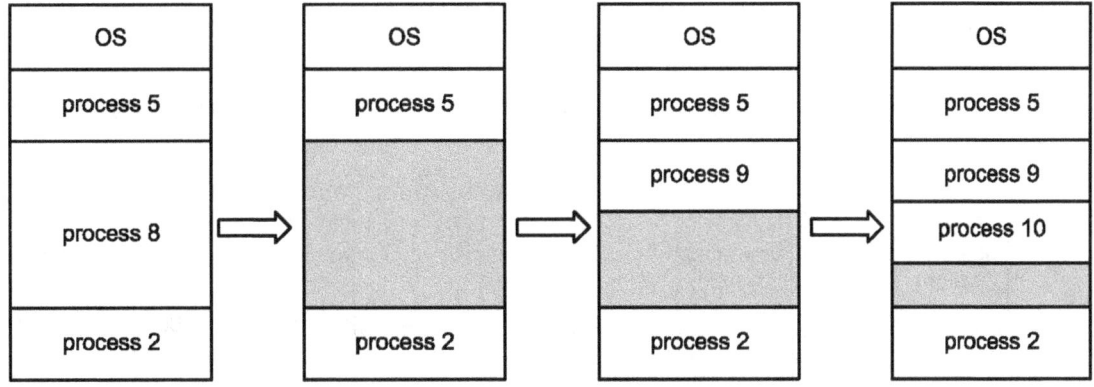

Fig. 7.10: Job scheduling with MVT

Advantages:

1. It increases degree of multi-programming.

2. It does not suffer from internal fragmentation.

3. Size of process can grow or shrink dynamically.

Disadvantages:

1. **External fragmentation:** When you start with, there is a very big hole of available memory. As job go on requesting and releasing the memory, this big hole is divided into small used blocks and unused holes. Such many holes are distributed in the memory, which do not satisfy memory requirement of any job. They form the external fragmentation. The worst part with external fragmentation is wastage of memory.

2. Lot of time is consumed by the system to search all these holes, when a memory request arrives.

7.3.3 Fragmentation   (April 16)

*   As jobs are allocated and de-allocated, memory is fragmented into small chunks. One of reason of fragmentation is improper selection of region size.

1. **Internal Fragmentation:**

*   Allocated memory may be slightly larger than requested memory; this size difference is memory internal to a partition, but not being used is known as internal fragmentation.

*   For example, if the hole is the size of 20,000 bytes, suppose that next process requests 19,800 bytes. 200 bytes are lost. This is called internal fragmentation; i.e. memory that is internal to a partition but is not being used. The general approach to avoiding this problem is to break the physical memory into fixed size blocks and allocate memory in units based on block size.

2. External Fragmentation:

- As processes are loaded and removed, the free memory is broken into little pieces. Total memory space exists to satisfy a request, but it is not contiguous then it is known as external fragmentation.

- As shown in Fig. 7.11, first fit and best fit method suffers from external fragmentation.

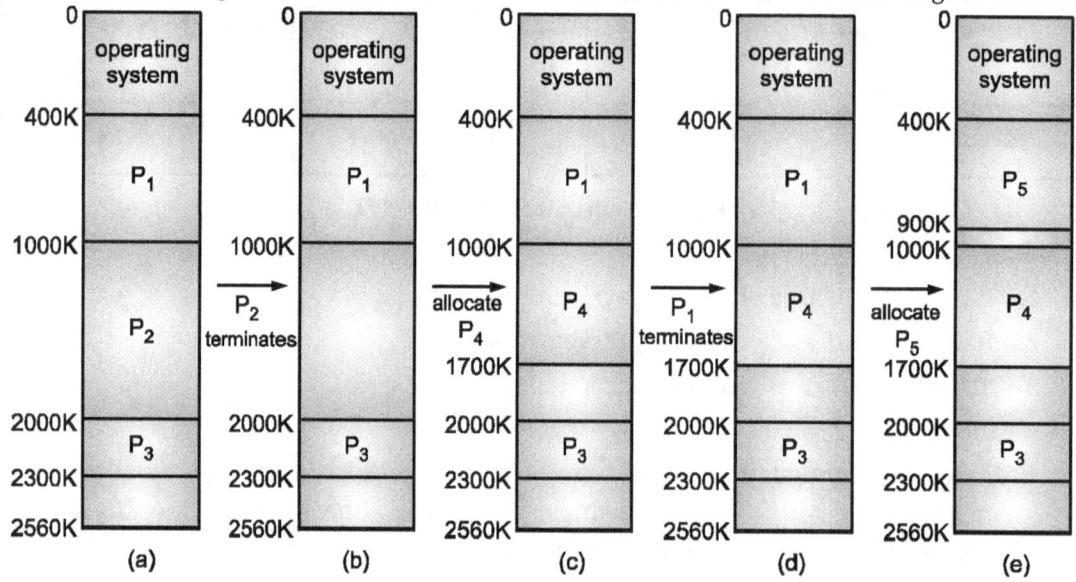

Fig. 7.11: External Fragmentation

- Depending on the total amount of memory storage and average process size, external fragmentation may be major or minor problem.

- Statistical analysis of first fit even with some optimization, given N allocated blocks, another 0.5N blocks will be lost to fragmentation.

- That is one-third of memory may be unusable! This property is known as the 50-percent rule.

- External fragmentation can be avoided by:

  1. **Compaction** is process of collecting all free holes and forms a single big free hole. It shuffles memory contents to place all free memory together in one large block. Compaction is possible only with dynamic relocation i.e. logical addresses be relocated dynamically, at execution time. If addresses are relocated only at load time, we can not compact storage. One must consider the cost of compaction while implementing compaction algorithm.

     - Simple compaction algorithm is to move all jobs towards one end of memory and all free holes to the other end of memory. This method is very expensive. As almost all jobs will change their address space, they will have to undergo relocation.

- Variation to this algorithm says that, a free space will be created in middle of the memory. If swapping is a part of the system, then that can be combined with compaction e.g. a job to be shifted will be rolled out to a backing storage and later rolled into some different address space. In this method, actual code for compaction will be very less, as system already have code for roll-out and roll in.

- Frequency of compaction algorithm to be executed will vary system –wise. One approach says, compaction should be called immediately after execution of job is over. Other approach may say, compaction must be called, only when it is required or may be after some regular interval of time. Compaction though is an extra overhead; it solves the problem of external fragmentation to maximum extent.

2. Another solution to external-fragmentation problem is to permit the logical address space of the process to be noncontiguous. Thus, allowing a process to be allocated physical memory wherever the space is available. Two complementary techniques achieve this solution: paging and segmentation.

- Let us compare MFT and MVT algorithm:

Factors	MFT	MVT
Region Size	In this method, memory is divided into several partitions of fixed size that size never changes.	region or partition size is not fixed; it can vary dynamically
Process Size	Can not grow at run time.	Can grow or shrink at run time.
Degree of multi-programming	Fixed (i.e. number of partitions).	Dynamic.
Memory utilization	Poor.	Good.
Fragmentation	Suffers from internal fragmentation.	Suffers from external fragmentation.

7.4 | PAGING

- Paging is a memory-management scheme that permits the physical address space of a process to be non-contiguous. It avoids external fragmentation.

7.4.1 Basic Method

- The basic method for implementation involves breaking physical memory into fixed-sized blocks called frames and break logical memory into blocks of the same size called Pages.

- The hardware support for paging is illustrated in Fig. 7.12.

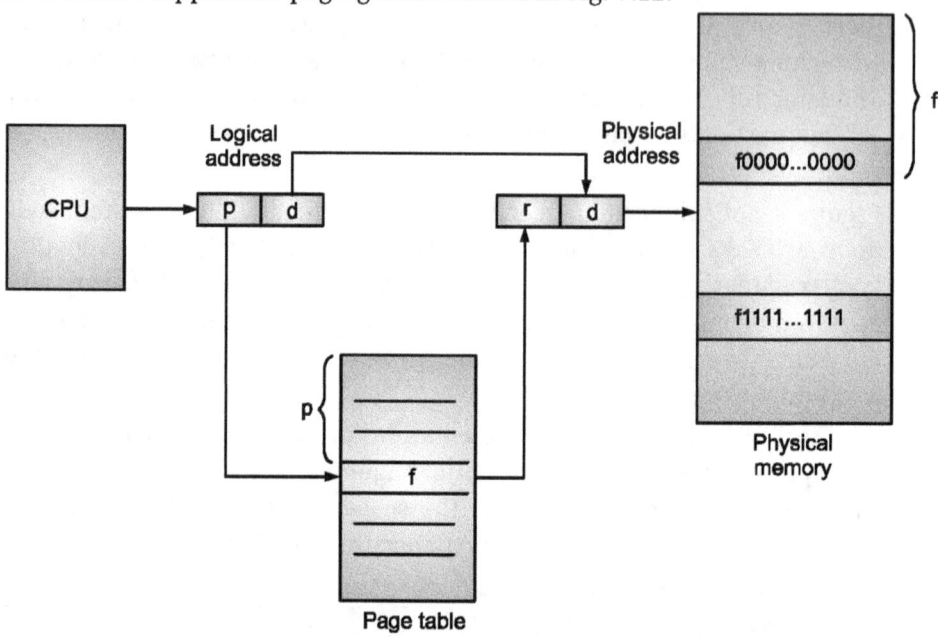

Fig. 7.12: Paging Hardware

- Every address generated by the CPU is divided into two parts: Page number (p) and Page offset (d).
- The page number (p) is used as an index into a Page Table.
- A page table is used to map a page on a frame.
- Page table has an entry for each page. The page table has the base address of each page in physical memory; which is combined with page offset (d) to define the physical memory address which is sent to memory unit.
- The paging model of memory is shown in Fig. 7.13.

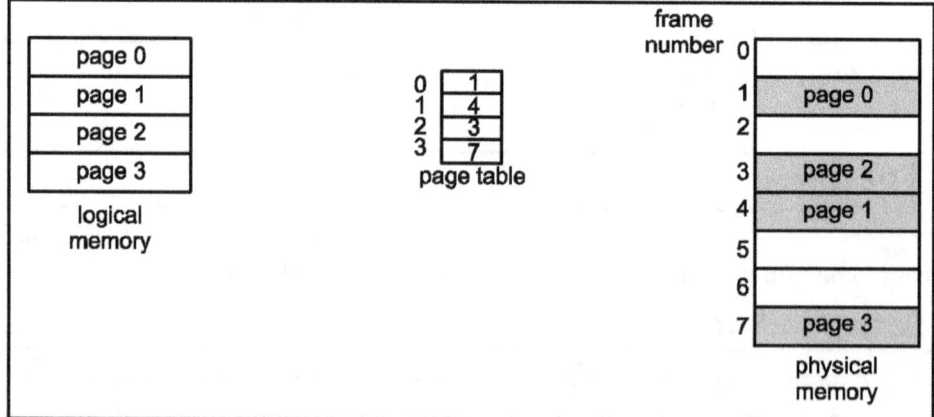

Fig. 7.13: Paging model of logical and physical memory

- Page size and frame is same and decided by hardware and is generally a power of 2 varying between 512 bytes and 16MB per page.
- Reason: If the size of logical address is 2^m and page size is 2^n, then the high-order m-n bits of a logical address designate the page number and n low-order bits designate the page offset. Thus logical address is as follows:

page number	page offset
p	d
m-n	n

Where, p is an index into page table and d is displacement within page.

- For example, consider the memory as shown in Fig. 7.14 using page size of 4 bytes and physical memory of 32 bytes (8 pages).

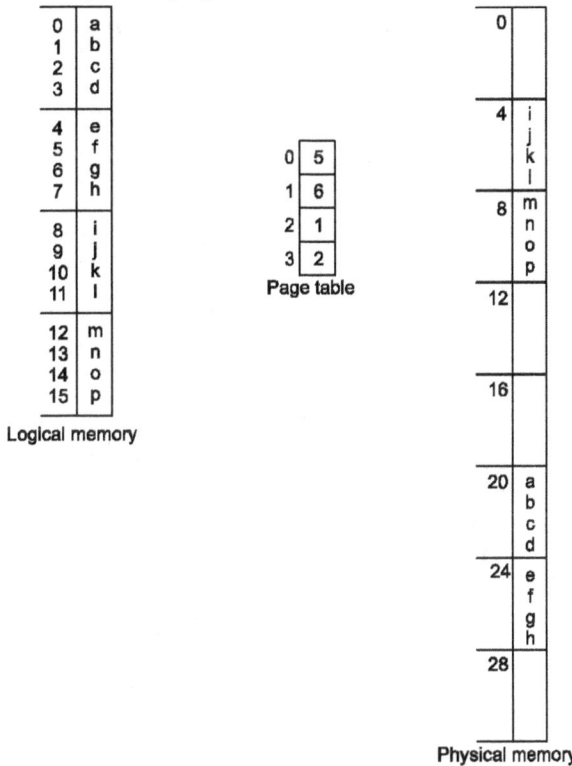

Fig. 7.14: Paging example for a 32-byte memory with 4-byte pages

- Let us see how the user's view of memory can be mapped into physical memory by following steps:
  1. Find out Page number (p) = Logical address /page size (integer division).
  2. Find out Page offset (d) = Logical address % page size.
  3. Check if offset is smaller than page size otherwise; a trap is to be generated.
  4. Using page number (p) as an index into page table; obtain equivalent frame number.

5. Find out the base address of the frame.
    - Base address of a frame = (frame number *frame size) or (frame number * page size)
    - Physical Address = Base address of a frame + Page offset.
- Suppose Logical address 3 can be mapped to physical address 23 as follows:
    - Page number (p) = Logical address /page size => 3/4 = 0
    - Page offset (d) = Logical address % /page size => 3%4 = 3
- Check if offset is smaller than page size (i.e. 3 < 4) if yes, then find frame number using page number 0 in page table.
    - Frame number = 5
    - Base address of a frame = (frame number * page size) => 5 * 4 = 20
    - Physical Address = Base address of a frame + Page offset => 20+3=23
        - When process arrives in the system, its size is expressed in pages.
        - Each page of the process needs one frame. If the process requires n pages, at least n frames are required in memory.
        - The first page of the process is loaded into the first frame listed on free-frame list, and the frame number is put into page table as shown in Fig. 7.15.
        - Operating system must be aware of which frames are allocated and which frames are free in physical memory. This information is kept in a data structure called a frame table.

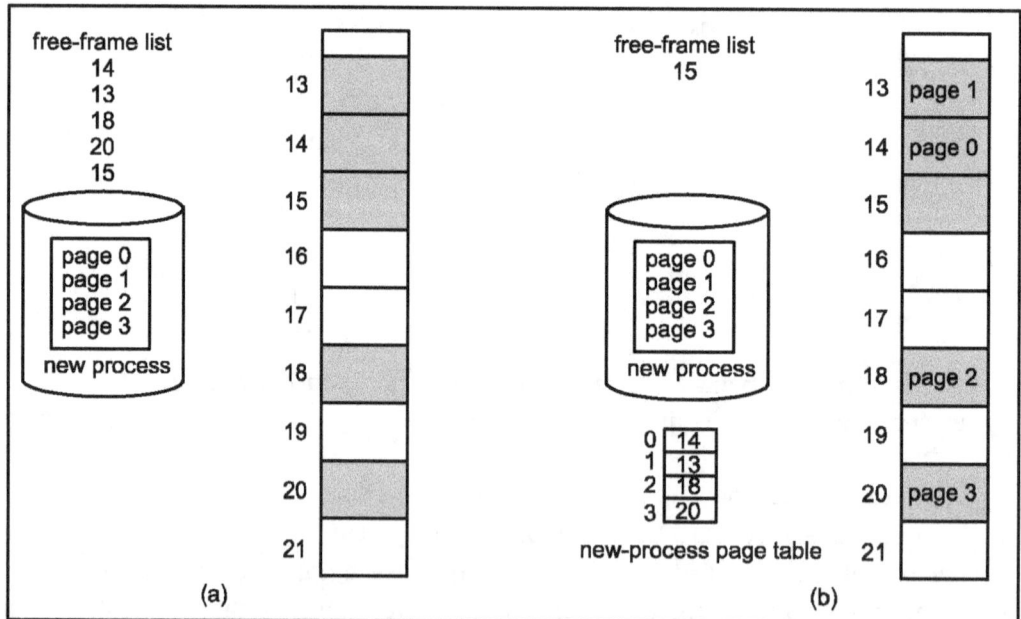

Fig. 7.15: Free Frames (a) before allocation (b) after allocation

7.4.2 Hardware Support   (April 13)

- Every access to any of page has to go through the page table. Therefore, implementation of the page table directly affects the performance of this kind of memory management.

- Though there are different ways on which page table can be implemented, generally the method depends upon the size of the page table.

1. **Page Table Implemented as Dedicated Fast Registers:**
   - As registers are very fast, access to table is also very fast.
   - This is a costly scheme.
   - As a page grows, number of registers may not be available, neither affordable nor feasible.
   - Therefore scheme is useful only for small page tables.

2. **Page Table Implemented in the Main Memory:**
   - This scheme is used when page table is big.
   - Page table is stored in the main memory.
   - PTBR (Pointer To Base Register) points to the base address of page table.
   - In case, location of the page table is changed in the memory, only the contents of PTBR are changed.
   - This scheme gives reasonably slow access. The memory access is to be done twice, once for accessing page table for getting frame number and secondly for accessing actual frame.

3. **Page Table Implemented in Associative Registers:**
   - The above problem can be solved by using special, small, fast lookup hardware cache, called a translation Look-Aside Buffer (TLB) or associative registers as shown in following Fig. 7.16.

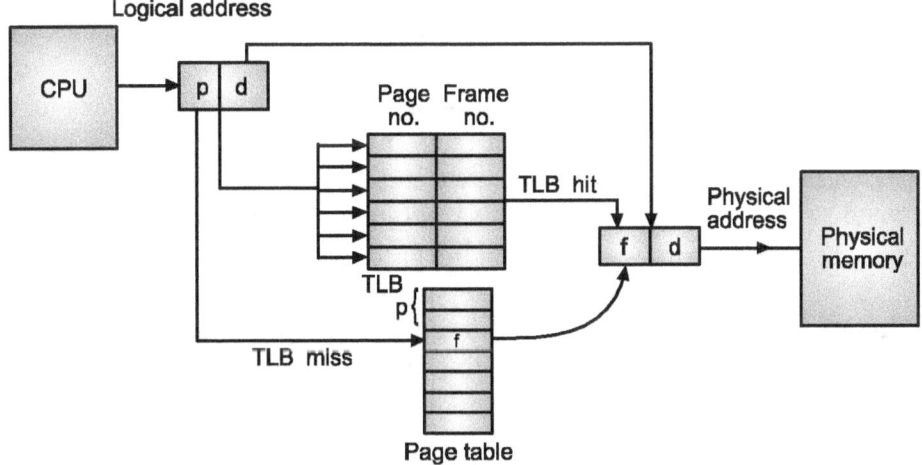

Fig. 7.16: Paging hardware with TLB

- o   Each entry in the TLB consists of two parts: Key and Value. When associative memory is presented with an item, the item is compared with all keys simultaneously. If the item is found, the corresponding value field is returned.

- o   The TLB is used with page tables in the following way: The TLB contains only a few of the page-table entries. When a logical address is generated by the CPU, its page number is presented to the TLB. If page number is found, its frame number is immediately available and is used to access memory.

- o   If the page number is not in the TLB (TLB miss) a memory reference to the page table must be made. In addition, we add the page number and frame number into TLB.

- o   If the TLB already full, the OS have to must select one for replacement.

- o   Some TLBs allow entries to be wire down, meaning that they cannot be removed from the TLB, for example kernel code.

- o   The percentage of times that a particular page number is found in the TLB is called hit ratio.

- o   An 80-percent hit ratio means that we find the desired page number in TLB 80 percent of time. If it takes 20 nanosecond to search the TLB and 100 nanosecond to access memory, then mapped memory access takes 120 nanoseconds when page is found in TLB. If TLB miss is there, then 220 nanoseconds will require for desired bytes. To find the effective memory access-time, weight each case by probability.

- o   Effective memory access time = $0.8 \times (100 + 20) + 0.2 \times (120 + 100) = 140$

- o   If our hit ratio is 98%, the effective memory access time = $0.98 \times (100 + 20) + 0.02 \times (120 + 100) = 122$.

7.4.3 Protection

- Memory protection in a paged environment is supported by protection bits associated with each frame. Normally, these bits are kept in page table.

- One bit can define a page to be read-write or read only. Every reference to memory goes through page table to find correct frame number. At same time, protection bits can be checked to verify that no writes are being made to a read only page. An attempt to write to a read only page causes hardware trap to the operating system.

- One more bit is attached to each entry in the page table: **a valid-invalid bit.** When bit is set to "valid" indicates that the associated page is in the process' logical address space, and is thus a legal page. When bit is set to "invalid" indicates that the page is not in the process' logical address space. Illegal addresses are trapped by using this bit.

- Consider a example as shown in Fig. 7.17.

  - o   Address Space: 14 bits, (Address is from 0 to 16,383).

  - o   Page size: 2K (2048 words)

- o Program size: 0 to 10,468 (pages from 0 to 5).

- o Total number of pages that can be addressed: 16,383/2048 = 8.

- o Any attempt to generate an address in pages 6 or 7, will find that valid-invalid bit is set to invalid, trap will be generated.

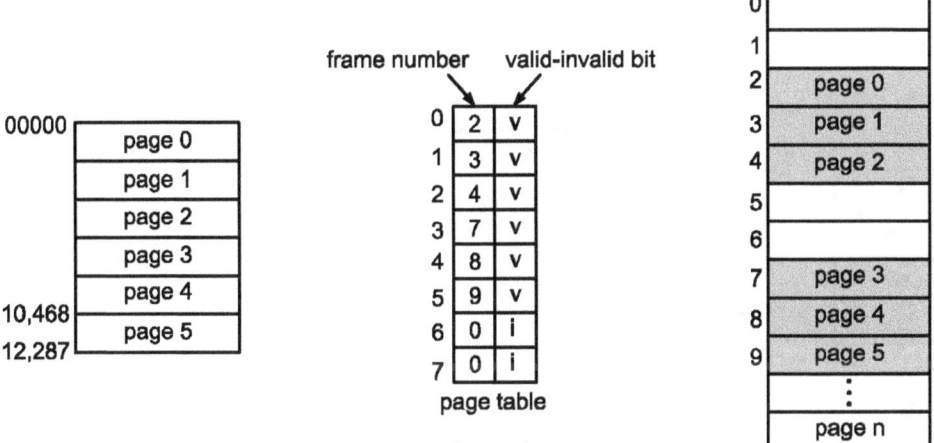

Fig. 7.17: Valid (v) or Invalid bit in page table

7.4.4 Shared Pages

- An advantage of paging is the possible of sharing common code, especially time-sharing environment.

- For example, consider a server with 40 user using text editor (with 150k reentrant code and 50k data space) as shown in Fig. 7.18, we see three page editors with 50k each. Each process has its own data page. So we need (150k + 50K) × 40 = 8000KB memory space. Lot of memory wastage.

- But reentrant code or pure can be shared.

- Reentrant Code or pure code is non-self modifying code; it never changes during execution.

- Thus, two or more processes can execute the same code at the same time. Each process has its own copy of registers and data storage to hold data for process executions.

- One copy of read-only (reentrant) code shared among processes (i.e., text editors, compilers, window systems, run-time libraries and database systems).

- Shared code must appear in same location in the logical address space of all processes.

- Thus, to support 40 users we need only   150k + 40 × 50k = 2150 KB memory space.

- Some operating systems implement shared memory using shared pages.

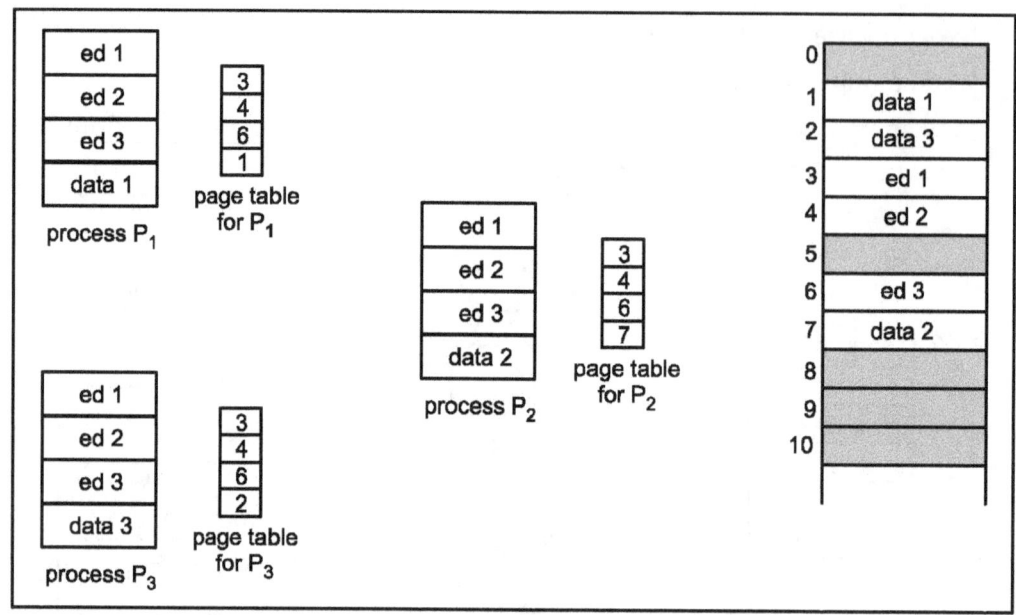

Fig. 7.18: Sharing of code in a paging environment

Advantages of Paging:

1. It permits physical address space of process to be non-contiguous and support virtual memory concept.

2. It maintains clear separation between user's view of memory and actual physical memory.

3. It does not require any support for dynamic relocation because paging itself is a form of dynamic relocation. Every logical address is bound by paging hardware to physical address.

4. It does not suffer from external fragmentation. Any free frames can be allocated to process that it needs.

5. We can share common code, so memory space is properly utilized.

Disadvantages of Paging:

1. Paging suffers from internal fragmentation. Internal fragmentation especially on last page of process; average of 50% on last page.

2. Smaller frames create less fragmentation but increase number of frames and size of page table.

3. Overhead to maintain and update page table.

4. Paging hardware increases the cost of operating system.

7.5 | SEGMENTATION

- As we have already seen, the user's view of memory is not same as actual physical memory in paging memory management scheme.

- The user's view is mapped onto physical memory which allows differentiation between physical and logical memory.

- Segmentation is memory management scheme that supports user's view of memory. A program is a collection of segments.

- A segment is a logical unit such as main program, procedure, function, method, object, local variables, global variables, common block, stack, symbol table, arrays etc. as shown in Fig. 7.19.

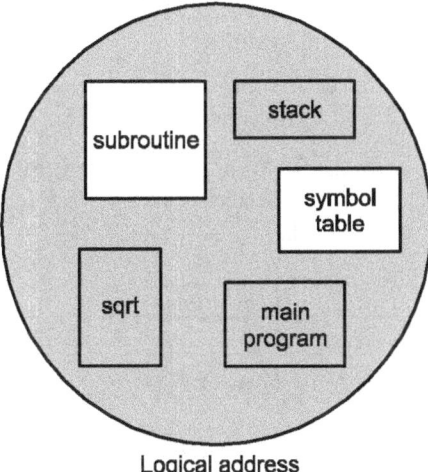

Logical address

Fig. 7.19: User's View of program

- Thus, user prefers to view memory as collection of variable-sized segments, with no necessary ordering among segments.

7.5.1 Basic Method

- A logical address space is collection of segments.
- Each segment has a name (e.g., a unique number) and a length.
- The user specifies each address by two quantities: segment name and length.
- For simplicity, segments are numbered and referred by segment number rather than segment name.
- Thus, Logical address is a .
- Offset is to specify offset of the data from start of a particular segment.
- Physical address is found by looking into a segment table.

7.5.2 Segmentation Hardware

- Although user specifies two-dimensional address, but physical memory is one dimensional array. So two dimensional address should be mapped by one dimensional physical address. This mapping is done by Segment table.
- Each entry in segment table has a segment base and segment limit.
- The segment base contains the starting physical address where segment resides.
- Segment limit specifies the length of segment. The use of segment table is shown in Fig. 7.20.
- As logical address consists of two parts: a segment number(s) and an offset into that segment(d) the segment number is used and index to the segment table.
- The offset (d)of the logical address must be between 0 and segment limit.
- If it is not, we trap to the operating system.
- When offset is legal, it is added to segment base to produce the address in physical memory of the desired byte.
- The segment table is thus essentially an array of base-limit register pairs.

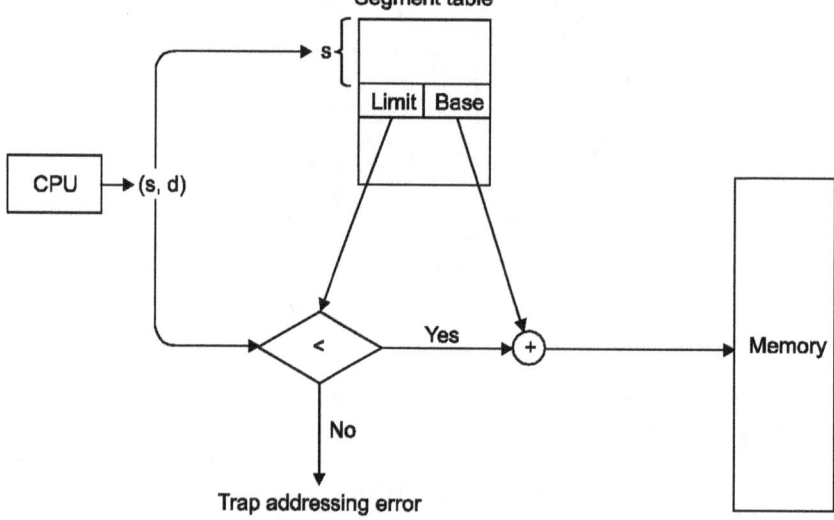

Fig. 7.20: Segmentation Hardware

- Consider an example, shown in Fig. 7.21. Segments are numbered from 0 through 4. The segments are stored in physical memory as shown. The segment table has separate entry for each segment.
- Let us see how to find physical address.
  1. Logical address is specified by a segment number(s) and an offset into that segment (d).

2. Use segment number as an index into segment table to find base address of segment.

3. If offset < segment limit then Physical address = Base address + offset; otherwise trap will be generated.

   - Suppose logical address is < 3,852>
   - Segment number = 3, offset = 852
   - Base Address of segment 3 = 3200
   - As offset < segment limit (i.e. 852 < 1100)
   - Physical Address= Base address + offset => 3200 + 852 => 4052

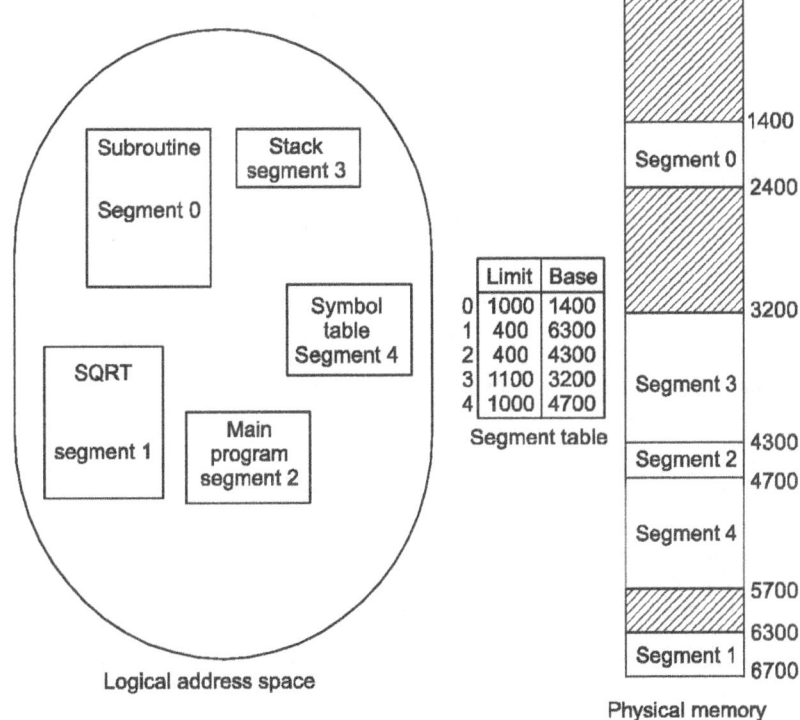

Fig. 7.21: Example of segmentation

- Segment table can be implemented same as page table.

1. **Segment Table can be Stored in Dedicated Fast Registers:**

   - As registers are very fast, access to table is also very fast.
   - This is a costly scheme.
   - As a segment number grows, number of registers may not be available, neither affordable nor feasible.
   - Therefore, scheme is useful only for small segment tables.

2. **Segment Table is Implemented in the Main Memory:**

   - This scheme is used when segment table is big.
   - Segment table is stored in the main memory.
   - STBR (Segment Table Base Register) points to base address of segment table.
   - In case, location of the segment table is changed from the memory, only the content of STBR is changed.

Protection:

   - Segments can be protected same as paging.
   - Protection bits can be associated with each segment table entry.
   - Protection bit can define a segment to be read-write or read only.
   - Every reference to memory goes through segment table to find base address and limit.
   - At same time, protection bits can be checked to verify that no writes are being made to a read only segment.
   - An attempt to write to a read only segment causes hardware trap to the operating system

Shared Segments:

   - Segmentation permits sharing of code segments. When entries in the segment table of two different processes point to same physical location; segments are said to be shared.
   - Shared segments are shown in Fig. 7.22.

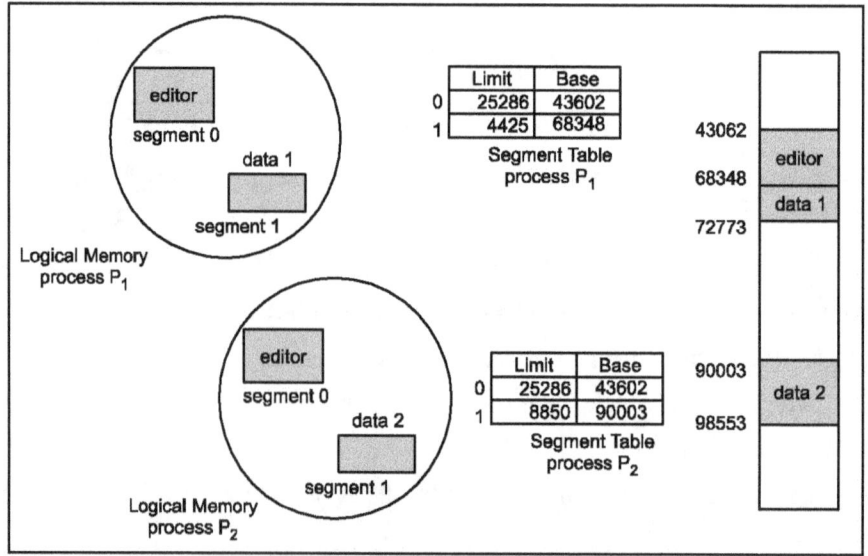

Fig. 7.22: Shared segments

- Sharing of module is easier than paging. Since segmentation is based on a logical division of memory rather than a physical one, segments of any size can be shared with only one entry in the segment tables of each user.
- With paging, there must be a common entry in the page tables for each page that is shared.

Advantages of Segmentation:

1. It permits physical address space of process to be non-contiguous and supports for virtual memory.
2. It supports user's view of memory and allow segments to grow.
3. It supports for dynamic relocation. Every logical address is bound to physical address by segment table.
4. Segment tables: only one entry per actual segment as opposed to one per page in paging.
5. Average segment size > average page size. So less overhead in maintaing segment table.
6. We can share code or data by segmentation which is easier than paging, so memory space is properly utilized.

Disadvantages:

1. Segments suffer from external fragmentation. External fragmentation occurs due to dynamic allocation policies.
2. Overhead to maintain variable sized segments on secondary storage; problematic in case of swapping.
3. Cost of mapping by segmentation hardware is more as compared to paging.

- Let us compare contiguous and non-contiguous memory management scheme i.e., paging and segmentation on following factors:

Factors	Contiguous memory allocation	Paging	Segmentation
Memory allocation	In this, each process is contained in a single contiguous section of memory.	This scheme permits physical address space of process to be non-contiguous but make clear separation between logical memory and physical memory.	This scheme permits physical address space of process to be non-contiguous but supports user's view of memory.

contd. ...

Hardware support	Relocation and limit register.	Address mapping is done by page table.	Address mapping is done by Segment table.
Dynamic relocation	Yes.	Paging itself is a form of dynamic relocation.	Yes, with help of Segment table.
Sharing of data or code	Not possible.	Possible. Sharing of reentrant code.	Possible, easier than paging.
Protection	By using limit register.	By Protection bits like r/w or r and valid-invalid bit attached to each entry of page table.	By Protection bits like r/w or r attached to each entry of segment table.
Fragmentation	Suffers from internal and external fragmentation.	Suffers from internal fragmentation.	Suffers from external fragmentation.
Performance	Time does not require for mapping of logical address to physical address. (only comparing address with limit register).	If page table is implemented in associative registers, then mapping is faster.	If segment table is implemented in fast registers then mapping is faster.

7.6   VIRTUAL MEMORY MANAGEMENT

- Virtual memory is a technique that allows the execution of process that is not completely in main memory.
- It abstracts main memory into an extremely large, uniform array of storage, separating logical memory as viewed by the user from physical memory.
- Virtual address space of a process refers to a logical view of how a process is stored in memory.
- A process begins at a certain logical address-say address 0 and exists in contiguous memory as shown in Fig. 7.23.

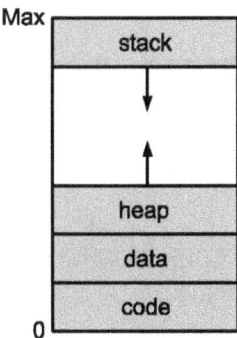

Fig. 7.23: Virtual address space

- As shown in Fig. 7.23, heap is allowed to grow upward direction in memory as it is used for dynamic memory allocation and stack is allowed to grow in downward direction through function calls.
- The large blank space between heap and stack is virtual address space.
- Virtual address space includes holes that are known as sparse address spaces.

7.6.1 Background

- Program to be executed must be in main memory. Program often have code to handle unusual error conditions. Since these errors rarely occur, so that code is almost never executed.
- Similarly, arrays lists and tables are often allocated more memory than actually required. Certain routines are not required at same time. But keeping entire program in main memory limits amount of physical memory and decreases CPU utilization and degree of multi-programming. So there is a need to execute program that is only partially in memory (i.e. virtual memory technique).
- Virtual memory technique offer following benefits:
  1. A program would no longer be constrained by the amount of physical memory. So programmer can concentrated on the problem to be implemented.
  2. More programs can reside in memory at same time, so degree of multiprogramming is increased. CPU utilization and throughput also increased.
  3. Less I/O would be needed to load or swap each user program.
  4. In addition to separating logical memory from physical memory, virtual memory allows files and memory to be shared.
  5. System libraries can be shared by several processes through mapping of the shared object into virtual address space.
  6. Similarly virtual memory enables processes to share memory.
  7. It provides an efficient mechanism for process creation.
- Virtual memory can be implemented via:
  1. Demand paging.
  2. Demand segmentation.

7.6.2 Demand Paging

- Demand paging policy or technique transfers memory pages instead of process to and from secondary storage. The entire process does not have to reside in main memory to execute and the kernel loads pages for a process on demand when the process references the pages.

- A demand paging is similar to paging system with swapping where processes reside in secondary memory as shown in Fig. 7.24.

- When we want to execute a process, swap from memory. Instead of swapping whole process, swapper brings only necessary pages into memory.

- A swapper is known as lazy swapper or pager who never swaps a page into memory unless that page will be needed.

- When process is to be swapped in, the pager guesses pages which will be used before process is swapped out again. Thus it decrease swap time and amount of physical memory needed.

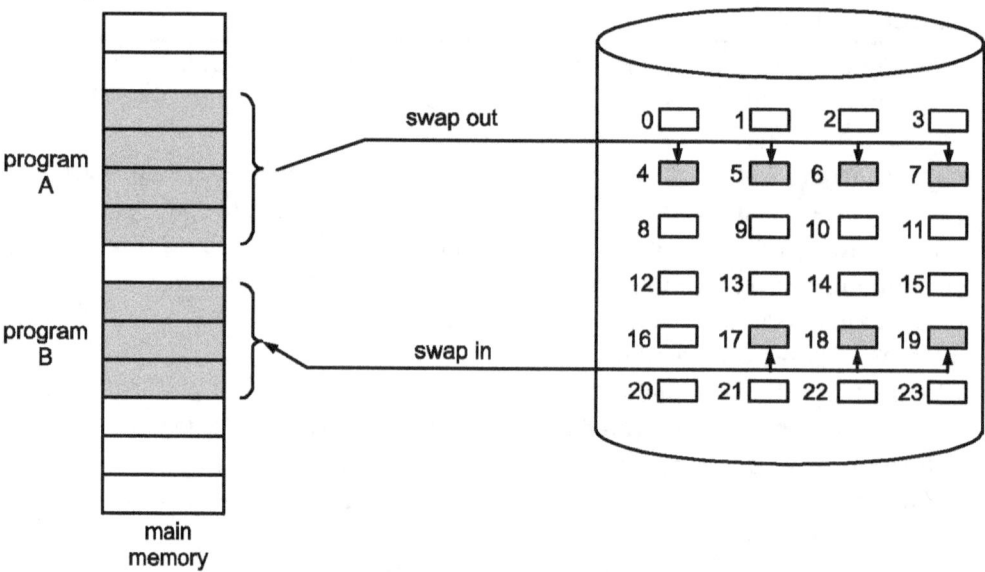

Fig. 7.24: Demand Paging

- The hardware to support demand paging is same as hardware for paging and swapping:

  1. **Page Table:** This table has the ability to mark an entry invalid through a valid-invalid bit or special value of protection bits.

  2. **Secondary Memory:** It is usually high speed disk; also known as swap device. It holds those pages that are not in main memory.

- To distinguish between the pages that are in memory and the pages that are on the disk, valid-invalid bit is used.

- When this bit is set to "valid", the associated page is legal and in main memory.

- When this bit is set to "invalid", page may not be valid or page is valid but currently on the disk as shown in following Fig. 7.25.

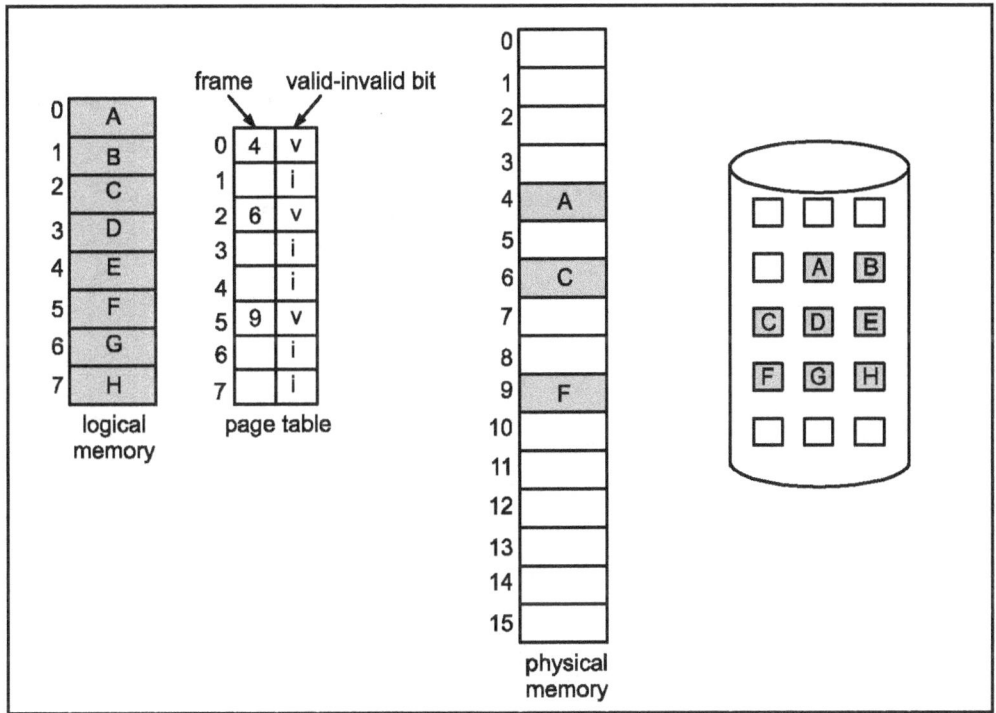

Fig. 7.25: Page table with valid-invalid bit

- Whenever, process tries to access a page which is not into memory, then page fault occurs.

- The paging hardware, which translates the address through page table, will notice that invalid bit is set and cause trap to the operating system.

- The steps for handling page fault are as follows: (shown in Fig. 7.26).

    Step 1: Operating system first has to determine why page fault occurs due to missing page (valid memory reference) or out-of-range reference (invalid memory reference).

    Step 2: If invalid reference, then terminate process. If valid reference, then causes a trap.

    Step 3: If valid page, but not yet brought in memory, then page is on backing store.

Step 4: To bring in a missing page:

- Suspend the process, saving user registers and process state.

- Locate a free frame in memory.

- Locate the missing page on backing store (its location on disk)

- Bring in the missing page into memory.

Step 5: When transfer completes, update page table by marking page to "valid".

Step 6: Reset process's program counter in PCB so that when it starts the instruction will be re-executed. Change process's state from waiting state to ready state.

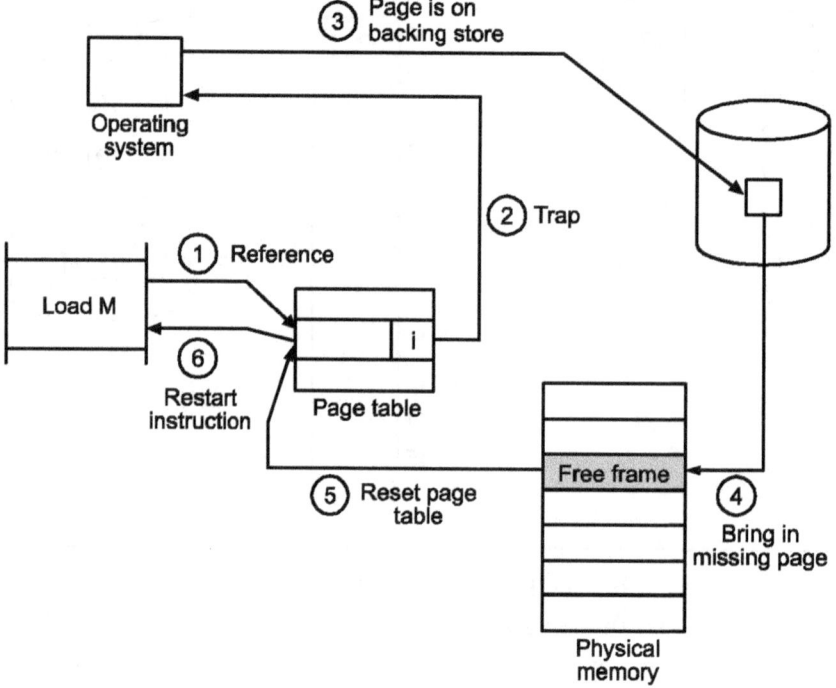

Fig. 7.26: Steps in handling a page fault

Pure Demand Paging:

- In demand paging, when process starts execution with no pages in memory, when operating system sets the instruction pointer to the first instruction of the process, process immediately faults for the page.

- After this page is brought into memory, the process continues to execute, faulting as necessary until every page that it needs is in memory.

- Thus, it never brings a page into memory until it is required.

7.6.3 Performance of Demand Paging

- Demand paging can significantly affect the performance of a system. For most computer systems, memory access time ranges from 10 to 200 nanoseconds.
- As long as we have no page faults, the effective access time is equal to memory access time.
- If page fault occurs, we must first read the relevant page from disk and access desired word.

  Let p be probability of page fault.

  If   p = 0 then no page fault occurs.

  If   p = 1, every reference is a fault.

  Effective Access Time (EAT) = (1 – p) × Memory access + p (Page Fault Overhead + Swap Page Out + Swap Page In + Restart Overhead)

- To compute the effective access time, we must know how much time is needed to service a page fault.
- Three major components affect the page fault service-time:
  1. Service the page-fault interrupt,
  2. Read in the page, and
  3. Restart the process.
- Let us assume that Memory access time = 200 nanoseconds
- Average page-fault service time = 8 milliseconds

$$\begin{aligned} \text{EAT} &= (1 - p) \times 200 + p \text{ (8 milliseconds)} \\ &= (1 - p) \times 200 + p \times 8{,}000{,}000 \\ &= 200 + p \times 7{,}999{,}800 \end{aligned}$$

- If one access out of 1,000 causes a page fault, then EAT = 8.2 microseconds. This is a slowdown by a factor of 40 because of demand paging. Thus effective access time is directly proportional to page-fault rate.
- Effective access time can be reduced by:
  1. Keeping page-fault rate low,
  2. Using better page replacement algorithm, and
  3. Allocating more pages to a process.

7.6.4 Page Replacement

- In multi-programming environment, it may happen that there is no free frame available and valid page fault occurs as shown in Fig. 7.27.

- The operating system could terminate the user process. But demand paging is an attempt to improve CPU utilization and throughput.
- Also users have feeling that all pages are in memory and large amount of memory available.
- To bring user page into memory, operating system swaps out some process by freeing its frames. The process of freeing frame is known as page replacement.
- The frame which is selected for replacement is known as victim frame.
- The major issue is how to select victim frame, normally frame that is not currently being used and free it.

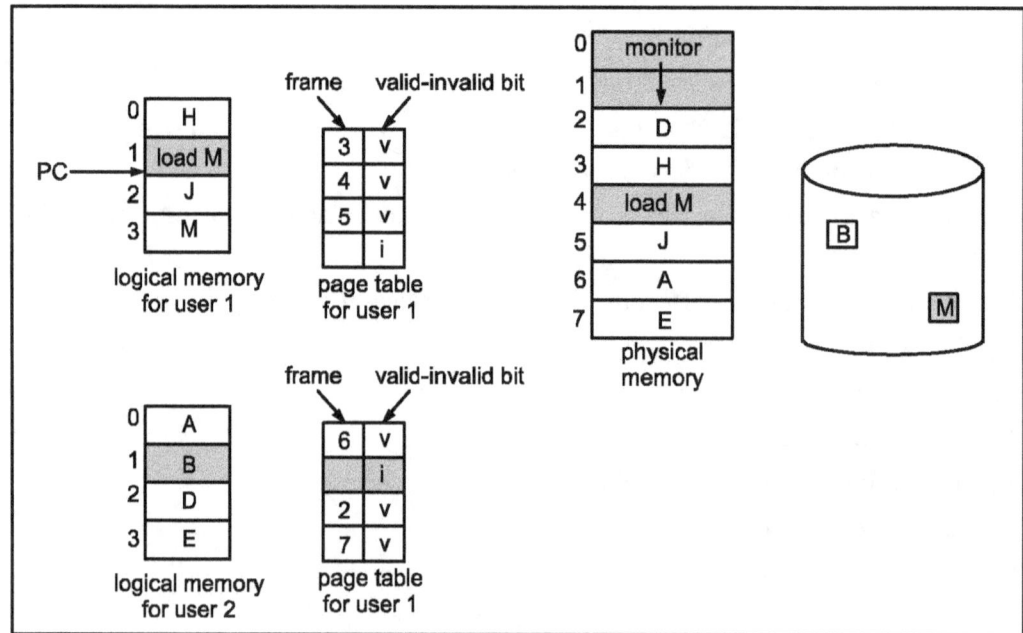

Fig. 7.27: **Need for Page Replacement**

- The page-fault service routine can be modified to include page replacement (shown in Fig. 7.28) as follows:
1. Find the location of the desired page on disk
2. Find a free frame:
   o   If there is a free frame, use it.
   o   If there is no free frame, use a page replacement algorithm to select a victim frame.
   o   Write the victim frame to the disk; change the page and frame tables accordingly.
3. Bring the desired page into the newly freed frame; update the page and frame tables
4. Restart the process.

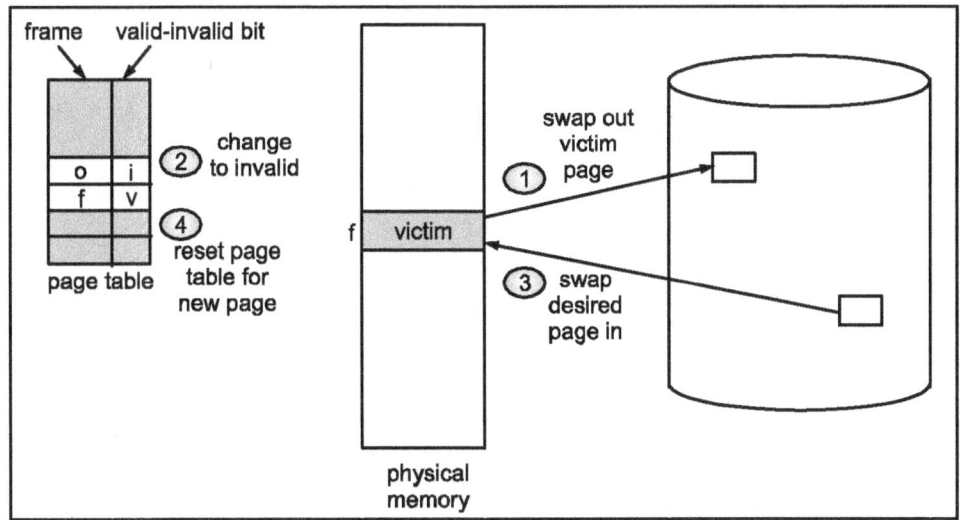

Fig. 7.28: Page Replacement

- If no free frames are free, two page transfers are required; first for to free the victim frame and second for to read the desired into frame. This overhead can be reduced by using dirty bit or modify bit.
- The dirty bit can be used as follows:
  1. Each page or frame has dirty bit associated with it in the hardware.
  2. Modify bit is set for a page, when any word has written to it after reading from secondary storage device.
  3. When we select a page for replacement, modify bit is checked.
  4. If the dirty bit is set, then page has been modified, so contents of page must be written to disk.
  5. If the dirty bit is not set, then page has not modified after reading from disk. i.e. contents of frame and copy of that page on the disk are same. So there is no need to swap out the page for purpose freeing frame. Only that particular frame is declared as free frame.

7.6.4.1 Page Replacement Algorithms

- Every operating system uses one of the page replacement schemes from following schemes. If the page fault rate is less, then page replacement algorithm will be better. The algorithm is evaluated on a string of memory references and is called as reference string.
- One may generate the reference string as follows: Suppose the address sequences which are recorded are:

    0100, 0432, 0612, 0102, 0611, 0105, 0613 .... etc.

    with 100 words per page. One may divide each address by 100 to get the particular page number and the reference string will be:

    1, 4, 6, 1, 6, 1, 6, ... etc.

1. FIFO (First In First Out):

- This is one of the simplest page replacement algorithms.
- In this scheme, all the available frames are given to the pages from reference string serially i.e. first frame to first page, second frame to second page and so on.
- When all the available frames are over at that time, the first frame is selected as victim frame and at next time the second frame and so on.

  For example: Consider the reference string:

    1, 2, 3, 4, 1, 2, 5, 1, 2, 3, 4, 5

  Number of frames are 3.

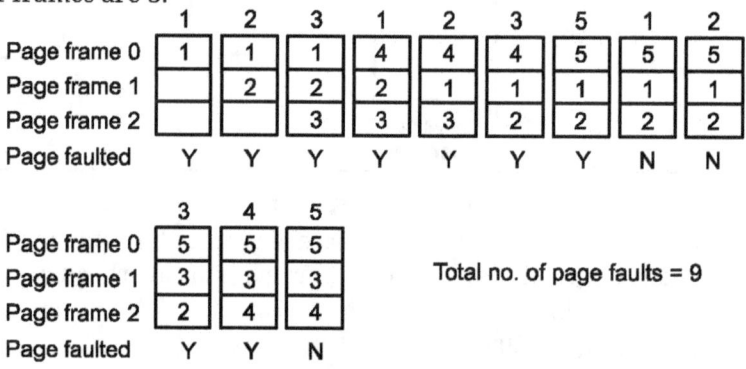

	1	2	3	1	2	3	5	1	2
Page frame 0	1	1	1	4	4	4	5	5	5
Page frame 1		2	2	2	1	1	1	1	1
Page frame 2			3	3	3	2	2	2	2
Page faulted	Y	Y	Y	Y	Y	Y	Y	N	N

	3	4	5
Page frame 0	5	5	5
Page frame 1	3	3	3
Page frame 2	2	4	4
Page faulted	Y	Y	N

Total no. of page faults = 9

Fig. 7.29: FIFO page replacement algorithm

Explanation:

- Number of page frames given are 3, numbered page frame 0, page frame 1 and page frame 2.
- Reference string is scanned serially.
- If the page is not present in one of the three page frames, then a page fault is counted and a page is brought into the page frame.
- In the above examples, first 3 pages 1, 2, 3 are brought in page frames 0, 1 and 2 respectively.
- When the page faulted for page 4, that time page frame containing page 1 is freed and 4 is brought in page frame 0.
- Page frame 0 was selected as victim frame because that was containing first of the first 3 pages.
- Next victim frame will be page frame 1 and so on.
- Total number of page faults in above example is 9. (for the pages 1, 2, 3, 4, 1, 2, 5, 3, 4).

Belady's Anomaly: (April 15)

- One of the factor that affect page faults is number of page frames available.
- Ideally, more the number of page frames, less should be the page fault rate.
- But practically, this is not found to be always true.

For example: We will again take the previous reference string:

1, 2, 3, 4, 1, 2, 5, 1, 2, 3, 4, 5

- Let the number of available page frames be 4.

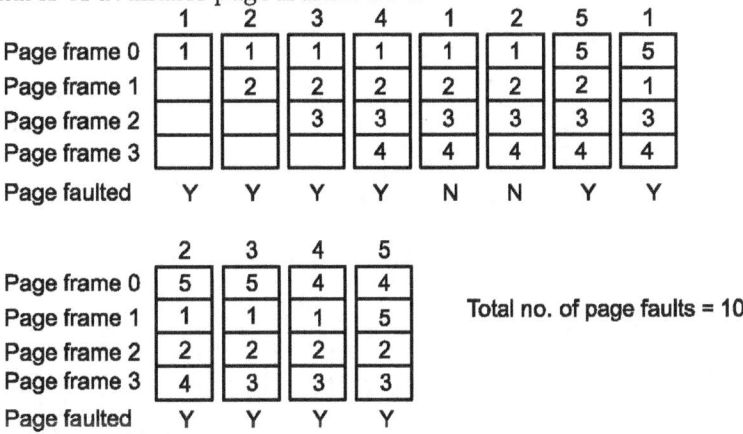

Fig. 7.30: Example of Belady's Anomaly

- In this example, page fault rate is increased though number of page frames is increased.

- In the previous example, with the same reference string and 3 number of page frames, the page faults were 9, such exceptions are called as Belady's Anomaly.

- For some page replacement algorithms, the page fault rate may increase as the number of allocated frames increases. Such exception is known as Belady's Anomaly.

2. **Optimal Replacement:**

- In this algorithm, the page that will not be required for longest period of time is replaced.

- Page fault rate in this case is less as compared to FIFO, hence the name optimal.

- With this algorithm, the page replacement decision requires complete reference string to be prepared before the execution of the algorithm starts because every page replacement needs to refer the reference string for the requirement of a particular page in future.

- Practically, this situation is difficult to achieve. Therefore, this algorithm is difficult to implement.

  For example: Reference string is:

  1, 3, 3, 2, 5, 4, 5, 4, 1, 4, 2, 2, 5. Number of page frames are 3.

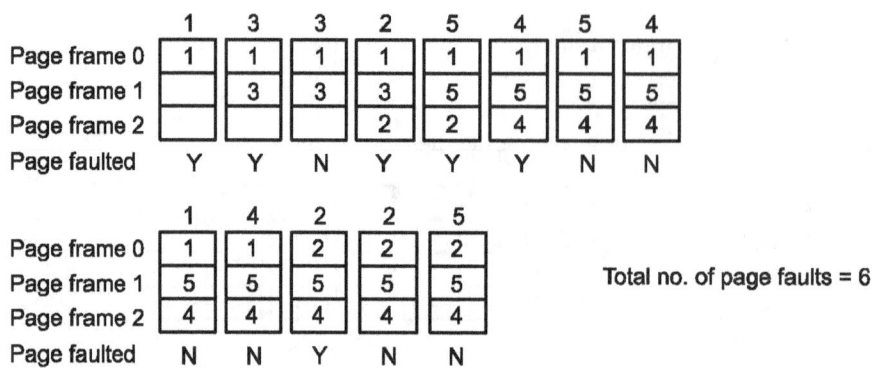

Fig. 7.31: Optimal page replacement algorithm

- If the same reference string is solved using FIFO, then 1, 3, 3, 2, 5, 4, 5, 4, 1, 4, 2, 2, 5.

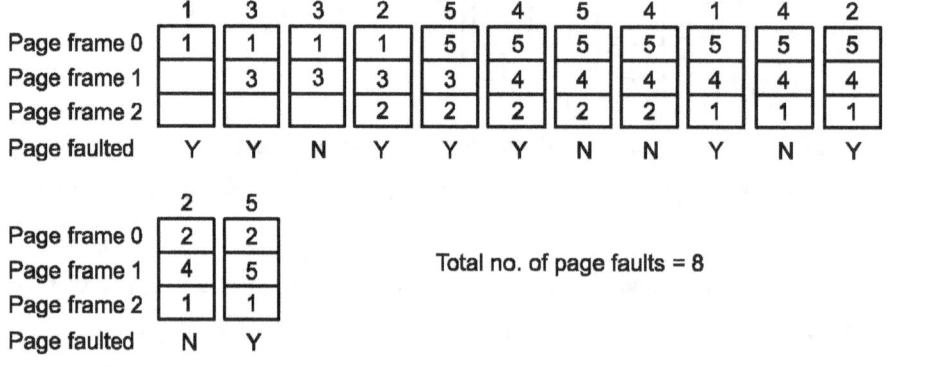

Fig. 7.32: Optimal page replacement algorithm using FIFO

Explanation (for optimal):

- First 3 pages 1, 3 and 2 are brought into frames 0, 1, and 2 respectively.

- To bring page number 5 in the memory, the reference string after this page is referred.

- Frame number 1 is selected as a victim frame because, it contains page number 3 which is farthest from page 5, in the future references of available pages. Similarly, while bringing page number 4, future reference after page number 4 is referred.

- The farthest page is page number 2, which is in page frame number 2.

- Therefore, page frame 2 becomes victim frame and 4 is brought in that frame.

3. **LRU:**

- LRU stands for Least Recently Used.

- In this algorithm, the algorithm refers to the past references of the pages.

- The one which is not used for longest time is selected for replacement.

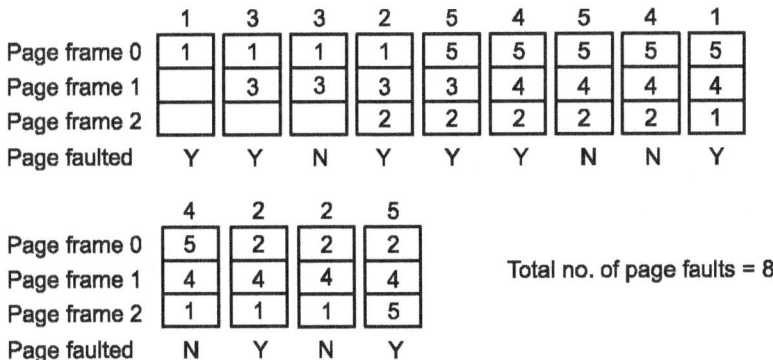

Fig. 7.33: Least recently used algorithm

- In simple words, optimal selects the page farthest in the right hand side direction from currently faulted page, and LRU selects the farthest page in the left hand side direction of currently faulted page.

- This algorithm is easy to implement, as compared to optimal as no future knowledge of reference string is require.

  For example: Reference string,

  1, 3, 3, 2, 5, 4, 5, 4, 1, 4, 2, 2, 5   number of page frames = 3

Explanation:

- First 3 pages 1, 3 and 2 are brought into page frames 0, 1 and 2 respectively. When page fault for page 5 occurs, that time frame 0 is selected as victim frame.

- If you observe the reference string upto page 5, page number 2 is nearest to page 5 and page number 1 is farthest from page 5. The farthest page is the one which is least recently used.

- Therefore, page frame 0 is selected as victim frame (containing the farthest page) and 5th page is brought into it.

- To bring page number 4 in the memory, frame 1 is selected as victim frame, because it contains the page 3 farthest from page number 4 (farthest in the past) and so on.

- Implementation of true LRU needs hardware assistance. Either of the following methods can be used to implement LRU.

  (i) **Counters:** A time-of-use register is added to the page table. An internal logical clock counter is added to the CPU. Whenever a memory reference is made, the counter is incremented. Whenever a page reference is made, the current contents are copied to time-of-use register of respective page in the page table. The page with smallest time-of-use value is selected for the purpose of replacement. (The page with highest value of time-of-use is the one which is most recently used and the one with smallest value of time-of-use is the least recently used).

(ii) Stack: A stack of page numbers is maintained. Whenever a reference to the page is made, it is brought onto the top of stack. At any moment, the page which is at the bottom of the stack, is the least recently used page and the frame containing this page is selected for the purpose of replacement.

   o   Both the above mentioned algorithms cannot be implemented without hardware assistance.

   o   Optimal and LRU both algorithms do not suffer Belady's Anomaly.

4.   LRU Approximation using Reference Bit/Bits:

- Some systems do not provide hardware support for LRU and then there is restriction of using algorithms like FIFO.

- With the help of a reference bit a one may try to implement LRU without hardware support.

- A reference bit is attached with each page. Initially all the bits (one for each page) are cleared i.e. set to 0. After a reference to a page is made, it is turned to 1.

- From this, one could immediately find out, which pages are referenced and which are not.

- But then there was no way by which order of the reference to the pages can be found out.

- To overcome this problem, a reference byte is (8 bits) used for each page. All the 8 bits of the byte are set to 0.

- After a reference to the page is made, the least significant bit of the reference byte is set to 1.

- Each reference to the page set the bit from 0 to 1 from least significant position to most significant position, one bit at a time.

  For example: Page P1 have reference byte 00000000.

  After first reference to P1, the byte becomes 00000001

  After second reference to P1, the byte becomes 00000011 and so on.

- Now, it is easy to decide the order of reference of pages. Smaller the byte value, least recently the page is used.

- Only problem with this algorithm is that, at a particular instance, there may be more than one pages with same bit pattern of reference byte.

5. **Second Chance Algorithm:**

- It is basically a FIFO algorithm. The only difference between FIFO and second chance is that, in FIFO, pages are replaced on First Come First Served Basis. In this algorithm, pages are given a chance on First Come First Served basis. Actual replacement may not be in FIFO manner.

- Reference bit of page is checked serially, if it is 0 then the page is replaced. If it is one, the bit is set to zero and current time is associated with page as its arrival time.

- Because of this, the particular page is given a second chance of replacement. This page will be replaced only after all pages are either replaced or given second chance by the system.

- In simple words, system imagine as if a list of pages is maintained. System starts with the first page in the list. If that page is having reference bit 0, then it is replaced. If not then this page is pushed to end of list and its bit is set to zero.

- System checks the second page, now either this page is replaced if reference bit is zero or pushed to the end of list if reference bit is 1 and its bit is set to 0.

- In worst case, all the pages will be pushed to the end of the list by the system and again the first page along with reference bit 0 will appear at first position and will be selected for replacement.

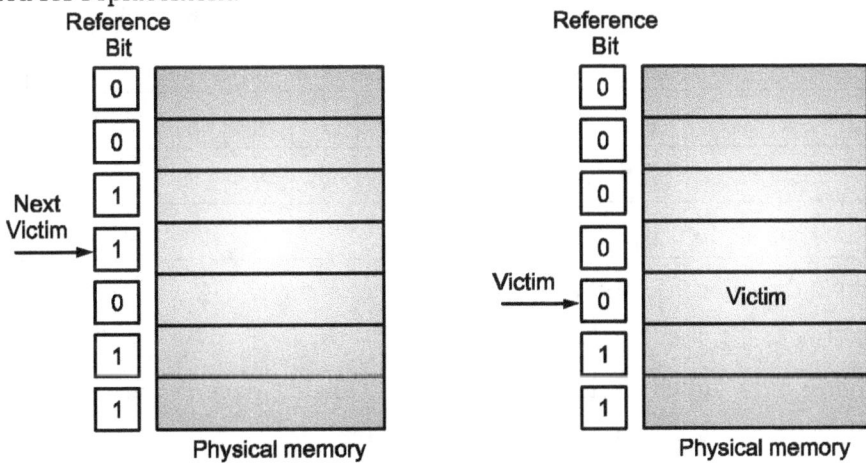

Fig. 7.34: Second chance algorithm

UNIVERSITY SOLVED PROBLEMS

Problem 1: Consider the following page reference string.

1, 2, 3, 4, 2, 1, 5, 6, 2, 1, 3

How many page faults will occur for following page replacement algorithms? Assuming 3 frames, all are initially empty.

1. FIFO
2. LRU

Solution: No. of frames = 3.

1. FIFO Method:

Reference string	1	2	3	4	2	1	5	6	2	1	2	3
Frame 1	1	1	1	4	4	4	4	6	6	6	6	3
Frame 2		2	2	2	2	1	1	1	2	2	2	2
Frame 3			3	3	3	3	5	5	5	1	1	1
Page Fault	1	2	3	4	X	1	5	6	2	1	X	3
	Y	Y	Y	Y	N	Y	Y	Y	Y	Y	N	Y

Total No. of page faults by FIFO = 10.

2. LRU Method:

Reference string	1	2	3	4	2	1	5	6	2	1	2	3
Frame 1	1	1	1	4	4	4	5	5	5	1	1	1
Frame 2		2	2	2	2	2	2	6	6	6	6	3
Frame 3			3	3	3	1	1	1	2	2	2	2
Page Fault	1	2	3	4	X	1	5	6	2	1	X	3
	Y	Y	Y	Y	N	Y	Y	Y	Y	Y	N	Y

Total No. of page faults by LRU = 10.

Problem 2: Consider the following page reference string:

1, 2, 3, 4, 5, 3, 4, 1, 6, 7, 8, 7

How many page faults would occur for the following page replacement algorithms, assuming four frames? All frames are initially empty.

1. LRU
2. Optimal replacement

Solution:

1. LRU Page Replacement Method:

Reference string	1	2	3	4	5	3	4	1	6	7	8	7
Frame 1	1	1	1	1	5	5	5	5	6	6	6	6
Frame 2		2	2	2	2	2	2	1	1	1	1	1
Frame 3			3	3	3	3	3	3	3	7	7	7
Frame 4				4	4	4	4	4	4	4	8	8
Page Fault	Y	Y	Y	Y	Y	N	N	Y	Y	Y	Y	N

Total page faults by LRU = 9.

2. Optimal Page Replacement Method:

Reference string	1	2	3	4	5	3	4	1	6	7	8	7
Frame 1	1	1	1	1	1	1	1	1	6	6	6	6
Frame 2		2	2	2	5	5	5	5	5	7	7	7
Frame 3			3	3	3	3	3	3	3	3	8	8
Frame 4				4	4	4	4	4	4	4	4	4
Page Fault	Y	Y	Y	Y	Y	N	N	N	Y	Y	Y	N

Total page faults by Optimal = 8.

Problem 3: Consider the following segment table:

Segment	Base	Length
0	600	120
1	1200	350
2	75	85
3	1760	90
4	2510	680

What are the physical addresses for the following logical addresses?

1. 0, 125

2. 1, 310

3. 3, 88

4. 2, 77

5. 4, 444

Solution:

1.   Logical address = 0, 255

                              Segment No. = 0,

                                    Offset = 255

            Base address of segment 0 = 600

        Since offset > Length (i.e. 255 > 120)

        Therefore invalid address and trap will be generated.

2.   Logical address = 1, 310

                              Segment No. = 1,

                                    Offset = 310

            Base address of segment 1 = 1200

                      Physical address = Base address + Offset

                                              = 1200 + 310

                                              = 1510

3.   Logical address = 3, 88

                              Segment No. = 3,

                                    Offset = 88

        Since Offset < length, therefore address is valid

            Base Address of segment 3 = 1760

                      Physical address = Base address + Offset

                                              = 1760 + 88

                                              = 1848

4.   Logical address = 2, 77

                              Segment No. = 2

                                    Offset = 77

                          Base address = 75

                    Physical address = 75 + 77

                                              = 152

5.   Logical address = 4, 444

                              Segment No. = 4

                                    Offset = 444

                          Base address = 2510

                    Physical address = 2510 + 444

                                              = 2954

Problem 4: Consider a logical address space of four pages of 512 words each, mapped onto a physical memory of 16 frames.

1. How many bits are in virtual address?

2. How many bits are in physical address?

Solution:

$$\text{Logical address space} = 4 \text{ pages} = 2^2 \ (m = 2)$$

$$\text{Page size} = 512 = 2^9 \ (n = 9)$$

$$n = \text{offset} = 9 \text{ bits}$$

$\therefore$ Logical address or

$$\text{Virtual address} = 9 + 2 = 11 \text{ bits}$$

$\therefore$ 11 bits are in virtual address.

$$\text{Physical memory} = 16 \text{ frames} = 2^4$$

$$\text{Frame size} = 2^9 = 519 \text{ words}$$

$\therefore$ Physical address bits $= 2^9 \times 2^4$

$$= 2^{13}$$

$\therefore$ 13 bits are in physical address.

Problem 5: Consider the following page reference string:

1, 2, 3, 4, 2, 1, 5, 6, 2, 1, 2, 3, 7, 6, 3, 2, 1, 2, 3

How many page faults would occur for the following page replacement algorithms assuming four frames? All frames are initially empty.

1. LRU

2. Optimal.

Solution: (April 13)

1. LRU Replacement Method:

Reference string	1	2	3	4	2	1	5	6	2	1	2	3	7	6	3	2	1	2	3
Frame 1	1	1	1	1	1	1	1	1	1	1	1	1	1	6	6	6	6	6	6
Frame 2		2	2	2	2	2	2	2	2	2	2	2	2	2	2	2	2	2	2
Frame 3			3	3	3	3	5	5	5	5	5	3	3	3	3	3	3	3	3
Frame 4				4	4	4	4	6	6	6	6	6	7	7	7	7	1	7	7
Page Fault	Y	Y	Y	Y	N	N	Y	Y	N	N	N	Y	Y	Y	N	N	Y	N	N

Total page faults = 10.

2. Optimal Replacement Method:

Reference string	1	2	3	4	2	1	5	6	2	1	2	3	7	6	3	2	1	2	3
Frame 1	1	1	1	1	1	1	1	1	1	1	1	1	7	7	7	7	1	1	1
Frame 2		2	2	2	2	2	2	2	2	2	2	2	2	2	2	2	2	2	2
Frame 3			3	3	3	3	3	3	3	3	3	3	3	3	3	3	3	3	3
Frame 4				4	4	4	5	6	6	6	6	6	6	6	6	6	6	6	6
Page Fault	Y	Y	Y	Y	N	N	Y	Y	N	N	N	N	Y	N	N	N	Y	N	N

Total page faults = 8.

Problem 6: Consider the following page reference string:

7, 0, 1, 2, 0, 3, 0, 4, 2, 3, 0, 3, 2, 1, 2, 0, 7, 0, 1

How many page faults would occur for the following page replacement algorithm, assuming 3 frames? All frames are initially empty.

1. Optimal
2. FIFO

Solution:

1. Optimal Replacement Method:

Reference string	7	0	1	2	0	3	0	4	2	3	0	3	2	1	2	0	7	0	1
Frame 1	7	7	7	2	2	2	2	2	2	2	2	2	2	2	2	2	7	7	7
Frame 2		0	0	0	0	0	0	4	4	4	0	0	0	0	0	0	0	0	0
Frame 3			1	1	1	3	3	3	3	3	3	3	3	1	1	1	1	1	1
Page Fault	Y	Y	Y	Y	N	Y	N	Y	N	N	Y	N	N	Y	N	N	Y	N	N

Total page faults by optimal = 09.

2. FIFO Replacement Method:

Reference string	7	0	1	2	3	0	4	2	3	0	3	2	1	2	0	1	7	0	1
Frame 1	7	7	7	2	2	2	4	4	4	0	0	0	0	0	0	0	7	7	7
Frame 2		0	0	0	3	3	3	2	2	2	2	2	1	1	1	1	1	0	0
Frame 3			1	1	1	0	0	0	3	3	3	3	3	2	2	2	2	2	1
Page Fault	Y	Y	Y	Y	Y	Y	Y	Y	Y	Y	N	N	Y	Y	N	N	Y	Y	Y

Total page faults = 15.

Problem 7: Consider the following job queue:

Job	Memory	Time
1	80 k	9
2	110 k	4
3	20 k	18
4	60 k	5
5	40 k	10

Show the memory map of various stages by using MVT scheduling. Assumption: Total memory is of 400 k and monitor of look and all jobs arrived at same time (0 ms).

Solution:

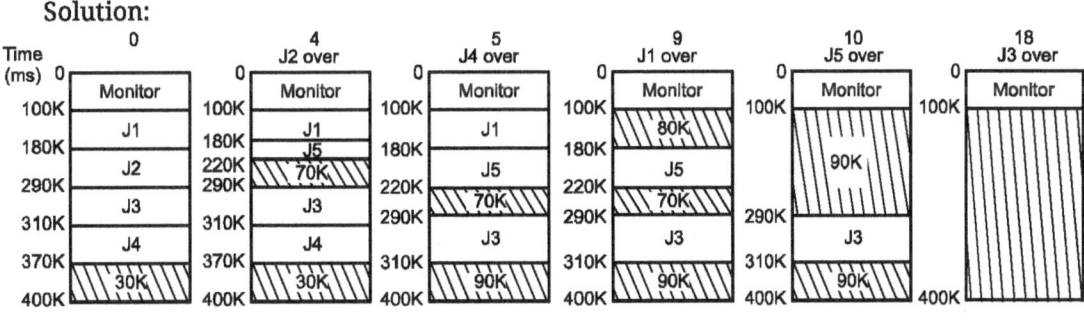

Fig. 7.36

Problem 8: Consider the following segment table:

Segment	Base	Length
0	363	500
1	1272	20
2	1675	1500
3	986	240
4	211	130

What are physical addresses for the following logical addresses?

1. 0, 425

2. 2, 500

3. 1, 150

4. 3, 285

5. 4, 125

Solution:

1. 0, 425

    Here offset is 425 and segment No. = 0.

    ∵   Offset < Length

    ∴ Address is valid

    Physical address = Base + Offset

                     = 363 + 425

                     = 788

2. 2, 500

    Segment No. = 2

    Offset = 500

    ∵   Offset < Length

    ∴ Address is valid

    Physical address = Base + Offset

                     = 1675 + 500

                     = 2175

3. 1, 150

    Segment No. = 1

    Offset = 150

    ∵   Offset > Length, it will generate trap an addressing error

4. 3, 285

    Segment No. = 3

    Offset = 285

    ∵   Offset > Length, it will generate trap an addressing error

5. 4, 125

    Segment No. = 4

    Offset = 125

    ∵   Offset < Length, address is valid

    Physical address = Base + Offset

                     = 211 + 125

                     = 336

Problem 9: Consider the physical memory of 15 frames with each frame of size 8 bytes. Consider page table entries as:

0	2
1	7
2	1
3	13
4	10
5	5

Map following logical addresses to their physical addresses:

(1) 5 (2) 40 (3) 23 (4) 36 (5) 68

Solution: Page size = 8 bytes

1.   Logical address = 5

Page No. = $5/8 \Rightarrow 0$

Page offset = 5 % 8 = 5

Base address = Frame number $\times$ Frame size

= 2×8

= 16

Physical address = Base + Offset address

= 16 + 5

Physical address = 21

2.   Logical address = 40

Page No. = 40/8 = 5

Page offset = 40 % 8 = 0

Frame No = 5

Base address = $5 \times 8 = 40$

Physical address = 40 + 0 = 40

3.   Logical address = 23

Page No. = $23/8 \Rightarrow 2$

Page offset = $23 \% 8 \rightarrow 7$

Frame No. = 1

Base address = $1 \times 8 = 8$

Physical address = $8 + 7 \Rightarrow 15$

4.   Logical address = 36

                        Page No. = 36/8 = 4

                      Page offset = 36 % 8 = 4

                      Frame No. = 10

                    Base address = 10 × 4 = 40

                Physical address = 40 + 4 ⇒ 44

5.   Logical address = 68

                        Page No. = 68/8 = 8

                      Page offset = 4

We can't find frame number since page 8 is not loaded in page table, so we can not find physical address.

Problem 10: Find the number of page faults for following string according to:

1. LRU,

2. Optimal.

Consider reference string:

   7, 0, 1, 2, 0, 3, 0, 4, 2, 3, 0, 3, 2, 1, 2, 0, 1, 7, 0, 1 assume 3 page frames.   (April 13)

Solution: 1. LRU Replacement Method:

Reference string	7	0	1	2	0	3	0	4	2	3	0	3	2	1	2	0	1	7	0	1
Frame 1	7	7	7	2	2	2	2	4	4	4	6	0	0	1	1	1	1	1	1	1
Frame 2		0	0	0	0	0	0	0	0	3	3	3	3	3	3	0	0	0	0	0
Frame 3			1	1	1	3	3	3	2	2	2	2	2	2	2	2	2	7	7	7
Page Fault	Y	Y	Y	Y	N	Y	N	Y	Y	Y	Y	N	N	Y	N	Y	N	Y	N	N

Total page faults = 12

2. Optimal Replacement Method:

Reference string	7	0	1	2	0	3	0	4	2	3	0	3	2	1	2	0	1	7	0	1
Frame 1	7	7	7	2	2	2	2	2	2	2	2	2	2	2	2	2	2	7	7	7
Frame 2		0	0	0	0	0	0	4	4	4	0	0	0	0	0	0	0	0	0	0
Frame 3			1	1	1	3	3	3	3	3	3	3	3	1	1	1	1	1	1	1
Page Fault	Y	Y	Y	Y	N	Y	N	Y	N	N	Y	N	N	Y	N	N	N	Y	N	N

Total page faults = 9.

Problem 11: Consider the following page reference string:

8, 0, 1, 2, 0, 3, 0, 4, 2, 3, 0, 3, 2, 1, 2

How many pages faults would occur for the following page replacement algorithms, assuming three frames?

All frames are initially empty.

(i) Optimal replacement.

(ii) LRU replacement.

Solution: (i) Optimal replacement algorithm:

Reference string	8	0	1	2	0	3	0	4	2	3	0	3	2	1	2
Frame 1	8	8	8	2	2	2	2	2	2	2	2	2	2	2	2
Frame 2		0	0	0	0	0	0	4	4	4	0	0	0	1	1
Frame 3			1	1	1	3	3	3	3	3	3	3	3	3	3
Page Fault	Y	Y	Y	Y	N	Y	N	Y	N	N	Y	N	N	Y	N

Total page faults = 8.

(ii) LRU replacement:

Reference string	8	0	1	2	0	3	0	4	2	3	0	3	2	1	2
Frame 1	8	8	8	2	2	2	2	4	4	4	0	0	0	1	1
Frame 2		0	0	0	0	0	0	0	0	3	3	3	3	3	3
Frame 3			1	1	1	3	3	3	2	2	2	2	2	2	2
Page Fault	Y	Y	Y	Y	N	Y	N	Y	Y	Y	Y	N	N	Y	N

Total page faults = 10.

Problem 12: For the following page reference string 7, 0, 1, 2, 0, 3, 0, 4, 2, 3, 0, 3, 2, 1, 2, 0, 7, 0, 1. How many page fault occur for the following page replacement algorithms, assuming three frames. All frames are initially empty.

(i) LRU

(ii) Optimal replacement.

Solution: (i) LRU:

Reference string	7	0	1	2	0	3	0	4	2	3	0	3	2	1	2	0	7	0	1
Frame 1	7	7	7	2	2	2	2	4	4	4	0	0	0	1	1	1	7	7	7
Frame 2		0	0	0	0	0	0	0	0	3	3	3	3	3	3	0	0	0	0
Frame 3			1	1	1	3	3	3	2	2	2	2	2	2	2	2	2	2	1
Page Fault	Y	Y	Y	Y	N	Y	N	Y	Y	Y	Y	N	N	Y	N	Y	Y	N	Y

Total page faults = 13.

(ii) Optimal Replacement:

Reference string	7	0	1	2	0	3	0	4	2	3	0	3	2	1	2	0	7	0	1
Frame 1	7	7	7	2	2	2	2	2	2	2	2	2	2	2	2	2	7	7	7
Frame 2		0	0	0	0	0	0	4	4	4	0	0	0	0	0	0	0	0	0
Frame 3			1	1	1	3	3	3	3	3	3	3	3	1	1	1	1	1	1
Page Fault	Y	Y	Y	Y	N	Y	N	Y	N	N	Y	N	N	Y	N	N	Y	N	N

Total page faults = 9.

Problem 13: Consider the following page reference string:

1, 2, 3, 4, 1, 2, 5, 1, 2, 3, 4, 5

How many page faults would occur for the following page replacement algorithms:

(i) LRU

(ii) FIFO

Assume three frames.

Solution: (a) LRU algorithm:

Reference string	1	2	3	4	1	2	5	1	2	3	4	5
Frame 1	1	1	1	4	4	4	5	5	5	3	3	3
Frame 2		2	2	2	1	1	1	1	1	1	4	4
Frame 3			3	3	3	2	2	2	2	2	2	5
Page Fault	Y	Y	Y	Y	Y	Y	Y	N	N	Y	Y	Y

Total pages faults by LRU = 10.

(b) FIFO algorithm:

Reference string	1	2	3	4	1	2	5	1	2	3	4	5
Frame 1	1	1	1	4	4	4	5	5	5	5	5	5
Frame 2		2	2	2	1	1	1	1	1	3	3	3
Frame 3			3	3	3	2	2	2	2	2	4	4
Page Fault	Y	Y	Y	Y	Y	Y	Y	N	N	Y	Y	N

Total pages faults by FIFO = 9.

Problem 14: Consider the following page reference string:

7, 0, 1, 2, 0, 3, 0, 4, 2, 3, 0, 3, 2, 1, 2

How many page faults would occur for the following page replacement algorithm?

(a) LRU (Least Recently Used)

(b) Optimal.

Assume three frames.

Solution: (a) LRU algorithm:

Reference string	7	0	1	2	0	3	0	4	2	3	0	3	2	1	2
Frame 1	7	7	7	2	2	2	2	4	4	4	0	0	0	1	1
Frame 2		0	0	0	0	0	0	0	0	3	3	3	3	3	3
Frame 3			1	1	1	3	3	3	2	2	2	2	2	2	2
Page Fault	Y	Y	Y	Y	N	Y	N	Y	Y	Y	Y	N	N	Y	N

Total page faults = 10.

(b) Optimal algorithm:

Reference string	7	0	1	2	0	3	0	4	2	3	0	3	2	1	2
Frame 1	7	7	7	2	2	2	2	2	2	2	2	2	2	2	2
Frame 2		0	0	0	0	0	0	4	4	4	0	0	0	1	1
Frame 3			1	1	1	3	3	3	3	3	3	3	3	3	3
Page Faults	Y	Y	Y	Y	N	Y	N	Y	N	N	Y	N	N	Y	N

Total page faults by optimal = 8.

Problem 15: Consider a logical address space of 4 pages of 512 words each, mapped onto a physical memory of 16 frames.

(a) How many bits are there in logical address?

(b) How many bits are there in physical address?

Solution:

$$\text{Logical address space} = 4 \text{ pages} = 2^2 \ (m = 2)$$
$$\text{Page size} = 512 = 2^9 \ (n = 9)$$
$$n = \text{offset} = 9 \text{ bits}$$

∴
$$\text{Logical address} = 9 + 2 = 11 \text{ bits}$$
$$\text{Physical memory} = 16 \text{ Frames} = 2^4$$
$$\text{Frame size} = 2^9 = 512 \text{ words}$$
$$\text{Physical address bits} = 2^9 \times 2^4$$
$$= 2^{13}$$

∴
$$\text{Physical address} = \textbf{13 bits}$$

Problem 16: Consider page reference string as follows:

7, 5, 6, 2, 9, 5, 7, 6, 2, 7, 6, 5, 2, 7, 2, 7, 8

Assume 3 frames. Find the number of page faults according to:

(i) Optimal page replacement algorithm.

(ii) Least Recently Used (LRU) page replacement algorithm.   (April 13) (5 M) (Oct. 16)

Solution: (1) Optimal page replacement algorithm:

Reference tring	7	5	6	2	9	5	7	6	2	7	6	5	2	7	2	7	8
Frame 1	7	7	7	7	7	7	7	7	7	7	7	7	7	7	7	7	8
Frame 2		5	5	5	5	5	5	2	2	2	2	2	2	2	2	2	2
Frame 3			6	2	9	9	9	6	6	6	6	5	5	5	5	5	5
Page Fault	Y	Y	Y	Y	Y	N	N	Y	Y	N	N	Y	N	N	N	N	Y

Total pages faults = 9.

(2) LRU algorithm:

Reference tring	7	5	6	2	9	5	7	6	2	7	6	5	2	7	2	7	8
Frame 1	7	7	7	2	2	2	7	7	7	7	7	7	2	2	2	2	2
Frame 2		5	5	5	9	9	9	6	6	6	6	6	6	7	7	7	7
Frame 3			6	6	6	5	5	5	2	2	2	5	5	5	5	5	8
Page Fault	Y	Y	Y	Y	Y	Y	Y	Y	Y	N	N	Y	Y	Y	N	N	Y

Total pages faults = 13.

Problem 17: Consider the following segment table:

Segment	Base	Limit
0	750	420
1	1780	535
2	3130	81
3	7070	70
4	6166	320

Map the following logical address to physical addresses. Consider the first leftmost digit as segment number.

(a) 4666

(b) 280

(c) 0251

(d) 1025

(e) 3003.   (April 13) (5 M)

Solution: (a) 4666:

Segment No = 4, Offset = 666, Length of segment = 320

∵ Offset > Length, it will generate trap addressing an error.

(b) 280:

Segment No = 2, Offset = 80, Length of segment 2 = 81

∵ Offset < Length

∴ Address is valid

∴   Physical address = Base address + Offset

                          = 3130 + 80

                          = 3210

(c) 0251:

Segment No = 0, Offset = 251, Length of segment 0 = 420

∵ Offset < Length

∴ Address is valid

∴   Physical address = Base address + Offset

                          = 750 + 251

                          = 1001

(d) 1025:

Segment No = 1, Offset = 025, Length = 535

∵ Offset < Length

∴ Address is valid

∴   Physical address = Base address + Offset

                          = 1780 + 025

                          = 1805

(e) 3003:

Segment No = 3, Offset = 003, Length = 70

∵ Offset < Length

∴ Address is valid

∴   Physical address = Base address + Offset

                          = 7070 + 003

                          = 7073

Problem 18: Consider the following page reference string:

7, 0, 1, 2, 0, 3, 0, 4, 2, 3, 0, 3, 2, 1, 2, 0, 7, 0, 1

How many page faults would occur for the following page replacement algorithm?

(a) FIFO page replacement

(b) Optimal page replacement.

Assume three frames.   (April 15) (5 M)

Solution: (a) FIFO page replacement:

Reference string	7	0	1	2	0	3	0	4	2	3	0	3	2	1	2	0	7	0	1
Frame 1	7	7	7	2	2	2	2	4	4	4	0	0	0	0	0	0	7	7	7
Frame 2		0	0	0	0	3	3	3	2	2	2	2	2	1	1	1	1	0	0
Frame 3			1	1	1	1	0	0	0	3	3	3	3	3	2	2	2	2	1
Page Fault	Y	Y	Y	Y	N	Y	Y	Y	Y	Y	Y	N	N	Y	Y	N	Y	Y	Y

Total page faults = 15.

(b) Optimal replacement:

Reference string	7	0	1	2	0	3	0	4	2	3	0	3	2	1	2	0	7	0	1
Frame 1	7	7	7	2	2	2	2	2	2	2	2	2	2	2	2	2	7	7	7
Frame 2		0	0	0	0	0	0	4	4	4	0	0	0	0	0	0	0	0	0
Frame 3			1	1	1	3	3	3	3	3	3	3	3	1	1	1	1	1	1
Page Fault	Y	Y	Y	Y	N	Y	N	Y	N	N	Y	N	N	Y	N	N	Y	N	N

Total page faults = 9.

SUMMARY

➢ Memory management algorithms for multiprogramming operating systems range from the simple single-user system approach to segmentation and paging.

➢ The most important determinant of the method used in a particular system is the hardware provided.

➢ We must ensure correct operation has to protect operating system from user access and user process from one another. This protection must be provided by the hardware. Two registers, base and limit register can be used to provide protection.

➢ The base register holds the starting base address or smallest legal physical memory address and limit register specifies size of the range.

➤ So to create active process in memory, symbolic addresses generated by program must be mapped into the process address space. This mapping is known as address binding.

➤ Address binding can be done at compile time, load time and execution time.

➤ An address generated by the CPU is commonly known as Logical Address or virtual address.

➤ The address seen by the memory unit that is one loaded into the memory- address-register of the memory is commonly referred as the Physical Address.

➤ The set of all logical addresses generated by a program is known as Logical Address Space.

➤ The set of all physical addresses corresponding to these logical addresses is Physical Address Space.

➤ Now, the run time mapping from virtual address to physical address is done by a hardware device known as Memory Management Unit(MMU).

➤ Simplest memory mapping is done using relocation register.

➤ To obtain better memory utilization, routines can be loaded in main memory as required. This is known as dynamic loading.

➤ In dynamic linking, linking is postponed until execution time.

➤ A process can be swapped temporarily out of memory to a backing store, and then brought back into memory for continued execution. This process is known as swapping.

➤ Swapping requires backing store.

➤ Main memory usually divided into two partitions as 1) Resident operating system, usually held in low memory with interrupt vector 2)User processes then held in high memory.

➤ Memory can be partitioned by two approaches: Single partition allocation and Multiple partition allocation

➤ Single partition allocation is the simplest method of memory management. The memory is divided in two sections: one section for operating system and second section for user program.

➤ In multiple partition allocation, to support multiprogramming, main memory is divided into several partitions; each of which is allocated to a single process. The number of programs residing in memory will be bound by the number of partitions.

➤ In Multiple contiguous fixed (static) partition allocation(MFT) method, memory is divided into several partitions of fixed size that size never changes. Each partition method holds one process.

➢ In Multiple contiguous variable (dynamic) partition allocation (MVT) method, region or partition size is not fixed; it can vary dynamically. It creates partition according to requirements of process.

➢ One of reason of fragmentation is improper selection of region size.

➢ Internal Fragmentation – allocated memory may be slightly larger than requested memory; this size difference is memory internal to a partition, but not being used is known as internal fragmentation.

➢ External Fragmentation – as processes are loaded and removed, the free memory is broken into little pieces. Total memory space exists to satisfy a request, but it is not contiguous then it is known as external fragmentation.

➢ Compaction is process of collecting all free holes and forms a single big free hole. It shuffles memory contents to place all free memory together in one large block. Compaction is possible only with dynamic relocation.

➢ Paging is a memory-management scheme that permits the physical address space of a process to be non-contiguous. It avoids external fragmentation. The basic method for implementation involves breaking physical memory into fixed-sized blocks called frames and break logical memory into blocks of the same size called Pages.

➢ Every access to any of page has to go through the page table. Therefore, implementation of the page table directly affects the performance of this kind of memory management.

➢ The percentage of times that a particular page number is found in the TLB is called hit ratio.

➢ Memory protection in a paged environment is supported by protection bits associated with each frame.

➢ Reentrant Code or pure code is non-self modifying code; it never changes during execution.

➢ Paging suffers from internal fragmentation.

➢ Segmentation is memory management scheme that supports user's view of memory. A program is a collection of segments.

➢ A segment is a logical unit such as main program, procedure, function, method, object, local variables, global variables, common block, stack, symbol table, arrays etc.

➢ Each segment has a name (e.g., a unique number) and a length. The user specifies each address by two quantities: segment name and length. For simplicity, segments are numbered and referred by segment number rather than segment name.

➤ Two dimensional address should be mapped by one dimensional physical address. This mapping is done by Segment table. Each entry in segment table has a segment base and segment limit.

➤ Segments suffer from external fragmentation. External fragmentation occurs due to dynamic allocation policies.

➤ Virtual memory is a technique that allows the execution of process that is not completely in main memory.

➤ Virtual memory can be implemented via: Demand paging and Demand segmentation

➤ Demand paging policy or technique transfers memory pages instead of process to and from secondary storage. The entire process does not have to reside in main memory to execute and the kernel loads pages for a process on demand when the process references the pages.

➤ Whenever process tries to access a page which is not into memory, then page fault occurs.

➤ To bring user page into memory, operating system swaps out some process by freeing its frames. The process of freeing frame is known as page replacement. The frame which is selected for replacement is known as victim frame.

➤ Page replacement algorithms are FIFO , Optimal, LRU and Second Chance.

➤ In FIFO scheme, all the available frames are given to the pages from reference string serially i.e. first frame to first page, second frame to second page and so on.

➤ In Optimal algorithm, the page that will not be required for longest period of time is replaced.

➤ In LRU algorithm, the algorithm refers to the past references of the pages. The one which is not used for longest time is selected for replacement.

➤ Second Chance is basically a FIFO algorithm. In this algorithm, pages are given a chance on First Come First Served basis. Actual replacement may not be in FIFO manner.

➤ Thrashing is high paging activity. A process is thrashing if it is spending more time paging than executing.

PRACTICE QUESTIONS

1. Explain the terms logical address and physical address. How logical address is converted to physical address?

2. Explain internal and external fragmentation, MFT suffers from which kind of fragmentation?

3. Explain protection offered by paging system.

4.   What is reentrant code, how it is useful in paging?

5.   Write note on compaction.

6.   Write note on swapping.

7.   What is page fault? Explain the different steps in handling a page fault.

8.   Write note on LRU algorithm of demand paging.

9.   Write note on virtual memory concept.

10. What is demand paging?

11. Explain second chance algorithm.

12. Consider the following string 1,2,3,4,2,1,6,51,2,1,3,7,6,3,2,1,2,3,6.how many page fault would occur for any one of the following page replacement algorithms, assuming 5 frames: (i) LRU, (ii) FIFO.

13. Consider the following string 4,3,2,1,6,9,1,2,4,2,3,1,6,4,2,.how many pages fault would occur for any one of the following page replacement algorithms, assuming 3 frames: (i) Optimal, (ii) LRU.

14. Consider a logical address space of 8 pages of 1024 words mapped onto a physical memory of 32 frames.

     (i)   How many bits are there in the logical address?

     (ii)   How many bits are there in the physical address?

15. Define the terms:

     (i)   Logical address

     (ii)   Reentrant code

     (iii) External fragmentation

     (iv)   Compaction

     (v)   Page table

     (vi)   Frame

     (vii) Swapping

16. State True or False:

     (i)   Demand paging is used to reduce the number of frames allocated to process.

     (ii)   Page size is always power of two.

     (iii) Paging suffers from external fragmentation.

     (iv)   Compaction is possible only if relocation is dynamic.

     (v)   Internal fragmentation occurs when allocated memory is less than the request memory.

     (vi)   First fit method is a faster method.

     (vii) Page replacement algorithms are implemented by operating system.

          Ans.: (i) True (ii) true (iii) False (iv) True (v) False (vi) True (vii) True

17. What are various dynamic allocation memory management methods?

Ans. First-Fit, Best-Fit, Worst-Fit.

18. What is dynamic loading?

Ans. Refer to Section 7.1.4.

19. What is the advantage of paging with segmentation model?

Ans. There will be no external fragmentation.

20. What is practical problem for implementing optimal replacement?

Ans. Refer to Section 7.6.4.1, Point (2).

21. What is the role of "valid" and "invalid" bits in demand paging?

Ans. Refer to Section 7.6.2.

22. Give the diagrammatic representation for: Swapping of two processes using a disk as a backing store.

Ans. Refer to Section 7.2.

23. Define Reentrant code.

Ans. Reentrant code is non-self-modifying code: it never changes during execution.

24. What hardware support is needed to implement demand paging?

Ans. Refer to Section 7.6.2.

25. The page size defined by hardware is typically a power of 2. Justify.

Ans. Refer to Section 7.4.1.

26. What is internal and external fragmentation? What are the various ways to avoid external fragmentation?

Ans. Refer to Section 7.3.3.

27. Differentiate between internal and external fragmentation. Does paging suffer from external fragmentation? Comment and justify.

Ans. Refer to Section 7.3.3.

28. Write a note on segmentation hardware.

Ans. Refer to Section 7.5.2.

29. Compare the memory organization schemes of contiguous memory allocation and pure paging with respect to following issues:
    (i) Memory allocation
    (ii) Hardware support
    (iii) Fragmentation
    (iv) Sharing of data or code
    (v) Protection.

Ans. Refer to Section 7.5.2 [Difference].

30. What is page fault? Describe the steps for handling page fault with suitable diagram.

Ans. Refer to Section 7.6.4.

UNIVERSITY QUESTIONS AND ANSWERS

1. What is TLB miss?   (April 2013) (1 M)

Ans.   Refer to Section 7.4.2.

2. Define physical address space.   (April 2013) (1 M)

Ans. Refer to Section 7.1.3.

3. What is Belady's Anomaly?   (April 2015) (1 M)

Ans. Refer to Section 7.6.4.1.

4. Define Hit ratio. Hit ratio of finding page in TLB is 77% hit ratio; It takes 24ns to search TLB, and 90ns to access memory. Compute the effective access time.

(April 2013) (4 M)

Ans. Refer to Section 7.4.2.

5. Explain the working of MVT with example.   (April 2015) (4 M)

Ans. Refer to Section 7.3.2.2.

■■■

File System

Contents ...

Objectives...

- To Understand Concept of File, File Attributes, Operations on File and Different Types of Files
- To Study Different File Access Methods
- To Learn Directory Structure and its Different Types
- To Know What is File System Structure?
- To Explain various File Allocation Methods
- To Explore Different Methods for Free Space Management

8.1 INTRODUCTION

- The non-volatility of the memory enables the disks to store information indefinitely. This information can also be made available online all the time.
- Users think of all such information as files. It provides the mechanism for on-line storage of an access to both data and programs of operating system and all users of the computer system.
- OS provides support for such management through a file system.
- File system is the software which empowers users and applications to organize and manage their files. So for most users, the file system is most visible portion of an operating system.
- The file system consist of two distinct parts: a collection of files, each storing related data, and a directory structure, which organizes and provides information about all the files in the system.

8.2 FILE CONCEPT

- Computer can store information on various storage media, such as magnetic disk, magnetic tapes, and optical disk.
- An operating system provides a uniform logical view of information storage. It abstracts physical properties of its storage devices to define a logical storage unit, the file.
- A file is a named collection of related information that is recorded on secondary storage.
- Commonly, files represent programs (both source and object forms) and data. Data files may be numeric, alphabetic, alphanumeric, or binary.
- Files may be free form, such as text files, or may be formatted rigidly.

- In general, a file is a sequence of bits, bytes, lines or records, the meaning of which defined by the file's creator and user.
- Files are mapped by the operating system onto physical devices.
- To be able to use some commands on a file, operating system needs to know the structure of each file. E.g. while printing a file; operating system print garbage for a binary object file. It can be prevented if operating system has been told that the file is a binary object file.
- There are two major disadvantages in letting the operating system know the structure of the files:
  1. There are various types of the files and for each type, operating system requires separate program to understand that file, so size of operating system increases. It must have code to support all different types of files.
  2. Operating system will not be able to manage any new type of the file, until and unless code for the particular type is not added to the operating system.

8.2.1 Tape Based System

- Early file systems were tape based. Each file was implemented by mapping it into its own reel of tape. But it had number of following problems:
- As only one file was stored on one tape, even the biggest file was using only two percentage of the tape. Remedy for this solution was to find a mechanism by which more than one file can be stored on a tape.
- Other problem was storing a very big file, partly stored on number of tapes. To be able to do this, many systems provided for multi-volume tape files.
- There was problem in determining which files are on which tapes. To get this information, a directory is added to tape. Some system also called it VTOC (Volume Table Of Contents). Apart from names of all files in the tape, directory could also have same extra information about each file.
- For any operation on the file, the means is added by which it can be searched from directory and then accessed.
- There was a need to separate the operations like rewind a file and rewind the tape.
- After file is added to the end of the tape, directory which is generally at the front of the tape required to be updated.

8.2.2 Disk Based Systems

- When files are stored on Hard disk, it is called disk based files. It allows direct access to the data. Storing multiple files on disk and drums is also comparatively easy.

- A disk has number of tracks on it. All the tracks are further divided into number of sectors. Number of tracks may vary from one disk to another. Large disks may have number of platters. Each of it has two surfaces. Cylinder is set of similar tracks on all platters.

- As sector is made up of fixed number of bytes, reading and writing is done in terms of sectors. Number of sectors per tracks and number of bytes per sector also vary from one disk to another.

- To address particular sector, surface number, track number and sector number must be known.

  t   is number of tracks per cylinder

  s   is number of sectors per track

  i   is cylinder

  j   is surface

  k   is sector

  The block number $b=k+s\times(j+i\times t)$

- Logical structure of drum and disk is almost same. Drums give good performance but it is costly, they can be called as one cylinder disk.

- Apart from providing direct access, disk has one benefit over tape. It is possible to read a block from the disk, modify it and rewrite it at same place.

- Disk can have list of files present on it.

Blocking:

- As a disk is divided into number of sectors and sectors are fixed size, sector can be called as a physical block on the disk. Such physical blocks are not on tape.

- The software program can decide the size of the physical blocks. Generally, the user data is in terms of records called as logical records.

- Number of logical records are mapped into a physical blocks.

- Total number of logical blocks that can fit into one physical block is called as packing density.

- The way logical records are fitted into physical blocks is called a packing technique.

- Size of logical records, physical blocks and packing technique determine packing density.

8.2.3 File Attributes   (Oct. 16)

- A file is named for the convenience of its human users, and is referred to by its name.

- A file's attributes vary from one operating system to another but typically consist of these:

  1. **Name:** The symbolic file name, usually a string of characters.

2. **Identifier**: It is unique tag, usually a number that identifies the file within the file system.

3. **Type:** This information is needed for system that supports different types of files.

4. **Location:** It is pointer to a device and location of the file on that device.

5. **Size:** The current size of the files (in bytes, word or blocks).

6. **Protection:** Access-control information determines who can do reading, writing, executing and so on.

7. **Time, date, and user identification:** It is information of time and date of creation, last modification and last use. These data can be useful for protection, security, and usage monitoring.

- The information about all files is kept in the directory structure, which also resides on secondary storage. Typically, directory entry consists of the file's name and its unique identifier. The identifier in turn locates the other file attributes.

8.2.4 File Operations   (Oct. 16)

- A file is an abstract data type. To define the file properly, we need to consider the operation that can be performed on files.

- The operating system can provide system calls to create, write, read, reposition, delete, and truncate files.

- **Creating a File:** Two steps are necessary to create a file.
  1. Find space for new file in the file system.
  2. Make an entry for the new file in the directory.

- **Writing a File:**
  1. To write a file, name of the file and the information to be written to the file should be provided to system call.
  2. Search the file name in the directory to find the file's location.
  3. Place the write pointer to the location in the file where next write is to take place.
  4. Update the write pointer whenever a write occurs.

- **Reading a File:** To read from a file,
  1. Specify the name of the file and where (in memory) the next block of the file should be put is given to system call.
  2. Search the file name in the directory.
  3. Place the read pointer to the location in the file where the next read is to take place.
  4. Update the read pointer whenever the read occurs.

- Because a process is usually either reading from or writing to a file, the current operation location can be kept as a per-process current-file-position pointer. Both the read and write operations use this same pointer, saving space and reducing system complexity.

- **Repositioning within a File:**
  1. Search the file name in the directory.
  2. Current-file-position pointer is repositioned to a given value.

  Repositioning within a file need not involve any actual I/O. This file operation is also known as a file seeks.

- **Deleting a File.** To delete a file,
  1. Search the directory for the named file.
  2. Release all the file space, so that it can be refused by the other files.
  3. Erase the directory entry.

- **Truncating a File.** The user may want to erase the contents of a file and then recreate it, this function allows all attributes to remain unchanged – except for file length. Length of file is set to zero and its file space is released.

- Most of the file operations mentioned involve searching the directory for the entry associated with the named file. To avoid this constant searching, many system require that an open() system call to be made before a file is first used actively.

- The operating system keep a small table, called the open-file table, containing information about files. When a file operation is requested, the file is specified via an index into this table, so no searching is required.

- When a file is no longer being actively used, it is closed by the process, and the operating system removes its entry from the open-file table. Create and delete are system calls that work with closed rather than open files.

- The implementation of the open() and close() operations is more complicated in an environment where several processes may open the file at the same time.

- This may occur in a system where several different applications open the same file at the same time. The operating system uses two levels of internal table namely a per-process table and a system –wide table.

- The **per-process table** tracks all files that a process has open as shown in Fig. 8.1.

- It stores the information regarding the use of the file by the process. For example, the current file pointer for each file, access rights and accounting information etc.

- Each entry in the per-process table in turn points to a **system-wide open–file table.**

- It contains process- independent information, such as the location of the file on disk, access dates and file size etc.

- Once, file has been opened by process, this table includes an entry for the file.

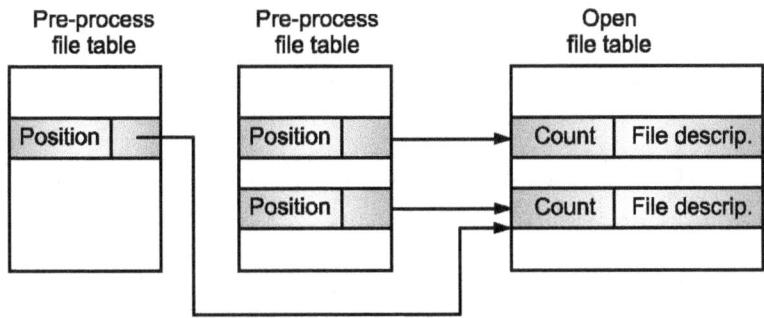

Fig. 8.1: OS data structure for files

- The following information associated with open file kept in open-file table is as follows:

  1. **File pointer:** On system that do not include a file offset as part of the read() and write() system calls, the system must track the last read – write location as a current file position pointer.

  2. **File-open count:** This counter tracks the number of opened and closed files by each process. It reaches zero on last close, then system can remove the entry from open-file table.

  3. **Disk location of the file:** Most file operations require the system to modify data within the file. The information needed to locate the file on disk is kept in memory so that the system does not have to read it from disk for each operation.

  4. **Access rights:** Each process opens a file in an access mode. This information is stored on the per-process table so the operating system can allow or deny subsequent I/O request.

8.2.5 File Types

- File type refers to the ability of the operating system to distinguish different types of file such as text files, source files and binary files etc.

- If an operating system recognizes the types of file, it can then operate on the file in reasonable ways.

- A common technique for implementing file types is to include the type as part of the file name.

- The file name is spilt into two parts – a name and an extension, usually separated by a period character.

- In this way, we can recognize the file type from name of file itself.

File type	Usual extension	Function
executable	exe, com, bin or none	Ready-to-run machine-language program
object	obj, o	Compiled, machine language, not linked
source code	c, cc, java, pas, asm, a	Source code in various language
batch	bat, sh	Commands to the command interpreter
text	txt, doc	Textual data, documents
word processor	wp, tex, rtf, doc	Various word-processor formats
library	lib, a, so, dil	Libraries of routines for programmers
print or view	ps, pdf, jpg	ASCII or binary file in a format for printing or viewing
archive	arc, zip, tar	Related files grouped into one file, sometimes compressed, for archiving or storage
multimedia	mpeg, mov, rm, mp3, avi	binary file containing audio or A/V information

- Operating system like MS-DOS and UNIX have the following types of files:
    1. **Ordinary Files:** These are the files that contain user information. These may have text, databases or executable program. The user can apply various operations on such files like add, modify, delete or even remove the entire file.
    2. **Directory Files:** These files contain list of file names and other information related to these files.
    3. **Special Files:** These files are also known as device files. These files represent physical device like disks, terminals, printers, networks, tape drive etc. These files are of two types:
        (i) **Character special files:** Data is handled character by character as in case of terminals or printers.
        (ii) **Block special files:** Data is handled in blocks as in the case of disks and tapes.

8.3 | ACCESS METHODS

- Stored information in the file must be accessed and read into computer's memory. It can be accessed in several ways like sequentially, direct or by other methods.

8.3.1 Sequential Access

- It is the simplest access method.
- Information in the file is processed in order, one record after the other.
- A fixed format is used for records and key field uniquely identifies the record

- Read and writes make up the bulk of the operation on the file which always start from beginning of file.

- **read next** operation reads the next portion of the file and automatically advance file pointer, which tracks the I/O location.

- **write next** operation appends to the end of the file and advances to the end of the newly written block(i.e. the new end of the file).

- **Rewinding file** reset file pointer to the beginning.

- Sequential access, which is depicted in Fig. 8.2, is based on a tape model of a file and works as well on sequential –access devices.

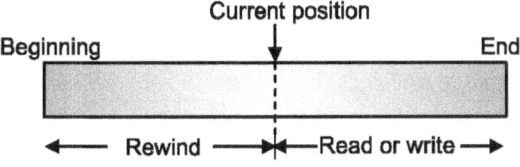

Fig. 8.2: Sequential-access file

Advantages:

1. It is simplest method of searching suitable for tape based systems.

2. If the application needs scanning of all records from file, then sequential access is best.

Disadvantages:

1. It is more time consuming since reading, writing and searching always start from beginning of file.

2. Insertion and deletion operation take more time.

8.3.2 Direct Access

- Another method is direct access (or relative access).

- A file is made up of fixed length logical records that allow program to read and write record rapidly in any order.

- This method is based on a disk model of a file, since disk allow random access to any file block.

- For direct access, the file is viewed as a numbered sequence of block records. So the file operation must include the block number as parameter.

- **read n,** where n is the block number, file pointer is placed at n^{th} block and reads data of that block.

- **write n** operation writes data into n^{th} block.

- The block number provided by the user to the operating system is normally a relative block number which acts as an index relative to the beginning of the file.

- Thus the first relative block of the file is 0; the next is 1, and so on, even though the actual absolute disk address of the block may be different.
- The use of relative block numbers allows the operating system to decide where the file should be placed and helps to prevent the user from accessing portions of the file system that may not be part of his/her file.

Advantages:
1. We can access any record randomly.
2. This method is more suitable for disk based systems.

8.3.3 Indexed Access

- The basic form of index includes a record key and storage addresses for a record. To find a record when storage address is unknown, it is necessary to scan the records.
- An index is a separate file from master file.
- To find a specific record, the index is first searched to find the key of the record required.
- When it is found, corresponding storage address is noted and then the program accesses the record directly.
- This method uses sequential scan of index and direct accesses to appropriate record. This is fast way to search or access a file.
- There are two types of indexed access files:

1. **Indexed Non-Sequential Access:**
   - In this method, master file is not any specific order.
   - There is one entry in index for every record in the master file.
   - When user wants to search any record, then operating system finds address using its key value from index table and move directly to that position.

2. **Indexed Sequential Access:**
   - In this, master file is sorted according to key values and index table contains only some key of the records.
   - When user wants to search any record, then operating system finds address using its key value from index table and apply sequential search to find out record from master table.
   - ISAM (indexed sequential access method) uses a small master index which points to parts of cylinder index. The cylinder index blocks point to track index and tracks index blocks point to the actual file as shown in Fig. 8.3.
   - The file is kept sorted on a defined key.

- To find a particular record, we first make a binary search of the master index, which provides the block number of the cylinder index.

- Then make a binary search of the cylinder index, which provides a blocks number of track index. Again within a track, binary search is used to obtain a desire record.

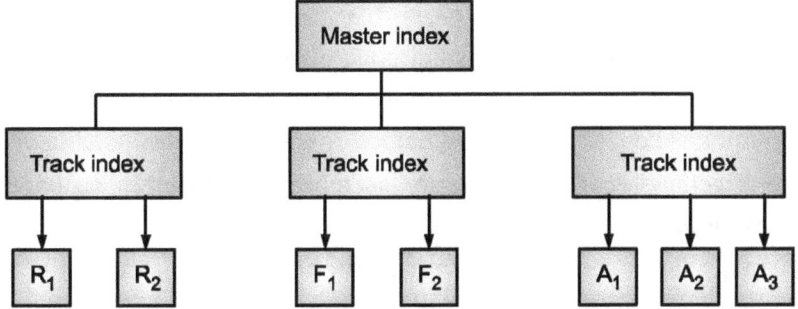

Fig. 8.3: Indexed Sequential Access Method

8.4 | DIRECTORY STRUCTURE

- Computer system stores million of files on disk. To manage all these data, we need to organize them. This organization involves use of directories.

- So directory can be viewed as collection of nodes containing information about files as shown in Fig. 8.4.

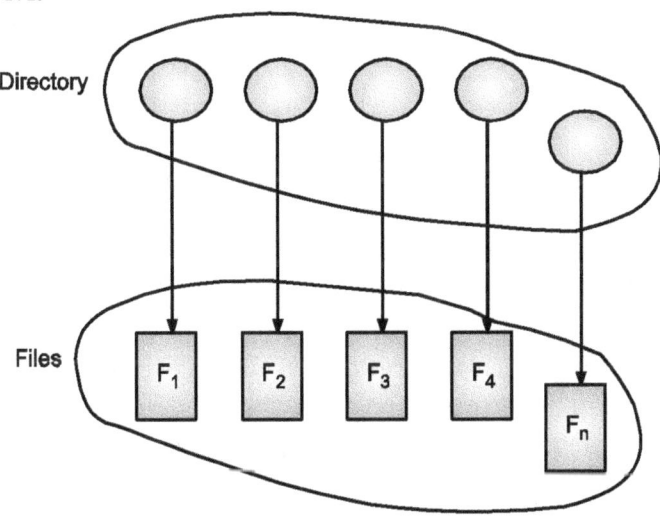

Fig. 8.4: Directory structure

- In the following section, basic storage structure and directory structure is explored.

8.4.1 Storage Structure

- A disk can be used in it's entirely for a file system.

- Sometimes, it is desirable to place multiple file systems on a disk or to use parts of a disk for a file system. These parts are known as partitions, slices etc. These partitions can be combined to form larger structure known as volume. Thus Volume is chunk of storage that holds a file system.

- Each volume that contains a file system must also contain information about files in the system.

- This information is kept in entries in a device directory or volume table of contents.

- The device directory records information such as name, location, size and type for all files in file system.

- Volumes can also store multiple operating systems, allowing a system to boot and run more than one.

- The Fig. 8.5 shows typical file organization.

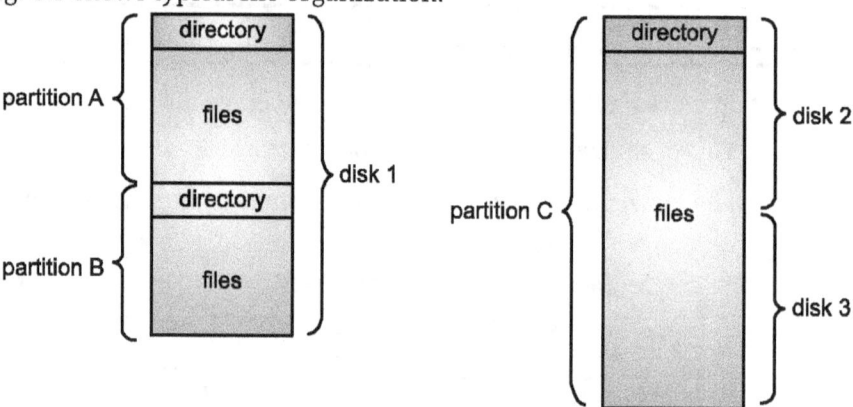

Fig. 8.5: A typical File System Organization

8.4.2 Directory Overview

- The directory can be viewed as a symbol table that translates file names into their directory entries.

- When considering a particular directory structure, we need to keep in mind the operations that are to be performed on a directory:

  1. **Search for a file:** To find the entry for a particular file or find all files whose names match a particular pattern.

  2. **Create a file:** New files need to be created and added to the directory.

  3. **Delete a file:** To remove a file entry from directory when it is no longer needed.

  4. **List a directory:** To list the files in a directory alongwith its information.

5. **Rename a file:** Renaming a file may also allow its position within the directory structure to be changed.

6. **Backup:** We may wish to access every directory and every file within a directory structure. For reliability, it is a good idea to save the contents and structure of the entire file system at regular intervals.

-   In the following sections, the most common schemes for defining the logical structure of a directory are described.

8.4.2.1 Single-Level Directory

-   The simplest directory structure is the single – level directory.

-   All files are contained in the same directory, which is easy to support and understand.

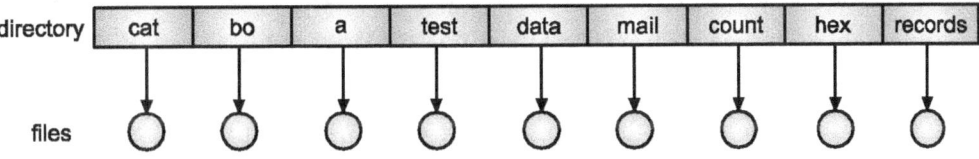

Fig. 8.6: Single-level directory

Advantages:

1. Simple to built.

Disadvantages:

1. As all files are in the same directory, they must have unique names.

2. It is difficult to remember the names of all the files as the number of files increases.

3. In multi-user system, many users may create files with same name.

4. Users can not create their own directory.

8.4.2.2 Two-Level Directory

-   The main drawback of single level directory is solved in the two-level directory structure.

-   In this, each user has his own User File Directory (UFD).

-   The UFDs have similar structure, but each lists only the files of a single user. When a user job start or a user logs in, the system's Master File Directory (MFD) is searched.

-   The MFD is indexed by user name or account number and each entry points to the UFD for the user.

-   When a user refers to a particular file, only his UFD is searched.

-   Different users may have files with the same name as long as all the file names within each UFD are unique.

- To create a file to user, the operating system searches only that user's UFD to verify whether another file of that name exists.

- To delete a file, the operating system limits its search to the local UFD; thus it cannot accidentally delete another user's file that has a same name.

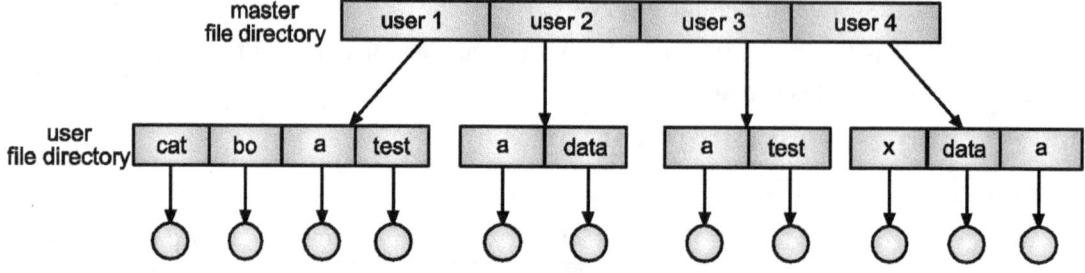

Fig. 8.7: Two-level directory structure

Advantages:

1. It solves the file name: collision problem by creating own user directory.

2. This method isolates one user from another and protects user's files.

Disadvantages:

1. As this structure isolates one user from another, sharing of tasks and access one another's files is not possible.

2. If access is to be permitted, user must have the ability to name a file in another user's directory (i.e. user must know pathname of the file desired.)

3. In case of system's files, which are required by all users, has to be copied in each users directory. It leads to wastage of memory.

8.4.2.3 Tree-Structured Directories   (April 16)

- The generalization of two level directory structure is an arbitrary tree structure directory.

- This generalization allows users to create their own subdirectories and to organize their files accordingly.

- It is the most common directory structure. The tree has a root directory, and every file in the system has unique path name.

- A directory (or subdirectory) contains a set of files or subdirectories. It is simply another file, but it is treated in a special way.

- All directories have the same internal format. One bit in each directory entry defines the entry as a file (0) or as a sub directory (1).

- Special system calls are used to create, delete and change directories.

- Path names can be of two types i.e., absolute and relative.
    1. **An absolute path name** begins at the root and follows path down to the specified file, giving the directory names on the path.
    2. **A relative path name** defines a path from the current directory to that specified file.
- For example, in the tree-structured file system of Fig. 8.8 if the current directory is root/spell/mail, then the relative path name prt/first/ refers to the same file as does the absolute path name root/spell/ mail/prt/ first.

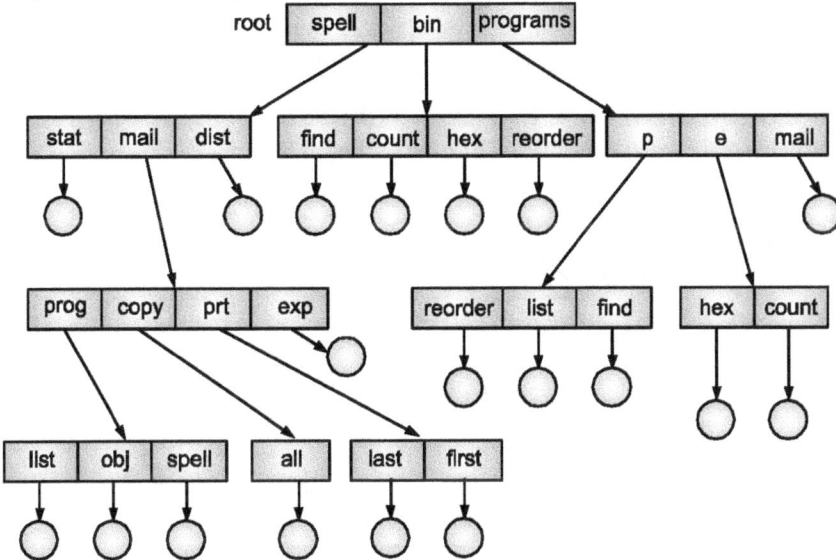

Fig. 8.8: Tree-structured directory structure

Deletion of Files:

- If directory is empty, its entry in the directory that contains it can be deleted.
- But if the directory to be deleted is not empty, then two approaches are taken:
    1. Operating systems such as MS-DOS will not delete a directory unless it is empty. Thus, to delete directory, the user must first delete all the files in that directory. If sub-directories exist, then same procedure must applied recursively to them, so that they can be deleted. But it results in significant amount of work.
    2. The other approach used by UNIX rm command is to provide an option: when a request is made to delete a directory, all that directory and sub-directories are also to be deleted.

Advantages:

1. User can create directory as well as subdirectory.
2. Users can access the files of other users.

Disadvantages:

1. The tree structure can create duplicate copies of the files.
2. The users could not share files or directories.

8.4.2.4 Acyclic-Graph Directories

*   A tree structure prohibits the sharing of files or directories. Consider two programmers who are working on a joint project.

*   The files associated with that project can be stored in a subdirectory, separating them from other project and files of two programmers. But since both programmers are equally responsible for the project, both want the subdirectory to be in their own directories. So there is need that the common subdirectories should be shared.

*   An acyclic graph that is, a graph with no cycles allows directories to share subdirectories and files as shown in following Fig. 8.9.

*   The same file or subdirectory may be in two different directories.

*   It is natural generalization of the tree- structured directory scheme.

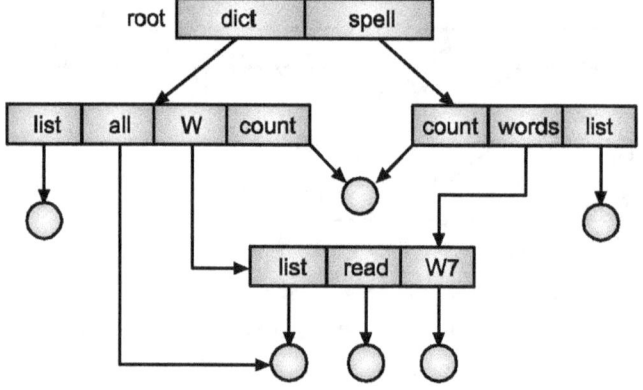

Fig. 8.9: Acyclic-graph directory structure

Implementation of Shared Files:

*   It is important to note that a shared file (or directory) is not the same as two copies of the file. With two copies, each programmer can view copy rather than the original one, but if programmer changes the file, the changes will not appear in others copy. So inconsistency is big problem with copies and memory wastage.

*   With a shared file, only one actual file exists, so any changes made by one person are immediately visible to the other.

*   Sharing is particularly important for subdirectories; a new file created by one person will automatically appear in all the shared subdirectories.

*   But also with a single copy, several concurrent updates to a file may result in user obtaining incorrect information, and the file being left in an incorrect state.

- Shared files and subdirectories can be implemented in several ways:
  1. A common way is to create a new directory entry called a link. A link is effectively a pointer to another file or subdirectory. For example, a link may be implemented as an absolute or a relative path name. When a reference to a file is made, we search the directory. In the directory, entry is marked as link, and then the link is resolved by using that path name to locate the real file.
  2. Another common approach to implementing shared files is simply to duplicate all information about them in both sharing directories. Thus both entries are identical and equal.

Deletion of Shared File:

- Another problem involves deletion of shared files. One possibility is to remove the file whenever anyone deletes it, but this action may leave dangling pointer to the nonexistent file.
- To overcome this problem, a reference count is maintained for shared files. Whenever a user shares file, reference count is incremented and whenever a user deletes a file, it is decremented.
- When reference count becomes zero, at that time only the file is actually deleted.

Advantages:

1. It is more flexible than tree-structure directories.
2. It allows sharing of files and directories.
3. Implementation of algorithm is simple to traverse the graph.

Disadvantages:

1. It is difficult to ensure that there are no cycles.
2. Implementation of shared file is complicated.

8.4.2.5 General Graph Directory

- When we add links to the existing tree structure directories, the tree structure is destroyed, resulting in a simple graph directory as shown in Fig. 8.10. This scheme gives complete flexibility in sharing files.
- If cycles are allowed, then algorithm should take care of the following:
  o Not allowing the reference to file to go in an infinite loop, because of cycle.
  o Garbage collection method should be implemented in case of deletion of shared files.
  o Garbage collection involves traversing the entire files system, marking everything that can be accessed. Then, a second pass collects everything that is not marked onto a list of free space.

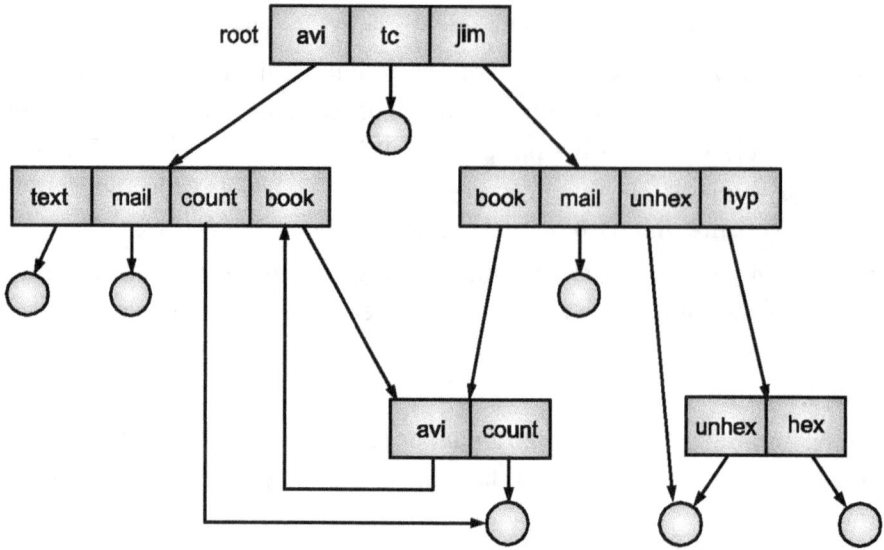

Fig. 8.10: General graph directory

Advantages:

1. Sharing of files.

2. Directories are more flexible than acyclic graph structure.

Disadvantages:

1. It requires separate algorithm for garbage collection.

2. Garbage collection for disk based file is time consuming.

3. While traversing, a poorly designed algorithm might result in an infinite loop continually searching through cycle and never terminating.

8.5 | FILE SYSTEM STRUCTURE

*   File systems provide efficient and convenient access to the disk by allowing data to be stored, located, and retrieved easily.

*   The file system design problem is divided into two groups.

    1. The first group is dealing with how the file system should look to the user. It includes the identification of a file and its attributes, operations allowed on a file and the directory structure.

    2. Second group is defining algorithm and data structure used to map the logical file system onto the physical secondary storage devices. The file system is divided into many different levels as shown in Fig. 8.11. These are:

        (i)   Application Programs (AP)

        (ii) Logical File System (LFS)

(iii) File Organization Module (FOM)

(iv) Basic File System (BFS)

(v)   Input/Output Control (IOC)

(vi) Devices.

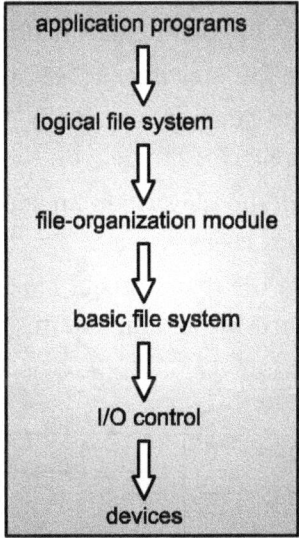

Fig. 8.11: Layered File System

- To create a new file application program, call logical file system.

- Logical file system knows about directory structure. The information about symbolic file name is given to the file organization by logical file system.

- Logical file system gets this information from directory structure. Logical File System is the highest level in the OS; it does protection, and security.

- File organization module knows about blocks and files. It is called by logical file system to map directory, input/output to disk blocks. File organizing module generate address of blocks for Basic File System to read.

- Basic File System does actual reading/writings of blocks to and from disk. Each block has a unique numeric disk address.

- Input/output control is made up of device drivers and interrupt handler and are responsible for actual transfer of data to memory and disk.

- At the end is actual device involved in input /output.

8.6 | ALLOCATION METHODS   (April 15, 16)

- The direct-access nature of disks allows us flexibility in the implementation of files. The main problem is how to allocate space to these files so that disk space is utilized effectively and files can be accessed quickly.

- Three major methods of allocating disk space are contiguous, linked and indexed. Each method has its advantages and disadvantages. More commonly, a system uses one method for all files within file system type.

8.6.1 Contiguous Allocation

- In this method, consecutive free blocks are allocated to a file.
- Directory contains name of the file, starting address and number of blocks.
- If the file is n blocks long and start at location b, then it requires blocks b, b + 1, b + n – 1 as shown in following Fig. 8.12.
- For sequential access of record, the file system must remember the disk address of the last block read so that next block is easily read.
- For direct access of block i of a file that starts at block b, we can directly access (b + i) block. Thus, this method supports sequential and direct access.
- It is used in IBM 370.

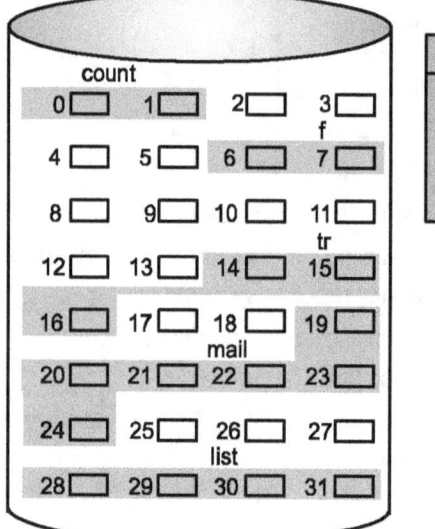

directory

file	start	length
count	0	2
tr	14	3
mail	19	6
list	28	4
f	6	2

Fig. 8.12: Contiguous allocation of disk space

Advantages:

1. Supports both sequential and direct access.
2. Reading all blocks belonging to each file is very fast.

Disadvantages:

1. Difficulty in searching space for new files.
2. To allocate a file, one needs to know the size of the file in advance.
3. If new block are freed from the file, they will remain unallocated (because their consecutive blocks are not free) creating external fragmentation.

4. Problem is there in the cases where files grow after some days. In this case, either user program is terminated or a new big free space is found and the file is copied to it.

Dynamic Storage Allocation Problem in Contiguous Allocation:

*   Disk space is nothing but large array of disk block. At any instance of time, few blocks are assigned to file and some blocks are freed by the file.

*   At any moment, we may find that allocated as well as free blocks are spread all over the disk. The unallocated (free) blocks are also called as holes. There may be number of consecutive holes.

*   Now whenever a user has a request of size n, either of the following method is used to search a hole big enough to satisfy the requirement of n units from the list of free holes.

1. **First fit:** In this case, as soon as the first hole (that is big enough) is encountered, searching is stopped and memory is allocated for creating a file.

    *   Most simple and less time consuming method to search a hole.
    *   Poor memory utilization.
    *   It creates internal fragmentation.

2. **Best fit:** In this case, the entire list is searched for and the smallest hole, that satisfy the request is selected and is allocated for creating file.

    *   Memory utilization is the best.
    *   Internal fragmentation is less.
    *   As compared to first and worst fit algorithm is more complex.
    *   It is a time consuming process.

3. **Worst fit:** Again the entire list is scanned, and the biggest hole/block satisfying the requirement (i.e. biggest > n) is selected.

    *   Time consuming.
    *   Memory utilization is very poor.
    *   Internal fragmentation is big problem.

Compaction:

*   Compaction is used to improve memory utilization, which is poor because of external fragmentation. Compaction is process of collecting all free holes into one big hole.

8.6.2 Linked Allocation   (April 13)

*   Linked allocation is essentially a disk-based version of the linked list.
*   In this method, a linked list of the all block belonging to the file is maintained. These blocks may be scattered through the disk.

- Directory entry contains the name of the file, address of starting block and the last block.
- If we want to read a file, we simply follow the pointers.
- If we want to write to a file, any free block is removed from free list and writes to it. This block is appended at the end of the file with pointer.
- It is used in DEC TOPS-10, Xerox Alto.
- The following Fig. 8.13 shows file jeep of five blocks 9-16-1-10-25.

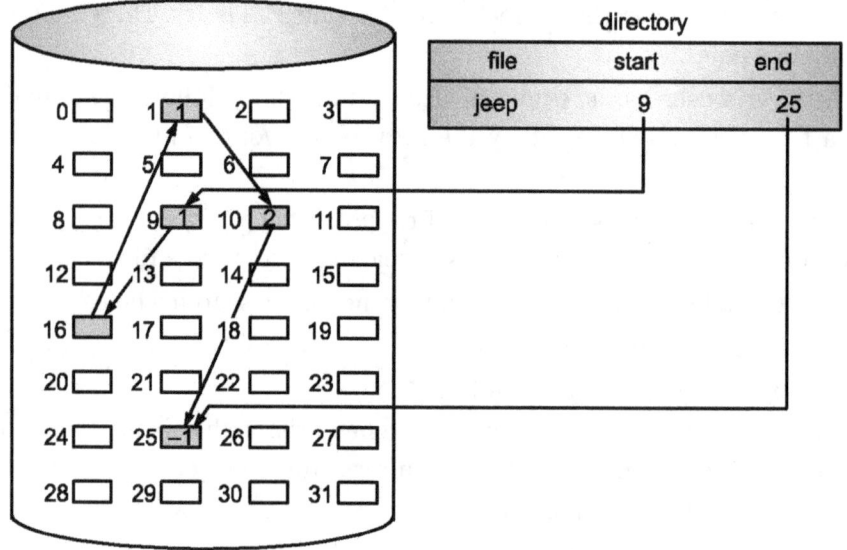

Fig. 8.13: Linked allocation of disk space

Advantages:

1. No external fragmentation because any free block is used to satisfy the request.
2. Files can grow any time.
3. No need to know the size of the file in advance.
4. No disk compaction.

Disadvantages:

1. Only sequential access is possible.
2. Memory is required for storing the pointers. Therefore, file requires slightly more space.
3. Reliability is big problem. Since disk blocks are linked by pointers, a single damaged pointer can make thousands of disk blocks inaccessible. So we can not access any portion of file or entire file.
4. Bug in an operating system may result in picking up wrong dangling pointers from the memory.

- A File Allocation Table (FAT) is a variation of Linked allocation. It uses a separate disk area to hold the links. This method doesn't use space in data blocks. Many pointers may remain in memory.

- A FAT file system is used by MS-DOS.

8.6.3 Indexed Allocation   (April 13, 15)

- One disadvantage with linked allocation method is that it does not support direct accessing since blocks are scattered all over the disk.

- This problem is solved by indexed allocation by placing all of the pointers together into an index block.

- In this method of allocation, an index block is there for each file. It contains addresses of all blocks belonging to that file sequentially e.g. i^{th} entry in the index block of a file will contain the address of ith block belonging to that file.

- A directory entry contains the name of the file and address of the index block.

- In case of large files, a single index block holds the addresses of all index blocks. These indexes may contain addresses of few more indexed blocks or addresses of actual block belonging to the file. This is called as level of indices.

- In the following Fig. 8.14 Block number 19th contain address, 9th, 16th, 1st 10th and 25th blocks. Address of index block 19th is present in the directory entry.

- It is used in DEC VMS, Nachos.

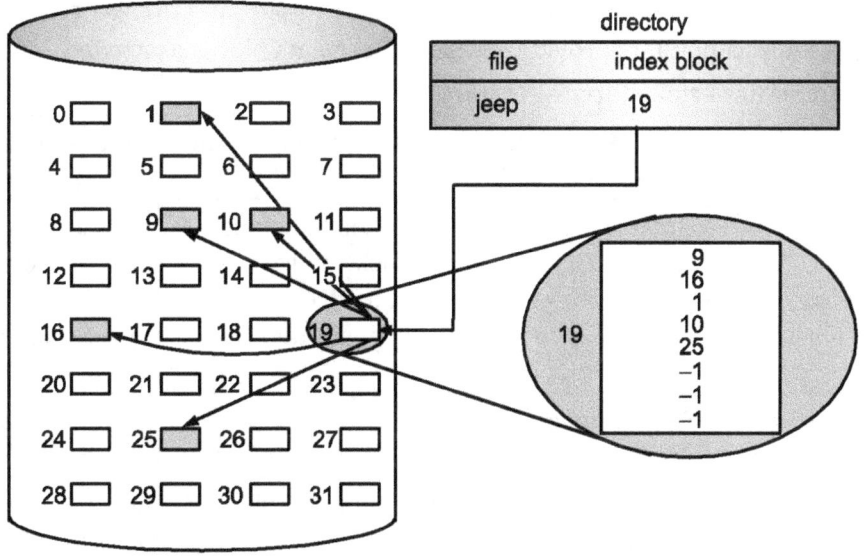

Fig. 8.14: Indexed allocation of disk space

Advantages:

1. Direct access possible.
2. No need for user to know size of the file in advance.
3. No external fragmentation.

Disadvantages:

1. Overhead of index blocks is not feasible for very small file.
2. Overhead of index block is not feasible for very big file also. It is also very difficult to manage levels of indices.
3. File access time is increased because, for any operation of the file, index block has to be accessed, which increases input / output.
4. Keeping index in memory requires space.

- A question is of how big the index block should be, and how it should be implemented. There are several approaches:

   1. **Linked Scheme:** An index block is one disk block, which can be read and written in a single disk operation. The first index block contains some header information, the first N block addresses, and if necessary a pointer to additional linked index blocks.

   2. **Multi-Level Index:** The first index block contains a set of pointers to secondary index blocks, which in turn contain pointers to the actual data blocks.

   3. **Combined Scheme:** This is the scheme used in UNIX inodes, in which the first 12 or so data block pointers are stored directly in the inode, and then singly, doubly, and triply indirect pointers provide access to more data blocks as needed.

- Let us summarize briefly three allocation methods.

Factors	Contiguous allocation Method	Linked allocation method	Indexed allocation method
Allocation method	Array of disk blocks.	Linked list of disk blocks which are scattered throughout disk.	All pointers to blocks are placed together in one block known as index block.
Access method	Sequential and direct.	Only sequential	Sequential and direct.
Directory entry	File name, start location of file and size of file.	File name, start block and end block.	File name and address of index block.

contd. ...

File Size	Should be known in advance and size is fixed.	No need to know in advance and file size can grow at any time.	No need to know in advance and file size can grow at any time.
Fragmentation	Suffers from external and internal fragmentation.	No external fragmentation.	No external fragmentation.
Reliable	Yes.	No, problem of dangling pointers.	Yes.

8.7 | FREE SPACE MANAGEMENT   (April 16, Oct. 16)

- To store a file on the disk, operating system needs to know which blocks on the disk are free and which are not.
- The operating system maintains free space list to keep the track of free disk space.
- When a file is created, the required amount of the space is searched from free space list and allocated to the file.
- This space is then removed from the free space list.
- When a file is deleted, the space which was allocated to a file is freed and added to the free space list.
- Following are some methods which manages free-space list information.

    1. **Bit Map / Bit Vector :**
        o This is method of keeping track of allocated and unallocated blocks. Each block is represented by one bit. If the block is free, the bit is set to 1.
        o If the block is allocated, the bit is set to 0.
        o For example, consider a disk where blocks 4, 5,8,9,10,12,13,15,18,19,25 are free, the free space bit map or bit vector is: **0001100111011010011000001**.

    2. **Linked List:**
        o Linked list of free blocks is maintained.
        o Pointer to first free block is preserved.
        o Fist free block contain address of the next free block and so on.
        o The following Fig. 8.15 shows linked list of free blocks in which pointer is at block 2 which is first free block. Block 2 would contain pointer to block 3 and so on.

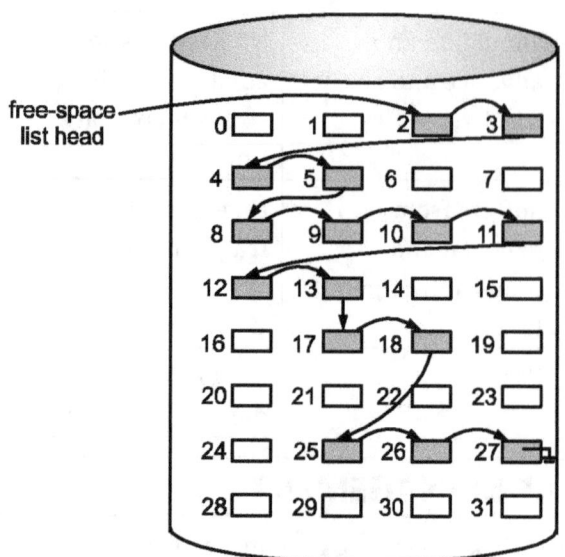

Fig. 8.15: Linked free-space list on disk

- However, this scheme is not efficient, since traversing of list is time consuming and requires reading of each block which requires substantial I/O.

3. **Grouping:**
   - To resolve the problem occurred in linked free space list, the addresses of n free blocks in the first free block.
   - The first **n-1** of these blocks are actually free.
   - The last block contains the disk addresses of another n free blocks and so on.
   - In this method, the addresses of a large number of free blocks can be found quickly.

4. **Counting:**
   - When many contiguous free blocks are present, rather than keeping a list of n free disk addresses, we can keep the address of first free block and count of the next n free contiguous blocks.
   - Each entry in the free space list then consists of a disk address and a count.

5. **Space Map:**
   - Sun's ZFS file system was designed for HUGE numbers and sizes of files, directories, and even file systems.
   - The resulting data structures could be VERY inefficient if not implemented carefully. For example, freeing up a 1 GB file on a 1 TB file system could involve updating thousands of blocks of free list bit maps if the file was spread across the disk.

- o ZFS uses a combination of techniques, starting with dividing the disk up into (hundreds of) metaslabs of a manageable size, each having their own space map.
- o Free blocks are managed using the counting technique, but rather than write the information to a table, it is recorded in a log-structured transaction record. Adjacent free blocks are also coalesced into a larger single free block.
- o An in-memory space map is constructed using a balanced tree data structure, constructed from the log data.
- o The combination of the in-memory tree and the on-disk log provide for very fast and efficient management of these very large files and free blocks.

SUMMARY

- ➤ A file is a named collection of related information that is recorded on secondary storage. It is an abstract data type defined and implemented by the operating system. It is a sequence of logical records. A logical record may be a byte, a line (of fixed or variable length), or a more complex data item.
- ➤ Commonly, files represent programs (both source and object forms) and data. Data files may be numeric, alphabetic, alphanumeric, or binary.
- ➤ Files are mapped by the operating system onto physical devices.
- ➤ Early file systems were tape based. Each file was implemented by mapping it into its own reel of tape. It allows sequential access to data.
- ➤ When files are stored on Hard disk, it is called disk based system. It allows direct access to the data.
- ➤ Every file has attributes which vary from one operating system to another but typically consist of these: Name, Identifier, Type, Location, Size, Protection and Time, date, and user identification.
- ➤ Operations on file are create, open ,read ,write , repositioning file, delete file, truncate file close file etc.
- ➤ File type refers to the ability of the operating system to distinguish different types of file such as text files source files and binary files etc.
- ➤ A common technique for implementing file types is to include the type as part of the file name.
- ➤ Stored information in the file must be accessed and read into computer's memory by following methods: sequentially, direct or by other methods like indexed sequential.

➢ A sequential access is that in which the records are accessed in some sequence i.e the information in the file is processed in order, one record after the other.

➢ Random access file organization provides, accessing the records directly. Each record has its own address on the file with by the help of which it can be directly accessed for reading or writing.

➢ Indexed Sequential mechanism is built up on base of sequential access. An index is created for each file which contains pointers to various blocks. Index is searched sequentially and its pointer is used to access the file directly.

➢ Each device in a file system keeps a volume table of contents or a device directory listing the location of the files on the device. In addition, it is useful to create directories to allow files to be organized.

➢ The directory can be viewed as a symbol table that translates file names into their directory entries.

➢ In single-level directory, all files are contained in the same directory, which is easy to support and understand. But in a multiuser system, it causes naming problems, since each file must have a unique name.

➢ A two-level directory solves this problem by creating a separate directory for each user's files. The directory lists the files by name and includes the file's location on the disk, length, type, owner, time of creation, time of last use, and so on.

➢ The natural generalization of a two-level directory is a tree-structured directory. A tree-structured directory allows a user to create subdirectories to organize files.

➢ Acyclic-graph directory structures enable users to share subdirectories and files but complicate searching and deletion.

➢ A general graph structure allows complete flexibility in the sharing of files and directories but sometimes requires garbage collection to recover unused disk space.

➢ File systems provide efficient and convenient access to the disk by allowing data to be stored, located, and retrieved easily.

➢ The file system is divided into many different levels as Application Programs (AP), Logical file system (LFS), File organization Module (FOM), Basic File System (BFS), Input/Output Control (IOC) and Devices.

➢ Three major methods of allocating disk space are contiguous, linked and indexed.

➢ In contiguous allocation method, consecutive free blocks are allocated to a file. Directory contains name of the file, starting address and number of blocks.

➤ In linked allocation method, a linked list of the all block belonging to the file is maintained. These blocks may be scattered through the disk. Directory entry contains the name of the file, address of starting block and the last block.

➤ In indexed allocation method, an index block is there for each file. It contains addresses of all blocks belonging to that file sequentially. A directory entry contains the name of the file and address of the index block.

➤ The operating system maintains free space list to keep the track of free disk space. When a file is created, the required amount of the space is searched from free space list and allocated to the file. When a file is deleted, the space which was allocated to a file is freed and added to the free space list.

➤ Free-space management techniques are bitmap, linked list, grouping, counting and spacemap.

PRACTICE QUESTIONS

1. What is file? Enlist its attributes.

2. Explain file operations in detail.

3. Following is sequence of free blocks on a disk (size of blocks are given: 120,30,60,40,50,90,70 if the disk place allocation request occur request in following order; 40,60,58,20,90,35. Find the allocation of free blocks to the above request using first fit best fit strategy.

4. Consider a file currently consisting of 100 blocks. How many disk I/O operation are involved with contiguous linked and indexed allocation strategies, if one block:
   - Is added at beginning?
   - Is added in the middle?
   - Is added at the end?
   - Is removed from the beginning?
   - Is removed from the middle?

5. A system supports the following allocation strategies for allocating disk space for files:
   - Linked
   - Indexed

   Discuss the criteria that has to decide, which strategy is to be adopted for a particular file.

6. Some systems provide file sharing by maintaining a single copy of a file. Other systems maintain several copies, one for each of the users sharing the file. Discuses the relative merits of each approach.

7. Compare linked, contiguous and indexed allocation.

8. What is the different allocation methods used in a file system? Explain indexed file allocation method in detail.

9. What are the advantage and disadvantages of a tree structure directory?

10. Explain different methods for free space management.

11. Explain contiguous allocation method in detail.

12. Explain indexed allocation method.

13. Write note on acyclic graph directory.

14. Explain different file access method.

15. Explain the information kept device directory.

16. Describe various directory structures in details.

17. Write note on file portion.

18. Defines terms:

    (a) Bit map.

    (b) Free-space management.

    (c) Compaction.

    (d) Allocation.

    (e) Access.

19. State true and false:

    (a) The external fragmentation is occurred in linked allocation file system.

    (b) Unix uses a tree structure directory.

    (c) In index allocation, file access is time increased

    (d) Link allocation method is more reliable than index allocation

    (e) In single level directory structure, we can have same file name for more than one file.

Ans.: (a) False (b) True (c) True (d) False (e) False

20. Linked allocation is more reliable than other allocation methods.

Ans. Refer to Section 8.6.2 (Advantages).

21. What information is stored in open-file table when file is opened?

Ans. Refer to Section 8.2.4.

22. Write a short note on acyclic graph directory.

Ans. Refer to Section 8.4.2.4.

23. What is file? List any two attributes of file.

Ans. Refer to Sections 8.2 and 8.2.3.

24. Give the diagrammatic representation of single-level directory. Also list out the disadvantages of single-level directory structure.

Ans. Refer to Section 8.4.2.1.

25. Explain any two file operations.

Ans. Refer to Section 8.2.4.

26. List any four file attributes.

Ans. Refer to Section 8.2.3.

27. List different ways for handling free-space-list in file system.

Ans.Refer to Section 8.7.

28. Explain in brief Indexed file allocation methods with advantages and disadvantages.

Ans. Refer to Section 8.6.3.

29. Discuss the various techniques of free space management in File System.

Ans. Refer to Section 8.7.

30. Explain different methods for handling free-space list in file system.

Ans. Refer to Section 8.7.

31. Explain Tree-structured directories along with advantages and disadvantages.

Ans. Refer to Section 8.4.2.3.

UNIVERSITY QUESTIONS AND ANSWERS

1. Justify: "Newly created directory will have two entries automatically in it"?

(April 2013) (1 M)

Ans. True. Two entries are for root directory and subdirectory. " . " refers to the directory itself ." .. " refers to the parent directory

2. Give any two disk allocation methods.   **(April 2015) (1 M)**

Ans. Refer to Section 8.6.

3. Explain Linked and Indexed file allocation methods along with merits and demerits.   **(April 2013) (4 M)**

Ans. Refer to Sections 8.6.2 and 8.6.3.

4. Explain in brief Indexed File allocation method with advantages and disadvantages.   **(April 2015) (5 M)**

Ans. Refer to Section 8.6.3.

■■■

April 2016

Time : Two Hours   **Maximum Marks : 40**

N.B.:   *(i)*   *Neat diagram must be drawn whenever necessary.*

     (ii)   *Figures to the right indicate full marks.*

     (iii) *All questions are compulsory*

1.   Attempt all of the following: [10 × 1 = 10]

(a)   What is function of bootstrap loader?

Ans.   •   To locate the Kernel and loads it into main memory and starts execution.

    •   To determine the state of the machine.

    •   To initialize all aspects of the system.

(b)   What will happen if all process are CPU bound in system?

Ans.   If all processes are CPU bound, the I/O waiting queue will almost empty.

(c)   List any two examples of many to many model.

Ans.   IRIX, HP-VX, Tru-64 unix (any two).

(d)   Define dispatch latency.

Ans.   The time taken by dispatcher to stop one process and start another process to run is called dispatch latency.

(e)   What is race condition?

Ans.   A situation where multiple processes access and manipulate the same data concurrently and the outcome of the execution depends on the order in which instruction execute.

(f)   Define starvation.

Ans.   A process may be held for long time waiting for its resources.

(g)   What are various dynamic allocation memory management methods?

Ans.   First-fit, Best-fit, Worst-fit.

(h)   Give any two disk allocation methods.

Ans.   Contiguous, linked, indexed (any two).

(i)   State two general approaches that are used to handle critical section in operation system.

Ans.   Pre-emptive Kernel and Non-pre-emptive kernels.

(j)   Define turnaround time.

Ans.   •   The amount of time to execute a particular process from its entry time.

    •   It is the interval from the time of submission to the time of completion.

2. Attempt any two of the following: [2 × 5 = 10]

(a) Explain PCB with proper diagram.

Ans.

Pointer	Process current state
Process ID (no.)	
Process priority	
Registers	
Program counter	
I/O status info	
Accounting info	
Memory limits	
Other information	

Fig. PCB

One line description of each task - 4 marks.

*   Pointer to PCB of next process in ready queue.
*   Current state of the process.
*   IP-Number allocated by the operating system to process on creation.
*   Priority is required to complete the process immediately than lower priority processes.
*   Register-number of CPU register, general purpose, accumulators, conditions code register etc.
*   Program counter is the address of next instruction to be executed.
*   I/O requires I/O device allocated to the process.
*   Accounting - no. of resource used, time limit, CPU time used, job number etc.
*   Memory limit - info about page table, bound register.
*   Other info - current directory, address of different scheduling queue etc.

(b) Consider the following set of processes, with the length of CPU burst time and arrival time in milliseconds:

Process	Burst time	Arrival time
P1	4	2
P2	6	0
P3	2	1

Illustrate the execution of these processes using Round Robin (RR) CPU scheduling algorithm (quantum = 3 milliseconds). Calculate average waiting time and average turn around time. Give the contents of Gantt chart.

Ans. Round Robin Algorithm

P2	P3	P1	P2	P1

0   3   5   8   11   12

Average turn around time = 8.33

Average waiting time = 4.33

(c) Consider a system with 7 processes A through G and six types of resources R through W with one resource for each type.

Resource ownership is as follows:

A holds R and wants S

B holds nothing but wants T

C holds nothing but wants S

D holds U and wants S and T

E holds T and wants V

F holds W and wants S

G holds V and wants U

Is the system deadlocked, and if so, which processes are involved?

Ans. Resource allocation graph.

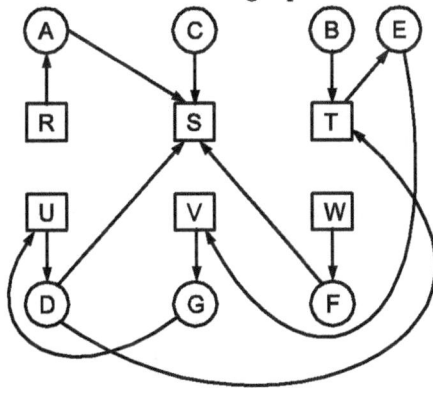

Wait for graph

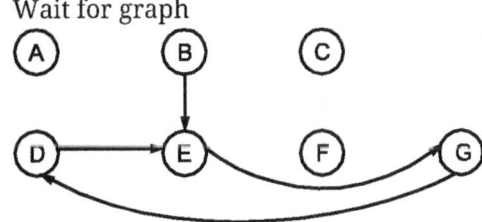

As cyclic exists in graph $0 \to \varepsilon \to G \to D$;

Process D, E, G are involved in a deadlock.

3. Attempt any two of the following: [2 × 5 = 10]

(a) What is a semaphore? Explain dining philosopher problem.

Ans. **Definition:** A semaphore is a protected variable, whose value can be accessed and altered only by the two atomic operation wait() and signal().

Dining philosopher problem:

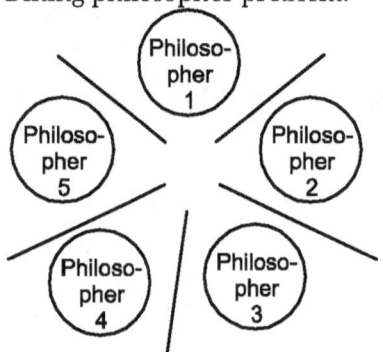

Description on above problem.

5 philosphers are sitting around a round able. This problem focus over the synchronization performed during the concept sharing of resources as well as data. It also focus over the implementation of mutual exclusion. This is also a solution to overcome the problem of deadlock.

(b) Discuss the various techniques of free space management in file system.

Ans. • Bit map/Bit vector
     • Linked list
     • Grouping
     • Counting
     • Space map

(c) Consider the following page reference string:
         1, 2, 3, 4, 1, 2, 5, 1, 2, 3, 4, 5
     How many page faults would occur for the following page replacement algorithm?
     (i) LRU   (ii) FIFO

Ans. (i) LRU

Ref. string	1	2	3	4	1	2	5	1	2	3	4	5
Frame 1	1	1	1	4	4	4	5	5	5	3	3	3
Frame 2		2	2	2	1	1	1	1	1	1	4	4
Frame 1			3	3	3	2	2	2	2	2	2	5
Page fault	Y	Y	Y	Y	Y	Y	Y	N	N	Y	Y	Y

         Total page faults = 10

(ii) FIFO:

Ref. string	1	2	3	4	1	2	5	1	2	3	4	5
Frame 1	1	1	1	4	4	4	5	5	5	5	5	5
Frame 2		2	2	2	1	1	1	1	1	3	3	3
Frame 3			3	3	3	2	2	2	2	2	4	4
Page fault	Y	Y	Y	Y	Y	Y	Y	N	N	Y	Y	N

Total page faults = 9

4. Attempt any one (A or B):   [1 × 10 = 10]

(A) (i) State and explain criteria for computing various scheduling algorithms.   [4]

Ans. • CPU utilisation

   • Throughput

   • Turnaround time

   • Waiting time

   • Response time

(ii) Explain internal and external fragmentation.   [4]

Ans. Internal fragmentation:

   • Allocated memory may be slightly larger than request memory, the size different is memory internal to a portion but not being used is known as internal fragmentation.

   External fragmentation:

   • As process are loaded and removed, the free memory is broken into little pieces. Total memory space exist to satisfy a request, but it is not contiguous, then it is known as external fragmentation.

(iii) Explain any two benefits of multithreading.   [2]

Ans. • Resource sharing

   • Economy

   • Scalability

   • Responsiveness

OR

(B) (i) Explain tree-structured directories along with advantages and disadvantages. [4]

Ans. Description of tree structure directory

   With path name types:

   • Absolute pathname

   • Relative pathname

Advantages:

* Create directory and subdirectory
* User access files of other user.

Disadvantages:

* Create duplicate copies of the file.
* User could not share files or directories.

(ii) Explain the term "Select a victim and Rollback" in the context of deadlock recovery. [4]

Ans. Selecting victim: Based on following criteria:

* priority
* own cost
* cost affecting other processes

Rollback: The process from which resource or resources are preempted will not be able to continue execution, such processes roll backed partially or completely to some safe state.

(iii) Explain any two benefits of virtual machines. [2]

Ans. • Protection

* Easy development
* Sharing hardware
* Easy communication
* Consolidation
* Portability
* Usefulness

■■■

October 2016

Time : Two Hours   **Maximum Marks : 40**

N.B.: *(i) Neat diagram must be drawn whenever necessary.*

(ii) Figures to the right indicate full marks.

(iii) All questions are compulsory

1. Attempt all of the following: [10 × 1 = 10]

(a) Define system boot.

Ans. The procedure of starting a computer by loading the Kernel is known as system boot.

(b) Write a primary function of medium term scheduler.

Ans. To remove number of jobs from memory temporarily and reduce the degree of multiprogramming.

(c) **What is Aging?**

Ans. A solution to the problem of starvation of low priority process is aging.

Aging is a process in which the priority of each process is gradually increased after the process spends a certain amount of time in the system.

(d) **State scalability and Responsiveness benefits of multithreading.**

Ans. **Scalability:** Threads are running in parallel on different process.

Responsiveness: Threads library provides function to create and terminate thread, synchronize their activity and to permit them to make request to the operating system.

(e) **Define Semaphore.**

Ans. A semaphore is a protected variable, whose value can be accessed and altered only by two automatic operations: wait() and signal().

(f) **"Wait for a graph is used for deadlock avoidance in the system" True/False? Justify.**

Ans. False: It is used in deadlock detection.

(g) **Define physical address space.**

Ans. The address seen by the memory unit that is loaded into memory address register of the memory.

(h) **List any four file attributes.**

Ans. Name, identifier, type, location, size, protection, time, date, user identification (any four).

(i) **Define the term swapping.**

Ans. A process can be swapped temporarily out of memory to a backing store and then brought back into memory for continued execution.

(j) **State functions of dispatcher.**

Ans. 1. Loading the register of the process.

2. Switching operating system to user mode.

3. Restart the program by jumping to the proper location in user program.

2. **Attempt any two of the following:**   [2 × 5 = 10]

(a) **What is Inter process communication? Explain the reasons required for Inter Process Communication.**

Ans. Definition and ... 1 mark.

- Concurrent executing process type
  o Independent processes
  o Cooperating process.
- Reasons ... 4 marks.
  o Information sharing
  o Computation speed-up
  o Modularity
  o Convenience.

(b) Consider the following set of processing with CPU burst time given in milliseconds.

Process	Burst time	Arrival time
J_1	1	5
J_2	0	7
J_3	3	3
J_4	2	10

Compute average time around time using RR (time quantum = 2) and shortest remaining time first.

Ans.

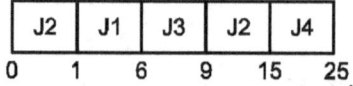

| J2 | J1 | J4 | J2 | J3 | J1 | J2 | J3 | J4 | J1 | J2 | J4 | J4 | J4 |

0   2   4   6   8   10   12   14   15   17   18   19   21   23   25

Average turn around time $= \dfrac{71}{4} = 17.75$.

Shortest remaining time first.

| J2 | J1 | J3 | J2 | J4 |

0   1   6   9   15   25

Average turn around time $= \dfrac{49}{4} = 12.25$.

(c) Consider the following sets P, R and E:

$P = [P_1, P_2, P_3]$

$R = [R_1, R_2, R_3, R_4]$

$E = [P_1 \rightarrow R_1, P_2 \rightarrow R_3, R_1 \rightarrow P_2, R_2 \rightarrow P_2, R_2 \rightarrow P_1]$

Also consider the following number of instances per resource type:

(i) One instance of resource type R_1 and R_2

(ii) Two instances of resource type R_2.

(iii) Three instances of resource type R_4.

Construct the Resource allocation graph for the above problem.

Check whether the system is in the deadlock.

Ans. Resource allocation graph.

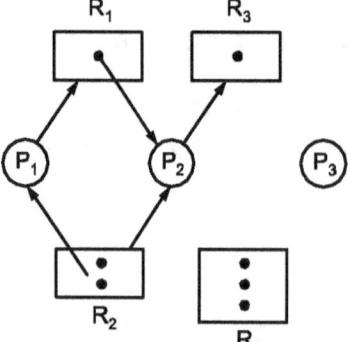

$R = \{R_1, R_2, R_3, R_4\}$

$E = \{P_1 \rightarrow R_1, P_2 \rightarrow R_3, R_1 \rightarrow P_2, R_2 \rightarrow P_2, R_2 \rightarrow P_1\}$

Since above resource allocation graph does not contain cycle - so no process in system is dead locked. So there is no deadlock.

3.   Attempt any two of the following: [2 × 5 = 10]

(a) Explain Bounded buffer problem. Give structure of producer and consumer.

Ans. Producer:
   •   Create item and add to buffer
   •   Do not want to overflow the buffer
   Consumer:
   •   Remove item for buffer
   •   Do not want to get ahead of producer
   with figure.
   •   Bounded buffer assumes, there is a fixed buffer size.
   •   It can be handled using semaphore, mutex semaphore, provide mutual exclusion, empty and full semaphores count number of empty and full buffers respectively.

(b) Explain different methods for handling free-space list in file system.

Ans. Proper description of following methods:
   •   Bit map/Bit vector
   •   Linked listening
   •   Grouping
   •   Counting
   •   Space map

(c) Consider page reference string as follows:
     7, 5, 6, 2, 9, 5, 7, 6, 2, 7, 6, 5, 2, 7, 2, 7, 8
     Assume 3 frames. Find the number of page faults according to:
     (i)   Optimal page replacement algorithm.
     (ii) LRU page replacement algorithm.

Ans. Optimal page replacement process and
                                    Total page fault = 9 .... $2\frac{1}{2}$ Mark

       LRU algorithm process and
                                    Total page fault = 9 .... $2\frac{1}{2}$ Mark

4.   Attempt any one (A or B):   [1 × 10 = 10]

(A) (i)   Define pre-emptive and non-preemptive scheduling. State disadvantages of pre-emptive scheduling.   [4]

Ans. (i)   Non-preemptive scheduling: When a CPU allocates a process and releases the process after completion or the process switches from running state of waiting state.

       Pre emptive scheduling: When a process switches from running state to the ready state or switches from waiting to ready then it is preemptive scheduling scheme. It means the process is interrupted.

       Disadvantage: Scheduling cost is increases.
                       Affect on the design of operating system kernel

(ii) **Explain MVT with advantage and disadvantages.** [4]

Ans. Proper description of MVT   – 2 marks
with figure
Advantages: – 1 mark
It increases degree of multiprogramming
It does not suffer from internal fragmentation
Disadvantages: – 1 mark
External fragmentation
Lot of time consumed

(iii) **State the features of loadable kernel modules.** [2]

Ans.
- it uses object oriented approach
- interfaces
- Each component loadable with kernel
- Each one component is separate

OR

(B) (i) **Explain file operations in detail.** [4]

Ans. Description of following file operation contains:
- Creating a file
- Writing a file
- Reading a file
- Repositioning a file
- Deleting a file
- Truncating a file

(ii) **What is deadlock? State different methods to handle a deadlock.**

Ans. Definition of deadlock   – 1 mark
To handle deadlock description of following methods   – 3 marks
- Deadlock prevention
- Deadlock avoidance
- Deadlock detection and recovery

(iii) **Which are the challenging areas faced by application programmer while designing multicore system program.** [2]

Ans. Any four from the following   – 2 marks
- Dividing activities
- Data splitting
- Balance
- Data dependency
- Testing and debugging

■■■